"I would never lie to protect myself ~~~~~ hurting you..."

Shay snorted a laugh. "You'd never lie, period. You're a true white hat, Michael."

"You say that as if it's a bad thing."

She looked away. "It was, for us."

"Shay." He reached for her hand when she wouldn't look at him and gave it a gentle tug. "I can't protect you if you're not straight with me."

She cocked her head. "And what exactly do you think you're protecting me from? Do you actually believe I could shoot someone in cold blood?"

Her eyes searched his face, and she nodded. "You do. There was a time I thought you knew me better than anyone else, Michael."

ACCLAIM FOR DEBBIE MASON

PRIMROSE LANE

"4 Stars! This is a book worth savoring as it has all the elements of a fantastic read."

—RTBookReviews.com

STARLIGHT BRIDGE

"4 Stars! Mason gives Ava and Griffin a second chance at love. There's a mystery surrounding the sale of the estate...that adds a special appeal to the book."

—*RT Book Reviews*

MISTLETOE COTTAGE

"Top Pick! 4½ Stars! Mason has a knockout with the first book in her Harmony Harbor series."

—*RT Book Reviews*

HAPPY EVER AFTER IN CHRISTMAS

"This charming story of two people struggling to trust their love and build a life together is certain to earn the author new fans."

—Bookpage.com

KISS ME IN CHRISTMAS

"This story has so much humor that at times I found myself laughing out loud, holding my sides and shaking my head...a complete joy to read."

—HarlequinJunkie.com

Driftwood Cove

Driftwood Cove

DEBBIE MASON

FOREVER
New York   Boston

Copyright © 2018 by Debbie Mazzuca
Excerpt from *Primrose Lane* copyright © 2017 by Debbie Mazzuca
"A Fairytale Bride" copyright © 2016 by Robin Lanier

Cover design by Elizabeth Stokes. Cover copyright © 2018 by Hachette Book Group, Inc.

Forever
Hachette Book Group
1290 Avenue of the Americas, New York, NY 10104
forever-romance.com
twitter.com/foreverromance

First Edition: February 2018

Forever is an imprint of Grand Central Publishing. The Forever name and logo are trademarks of Hachette Book Group, Inc.

The publisher is not responsible for websites (or their content) that are not owned by the publisher.

The Hachette Speakers Bureau provides a wide range of authors for speaking events. To find out more, go to www.hachettespeakersbureau.com or call (866) 376-6591.

ISBNs: 978-1-5387-4417-8 (mass market), 978-1-5387-4418-5 (ebook)

Printed in the United States of America

OPM

10 9 8 7 6 5 4 3 2 1

For my parents, Jean and Norm LeClair, who taught me everyone has a story and most people deserve a second chance.

Driftwood Cove

Chapter One

♥

There'd been no foreboding signs to alert Shay Angel to the danger, no warning that this was the day her past caught up with her and her life might be on the line.

Her morning had started off the same as usual. The alarm on her bedside table went off at seven, and she hit the snooze button three times at ten-minute intervals just like she always did. She didn't fall out of bed or trip over her boots on the way to the shower. Her one-bedroom apartment was sparsely furnished, and her boots were right where she'd left them—directly at the end of her bed, toes pointed toward the door in case she needed to make a quick exit.

Even the unreliable showerhead had cooperated today. Her five-minute shower had been exactly the way she liked it, hot and strong. Just like her coffee, which she drank from an oversized travel mug that read *Do I look like I "Rise & Shine"?* Her assistant at the security company she worked for had a sense of humor. Shay didn't.

Nor, for the most part, did she do friends, which

her assistant was desperately trying to change. Lately—okay, so in the past ten years—Shay didn't do boyfriends either. Something else her assistant was desperately trying to change by signing Shay up on every matchmaking app known to mankind. Without Shay's permission, of course.

Just one more reason Shay had been lulled into thinking the day, for the most part, would be pretty good. She'd had forty-five minutes of peace and quiet before she'd left for work. No pings or beeps and bells and whistles from texts or emails from the apps she was signed up for alerting her to a new and perfect match.

She'd met her match a long time ago. Only he turned out to be perfectly imperfect. And he was calling her at a perfectly imperfect time. She reached for the vibrating cell phone on her desk and hit Decline. She'd stopped taking his calls ten months before but couldn't quite make it official by blocking him completely. He was one of the reasons she'd accepted the job in Vegas. The move put twenty-three hundred miles between her and her past, in which Michael Gallagher had played a starring role.

But she didn't have time to think about him now, or ever, really. She had bigger worries to contend with. Like the cop who sat on the other side of Shay's desk with a familiar, suspicious look in her eyes.

"In less than three months, four of the homes your company installed security for have been robbed of more than a million dollars in diamonds. I don't believe it's a coincidence that your clients are the ones being targeted, Ms. Angel." Detective Sims slapped a file onto Shay's desk.

Working to keep any sign of worry from showing on her face, Shay drew the manila folder toward her. There was no way she'd give Detective Sims the satisfaction of seeing her sweat. Shay's petty-criminal parents had imprinted her DNA with a deep dislike and distrust of law enforcement, but she didn't have to like or trust Sims to know the woman wasn't making up the evidence in the file.

Over the past five days, Shay had been trying to convince herself that no one at Sterling Security was involved in the break-ins. Then yesterday she'd overheard a conversation between her boss and an installer and could no longer deny the likelihood that they were in this up to their ears.

Which totally blew, because her suspicions put her bright and shiny dream for her future at risk. She'd left her job in New York to work for Ray Sterling, a man who was renowned in the security business. She'd planned to learn all that she could from him and then branch out on her own. Now...

Without saying a word, she closed the file and held the gaze of the woman sitting on the other side of her desk.

Shay's uncle Charlie had taken up where her parents left off. He'd taught her how to not only run a con and make a cop with a single glance, but also how to elude and confuse them. Other than the summer she'd turned nineteen, his lessons had served her well.

Sims's dark eyes narrowed beneath her frosted blond fringe.

Leaning back in the chair, Shay crossed her arms as she waited for the detective to show her hand. It didn't take long.

"Do not try to intimidate me. I've heard all about your Superwoman act. How you saved your assistant and got Ace Rodriguez and his gang of thugs out of your neighborhood. But you don't scare or impress me like you do the beat cops. I know who and what you really are." Sims leaned forward and tapped the file with a hot-pink fingernail. "You were put away for grand theft auto at nineteen. Not much of a leap between stealing cars and stealing diamonds, now, is there? So tell me, Angel, where were you on the nights in question?"

Charlie and her parents had been good teachers, but it was prison that taught Shay the most valuable lessons of all. Number one, how to stay alive. And number two, that she'd do whatever it took to ensure she was never put away again. Even if it meant turning on the man who held the key to making her dreams come true.

First, though, she needed more proof to support her suspicions that her boss's son was behind the break-ins. If he was, it meant Ray had found the perfect fall guy, or girl in this case. He'd correctly predicted that Detective Sims would focus on Shay. It wasn't like he had to be especially smart or a mind reader to guess that she'd draw the detective's interest. Everyone and their mother knew that in law enforcement's eyes, once a con, always a con.

In the five years since she'd walked out of the prison's gates, Shay had been on the receiving end of the expression. If it wasn't said to her face, it was whispered behind her back or delivered with raised eyebrows and knowing smirks.

Another cliché she knew to be true: It takes a thief to catch one. And that's exactly what she planned to do. Once she got rid of Sims.

Given her own concerns over the robberies, Shay had been prepared for a visit from the Las Vegas Metro Police Department. Still, it ticked her off that she was on the top of Sims's suspect list, the emotion evident in her voice when she said, "I was working the crisis hotline the night of the first robbery, and I had a one-on-one MMA session that clears me of the third break-in."

"You don't expect me to take your word for it, do you? And what the hell is a private MMA session anyway? Do I even want to know?"

"Mixed martial arts. I'm an instructor at Elite Gym," Shay responded through clenched teeth, reaching for the kitschy holder on her otherwise empty desk. Her assistant, Cherry, a former stripper who was into all things crafty, had made the card holder for Shay as an early Valentine's Day gift. Which meant it was pink and sparkly and covered in hearts. And smelled like Love's Baby Soft perfume. Cherry must have given it a fresh spritz that morning.

According to her assistant, the fragrance was imbued with the power to bring out Shay's inner girly girl and break her dating dry spell before the most romantic day of the year. Despite wanting to hurl at the task before her, Shay felt a smile tugging on her lips as she withdrew a business card from the holder. The reluctant smile faded

as she turned the card over to write the names and numbers of the people who would provide her alibis.

She'd have to talk to them. Let them know the police
would be calling to verify her whereabouts for the
nights in question. Instead of throwing the card at Sims
like she wanted to, Shay flicked it across the desk with
the end of her pen.

After glancing at the names, Sims raised an eyebrow.
"Judge Watkins. I'm surprised he didn't ask for another
instructor when he found out you were an ex-con. He's
a hardass. You would've served ten years instead of five
if he'd presided over your case."

Other than Ray, and obviously Sims, no one in Vegas
knew that Shay had done time. Any chances of keeping
her record private were gone now. Sims would see to
that. Shay had met her type before.

"I have an appointment in twenty minutes, Detective.
If there's nothing else..."

"You're not off the hook yet, Angel. You're missing
alibis for two of the break-ins."

"You know as well as I do that one person is responsible for all four robberies, and it's not me."

"And how exactly did you come to that conclusion?"

"How do you think? I've spoken to my clients
and read the reports." There was something off about
Sims's reaction, her tone of voice, and it gave Shay
pause. What if there was more to this than she knew?
She came up with a question that might immediately
rid her of the worrisome suspicion now niggling at
her brain. "If you're planning on questioning Ray
and his son, you might want to get on that. They're

leaving today for the security conference in New York."

"Why would I want to question the Sterlings? They're one of the richest families in the state. It's not like they need the money nor would they benefit from the negative publicity. Ray's well respected and—"

"Let me guess, a generous benefactor to the mayor's last campaign." It was as if history were repeating itself. If it came down to her word against the Sterlings', Shay didn't trust the law to be on her side. She'd learned the hard way that the same rules didn't apply to the rich and connected.

It's why she'd accepted Ray's offer last March—to earn the respect and power that went with having a fortune. She wanted to learn from the best, and once she had, she planned to develop a concept she could franchise. The security industry was a 350-billion-dollar business, and she wanted a big piece of it. But she had a long way to go before she earned the kind of coin that guaranteed her a get-out-of-jail-free card.

"Watch your step, Angel," Sims said as she came to her feet. "And don't leave town."

"I'm curious, just how well do you know Ray?" Shay said to the woman's back.

Her hand on the knob of the office door, the detective hesitated before turning to face her.

A faint, knowing smile lifted Shay's lips. She'd been bluffing, but from the slight flush of color on Sims's cheeks and her initial hesitation, Shay had obviously hit a nerve. It shouldn't come as a surprise. The detective was Ray's type . . . a man who'd been divorced four times.

It also explained why Sims had ended up here today, targeting her. Shay nosing into the investigation had made Ray nervous, and he knew the perfect way to shut her down and protect his son. She'd made the mistake of confiding in him a few months back, sharing her greatest fear.

"What are you insinuating?"

A younger version of herself would have told Sims exactly what she was suggesting, but Shay liked to think she'd become smarter, more strategic. Self-preservation won out over righteous indignation and revenge every single time. "Nothing, but now that you mention it, you're awfully defensive. Can't say I blame you, though. Connected as he is, Ray probably has your boss on speed dial, doesn't he? Don't worry. I won't tell him you're harassing me. I know you're just doing your job."

Sims looked like she was trying to decide whether she'd just been threatened or whether Shay was clueless.

"I am just doing my job. It has nothing to do with office politics or my relationship with the Sterlings."

So, clueless it was. Except Sims's mention of her *relationship* with the Sterlings was either a Freudian slip or strategic. If it was strategic, the woman had correctly surmised that Shay wouldn't let up on the investigation and somewhere there was evidence of her relationship with Ray. Which would also mean Sims knew Shay was playing her.

"Relax, I believe you. Now I really do need to head out for my appointment or I'll be late, and that would make my boss an unhappy man." Shay had every intention of making Ray Sterling a very unhappy man before he left for NYC. She refused to have the threat of prison hanging over her any longer than she had to.

* * *

Sitting in a black Challenger outside Ray Junior's apartment building, Shay hacked into the security system and remotely took control. She kept an eye on the front of the building while angling the exterior cameras so that one captured the entrance to the casino across the road and the other one focused on the parking garage.

There was no time for her to celebrate successfully overriding the security system. She might get in the building undetected, but she still had to deal with the cameras in the elevators and on Junior's floor. And then there was the matter of searching his apartment in under an hour in order to confront her boss before he left town.

As she leaned over to grab her knapsack off the floor, the passenger door opened and a blond bombshell slipped in. A decade older than Shay, her thirty-nine-year-old assistant wore a hot-pink leather jacket, matching miniskirt, and thigh-high white shiny boots.

"What are you doing here, Cherry? I need you back at the office." If things went south, Shay didn't want the Sterlings looking at her assistant. Cherry needed this job even more than Shay did. "Wait a minute, how did you even know where I was?"

Cherry made a limp wrist hand drop, the stacks of

rings on each finger no doubt weighing down her hand. "How many times do I have to tell you? If you don't want anyone to know where you are, stop driving Hell Baby."

A powerful muscle car, the sleek black Hellcat with its yellow rims was Shay's pride and joy. "Okay, you found me; so what do you want?"

Glancing from the building back to Shay, Cherry blinked eyes framed with long blue lashes that sort of matched her eyes. "I know you're desperate for a man, but Ray J, Shaybae? Do you seriously not look in a mirror?" She tugged on Shay's ponytail that stuck through the hole at the back of her ball cap. "You have this lush black mane that you never let down to play, stunning gray eyes, and pillow lips. Like it or not, girlfriend, you're a ten even sans makeup and with the Goth uniform. And poor Ray J, he's a two on a fab hair day, and that's me being kind."

About a fifth of what Cherry said actually registered with Shay. The part where her assistant thought she was desperate and, worse, the part where she knew this was Junior's apartment building. That was the thing about Cherry—with her blond-bombshell looks, people underestimated her.

Including Shay, it seemed. "I'm not desperate. What I am is busy. I have to drop off an estimate for Junior. He messed up his numbers again, and I fixed the quote as a favor. Don't let him or his father know I said—"

Cherry's cell phone rang, and she held up a finger. "I routed the office calls to my phone. Sterling Security, how may I be of service?" She made a face and then smiled like the person on the other end of the line was standing in front of her. "An adorable pink heart that was attached to your purse? Umm, right, you didn't say adorable. But you have such a fashionable flair, Detective Sims, that I just knew it must be."

"Seriously?" Shay muttered, flicking the *adorable* pink heart hanging from Cherry's bag.

Cherry pointedly ignored her and continued. "Don't you worry, I'll find it if it's here. All right, you have yourself a good day." She disconnected and held up her hands, her rings catching the sunlight and making a rainbow in the car. "What? She made me nervous, and you know what happens when I'm nervous or upset."

"Yeah, you steal things, and one day it's going to get you in trouble that even I can't get you out of. You need to see a shrink."

"We both might need one when I tell you why she makes me nervous."

"She's a cop. Of course she makes you nervous." It's something they had in common.

"No, it's more than that. So much more. But I don't want to tell you. I can't. If I do, it's going to—"

"Just spit it out."

"All right, but don't say I didn't warn you. It's about the robberies. It's Ray J. He got mixed up with some bad dudes, and he's feeding them the inside scoop on our clients."

"Are you sure? Does Ray Senior know?"

"I'm not sure if he knows. I saw Ray J at the Purple Peacock with the scary dudes. I know, I know. It was just that one time. But, hey, it's a good thing I went.

Harry, the bartender, he's an old friend of mine. He gave me the scoop." She wrung her hands. "I know how much you admire Ray Senior, and I'd rather remove my implants than hurt you, Shaybae, but you need to know. He's setting you up to take the fall."

"I figured that out when Sims was questioning me. Last night I overheard Ray talking to one of the installers. Junior is no longer allowed on the jobs."

"Okay, so what are we going to do?"

"I need hard evidence against Junior. Evidence that I can blackmail his father with. Either he calls off Sims or I take what we know to the ... DA," she said, thinking about Michael's earlier call.

He was an assistant district attorney in Boston. If worse came to worst, she'd ask for his help. He, out of anyone, would know someone here that she could trust. Her hands got sweaty at the thought. She didn't like depending on anyone. They always let her down. It's why she fought her battles alone. This time, though, she couldn't afford to take the risk. She'd do whatever it took to protect herself. And Cherry.

"You need to go back to the office and forget everything you just told me. That way, when this is over, you'll still have a job."

Cherry sniffed and flicked her overprocessed hair. It might have made for a dramatic performance if her rings hadn't gotten caught in her teased blond locks. Her words made up for it, though. "I meant what I told you the night you saved me in the alley. I'm your slave for life. You got me the job at Sterling, and I'm not staying there without you. I won't work for a man who rewards all the overtime you put in by throwing you under the bus. Where you go, I go." She tilted her head. "Just for curiosity's sake, do you know where we're going? Don't worry if you haven't thought that far ahead; I'll do a tea reading. That way we can be assured of ending up in the perfect place. How does Greece sound? I hear Greek men like blondes." She twisted a lock of hair around her finger and then glanced at Shay. "Not on your bucket list?"

"Let's deal with one thing at a time, okay?" she said, feeling a little panicked and slightly claustrophobic at the idea of not only being jobless but being responsible for Cherry too. Right now, though, she had more important things to worry about. She glanced at her phone. "We have half an hour to get in and out of Junior's apartment without getting caught."

Cherry fluffed her hair and stuck out her impressive triple Ds. "Don't you worry, I haven't met a man I couldn't distract."

Her assistant was nothing if not confident, Shay thought as they walked to the front doors of the building. Stepping behind the potted palm at the entrance, she remotely changed the angles of the cameras in the lobby and outside the elevator doors. Once Cherry began singing Shania Twain's "Man! I Feel Like a Woman" off-key and strutting her stuff, Shay took one last look around before heading for the door to the left of the elevators. Cherry would hang out in the lobby to distract security and keep an eye on who came into the building.

Shay hip-checked the door to the stairs open while

digging in her knapsack for her lock kit. If she'd had more time, she would've lifted Junior's keys and made a copy for herself. She reached the twelfth floor in record time and eased open the door to look down the deserted hallway, noting the locations of the cameras as she did.

Once she shut down the security feed, she'd have just under seven minutes to break into Junior's apartment before they rebooted the system and got the cameras back online. Shay leaned against the door, doing a trial run in her head. Confident she had everything planned out to the last second, she set the alarm on her phone for four minutes and then raced down the blue paisley carpeted hall to the door at the far end.

It took her twenty seconds. Less than four minutes later, she opened the door to Junior's apartment and disabled his alarm. She was just about to close the door when the bell on the elevator dinged and the doors slid open to reveal a frazzled Cherry on the phone.

"Yes, yes, I see her. She's okay. She picked the lock, and she's inside his apartment to get the evidence."

Shay had to practically lift her jaw off the floor to speak. "Have you lost your mind? Who are you talking to?"

"The Sterlings are on their way up," Cherry said in a frantic whisper, shoving the phone at Shay. "Talk to him."

Like she had time to talk to anyone with the Sterlings headed their way. She glanced at the second elevator; it was on the third floor. Jerking Junior's apartment door closed, she grabbed Cherry by the arm and raced back down the hall to the stairway.

"Slow down; I'm in heels, and you're in motorcycle boots," Cherry complained, as if that were the only reason she couldn't keep up. The woman considered shopping an exercise.

Shay put a finger to her lips, dragging her assistant behind the door just as the elevator dinged. Shay peeked around the edge of the blue steel door to see the Sterlings step off the elevator. Someone calling her name drew her up short. She glanced at the phone. *It couldn't be.* She let the door close and leaned against it. Holding up the phone, she stared at Cherry.

"It's Special Agent Gallagher. He called to speak to you, and I thought we could use the help when I saw the Sterlings getting out of their car. He says he's a friend of yours. Talk to him. Let him help."

The voice sounded like Michael's, but it couldn't be. He was an assistant district attorney, not a special agent. Maybe it was his cousin Aidan, who was a DEA agent. Shay had done some undercover work for him two years before. The reasoning made sense, and her racing heart slowed.

Hefting her knapsack over her shoulder, she nudged Cherry to get her moving down the stairs and put the phone to her ear. "Aidan?"

"Aidan? No, it's Michael. What's going on, Shay? Are you okay? Are you safe?"

It *was* Michael. She'd recognize his deep, sexy-assin voice anywhere. Even with a note of concern giving it a rougher edge, it affected her the same as it always had. Like he'd reached through the line and stroked her with his strong and elegant fingers. A door slamming on the floor they'd just left drew her attention. She cocked her head, waiting for the Sterlings to start yelling, to come running their way. There was nothing but the crinkle of leather and the click of Cherry's heels on the concrete stairs.

"Shay?"

"Sorry. Yeah, I'm good. We're okay."

"Sure you are. You just have someone trying to frame you. For once can you be straight with me and admit you need help?" She heard the worry and frustration in his voice, and it reminded her of the night she'd ended up in his arms, and eventually in his bed. The night she'd tangled her fingers in hair as black as a starless winter's night, gazed into eyes as blue and as warm as the Atlantic Ocean on a summer's day, and trailed kisses along a jaw as chiseled as the rocks that lined the harbor.

There'd been a time when she'd loved him beyond reason. Sometimes she was afraid that she still did. It's why she'd stopped taking his calls. She gave her assistant the evil eye. It didn't do her much good. Sprawled over the handrail trying to catch her breath, Cherry sounded like she needed oxygen.

Shay nudged her to keep her moving while defending herself to Michael. "I didn't do anything wrong. I didn't break any laws."

"So you're telling me that you didn't enter the apartment after picking the lock?"

She heard a hint of amusement in his voice. "They're setting me up, Michael. I won't go down for something I didn't do. I won't."

"Trust me, they won't get away with it. I won't let them. Just...Hang on a minute."

She wanted to believe him, but she'd lost her innocence a long time ago. There'd been a time when she'd trusted him, though. When she'd believed it didn't matter that they came from two different worlds. She'd thought a love like theirs could survive anything and anyone.

She frowned at the thought, unable to believe that she'd ever been that naïve. She supposed it was possible. But the sentiment seemed more like something Michael would have believed. He'd been an idealist and an optimist. He'd also been incredibly persuasive. So different from her in so many ways.

All things considered, it wasn't really surprising that she'd been the one who'd paid the price the summer their worlds collided. Her life had ended up in tatters. Michael's, as far as she knew, had remained as privileged as ever.

There were muffled voices in the background and then Michael came back on the line. "All right, in the next couple of minutes an agent will call you on this number. He'll arrange a meet. His name is Tom Bryant. You can trust him, Shay. I promise, everything will be okay."

A lump formed in her throat, surprising her. She would have expected relief, not this odd sense of longing for what might have been. "Thanks. I appreciate your help."

"Yet if it was up to you, I wouldn't have had the chance to give it to you, would I? The only reason you're talking to me right now is because your friend—"

"Wait. Why did you call? And why did you lie to Cherry and say you're with the FBI? Did you think I—"

"I didn't lie to your friend. I am with the FBI, and you would've known that if you hadn't cut me out of your life, Shay. As to why I was calling, it'll keep. We'll talk after you've met with Tom and gotten the situation there under control."

A door slammed several flights below, immediately followed by the sound of booted feet running up the stairs. *Crap.* She yanked Cherry upright and practically carried her back to the floor they'd just passed. "Your friend Bryant? You better send him here, like, now, Michael. Our situation has..." A bullet shattered the concrete an inch from her head.

Chapter Two

♥

Shay clamped a hand over Cherry's mouth, smothering her scream. "Run like there's a fire sale at Juicy Couture," she whispered in the woman's ear, and took her hand, running up the last four stairs and racing across the landing to the door. Staying low, Shay inched it open to check if anyone was there before pushing Cherry into the empty hall. She followed after her. A bullet hit the door as it quietly closed. The gunman wasn't far behind. Cherry kept running down the hall, emitting tiny chirps. She sounded like a chicken.

"Cherry, stop." Now that someone knew which floor they were on, she didn't want her near the elevators. "Get over here. Stand beside me with your back against the wall." Shay's throat was tight from calling to her in just above a whisper. Cherry didn't stop running as she headed back Shay's way. Her face was flushed and sweaty, her cheeks puffed from holding her breath.

"Breathe. It'll be fine," Shay told her.

Though the only way they would be was if the gunman came through that door thinking they were on the

run, and he had to do it before the elevator reached
their floor. It was on the second floor. She hoped Cherry
didn't notice.

The door from the stairs banged open, and a tall
man burst into the hallway. Shay recognized him as
Sterling's installer. She offered up a silent thank-you
before swinging into action. She grabbed the man's
hand that held the gun, jerking it straight up at the
same time as she raised her knee. Groaning, he bent
over at the waist. She twisted the gun out of his hand
and raised her knee again. Only this time instead of
the family jewels, her knee connected with his jaw.
Now that their dance was over, she opened the door,
placed her hand on his bowed head, and pushed. They
didn't have to worry about him at least for another
hour. And Shay planned to be long gone by then. She
grabbed Cherry by the hand and pulled her onto the
landing of the stairwell just as the elevator announced
its arrival with a *ding*. Shay pulled the door closed,
sidestepping the installer's body to look over the railing at the levels below. All clear.

She waved Cherry on with the gun, placing a finger to her own lips when the other woman opened
her mouth. Emitting a small sob, Cherry headed down
the stairs. They'd just reached the fourth floor landing
when Shay heard the sound of the door above creak-
ing open. Someone cursed. And then another male
voice did the same. They'd seen the installer. And
if Shay wasn't mistaken, the voices belonged to the
Sterlings. She felt movement above her and grabbed
Cherry, dragging her to the opposite side, flattening

their backs against the exit door. If one of the Sterlings leaned over the rail like she had, he wouldn't see them.

"They've gotta be on their way down," Ray Senior told his son. "Tell the boys in the lobby to keep an eye out for them."

* * *

The last thing Special Agent Michael Gallagher expected was for his investigation into the death of mob enforcer Tony Dulbecco to lead him straight to the town of Harmony Harbor and Charlie Angel. Or that his phone call to Shay would—hopefully—save her life.

Right before the call dropped, he'd heard her friend scream. The only sound that had come from Shay was a sharp intake of breath. Just one quick inhalation after what sounded like a bullet shattering concrete within inches of her.

The woman had nerves of fortified steel. She was tougher than anyone he knew, and so damn beautiful she'd haunted his dreams from the moment he first saw her ten years before. She'd been riding a Harley down Main Street on a hot summer's day, her long hair whipping behind her in the wind, cool and confident with a lithe body that stole his breath as surely as she'd stolen his heart.

To this day, she still held a piece of it. She didn't want it, though. She'd made it clear she didn't want anything to do with him. He didn't blame her. But a heart wants what it wants, and no matter how hard he tried to get over her, nothing seemed to stick for long. That was the problem with a first love that couldn't, or wouldn't, be his last.

Automatically, he reached for the cell in the console of his SUV, curling his fingers into a fist when he realized what he was doing. He'd been fighting the urge to call her the entire drive from Boston to Harmony Harbor. He didn't want to risk distracting her or alerting anyone to her location if she was hiding out until Special Agent Bryant got there.

Fifteen more minutes. He'd give her fifteen more minutes, he decided as he drove past the town hall and the copper-domed clock tower situated on the hill overlooking the harbor. It was a view he was familiar with. William Gallagher, his great-grandfather many times over, had settled the town of Harmony Harbor in the early seventeenth century.

Michael had mostly fond memories of the summers he'd spent there and at Greystone, the family's estate. Built to resemble a medieval castle, the manor sat on five thousand acres of woodland and oceanfront property west of town and now served as a hotel. Members of his family still lived here, including his uncle, cousins, and grandmother.

If his great-grandmother Colleen had her way, every single member of the extended Gallagher family would move back home someday. She was still controlling them from the grave. Fifteen months earlier, she'd died and bequeathed the property to Michael, his brothers, and his cousins. There was a catch, though. They all had to agree to keep the estate in the family or sell. So far there were five of them, including himself, who were on the Save Greystone Team.

Lately, he'd been playing with the idea of moving into one of the cottages on the estate. He was tired of his life in the city. Tired of being harassed by his neighbors, who wanted their building designated pet free. He wanted Atticus, his aging Irish wolfhound, to run free while he still could. But Michael wasn't a fan of the commute. It was a solid hour's drive from headquarters in Boston, and that's if both the weather and traffic were cooperating. Neither had been cooperating today.

At least for Michael. Oliver James, the senior agent he'd been assigned to, had beaten Michael here. James's black Crown Vic idled in front of the Salty Dog. The pub sat on the corner of Main Street and South Shore Road—a twenty-foot wooden sailboat mast secured to the red brick building. At the top of the mast, in the crow's nest, sat a fiberglass bulldog that looked a lot like the bar's owner, Charlie Angel.

As Michael pulled into a parking space across from the pub, James's long-legged swagger brought him to the passenger side of the Range Rover. Six foot five and built like a linebacker, the guy could pass for The Rock and had the personality of a pit bull. They'd been working together for less than a week, and James had already tried to have Michael transferred out of organized crime and into white-collar crime three times. He had the door open before Michael had come to a complete stop.

"You got some explainin' to do, pretty boy. You weren't exactly forthcoming about your past with the Angels. I did a little investigating after you had me call in a favor for the old man's niece," James said as he filled the passenger seat with his bulk and pulled out his cell phone. Tapping the screen, he brought up an old newspaper article from the *Harmony Harbor Gazette.* "I'm surprised the lady still talks to you after your family had her put away. Five years for a first offense..." He shook his head, making a face like the thought of a teenage Shay Angel in prison made him sick.

Michael remembered the feeling. It had taken him years to shake the guilt. Still, he felt the need to defend the indefensible. "She stole my car. They found her with it at a chop shop. There was nothing I could do. I tried."

He'd been hurt at first. He'd loved her and thought she'd loved him too. But as his mother had been only too happy to point out at the time, Shay had been using him. She'd played him. She was a con just like her uncle. Years later, he saw things differently, more clearly. There was no denying who Shay was back then. She had been a con, a grifter. Her uncle had trained her well. Nevertheless, that long-ago summer, she'd loved Michael too. She'd been nineteen; he'd been twenty-four.

The Christmas before last they'd had a reunion of sorts. It had been the first time they'd actually spoken since that horrific morning a decade before. Though the circumstances they found themselves in turned out to be more hair-raising than conducive to intimate conversations about their past. Shay had been working undercover for his cousin.

But talking wasn't what Michael had come looking

for that cold December afternoon. He'd been seeking absolution, and she'd readily given it. As he'd soon discovered, though, forgiven wasn't the same as forgotten. Same time next year, she'd promised. Only she never showed at the bandstand in the village green on Christmas Day.

By then she'd stopped taking his calls for months, so he should've known she wouldn't show. Still, like an idiot, he'd waited there for hours. Atticus sat in the passenger seat of the Range Rover with a big red bow around his neck, waiting for his hero. Shay had rescued his dog from his ex-fiancée, who'd held Atticus hostage after she'd jilted Michael the night before their wedding.

In his ex's eyes, he'd done the unforgivable by deciding to give up his job as ADA to go into law enforcement. He had a feeling Shay would feel the same but for an entirely different reason than his ex. Especially once Michael told her about her uncle Charlie.

His partner eyed him and nodded. "You loved her, didn't you?" Without waiting for Michael to respond, he continued. "Bet that went over well with the governor. Shay Angel was lucky she wasn't put away for life."

James wasn't far off the mark. Only it wasn't Michael's father but his mother who'd been pulling the judge's strings. Maura Gallagher had big plans for her youngest son. Michael had been chosen to follow in his father's footsteps to become governor one day. No way was Maura about to let him squander his life and his love on a petty criminal with no social standing or family fortune.

He didn't plan on sharing any of that with James. The man already knew more about his personal life than Michael wanted him to. "Why don't you give Bryant a call, see if he has any news?" he suggested, keeping his growing concern for Shay from his voice. James had been the one to call in a favor with Special Agent Bryant. The two had gone through the Academy together.

"Huh, not bad, pretty boy. Some people might actually believe that you're not crapping yourself with worry over the woman."

"You almost make me want to transfer to white-collar crime," Michael said, rubbing the bridge of his nose between his thumb and forefinger.

His partner grinned and then put him out of his misery by calling his friend. "Tom, my man, got an update for us?"

If Michael thought his wait was over, he was wrong. James did a lot of nodding, threw in a couple *You don't say*s and the occasional *Really?* before Michael bit out, "Is. Shay. All. Right?"

"Hang on a minute, Tom. Mr. Playing It Cool isn't so cool anymore."

"James," Michael said through gritted teeth.

"Relax. She's fine. By the time Tom and the cops got there, she had the Sterlings and their hired thugs taken care of." He turned his attention back to the phone. "Yeah, sure, I'll let him know. Thanks. You too."

"That's it?" he said when James disconnected. "What about the LVMPD and Detective Sims's investigation? Did they shut her down? Have they opened an investigation into her?"

"Sounds to me like everything's good. The ladies are out with Tom and his guys for celebratory pizza and beer. Besides, from what he told me, Shay Angel is more than capable of taking care of herself." He chuckled. "Tom's partner didn't identify himself, and she had him disarmed and on the ground before he had a chance to blink."

Michael had seen her in action a year before and knew exactly what she was capable of. It didn't mean she was invincible, though. She'd been railroaded before, and there'd been nothing he could do to stop it. This time, there had been. Only she might not have wanted his help once she heard about her uncle.

He grimaced at the reminder, pressing the heel of his palm to his chest. "You might as well get started questioning the staff at the Salty Dog." When they'd initially called the pub to check on Charlie's whereabouts, no one had seen him in the past twenty-four hours. He also wasn't answering his landline or cell. "I'll give Shay a call. She might know where he is."

"If I wasn't in desperate need of a caffeine fix, I'd stick around for that conversation. Something tells me Shay Angel won't be happy to hear you're investigating her uncle for murder."

The pressure of his palm did nothing to alleviate the burning ache in his chest. "He's a person of interest, not a suspect."

"Come on, you don't buy that, and neither do I. Fat Tony was offed in the alley outside his apartment building twenty minutes before he was supposed to meet with Angel. Angel confirmed he'd be there, and now the guy is on the wind."

They had ironclad evidence of the meet. Fat Tony's murderer had conveniently left the victim's phone behind. "Yeah, and we both know that Charlie wasn't the only one he planned to meet. Tony was on a mission. He was warning anyone with ties to the old guard to get out of town."

Six of the former bosses of the Costello crime family were set to be released from prison next month and things were heating up. Word on the street was that the younger generation had no interest in handing back the reins to the old guard. They'd recently moved the seat of their operations from Providence to Boston. As a former ADA, Michael was well acquainted with the Costello crime family.

"Huh, never would have thought you had it in you, but you've got some game, my man. Women love that white-knight crap. You tell the lady you're doin' everything you can to keep her uncle safe, and you'll have her eating out of your..." He pulled a face. "Now that I think about it, I may have spoken too soon. Shay Angel doesn't sound like any woman I've ever met, so this might blow up in your face, pretty boy." He adjusted his seat into the recline position.

"What are you doing?"

"Getting comfortable. Everyone's been telling me what a brilliant lawyer you were, so I figure it's the perfect opportunity to see you in action. That way I can judge for myself."

All he'd need was James heckling him from the sidelines. Michael pushed back his navy wool coat and pulled his wallet from his back pocket. "Coffee's on me," he said, offering his partner a ten-dollar bill.

James cocked his head and eyebrow at the same time.

Michael pulled out another ten and handed him both. "Order me one, too, and try the rest of the numbers Fat Tony called in the twenty-four hours before he was killed."

"You do remember I'm the senior agent in this partnership, right? And just to clarify, that means I tell you what to do and not the other way around. And even if that wasn't the case, I couldn't contact anyone he called if I wanted to. His phone is in evidence."

Michael typed seven sets of digits into his phone and texted them to James. "Now you can. Those are the numbers."

"What are you talking about?" James scanned the text, and then his bald head jerked up and around to Michael. "How and when did you get these?"

"Before the CSS guys arrived."

"I was there, Gallagher. All you did was look through his contacts and recent calls the same as me. You didn't take notes." He frowned. "Wait a minute. Are you telling me you've got a photographic memory?"

Michael made a noncommittal sound in his throat. It wasn't something he liked to talk about. His memories of performing on demand for his mother's friends were almost as bad as the teasing he'd endured in grade school.

"Whoa, that is all kinds of freaky," his partner said as

he heaved his big body from the passenger seat. However, judging from his intrigued expression as he got out of the Range Rover, he could tell James was already thinking of ways to use Michael's *freaky* ability to his advantage. Which made him nervous. In the short time he'd been working with his partner, he'd seen signs James wasn't exactly a by-the-book kind of guy, and Michael was.

The freezing rain they'd dealt with earlier in the day started back up, the pebble-sized ice cubes pinging off the roof and windshield of the SUV...and off James's bald head as he ran across the road. Michael turned the key and then adjusted the heat to high, glancing up at his partner cursing from where he half-lay on the sidewalk.

Michael powered down the window. "Ouch, that looks like it hurt, partner. You need a hand?"

James gave him the finger.

Smiling, he rolled up the window. It served the guy right. He'd been a pain in Michael's butt for the past week. *Yay for karma.* Michael's smile faded at the thought of fate stepping in to even the score, of being punished for past actions. Probably not the smartest thing to be thinking about right before he called Shay.

His thumb hovered over the cell phone keys as he debated whether to press number one. He'd programmed her in at the top of his contacts the day she'd left him at the village green. He saw it so clearly then, them together again. He hadn't liked that she'd needed a year, but he'd given in, mostly because she hadn't given him a choice.

In the end, it hadn't mattered. She'd stopped taking his calls three months later. She'd been right, though. He'd needed time to get his head straight after being kicked to the curb by his ex. He was more than ready for a relationship now; too bad Shay obviously wasn't.

At least physically she's okay, he thought, looking for something positive. But she still had a lot on her plate. The last thing she'd need to hear about was the trouble Charlie may or may not be in. Michael figured he could give her at least a day, maybe two, to deal with the situation in Vegas before he called.

Just as he returned the cell to the console, it rang. He glanced down, his heart giving an electrified thump at the name showing up on the screen. It felt like the sun had just come out. He rolled his eyes at himself, wondering when he'd lost his game. All he could think was thank God James wasn't there.

"Hey, Shay, I'm glad you're okay. My partner said—" Michael began before she cut him off.

"I know exactly what your partner's saying, Michael. Agent Bryant just filled me in. But what I don't understand is why you didn't tell me my uncle is a suspect in a murder investigation? The least you could've done is given me a heads-up."

Karma hadn't done near enough damage to his partner, Michael thought before saying to Shay, "And when was I supposed to do that? While the guy was shooting at you, or after, when you were bleeding out or lying in a hospital bed?" All right, so maybe he was being dramatic. She hadn't been shot and hadn't ended up in a hospital today. He leaned back against the seat, releasing an aggravated breath. This wasn't only about her uncle. At least for him it wasn't. For her, no doubt it was. "I called this morning to ask if you'd heard from Charlie or knew where he was. You didn't pick up."

"I listened to your message. You never said anything about Charlie."

Okay, so that didn't help his mood any. "I would have, if you'd returned my call like I asked. You didn't. But I guess I should've known you wouldn't. It's not like you returned any of them over the past ten months."

"I told you to stop calling. I wasn't going to change my mind." She gave a low, humorless laugh. "We would've ended up right where we are, Michael. You on one side of the law, me and my family on the other."

"That's what it all comes down to for you, doesn't it? You can't get past that day to remember the time before. It was good, Shay. We were good. We had something special. Something worth—"

"We were kids. We didn't know any better."

He heard the steely resolve in her voice. Trying to change her mind would be like trying to break down a cement wall with a toothpick. He should've known that his investigation into Charlie's possible role in a murder would be the final straw for her. God only knew what would happen if he ended up being the man to arrest her uncle.

Talk about karma, he thought as the reality of the situation finally hit him. If he'd subconsciously been holding out hope that he and Shay would eventually find their way back to each other—and he knew damn

well that he had—it was now completely and fully erad-
icated. He'd lost her for good.

And for the very first time, even after all the drama
his decision to join the FBI had caused, he wondered
if it had been worth it. He reached in his pocket for
an antacid and popped it in his mouth. "You're right,
we were just kids," he agreed, even though to his mind
twenty-four and nineteen no longer qualified as kids.
"And, Shay, I don't know where you're getting your information, but at this point, Charlie is merely a person
of interest, not a suspect."

"Yeah, and you probably have some land in Sweet
Bay you want to sell me too," she scoffed, referring
to swamp land north of Harmony Harbor. "You forget
who you're talking to, Michael. I know the score."

"Okay, fine, believe I'm the bad guy in this if you
want to, Shay. All I need to know is if you've heard
from Charlie in the past few days."

"I haven't. But, I just left a message on his landline
and cell phone for him to call me. When I hear from
him, I'll let you know, or you'll hear from him yourself."

"Is it unusual for him to take off and not let anyone
know?"

"Charlie? No. Every now and again he gets a wild
hair and takes off. He was complaining about the
weather when I talked to him last week. He said he
might come out for a visit. He likes to gamble, you
know."

Oh yeah, Michael knew the man liked to gamble.
Charlie had been the reason Shay had stolen Michael's

Corvette. Her uncle couldn't pay off a gambling debt. Shay had intimated that the men Charlie owed money to weren't exactly the forgiving kind. Which reminded Michael of why they were even talking. "Did Charlie ever mention a man named Tony Dulbecco? He may have referred to him as Fat Tony."

There was a long pause; the sound of laughter in the background, along with the clink of glasses and someone playing sax. "No, doesn't ring a bell."

As a former prosecutor, he'd developed the ability to know when someone was lying to him. Like everything else in his life, Michael had put extensive time and effort into learning how to pick up the slightest inflections in witnesses' voices, or the minute movements that gave them away.

Which was how he knew Shay had just lied to him. "You're sure? And before you answer, remember I'm not the enemy. Charlie could very well be in danger. There's more going on here than you know."

"You mean like Danny Costello going after anyone who might side with his uncles in their bid to take back the family business?"

"Okay, so maybe you're aware of some of what's going on." He should've known that she'd start nosing around as soon as she'd been apprised of the situation with her uncle. Shay had been a PI before going into the security business. "Do you have any idea why Tony would get in touch with Charlie?"

There was a heavy silence over the line before she said, "Maybe Dulbecco liked a game of cards and heard Charlie knew where the action was."

"I see. Charlie was running the games out of the bar, then?"

She laughed. It wasn't a laugh shared with friends. "Come on, I'm not the one getting paid the big bucks, Special Agent Gallagher. You can't expect me to do your job for you."

So it was going to be like that, was it? He rubbed his fingers across his chest. "Enjoy your night out with Bryant and the boys, Shay. I'm glad you're okay," he said, and went to disconnect.

"Michael, wait. I'm sorry. I just...Look, thank you for getting in touch with Bryant and trying to help. I appreciate it. I really do."

"From what I hear, you already had the situation well in hand."

"Maybe, but having Bryant back me up when Detective Sims got to the scene made a difference."

"So you're in the clear with the LVMPD?"

"Yeah, it's all good. They arrested both Sterlings and recovered half the stolen diamonds from Ray Senior's safe. They have an APB out on the men Junior was working with, and Sims is being investigated by IA."

"Stolen diamonds?" He winced when he realized there'd been a slight hesitation, the smallest hint of unease, in his voice.

She huffed a breath. "I didn't steal your ex's diamond engagement ring. You gave it to me, remember? You told me not to take anything under fifty grand for it."

"Of course I remember, but I gave it to you because I thought you were alone and on the run. I didn't know then that you were working undercover."

"Well, you didn't ask for it back when I returned Atticus to you later that day, so I just assumed you considered it payment for him and for the information I gave you on your ex's father and lawyer."

The information she'd gathered had saved him at least five times the cost of the ring and no doubt his reputation. "You're right. It's fine. I didn't want the ring anyway. I hope you got at least fifty for it."

She made a noncommittal sound in her throat and then asked, "How's Atticus?"

"Slowing down a bit." Michael was doing everything he could think of to keep his best friend healthy and around for as long as possible. "I'm sure he'd like to see you. If you're ever in Boston—"

"I don't think that's a good idea. I—"

"No, you're right. I shouldn't have mentioned it. Take care, Shay." As he disconnected, he fished in his pocket for another antacid. The pain was different than the typical dull burn of his ulcer. This time it was the deep ache of yearning for something he finally had to admit was lost to him for good. Like he so often did, he looked for something positive to focus on. The only thing he came up with was that he'd put that part of his life on hold for a year waiting for Shay, and now he could move on. Funny thing was, until today, he thought he had.

Chapter Three

♥

Roxy, you be a good girl and go tinkle for Auntie Shay," Cherry said from where she was stretched out in the backseat.

Shay looked from the shivering pink poodle, squatting in the only patch of snow at the edge of the gas station's parking lot, to the woman wrapped in a blanket with a pink satin eye mask pushed to the top of her head, and thought, *I should've gone to Greece.*

But really, that wasn't an option, and hadn't been since she'd spoken to Michael. She was pretty sure he had no idea just how much anger and resentment had been festering inside her on the other end of the line. It didn't matter how he tried to frame his questions—she knew exactly what was going on. They were looking at her uncle for Fat Tony's murder. And they were looking at him for exactly the same reason Sims had been looking at Shay.

It'd been four days since she'd last spoken to Michael, and she could still feel it, just under the surface, like a deep, angry itch she couldn't scratch or soothe. After disconnecting from him and calling everyone her uncle knew, she'd discovered Charlie had basically dropped off the face of the planet. Which meant she wasn't only angry and resentful, she was worried too.

It was an emotional combination she was familiar with when it came to her uncle. And just one more reason she'd accepted the job in Vegas. Charlie's drama somehow managed the two-hundred-and-fifty-mile trip to New York but petered out halfway through the twenty-three-hundred-mile journey to Vegas. Until now, she reminded herself. Her uncle and Michael had managed to drag her back home, to a past she couldn't seem to escape. Come to think of it, she hadn't had much luck escaping it in Vegas either.

At least that situation had been taken care of—mostly. Sterling Securities had closed their doors for the foreseeable future, leaving her and Cherry out of work and Shay's bright and shiny future shattered like a pane of glass.

"Shaybae!"

She shot to attention, scouring the gas station's parking lot for whatever made Cherry yell. When she didn't see anything out of the ordinary, she said, "What?" unable to keep the testiness from her voice. She'd been driving for thirty-six hours with very little sleep thanks to the woman in the backseat.

"I told you before. I don't understand why you keep forgetting. Turn your back on Roxy or she won't tinkle. She's shy."

Why? Shay asked herself for probably the thousandth

time in the past thirty-six hours. *Why had she agreed to bring them with her?* It had been the road trip from hell. She was tempted to drive past the turnoff to Harmony Harbor and head straight to Logan International Airport in Boston and put them on a plane back to Vegas.

She rubbed the Harry Winston Belle engagement ring between her fingers. It hung from a thin chain under her sweatshirt. The two-carat diamond was her backup plan. But what good was a backup plan if she lost her ever-loving mind dealing with a diva and the diva's dog? Last time Shay checked, she could easily get a hundred grand for the ring. It was enough to pay start-up costs for her business and to help Cherry out until she found a job. There were only two problems with that plan.

The first was that she couldn't send Cherry and Roxy back because Special Agent Bryant had recommended they get out of town until things cooled down. Junior's partners were still footloose and fancy-free, and no doubt knew by now that Shay and Cherry were the ones responsible for derailing their money train. And Shay didn't trust anyone but herself to protect her pain-in-the-butt friend.

The second was related to the ring her fingers caressed. The only way to provide for Cherry and Roxy in Vegas until her friend found a job was to sell the Harry Winston Belle. Which, up until now, Shay had been unable to do. It bothered her to think about, so, for the most part, she didn't. There had to be a reasonable explanation as to why she hadn't been able to part with the ring. She'd tried, oh yeah, she'd tried.

Three times. But in the end, she hadn't been able to go through with it.

Annoyed at herself, she released the ring. She needed to sell it or at least put it in a safe. "If she doesn't hurry up, she'll freeze that way," she said about the dog, who hadn't moved from its spot in the snow.

Wondering if that may well be the problem, Shay squinted at Roxy in the faint glow of the sign's neon lights. The dog stared back at her. She noted the petulant ire in the poodle's eyes, similar to that of her owner, who'd sat up to glare at Shay from around the headrest.

"You know what, I'll sit in the car, and you can be on"—she refused to say *tinkle* out loud—"pee patrol."

"My false eyelashes stuck together the last time I went out. I hate to think what it's doing to my implants. You really should've warned me how cold it was..." The lines at the outer edges of Cherry's mouth relaxed into a proud smile. "Oh, Roxy Roo, you're mama's best girl. See," she said, giving Shay one of those pursed-lip faces she'd become accustomed to over the past three days, "if you would've just done as I told you, we wouldn't have been sitting here freezing our patooties off for the past ten minutes."

"Or your boobs, apparently," Shay said under her breath, though for the amount of time Cherry had been outside, she didn't think she had to worry.

Shay waited a second before scooping up Roxy and then slid into the driver's seat of the Challenger, passing the poodle back to Cherry. "Okay, are we good now? We're not stopping again, so speak now or—"

Cherry's hand went to her hair. It was such a mess that

it looked as if Roxy had been digging in it for a doggy treat. "We're at least three hours away. Can't we stop just outside of town? I want to make a good first impression. We need to freshen up before we see anyone."

"Unless my uncle is at home and ignoring his phone, you don't have to worry about making an impression on anybody. By the time we get into town, it'll be close to midnight."

"I thought we'd go to the pub. Your friends must be anxious to see you. Did you let them know—"

The engine revved as Shay's foot came down on the gas and the car shot out of the parking lot. Thrown against the backseat, Roxy yelped and Cherry gasped.

Shay winced. "Sorry, you guys all right? I hit black ice." Her hands tightened around the steering wheel as she eased off the gas. If she allowed the suggestion that her nonexistent friends were anxiously awaiting her arrival to get under her skin, she'd need to grow an extra-thick layer of epidermis to get through the next few days. "We're too late to go to the pub. Last call on Sundays is eleven."

"Shaybae, what's wrong?"

Cherry's voice was close to her ear as she moved in behind her. Wrapping her arms around the seat and Shay, she was enveloped in Cherry's concern and sweet, cotton candy scent.

"I'm fine. Sit back and put on your seat belt."

"I'm sorry, all I've been doing is complaining about being trapped in this coffin, eating in dives, staying in no-frill motels with none of those fancy shampoos and stuff, and freezing my patootie—"

"And your boobs, don't forget your boobs," Shay said, amused despite herself. Even Cherry's apology was a complaint. But at least she was self-aware enough to realize she'd been a pain in the *patootie*. It gave Shay hope that she'd make a better roomie than a roadie.

"—while you're worrying about your uncle. It's probably like you said, and he just got tired of the cold. Maybe he took a trip to Mexico."

"That's why I'm here. I'll have a better idea what he's up to once I search the house." And see if his passport and stash of cash were missing or if he'd left her a note.

There'd been things she'd held back from Michael when they spoke. Like the fact that Charlie knew exactly who Tony D was, and so did Shay. Back in the day, he'd been known in the Angel household as Uncle Tony, an old friend of her father, Charlie's older brother. By then Tony had been trying to get out of the business.

She remembered him as the nice man who smelled like doughnuts and pulled quarters from behind her and her sisters' ears, but she'd seen another side of him when he'd shown up at her hearing. He'd sat behind her in court, giving her piece-of-crap attorney a coronary by telling him that, if he didn't get her off, he was a dead man.

There'd been a cold promise in Tony's eyes that day. At nineteen, she'd seen her fair share of the seedier side of life and the men who inhabited it and knew without a doubt she was looking into the eyes of a killer. After she and Charlie made it clear that wasn't something either of them wanted him to do, Tony backed off. It didn't stop him from offering to off Maura Gallagher and the judge, though. Still, Shay had been glad he'd been there when the sentence came down, for her uncle's sake. And later, for her own.

He'd known a woman, Gwen, who was serving time for armed robbery. He'd asked her to keep an eye on Shay as a personal favor to him. The older woman had put Shay under her protection, teaching her the ropes, keeping her safe. At least she did for the first year.

"Don't you have family or friends who could've checked for you?" Cherry asked.

There she goes again, circling back to the friends thing, Shay thought. Cherry must've picked up on something in her voice. And knowing the woman like she did, Shay didn't hold out hope she'd get any peace until she gave Cherry something. "Look, I'm not like you. I don't need friends. I didn't have many growing up, and that was just fine by me."

She didn't need them for the first twelve years of her life because she'd had her sisters. They'd been sent to live with Charlie after their parents died. He'd tried his best, but raising three little girls between the ages of four and ten was a lot to expect of a confirmed bachelor. Shay looked after her younger sisters as best she knew how. She'd thought they were doing okay until the day social services arrived at their door and removed them from Charlie's care.

Six months later, they were separated forever. Her sisters were adopted, and she never saw or heard from them again for sixteen years. She'd spent the year after she'd lost them running away from the group home and back to her uncle and Harmony Harbor. After the seventh time, the powers that be finally gave up and allowed her to stay with Charlie.

"Right?"

"Sorry, I missed what you said." A wind as strong as her emotions buffeted the car. She held the wheel steady, trying to banish thoughts of her sisters and Charlie. She flexed her fingers on the wheel, focusing on the taillights of the truck ahead of her through the spray of slush and salt. She couldn't afford to be distracted right now.

The road conditions weren't ideal, especially for the Challenger that handled winter weather about as well as Cherry. Shay's car had been another reason she'd second-guessed her decision to drive instead of fly. In the end, she refused to leave her pride and joy unattended in Vegas, afraid that Junior's friends would take their revenge out on her car.

"I said, you must have some family, right?"

"Wrong. I only have Charlie."

"Oh, Shaybae. My heart is breaking. Do you hear it? I just heard it crack." She flopped back against the seat with her hands pressed dramatically to her triple Ds.

"Maybe your implants really did freeze, and the crack you heard was them—"

"Don't even joke about that," Cherry said, her voice muffled.

Shay glanced in the rearview mirror. Sure enough, Cherry's head was bent as she checked beneath her unzipped jacket, no doubt looking for signs of deflation or saltwater damage. A chuckle bubbled up in her throat. The woman might frustrate Shay to no end, but she was good for a laugh every now and again.

"Everything's fine down there," Cherry said, sounding relieved as she scooted forward to rest her arms on the back of Shay's seat. "Okay, so with your looks and bite-me attitude, I can see why you wouldn't have a lot of girlfriends, but you must have had the boys sniffing around you twenty-four-seven. Like your friend the FBI agent with the panty-melting voice. Tell me about him. I sense a story there."

Shay gauged the safety of the maneuver and then tapped the brake, sending Cherry flying back against the seat. "Lots of black ice on the road tonight. Better buckle up and let me concentrate." And hopefully that would be the last Shay heard of Panty-Melting Gallagher for the rest of the night.

* * *

It was Sunday night, and instead of putting his feet up and reading a good book, Michael was driving under the stone arch to Greystone Manor. An early evening altercation with a neighbor had turned Michael's abstract thoughts of leaving the city for the country into a reality. He'd called his grandmother an hour before to ask if his family's cottage was available.

The spotlights in the front gardens lit up the imposing mansion built of local sand-colored granite. Across the parking lot, he spotted his cousin leaning against his truck. Aidan looked up from his phone when Michael pulled in beside him. With his blue eyes and dark hair and height, he could've passed for Michael's brother. All the Gallaghers looked alike.

Aidan cocked his head and pointed to his eye. Obviously, the parking lot lights illuminated the interior of the Range Rover and his cousin had caught a glimpse of Michael's shiner. At the reminder, Michael brought his hand to his eye and winced. He should've iced it or tried to conceal the swelling and bruise before heading for Harmony Harbor.

Strapped in the passenger seat beside him, Atticus whined and leaned in to give Michael a sloppy doggy kiss.

"Don't feel bad, buddy. I'd take a punch for you any day of the week." He ruffled the wolfhound's coarse, gray coat. "Stay here while I get the key, and then we'll check out our new digs."

Aidan met Michael as he got out of the SUV. "What happened to you? You finally meet a situation you couldn't smooth-talk your way out of?"

"Yeah, an eighty-year-old former marine who didn't appreciate Atticus bowling his wife over." It hadn't been intentional on his dog's part. Atticus wasn't only the size of a small horse, but he also had degenerative eye disease and was going blind.

"They gonna sue?" his cousin asked.

"They planned to until I laid out the reasons why they couldn't win against me."

Aidan laughed. "I forgot you can still be an arrogant smartass when you want to be."

He didn't take offense to his cousin's remark. Michael

had been an arrogant ass in his teens and early twenties. "You're just jealous because GG loved me best."

"Right now, you're Gram's favorite. She's over the moon that you've decided to move into the cottage. No doubt GG's dancing a jig in heaven now that another member of the Save Greystone Team's come home."

"Founding member. I still can't understand why we haven't gotten everyone on board yet. Even my brothers are holding out."

"How are they? I haven't seen them since GG's funeral."

Michael was the baby of the family. Logan was the oldest, and then there was Connor. In Harmony Harbor, they were known as the summer Gallaghers. "Logan's leaving his last overseas posting for good next week. He's been reassigned to the president's security detail."

"They couldn't ask for a better man. Your parents must be glad he'll be closer to home."

Aidan was right about Logan. There wasn't a Secret Service agent any tougher, smarter, or more capable and dependable than his brother. Michael looked up to his oldest brother and always had. "Yeah, Mom's planning a welcome-home thing for him. No doubt you'll get an invite. You can catch up with Conner then too."

Aidan grinned. "How is the black sheep of the family?"

Connor was a big-time corporate lawyer, who was more interested in the money than the law. That wasn't entirely true; he was very interested in the law and manipulating it to work to his advantage. Which he was very, very good at. "Rich and full of himself."

Even though he didn't exactly approve of his brother, Michael loved him and felt guilty for dissing him. "He probably just needs the love of a good woman to turn him from a beast into a prince. I hear congratulations are in order, Beast," he teased his cousin.

"Har har. Let me guess, you've been talking to Liam. You two always were a pain when you got—" He broke off at the approach of a woman with wild dark hair and big purple eyes in a pretty, pale face.

Aidan grinned when she reached his side. "You've stopped pulling out your hair, so I take it you were able to access your manuscript and get it off to your editor. Julia's a writer," he informed Michael. "I don't think you two have met. This is my cousin Michael. Michael, Julia." His cousin lowered his voice and said to Julia, "Don't embarrass him by saying anything about the shiner, babe. He got beaten up by an octogenarian. He always was more of a lover than a fighter."

Michael rolled his eyes as he extended his hand to Julia.

"His fiancée," she said, giving Aidan a nudge before putting her hand in Michael's. "We've never met, but I've heard all about you. Sophie was going to set us up together."

"It's not too late. You're not married yet," Michael said, grinning at his cousin's low growl. "Sounds like the Beast objects."

She laughed. "I should hope so. The date's set, and plans for the wedding are well under way." She smiled up at Aidan. "Father O'Malley agreed to marry us in the water."

His cousin rubbed the back of his neck, looking decidedly uncomfortable with the news. "I thought you were joking about the mermaid theme."

"Of course not. That's where we had our meet-cute."

"I thought our meet-cute was under the mistletoe at the manor."

"It was, but we're getting married in July, not December."

This was a side to his cousin that Michael had never seen before. The former DEA agent used to be taciturn and tough. He wouldn't be talking about meet-cutes or agreeing to mermaid weddings.

Must be love, Michael thought, working to keep the laughter from his voice when he said, "I'll leave you guys to it. Nice meeting you, Julia. Give me a call if you ever get tired of this guy." He clapped his cousin on the shoulder. "I was planning to stop by the station before I head to work in the morning. You going to be in? I thought we could share information on Charlie Angel's case."

"Yeah, sure. Sounds like a—" Aidan began before Julia cut him off with a frown.

"What are you talking about? What's going on with Charlie?"

"He's missing. I thought I told you... Right, you've had deadline brain for the past few days." He glanced at Michael, amusement and maybe a hint of pride glinting in his eyes. "She doesn't see, hear, or do anything other than write for the entire seventy-two hours before she has to hand in her book. Hence the hair and pale face."

She touched her head. "What's wrong with my

hair?" Then she waved off her own question. "That's not important. Tell me why both the FBI and the HHPD are looking into Charlie's disappearance. This isn't just about him taking off like he sometimes does, is it? Not with both of you involved."

"Might be. At this point, we're not sure. But his name's come up in an investigation, and we need to talk to him. So far, we haven't been able to reach him," Michael told her. "Your bookstore's just up the street from the Salty Dog, isn't it? Do you remember when you last saw him?"

She tilted her head to the side. "I think it was... When exactly did he go missing?"

"Best we can tell, sometime after nine o'clock Tuesday night," Michael told her, catching a hint of dismay cross her face just before it vanished. He glanced at his cousin to see if he noticed.

Of course he had. Aidan's eyes narrowed on his fiancée. "Julia, what is it? Do you know something?"

She played with her earring. "No, nothing. Nothing at all. I didn't see anything. Oh, look at the beautiful dog. He's huge," she said, walking toward the Range Rover.

His cousin grabbed her hand and tugged her back. "Hold it. What aren't you telling us?"

"Trust me, just let it go. You really don't want to know."

"Babe, I assure you, we really do. I've put together a special sending-off-the-manuscript celebration that's going to be ruined if you stall for much longer, so spill."

Special sending-off-the-manuscript celebration?

Michael stared at Aidan, wondering who'd taken over his cousin's body.

As though he knew what Michael was thinking, Aidan shrugged and then muttered, "Just you wait, smartass." Then he looked down at his fiancée. "Julia, I don't know who you're trying to protect, but Charlie might be in trouble."

"If he is, then someone who is important to you, and to you"—she nodded at Michael—"might be in trouble too."

"My brother?" Aidan asked at almost the same time as Michael said, "Liam?"

"No." She glanced back at the manor and then lowered her voice. "I took a walk down to the harbor to clear my head Tuesday night. About an hour before you came to pick me up, Aidan. So probably around ten. I saw Jasper and Charlie on the wharf. They were arguing. It looked...it looked like it might get physical."

Chapter Four

♥

After four rounds of heads-or-tails ended in a tie, his cousin decided that the FBI had jurisdiction, so it was Michael's job to question Jasper. Michael knew better. It didn't have anything to do with jurisdiction. His cousin didn't want to interrogate the man who'd been like a great-uncle to the Gallagher grandchildren any more than Michael did.

Jasper had been a permanent fixture at the manor for as long as any of them could remember. Tall, with white hair brushed back from an angular face and a hint of the British Isles in both his manner and speech, the seventysomething man could easily pass for the butler in his favorite period drama, *Downton Abbey*.

He'd been their great-grandmother Colleen's right-hand man, running the manor and the family with an iron fist. Which included keeping Michael and his brothers in line whenever they came to visit. Especially when they were younger and spent summers at the family cottage. The cottage Michael had hoped to be settled into by now.

He imagined Atticus did too. "Come on, boy," he said, releasing the seat belt as his cousin pulled away with a wave. From the truck's passenger window, Julia sent Michael a commiserating smile. He hoped she was wrong about what she thought she'd seen. His cousin didn't think so. Apparently Aidan had heard rumors of a feud between Jasper and Charlie years before. Something to do with Ronan, their grandfather.

Atticus's gaze moved from Michael to the asphalt, his long eyebrows and beard making him look like an old man. Lately, he'd been acting like one too. Michael banished the thought and the depressing worries that accompanied it. He wouldn't allow himself to think about what the vet had said at their last visit.

"You know what, boy? Living here will be good for you. Lots of places to roam free and plenty of fresh air." It might end up being as good for him as it was for his dog, Michael thought as he helped Atticus out of the SUV. The wolfhound wasn't the only one who'd been in a rut.

Michael pressed the lock button, standing for a minute to listen to the waves crash against the rocky shore at the back of the manor. The sound reminded him of how much he'd loved coming here as a kid. There was something wild and primal about the place that appealed to him. He liked the history, too, the sense of family and belonging. A cold wind blew off the ocean, ruffling his hair and tugging at his coat, the tang of fish and salt on the damp sea air.

Atticus nudged him, unwilling, it seemed, to let Michael put off the interrogation any longer. With a low *woof,* the wolfhound lumbered up the walkway. The flagstone path was lit by the same white fairy lights that were wrapped around the fifteen-foot cedars and flowering shrubs, their buds tightly cocooned.

Michael reached the dark wood medieval-looking door just as it creaked open. Atticus must have knocked with his big head or equally big paw. "Thanks a lot, pal," he murmured, not quite ready to hear what Jasper had to say.

It was then that Michael realized what he hadn't allowed himself to think about. His worry that a member of his family might somehow be involved in Charlie's disappearance, and what that would mean for his relationship with Shay. He drew in a frustrated breath at the sign that he still held out hope, even after their last phone call.

"Master Michael, Atticus, we've been awaiting your arrival. It's good to have you home where you belong. I aired out the cottage and stocked the kitchen," Jasper said while giving Atticus a quick rubdown.

The older man wasn't normally a fan of animals in the manor, but he had a soft spot for Michael's dog. His great-grandmother had presented Michael with Atticus on the day he'd passed the bar. However, it was Jasper who'd decided on the breed and breeder and looked after the baby wolfhound before he was given to Michael.

Jasper's smile faded as he lifted his gaze, his brow furrowed. "Master Michael, what on earth happened to you?"

"Nothing to be concerned about," he said, once again making the mistake of bringing his fingers to his eye.

Atticus whined and stood on his hind legs, placing his front paws on Michael's shoulders to give him another sloppy apology kiss. Michael hugged the dog. "I'm fine, buddy, but you need some doggy breath mints. Come on, get down."

Atticus dropped to the slate floor on all fours, rocking the glass vase in the middle of the pedestal table.

Jasper grabbed it when two red petals fell from the roses, shooting a disgruntled look at the black cat that sauntered past the table.

"Sorry about that. We won't be long. I just need to pick up the key, and I have a couple of questions for you." Michael may have mumbled the last under his breath.

"In regards to?"

He cleared his throat. "The disappearance of Charlie Angel."

* * *

"Yes, it's me, Atticus my boy. Just because you can't see me doesn't mean I'm not here," Colleen said to the wolfhound, who sniffed at the window seat on which she was currently perched in her ghostly form. Simon, the black cat who'd arrived at the manor a week before Colleen had passed, took a swipe at the dog.

"You're a brave one. He could eat you in a single bite if he was so inclined." Which of course he wouldn't. Atticus was a noble dog with a sweet and gentle disposition. They said a person's pet often reflected its master, and she thought that to be true in this case.

Michael was a fine man, noble, commanding, and whip smart, but there was a warmth and kindness about him too. And to her utter delight, the boy had finally decided to come home where he belonged.

Out of all her great-grandchildren, Michael had loved Greystone Manor the most. She saw signs of her son Ronan not only in Michael's strong, masculine features but also in his quiet intellect, smooth-talking tongue, and his love of history. Thinking of Ronan brought on a familiar twinge where her heart had once beat.

At the time that she died, more than a year before, she'd seen the light and had been overjoyed at the thought of seeing her loved ones once more. A hundred and four when she passed, she imagined there'd been quite the crowd gathered at the Pearly Gates, anxiously awaiting her arrival. Only she'd made the mistake of looking back at those she'd leave behind as they tried desperately to revive her.

In that instant, she'd known they needed her more than the ones who'd gone before. They weren't prepared to take on the battle for Greystone's future, and they were at a complete and utter loss when it came to finding their true loves.

Michael was the worst of the lot and had come within hours of making the biggest mistake of his life. The lad might be book smart, but when it came to life and love, he could use some help. Either that or a kick in the hinie. The rest of them hadn't been much better off at the time, so she'd felt she didn't have a choice. She'd stick around and set them on the path to true love. In doing so, she'd not only ensure they lived happily ever after, she'd also guarantee that the estate would stay in the family forevermore.

So here she was, living betwixt and between, a ghost of her former self. But not in a vampire or zombie sort of way. She was tied to the manor, invisible and inaudible to most but Simon and some of her great-great-grandchildren. Jasper, who was just then taking a seat across from Michael in the study, could sense her presence. Mostly because of Simon. He knew where one went, the other wasn't far behind. Not always, though.

Jasper wasn't paying any mind to Simon now. He was intent on Michael, who was seated behind Colleen's imposing mahogany desk. There was something about the way her great-grandson was studying Jasper that made Colleen nervous.

The animals drew her attention with their battle sounds. "Enough now. I need to hear this," Colleen said, her forefinger going through the hissing Simon's nose as she tried to gently tap it. Both the cat and dog reared back. Tail tucked between his hind legs, Atticus made his way to his master's side, bumping into a chair and a floor lamp along the way.

"Poor laddie, he's going blind. You be kind to him from now on, do you hear?" she said to Simon.

He gave her a shirty look and plunked down beside her.

The door to the study opened, and Colleen's daughter-in-law Kitty appeared. She'd been married to Ronan for decades but still managed to look like a woman much younger than her years. Colleen suspected her wardrobe played a part. Tonight, she wore skinny jeans and a blue mohair turtleneck that matched her eyes. "What's all the commotion...Michael darling, you're here. Oh my, your eye." She raised a hand to her throat. "Jasper, did you—"

"I most assuredly did not. I would never strike the boy. And I must say I resent your implying that I would do so, Kitty." Jasper harrumphed and crossed his arms.

His dark eyebrows drawing inward, Michael looked from Jasper to his grandmother.

"You see it, don't you, my boy? Things have indeed changed between the two. Kitty now knows Jasper has been in love with her for years, and she has feelings for him too."

Which created something of a problem for Colleen. Where Jasper had once been on her team, willing to help out as best he could given her ghostly circumstance— though he'd managed to mess up a time or two—he was definitely on Kitty's side now. The two of them had been in cahoots since Jasper discovered Kitty had Colleen's memoir, *The Secret Keeper of Harmony Harbor*. And just like the title implied, the book contained not only the Gallagher family secrets but also the secrets of half the town.

Kitty and Jasper had taken it upon themselves to right the wrongs of the past. Now, if Colleen was honest, she'd admit their first attempt had turned out all right in the end. Of course, not as well as if she'd been the one pulling the strings, exposing secrets and revealing truths.

"I'm sorry, darling. I...," Kitty said to Jasper, trailing off when Michael's blue eyes went wide.

"All right, am I missing something? Since when do you refer to Jasper as darling?" Michael asked.

Colleen's old confidant looked at Kitty, no doubt holding his breath awaiting her response. Kitty wasn't keen to let word of her and Jasper's romance get out. As far as Colleen could tell, she was worried about how her sons and grandchildren would feel. Colleen thought she might've given Jasper's feelings as much consideration as she gave to the family's.

"It was just a slip of the tongue. Nothing to concern yourself with." She cast an apologetic glance at Jasper. He stared straight ahead, ignoring the light brush of her fingers on his arm when she took the chair beside him. "So, how did you get the black eye, darling?"

"A disagreement of sorts. It precipitated our move here. I realize it was short notice and it's getting late. I hope I didn't put anyone out."

"Not at all. We're absolutely thrilled you're here. Jasper has everything in order at the cottage, so if you'd like to head over—" Kitty began, obviously anxious to get rid of Michael. No doubt she wanted to make amends to Jasper as quickly as possible.

"Actually, if you don't mind, I need a word with Jasper, Grams. Alone."

"He wishes to question me about Charlie Angel," Jasper said, continuing to stare straight ahead.

"Oh." Kitty swallowed hard. "I'm not going anywhere, Michael. Jasper's my...friend. If he's in some kind of trouble, I want to know."

Colleen took in the nervous way Kitty rubbed her hands together. And in doing so, she almost missed the silent exchange between the couple. Almost. "For the love of all that's holy, do not tell me you told Charlie what I did all those years before?" Colleen muttered at the pair.

"Why would you think Jasper's in some kind of trouble, Grams?"

Jasper reached for Kitty's hand and gave it a squeeze, whether to comfort her or shut her up, Colleen wasn't sure. Then he looked at Michael. "I'm aware Charlie's missing, and if you're here to question me, I imagine you have a witness who saw me with him on the wharf."

"I do, and Jasper, I'd be remiss if I didn't inform you that it might be best if you had an attorney present. Would you like to call one before we continue?"

"Michael, Jasper is a...like a member of this family. How dare you threaten—"

"Grams, I'm protecting him, not threatening him. This is an informal conversation, but it wouldn't be a bad idea if he had representation."

"I have nothing to hide, Master Michael. Please, go ahead."

"If he's going to jail, so am I. We're in this together and we'll go down together if—"

Jasper made an exasperated sound in his throat. "Kitty, not another word."

"No, you're not facing the consequences alone. We were just trying to right Mother Gallagher's wrong."

"If I wasn't already dead, the two of them would

be the death of me, Simon," Colleen said to the cat, whose ears had perked up the moment Michael suggested Jasper hire an attorney.

Jasper and Kitty began a back-and-forth spat, which Michael put a stop to by placing his fingers between his lips and whistling. Atticus whined, and Simon put his paws over his head. Jasper and Kitty looked at Michael. "Stop arguing, and let's start from the beginning. Jasper, what were you and Charlie fighting about?"

"We weren't fighting."

"Don't hold out on me, okay? The person who saw you on the wharf said the conversation was heated and looked to be getting physical."

"That's true, but not on my part." He glanced at Kitty, and she nodded. "Your grandmother and I came across information that we felt Charlie had a right to know. He was, to put it mildly, upset."

"What did you tell him?" Michael asked.

"My great-grandson won't be happy about this, Simon. Or happy with me, I'm afraid. But I did what I thought was best at the time. I only meant to protect the girls."

"Your great-grandmother was the one who called social services on Charlie all those years before and had Shay and her sisters removed from his care."

Michael stared at him and then closed his eyes. Leaning forward to place his elbows on the desk, he brought his hands to his face and rubbed his forehead as if to banish the words Jasper said from his head.

Colleen knew her great-grandson well enough to understand what was going on in his mind. There would be no coming back from this. No hope of him having a second chance with Shay after she learned the truth. Though Colleen imagined Michael had begun to come to terms with that possibility when Shay failed to meet him at the village green as she had promised. A piece of news Colleen had gleaned from sitting in this very room while her great-granddaughters-in-law conducted their weekly coffee klatch. Still…"I'm sorry, my boy. It happened long before I realized Shay was your one true love. Even had I known, in good conscience, I couldn't have stayed silent."

Atticus shoved his snout under Michael's arm, no doubt in an effort to comfort him. His master absently patted the dog's head.

"Madame had her reasons, Master Michael. As you well know, Charlie wasn't a pillar of society."

"I don't think that will bring much comfort to Shay, Jasper. She lost her sisters and, as far as I know, has never been able to find them."

"Yes, and that's why we decided to bring the matter to Charlie's attention. Madame had recorded the name and number of her contact at social services in her book"—he cleared his throat—"a letter that I recently came across in her desk. The adoptions were closed, but your great-grandmother managed to get some informa-tion, which she recorded. Both of the adoptive families moved not long after the girls were placed in their care. I gave Charlie their last known addresses. We were just trying to make things right."

"Obviously, Charlie wasn't happy to learn the truth," Michael surmised.

"I'd say that would be an understatement."

"So, when you gave him the information, did it seem like he was going to tell Shay or was he going to try and find the girls himself?"

"I believe he meant to keep the information to himself in hopes that he would be able to find the girls. You aren't the only one who feels they have something to make up for where Ms. Angel is concerned, Master Michael. Though, as I've told you countless times in the past, the guilt is not yours to bear."

"The sins of the father, or in this case, the mother, Jasper. And now it seems my great-grandmother."

"I'm sure Shay will understand that none of this is your fault, darling."

"I wouldn't be so sure about that, Grams," he said, a determined look coming over his face as he pushed back from the desk. "I have something I need to check into. If you don't mind, I'll leave Atticus here. I shouldn't be more than an hour."

"I've known you for thirty-four years, and I recognize that look in your eyes, Master Michael. I feel it's my duty to warn you that going against your code of honor has never served you well in the past. Don't do it. Don't put your job in jeopardy."

"I appreciate your concern, but you don't have to worry about me putting my job at risk. Shay and I used to date, so it's reasonable to assume that I could still have a key to Charlie's place."

Jasper drew a long and somewhat exasperated breath through his nose before coming to his feet. "You were, without a doubt, one of the finest prosecutors I have ever had the pleasure of watching, and I'm sure, given your desire to serve and protect, you will be an excellent FBI agent. But I'm afraid I don't have the same level of confidence in your abilities as a thief. So tell me what it is you're looking for, and I'll go in your stead."

Michael appeared both touched and amused. "Thanks, but I'm not sure I'm any more confident in your abilities as a thief as I am in my own."

"Oh, darling, you have no idea what Jasper is capable of. He's an excellent thief as well as—" Kitty caught Jasper's raised-eyebrow glance and cleared her throat. "He's very good at whatever he sets his mind to."

"Look, I appreciate the offer, but this is something I have to do on my own. You two have done enough already. I'll take it from here."

"What exactly is it you're planning to do, Master Michael?"

"First, my job. If Charlie is, as you think, searching for his nieces, there should be some evidence of that at his place. Which means he's not in danger and my interest in him in connection to my case diminishes. But if he wrote anything down about GG's involvement or happened to leave any of the papers you gave him lying around, I don't want Shay to find them. According to staff at the Salty Dog, she left Vegas for Harmony Harbor and is expected in the next couple of days. Don't look so shocked," he said to Kitty and Jasper. "I still might need her cooperation in my case, and she won't be feeling very cooperative if she finds out what GG did. And if Charlie doesn't find her sisters, I will. So don't worry, she'll learn the truth eventually. Just not right now."

"It appears your mind is made up. As that's the case, wait here for a moment. I have something that should help in the night's business."

Michael watched Jasper leave before turning to his grandmother. "What did you mean when you said Jasper was an excellent thief?"

Kitty made a zip-it motion with her fingers.

Colleen wished Jasper had kept his lips zipped. She had a feeling her great-grandson's trip to the dark side wasn't going to end well.

* * *

Shay pulled onto the parking pad that looked down on the cedar-shingled home she'd lived in for nine years of her life. It was more of a cottage really and sat just beyond the salt marshes. There was a small enclave of ten homes that had seen better days. Although those days must have been long past because she couldn't remember them.

It was dark, the quarter moon and stars barely visible in the cloudy night sky. The lack of streetlights didn't help. Two were out, the broken glass lying at their ornate cast-iron bases. A leftover symbol of days gone by.

Shay stretched, glad to finally have arrived. She glanced in the rearview mirror at Cherry and Roxy. They were sleeping, soft snores emitting from their open mouths. If she wasn't so tired, she'd take a picture. It would make for good blackmail material. Cherry didn't like anyone to see her looking less than her best. And if the road trip from hell was any indication, Shay would need all the blackmail material she could get her hands on.

She popped the trunk, about to get out of the car, when a flicker of light from inside the house caught her eye. Muscles that she hadn't even known were tight relaxed as her worry over her uncle faded. She picked up her phone, checking to see if it was on, checking to see if there were messages or calls she'd missed. There weren't any.

She looked back at the house, eyes narrowing on the halo of light that moved from left to right. She'd been wrong. Her uncle wasn't home. Whoever was in there hadn't been invited. They were looking for something, or someone.

Movement from behind her brought her gaze to the backseat. Cherry sat up with a sleepy smile and reached between the seat and door. "Let's blow this popsicle stand, Shaybae. I can't wait—"

"No, you're not going anywhere. Not yet," she said, and leaned across the passenger seat to open the glove box. She took out a Five-seveN handgun.

"That's a gun. Why do you have a gun?"

The question should probably be *how*. As a convicted felon, no matter that she'd served her time, Shay wouldn't legally be allowed to carry had she not worked undercover for the DEA. They'd petitioned a judge for a license on her behalf.

Cherry flapped her hands in front of her face. It sounded like she was hyperventilating.

"Relax, it's just a precaution. I want to check the house." Shay carefully opened the car door, stepping outside. Keeping an eye on the house, she reached for the lever and moved the seat forward. "Sit up front. If anyone other than me comes out of the house, you drive away, and you drive away fast. Don't stop until you're sure no one is following you, and then find someplace well lit and populated and call the cops."

"Let's call them now."

"No." If Danny Costello had sent someone looking for Charlie, Shay didn't want the cops involved. She needed to do this on her own. She needed answers, and one way or another, the person inside her uncle's house would provide them.

Chapter Five

♥

It had been over an hour since Michael had broken into Charlie's house, and he was beginning to think Jasper would've had better luck. Michael's guilty conscience kept slowing him down. At every squeak and creak, he'd freeze, afraid Charlie was going to walk in and find him there. Though it was possible Shay's uncle wouldn't recognize him. Part of Jasper's break-and-enter kit had consisted of a disguise.

On one level, the fact the older man actually had a B&E kit was worrisome and warranted further investigation. On the other, his expertise had come in handy. Michael was beginning to think he should call Jasper and ask where he thought Charlie might hide the papers if he'd left them behind. So far Michael had searched the living room, kitchen, and Charlie's bedroom and come up empty.

He didn't want to push his luck by being there much longer. He'd almost gotten caught when he was picking the lock. Probably because, after failing to open the door for what felt like the twentieth time in so many minutes, he swore in frustration. Repeatedly. And the lights had gone on in the house next door. He was pretty sure he'd heard their sliding glass door open too. He couldn't tell for certain because, at that point, he was lying facedown on the wooden deck that was littered with dirt and leaves.

If he was honest, though, which he was, sometimes to a fault, he'd admit there were a variety of reasons for his frustration, reasons that had several layers. However, once all the layers had been peeled back, the heart of the matter remained the same. Shay and how he felt about her.

Jasper was right. Michael had been extremely good at his job as ADA. So good, in fact, he probably could make a case that he hadn't been able to completely get over Shay because circumstances and people had torn them apart. They hadn't had a chance to quietly grow tired of each other and fall out of love.

Which, given his track record back then, would've happened a week later if she hadn't stolen his car. Instead, all he remembered was being completely and utterly head over heels in love with the woman. Of course, he'd known in the eyes of the world and his mother she was completely and utterly wrong for him. Young and stupidly in love, he hadn't cared.

"Get a grip and stay focused," he muttered to himself as he left Charlie's bedroom empty-handed.

He glanced to his left and headed for Shay's childhood bedroom at the end of the hall, speculating that Charlie may have gone in there after learning the truth from Jasper. He might have sat on her bed to think about the past—the part he'd played in ruining her life. Everything Shay had suffered because of the Gallaghers.

A low creak caused Michael to freeze in his tracks. He stayed still, listening intently before shaking his head at himself when all he could hear was the hum of the refrigerator. He really wasn't cut out for this sort of thing. Breaking the law wasn't in his DNA, even if he could make a justifiable excuse that he'd done so for the greater good. He took another step on the pine floor. No creak, no squeak, no...

"Flashlight down and on the ground," ordered a familiar terse, feminine voice.

"Shay, I can...," he began as he turned around.

Bang!

The flashlight exploded in his hand. "Jesus! Shay, it's me!" He dropped what was left of the flashlight and held up his hands, trying to gauge her reaction from her stance, but he couldn't really see her. She stood in the shadows. He remembered his disguise and lifted his hand to remove the beard.

Bang!

A bullet whizzed by his head and into the wall behind him. "What the hell? It's me, Michael. You recognize my voice. I know you do. And if you'd just give me a chance to—"

"I know exactly who you are, Special Agent Gallagher. You're the man who is trying to build a case against my uncle for murder, and you've broken into our home in the middle of the night wearing a disguise, gloves, and boot covers. So excuse me if I'm—"

"Okay, I can see how it looks bad, but if you'd just give me a chance to—" At the sound of the front door crashing open, followed by high-pitched barking and higher-pitched shrieking, he jerked his gaze from Shay's shadow to the space behind her. Within seconds, a small blur of fur barreled toward him and was quickly surpassed by a blonde in fluorescent pink.

"I've got him! I've got him, Shaybae!" the blonde screamed just before she tackled Michael to the ground.

* * *

Shay was just about to pull Cherry and Roxy off Michael when she heard the familiar slide of a chamber. "Drop your gun and get them off Charlie. Get them off him now!" yelled a young girl.

Slowly lifting her arms, the gun still in her hand, Shay said, "Calm down. That's not Charlie."

Inching her way around, Shay came face-to-face with a double-barrel shotgun in the shaking hands of a teenager. About five-three and ten pounds too skinny, the young girl looked to be seventeen. She had long, dark hair with a gold stud in her nose, and she was doing her best at playing it tough despite her ashen face and the tremor in her voice. It didn't mean she was any less of a threat. A gun in the hands of someone who was both angry and afraid...

If Shay got out of this alive and found her uncle, she planned to have a word with him not only about dead bolts but also about gun safety. "Put my uncle's gun down." She saw a flicker of confusion cross the young girl's face. "I'd only know that's Charlie's gun if I was his niece, so trust me"—she nodded at the tangle of bodies on the floor—"that is not my uncle."

"You know, you could've called off your friend and your dog before they attacked me," Michael said, his voice gruff with irritation.

She glanced over her shoulder at Cherry's gasp. Her friend pushed off Michael's chest to sit up and straddle him. "I know that voice! It's you, Agent Panty-Melting Gallagher."

"Cherry, there's a kid here, so—"

Her entire focus on Michael, Cherry waved off Shay without turning. "No offense, but you sound a lot hotter than you look. Younger too."

"Shay." Ignoring Cherry, Michael lifted his chin, presumably at the young girl behind her.

She saw why as soon as she turned back to the teenager. Shay caught the minute movement of the barrel and her finger. One twitch and she'd blow off the back of Cherry's head.

"What do you mean, agent? What kind of agent?" the girl asked, sounding panicked.

Shay stored the kid's reaction for later. "This is your last warning. Put the gun down. Now."

Her bottom lip quivering, the teenager wasn't quite able to pull off a cocky smile. Still, Shay gave her points for trying.

"Yeah, what are you going to—" the kid began.

Shay stepped in, grabbed the barrel, and aimed it at the ceiling, at the same time hooking her fingers around the young girl's and removing them from the trigger. Once she got the gun away from her, Shay laid her free hand on the kid's shoulder, holding her firmly in place. "Don't do anything stupid. I don't want to hurt—" The sound of a child's sob jerked her attention from the teenager.

"Teddy! Where are you, Teddy?"

The girl wrenched away from Shay, turning to run toward the back of the house. "I told you not to follow me, Gabby!"

Shay found the teenager she assumed must be Teddy kneeling on the kitchen floor in front of a little girl of about five who wore only an oversized black T-shirt, her round face tearstained beneath a mop of curly, dark hair. The sliding door was open, indicating that this was how Michael had gotten inside, and then the girls. He had some major explaining to do.

"Okay, take it easy, Roxy. I don't want you to get glass in your paws. Just give me a sec, Cherry. I'll help you next." Michael's deep and smooth voice came from the back hall.

Shay rolled her eyes as she flipped the light switch. Did he always have to be so damn polite and chivalrous? It irritated her to no end. Even more annoying was that she noticed. She reminded herself of all the reasons she had to distrust and dislike him.

She refocused on the girls on the floor. "Do you live next door in Hattie West's house?"

Gabby buried her face in Teddy's shoulder. "She was my great-grandmother," the teenager said, watching Shay through suspicious, pale blue eyes.

"I'm sorry for your loss. I didn't know she died."

Unless the years had changed her for the better, Shay remembered Hattie as a bitter old woman who had no use for children, so she wasn't surprised to see Teddy raise a negligent shoulder in response to Shay's offer of sympathy. "Have you lived there long?"

"A couple months," Teddy said, coming to her feet. Like Shay, the teenager seemed to favor the black-on-black look—jeans, hoodie, and sneakers.

"Why don't you let me get a blanket for your sister? She is your sister, isn't she?"

"Yeah, what did you think? She's my kid?"

"No…Okay, so maybe I did. It does happen, you know. Just give me a minute, and I'll walk you guys back—"

"No, we're good." Her eyes skittered past Shay and went wide.

Michael walked into the kitchen with a blanket in one hand and Roxy in the other. She winced at the sight of his black eye, wondering if Cherry or Roxy had landed the blow. Despite the black eye and without his fake gray beard and silver-streaked bushy eyebrows, he was as drool-worthy as Shay remembered. A black knitted hat covered most of his hair that no doubt was just as thick and lustrous as she remembered. Her fingers itched to rip the hat off his head and check for herself.

It didn't take much to get the desire to do so under control. One look at the black gloves that covered his large yet elegant hands, dark jacket, sweater, pants, and shoes half hidden in blue paper booties reminded her of what he'd been up to.

Apparently Cherry had forgotten that part. She was

following after him with her tongue practically hanging out of her mouth. Even Roxy appeared to be in love with the man. Shay was gratified to see Teddy looking at him with wary eyes and a sneer.

Obviously still confident in his ability to win over any woman—young or old—with his charm and good looks, he handed Roxy to Shay. There was an emotion in his improbable blue eyes that she couldn't read. Maybe it had been so long since she had those lapis orbs focused on her that she couldn't think straight. Or maybe it was because she knew exactly what was going on in his head when he looked from her to the sisters standing in her kitchen after midnight with no parent in sight.

He raised his fingers as though to caress her face but then slowly lowered them. He'd always been better at reading her emotions than she had been at reading his.

He offered Teddy and Gabby a smile that had no doubt ensured there was standing room only in the courtroom when he tried a case. "I'm an FBI agent, Teddy, but you're not in trouble, okay? I understand you were looking out for Charlie, and that was an incredibly brave thing for you to do. Next time, though, it might be better if you picked up the phone and called 911 instead of picking up a gun that could have just as easily been used against you."

The wealth of attitude in the look that Teddy gave Michael made Shay smile.

Cherry moved in to retrieve Roxy, who was squirming in Shay's arms. "Scary. The kid's your mini-me," Cherry said sotto voce.

Shay's smile fell as she saw what Cherry and Michael must have, and the memories crept up on her. Whoever said you can't go home was right. And if you could, you shouldn't. Then she reminded herself why she was here and who might be behind Charlie's disappearance. If it had been someone sent by Danny Costello instead of Michael here tonight… "He's right, Teddy. I appreciate you looking out for my uncle, but next time, call the cops if you see anything suspicious. Charlie wouldn't forgive himself if something happened to you on account of him."

The little girl's head lifted off Teddy's shoulder, and she opened her mouth.

"We better go," Teddy said, tightening her arms around her sister.

Shay wondered what it was that Teddy didn't want her sister to tell. She'd have to wait to question her when they didn't have an audience.

"Not so fast," Michael said, carefully wrapping the blanket around the two girls. "I have to walk you home. I'd get in trouble if my boss found out that I didn't. You don't want me to get in trouble, do you?" He winked at Gabby, who blinked and then gave him a smile that said it was love at first sight. Which of course was adorable on a five-year-old, but Shay was pretty sure she'd given him a similar smile the day they'd first met.

Teddy huffed a disgusted breath. Cherry laughed, and Shay realized she'd just done the same.

"I know what you're doing. You're just checking up to see if we're alone. My mom is on her way home. She had to work overtime. Her boss is a tool. But I'm fourteen so you can't charge us or anything."

Shay didn't know how much more she could take. It was like someone's idea of a bad joke. She could see herself standing where Teddy was, defending her uncle to the woman from social services. Seventeen years later and she still remembered her name, Olive Olivetti.

Beside her, Cherry made a sympathetic noise. Shay nudged her in the ribs. Sympathy wasn't what Teddy needed or wanted. Something Shay knew from firsthand experience.

"From what I saw tonight, you're more than capable of taking care of yourself and your little sister, Teddy," Michael said.

Which was the perfect thing to say. Trust Michael to get it right.

"I've got a couple of questions about Charlie, and Gabby looks like she's ready for bed. So how about I walk home with you and you can tell me what I need to know, and then you and your sister can get some sleep?"

Teddy's distrust of Michael remained evident on her face. The kid was obviously a much better judge of character than Shay had ever been.

* * *

Michael walked up the stairs to the back deck. Shay was crouched at the patio door, the overhead light shining down on her inky black hair. She wore it tied back in a ponytail that fell over the shoulder of her black hoodie.

He took in her profile, the long, lush lashes; the straight, narrow nose; the curve of her high cheekbone; the hint of her full, sensuous lips; and the delicate jawline that belied the strength of the woman. Her long, lithe frame that did the same. She glanced to where he stood watching her.

"Let me do that," he said, clearing the roughness from his voice as he nodded at the screwdriver in her hand. He knew he had to tell her what GG had done as soon as he saw those two little girls in her kitchen, saw the reaction on Shay's face when the memories came rushing back. But for just a few minutes, he wanted to talk to her without another betrayal coming between them.

He waited for her to scoff at his offer. She didn't like to be beholden to anyone or made to feel like there was something she couldn't do on her own. She was fiercely independent and scarily self-reliant. They were her greatest strengths and conversely her biggest weaknesses.

She came to her feet, her fingers lightly brushing his as she handed him the screwdriver. He felt that small electrical charge of attraction and heat, both relieved and disappointed it was still there. She felt it, too, he knew. He heard the quick inhalation, saw the light flicker in her silver-gray eyes. Once, he'd seen a snow leopard with eyes the color of hers. There was something catlike about her movements. She was graceful, fast...and the way she was looking at him right then reminded him of the leopard with its prey.

"Where's your friend?" he asked in order to give

himself some time. He crouched at the patio door, screwdriver in hand, ready to wow her with his handyman skills and maybe earn some brownie points. He frowned, reaching around to move the lock up and down on the inside of the door. He came to his feet. "You could have told me you already fixed it."

"Yep, I could have. And you could've told me why you picked the lock in the first place and what you were doing in there." She lifted her chin at the house next door. "Are they okay?"

He was pretty sure Teddy was holding something back, but without an adult around, he hadn't wanted to press too hard. He'd be back, though. Unwilling to share his suspicions with Shay, at least for now, he nodded. "I stalled as long as I could. House is clean, food in the fridge, and locks are solid."

She knew as well as he did that a clean house and food in the fridge didn't always tell the whole story. He had no doubt that tomorrow she'd nose around, strike up a conversation with the girls' mother, and get a feel as to whether the kids were truly safe. He'd do some digging of his own.

"What did Teddy tell you about Charlie? When was the last time she saw him?"

It looked like his reprieve was over. "Why don't we go inside? It's cold out, and you've had a long drive. You look tired," he said, and, unable to help himself, brought his hand to her face. She leaned into it, her face soft in his palm, her breath warm against his skin. He stroked her satin-smooth cheek with his thumb, wishing, not for the first time, that he hadn't questioned Jasper tonight.

She covered his hand with hers, lifting those starlight eyes to his. "What are you keeping from me, Michael? Is it bad news?"

"No, not really. In a way, it's good news. I just need you to know that tonight is the first I heard about it."

She frowned, releasing his hand to step away from him. "What is it?"

He mourned the loss of her closeness. The air suddenly felt colder, and without her scent of wildflowers filling his senses, he smelled the faint, sulfuric odor coming off the salt marshes. He struggled to think of a way to break the news of GG's interference in their lives without alienating Shay for good.

In the end, Michael had no choice but to tell her the truth; she'd lost her sisters because of his great-grandmother. It would've been easier if there was a particular incident that he could point to, a concrete reason for GG to have done what she did, but he only knew what Jasper had told him, which he shared with Shay. As well as what went down at the wharf between the two older men.

She stood stiff and silent as he talked.

"I don't know what else to say but that I'm sorry, Shay. I guess the only positive out of this is that now Charlie has something to go on, he might actually find your sisters. I'll do whatever I can to help. And given the timeline of his meeting with Jasper and when Teddy saw him last, Charlie's been cleared as a suspect in Tony's murder. He couldn't have made it from here to Boston in...Shay?"

It felt like she was pulling his heart from his chest when she raised her gaze to his. Her eyes glistened like quicksilver. He'd never seen her cry before. "Shay, honey." He reached for her, and she jerked away as though sickened by his touch.

"Just an hour ago I was thinking it was probably Hattie who called social services, but I should've known better. I should've known it was a Gallagher. First your mother, and then your great-grandmother. And you, you must be really disappointed not to be able to pin Tony's murder on Charlie. You always did blame him for what happened to us."

"Stop. Don't say anything else, not now. You're tired. Sleep on it, and we'll talk in the morning."

"No. I don't ever want to see you or talk to you again. I don't want to see any of you."

He couldn't let it end this way. "Shay, please, let me try and find your sisters. I—"

"I found my sisters last year." She walked into the house and closed the sliding door.

Chapter Six

♥

Michael glanced at his watch as he tossed the blue rubber Kong a few yards from the back door of the cottage. It was his first day driving to work from Harmony Harbor, and he calculated that he had to be on the road in twenty minutes if he wanted to make it to headquarters before his partner. All he'd need was to give the guy something else to razz him about. Oliver James could have taught Michael's brothers a thing or two about getting under someone's skin, and that was saying a lot.

"Buddy, what are you waiting for? Go get your Kong."

Michael had been trying to ensure that Atticus's failing eyesight didn't rob him of his enjoyment of life. The Kong was filled with peanut butter, so he should be able to sniff it out. If he was the least bit interested in doing anything other than sitting on the back deck. Which, apparently, he wasn't.

Michael took the dog's long face in his hands. "I get it, buddy. In a few days, you'll know where everything is and won't be bumping into things. It's okay to be scared. We all get scared sometimes. It's what you do with your fear that matters." He gave Atticus a pat and then walked across the yard to pick up the Kong, tossing the peanut-butter-filled toy closer to the back deck. "Give it another try, boy," Michael said. Then he murmured, "You've got this," when Atticus tentatively came down the steps, cheering when he claimed his prize.

It gave Michael hope. Like his dog, he was feeling a bit out of his element too. And maybe a little afraid. Afraid that the odds of Shay ever speaking to him again were negligible.

She'd slain him when she had looked up with tears in her eyes and admitted she'd found her sisters. In his gut, he knew the reunion hadn't gone well. It wasn't fair that she'd dealt with that on her own, and he didn't doubt that she had. She'd always been a loner. She rarely let anyone in, let alone confided in them. Maybe that's how she'd survived the losses and the pain.

He thought of Cherry racing toward him, heedless of the danger. Her only concern protecting Shay, a woman who prided herself on her street smarts and ability to take care of herself. He smiled, thinking that Cherry would probably hear about it today if she hadn't last night.

Sometimes it surprised him how well he knew Shay. Then again, he'd known her before her walls had been cemented into place. There were no cracks or fissures now, no room for anyone to sneak past her defenses.

Michael pulled his phone from the pocket of his navy wool coat, scrolling to Cherry's number. He sent her a text, asking her to let him know if Shay was okay. He hoped her phone was off or at least on vibrate. It was early, and they'd gotten in late last night.

He could've waited, he supposed. But he'd just end up second-guessing himself later. Something he'd done for the better part of the night. Best to do it before he remembered the way Shay had looked at him last night, the anger in her eyes…and the hurt. If he thought about it for too long, he might come to the same conclusion that she had. The last thing she wanted or needed was a Gallagher in her life. All they'd ever done was cause her pain.

A minute later, his cell rang. FaceTime. He accepted, and Shay's friend appeared on the screen. Thin strips of curly blue eyelashes were stuck to her forehead. He assumed the culprit was the pink satin eye mask that held back her hair. The blond locks looked like they'd been electrified.

"Sorry, I didn't mean to wake you, Cherry."

She waved fingers weighed down by stacks of rings and yawned. "No problemo, Agentlicious. Roxy's going tinkle, and she takes forever when it's cold." She turned the camera to the apricot-colored poodle squatting beside a garden gnome. "Say hi to our special agent man, Roxy. Shoot, I forgot. She won't tinkle when anyone's watching. Sorry, Roxy Roo." She turned the camera so fast that everything was a blur.

It might have been better had the picture stayed that way. When it came back into focus, he got a bird's-eye view of an impressive chest. Cherry wore a pink feather-trimmed negligee that left little to the imagination.

"Cherry." He cleared his throat, motioning upward with his index finger in hopes she'd clue in. "You might want to put on a jacket," he said when she didn't.

She looked down and patted herself. "It's okay. They haven't froze yet." She smiled at him. "Now tell me all about you and my Shaybae. No." She raised a finger when he opened his mouth. "You two can deny it all you want, but I saw the way you looked at each other last night. The amount of heat flying between you two was enough to give me a hot flash, and I'm only thirty-nine."

"We're friends," he said, knowing that's all Shay would want him to admit to.

"Of the benefits kind, I know. That's what Shaybae said. But I've been around the block a time or two, and I'm guessing you were her first love and she was yours. Only you've never gotten over her, have you, Agent-licious?"

At the sympathy in her voice, he rubbed the heel of his palm across his chest. The truth hurt, though it shouldn't. It wasn't like it was news to him. Still, as embarrassed as he was to come across as a sap—at least he hoped Cherry was thinking a sap and not a stalker—who was unable to let go of his feelings for the woman he once loved, he couldn't bring himself to disconnect.

"I'm concerned about her, that's all. She's been through a lot. And while she won't admit it, she's worried about her uncle. Do me a favor, Cherry. Keep an eye on her. Let me know if she needs anything." Huh, that was pretty impressive. He was almost 99 percent certain that his *concerned but definitely not hung up on her* voice would convince Cherry that she'd misread the situation.

"Oh, don't you worry. I—" The door opened behind her, and Michael got a glimpse of Shay's bed head and heavy-lidded eyes just before he got an up-close-and-personal view of Cherry's cleavage.

"Seriously," he heard Shay mutter at the same time he came back into the wintery-white light.

Shay reappeared on the screen. If he had any doubts she'd become a morning person in the past ten years, the ticked-off look on her face kind of cleared that up.

"Shay, I can"—*Beep. Beep*—"explain."

Michael stared at the dark screen for a minute, debating whether or not to call back. "When did I become a masochist, Atticus?" he asked his dog, who dropped the Kong at his feet.

Michael turned as a metallic-gray Cadillac pulled in the gravel drive with his mother, Maura, behind the wheel. She rarely drove around the block herself let alone left Boston, so it was slightly unnerving to see her here. Their relationship had been strained since Michael's ex, Bethany Adams, had called off their wedding fifteen months before.

His fiancée had been handpicked and groomed by his mother to be the perfect governor's wife. Only, Michael had decided he didn't want to follow in his father's footsteps and worked up the courage to tell them the night before they were to be married. Bethany's temper tantrum had ensured he hadn't been heartbroken when she threw her engagement ring at his head. Unlike his mother, who'd been beside herself with grief, though her grief looked a lot like anger.

Over the past year, things had gotten better between him and Maura. Though it was far from the loving mother-and-son relationship it had once been when he was younger. Too much water had gone over the dam. For him, it went back to the part Maura played in Shay's sentencing. For his mother, she'd lost her standing with the Boston elite because of his broken engagement. The Adamses were higher up in the social stratosphere than the Gallaghers, and Bethany turned on Maura as quickly as she'd turned on Michael.

His mother remained in the car, looking at him through the windshield. Of course she'd expect him to help her from the car. Which he already would've done had he not been trying to decide how bad a sign it was that she'd shown up. He dug in his pocket for an antacid and discreetly put it in his mouth as he walked toward the Cadillac. "Mother, this is a surprise," he said upon opening the door.

"Is it? I thought you would've heard from your father by now." She shrugged her shoulders beneath a fur coat the exact shade of brown as her chin-length hair. She was an attractive woman who looked at least two decades younger than her age. She spent a small fortune to stay that way. "Obviously I made the right decision if he can't be bothered to let his sons know that I've left him."

Michael's extended hand fell to his side. Until that

moment, he'd never been at a loss for words. Now it was possible the consequences of his mother driving herself to the place she hated most in the world to deliver her announcement to him, her wayward son, were already beginning to form in his head and negatively impacting his power of speech. However, given that he hadn't fully recovered from his trip down Cherry's cleavage and the FaceTime evidence that he'd once again managed to tick off Shay, he held out hope he'd misunderstood what his mother had said.

"Left him? As in you've left him to his own devices to come for a visit today?"

She gave him the same look she'd been giving him for the past thirty-four years whenever he failed to live up to her expectations. "You used to be such a bright boy. It must be that new job. It's not challenging enough, and you're losing brain matter." She lifted her hand, motioning at him with her manicured fingers. "Well, I'm here now, and I'll have your life back on track in no time at all. You've been floundering ever since you and Bethany broke up. I'm partially to blame, I know. Your father's career took up so much of my energy, I'm afraid I've neglected you and your brothers. But now that he no longer needs me, I plan to make it up to the three of you." With the tip of her red fingernail, she swiped away a tear that clung to her bottom lashes.

Michael stared at her. He couldn't remember ever seeing her cry. Wail and rage, definitely. Real tears? No, never. "Mom, trust me on this. Dad needs you."

"No, he doesn't. Your father has decided to retire."

She took his hand and came unsteadily, he thought, to her feet.

He looked at her more closely, noting her lack of bronzed glow and lipstick. She never left home without her makeup on. Then again, this was a woman who didn't start her day until eleven, and it was much earlier than that. Still, she was his mother, and she was obviously hurting. "I'm sorry you and Dad are going through a rough patch, Mom. I'm sure the old man will be lost without you and beg you to come home." Hopefully by tomorrow. Tonight would be even better. "You're welcome to stay here a couple days, but you might be more comfortable at Connor's penthouse in the city."

She tilted her head and attempted a frown, but she must have had a Botox treatment recently.

"Okay, so maybe not Connor's, but what about Logan? You could help him find a place in Washington."

"There's nothing your father could do or say to make me change my mind. I've been taking care of him for more than forty years; it's you boys' turn. And don't worry about your brothers. I'll get to them as soon as I've gotten your life back on track. It's past time you were married and had a family of your own, Michael. I want to see you settled. As I said, you're floundering."

"Mom, I'm not floundering." But he was panicking at the idea of Maura taking control of his love life and playing matchmaker. Been there, done that, and it wasn't an experience he wished to repeat ever again.

"Trust me, you're floundering, and floundering badly," she said with a pointed look at the cottage.

He was almost relieved that her evidence of his life being in complete disarray was his move to Harmony Harbor. For a minute there, he'd thought it might have something to do with Shay being back in town. "Moving here isn't a reflection on my life needing an overhaul, Mom. The board at the condo wants the building pet free, and Atticus and I were being harassed. Besides that, it'll be better for him here. He'll have company when I'm at work. Jasper's going to walk him, and he's arranging playdates for him with Miller."

"Really, Michael. You're more concerned about Atticus's social life than your own." As she turned to walk toward the cottage, he heard her mutter under her breath, "It's worse than I thought. He's the perfect target for that Angel woman. If she thinks she can get her hooks into him again, she needs a reminder who she's up against."

* * *

"Hate to be the one to ruin your day, pretty boy," James said with a grin as Michael made his way across the field toward him. They had another murder. The call had come in right after his mother had inadvertently given him a clear idea of her agenda.

Michael was about to tell his partner he should've gotten up earlier if he wanted to ruin his day, but James was on a roll, performing for the CSS—Crime Scene Services—who were busy protecting the crime scene and body from the inclement weather that was forecasted to arrive within a few hours. "Just kidding, I love ruining your day...and your suit. Tom Ford? How much, ten grand? Look at my boy, guys. Isn't he stylish?"

Michael looked up at the bloated gray sky when a couple of James's CSS friends joined in the ribbing. It didn't bother him as long as it didn't interfere with getting the job done, but today, he could've done without it. He was preoccupied, trying to figure out what his mother was up to while he was at work. He was tempted to warn Shay to go the other way if she saw a metallic gray Cadillac coming her way. Yeah, that would go over really well.

One of the investigators moved aside, and Michael got his first look at the victim. Like Fat Tony, the gray-haired man appeared to be in his late sixties. He'd also been shot execution-style. The same as Fat Tony. "Any ID on him?" Michael asked.

"More than that, partner. And this really is going to ruin your day," James said as he snapped on a pair of gloves. "Give me the cell, will you, Lou?" A man in white coveralls handed a smartphone to James. "Looks like your old pal Charlie Angel knew our latest vic too." He turned the screen. "So, either all three of your witnesses are lying about the last time they saw Angel or he's on Danny's payroll and arranging the meets."

So much for thinking his day couldn't get worse. "You're assuming he's guilty, and I don't believe he is."

"Yeah, because you don't want to. We've already established you have a thing for his niece. But that doesn't make him innocent, pretty boy."

"Knock off the *pretty boy*. And this has nothing to

do with Shay. Two of the witnesses are completely reliable, but not the third."

"The kid?"

He nodded. "Something didn't feel right. I got the feeling that she saw something that night. Whatever it is, she's protecting Charlie. Now we just have to find out why."

"You questioned her last night. Why didn't you—"

"She's fourteen, and her mother wasn't there. Plus, it was late, and whether she'd admit it or not, the kid had a scare."

"Okay, so back we go to Harmony Harbor."

Chapter Seven

♥

Of course I'm still angry. After everything I told you, you were conspiring with the enemy," Shay said as she brought Roxy's booties to Cherry as ordered. This was the third bathroom break since Michael's phone call this morning.

Which might explain the intrigued gleam in Cherry's eyes. She obviously felt Shay's fit of temper should be over by now. "FYI, your false eyelashes are still stuck to your forehead," she said in an attempt to distract her friend.

Great. Cherry looked even more intrigued. As though Shay were some kind of ice queen who never experienced emotion of any kind. Which in and of itself was annoying. She was no different than anyone else.

Cherry had her over-the-top emotions on display practically every day. It wasn't like Shay didn't experience that same wide range of emotions. It's just that she'd trained herself to never let them show, unwilling to let anyone read her and gain the upper hand. It was safer that way.

She should've reminded herself of that last night. Admittedly, it probably wouldn't have made a difference. She'd reached her breaking point thanks to the close call in Vegas, lack of sleep, and worry over Charlie. She was only human after all.

A switch had been tripped when she found out that Michael's great-grandmother was the reason she'd lost her sisters. She'd been swamped by emotions so fierce she'd been unable to contain them. They'd spewed out of her like a volcano erupting after lying dormant for years. Everything she'd thought she'd buried long ago. And Cherry had been there to bear witness to it all. Shay had totally overshared.

Which may have been why her heart pumped an extra beat when the intrigued gleam in Cherry's eyes was replaced with a knowing smile. "You're in love."

"With who? Michael?" She didn't wait for Cherry to answer and vehemently shook her head. "Nooo, no, I told you. We were nothing more than friends with benefits. Anyway, how did you get that I love"—she kind of choked on the word and cleared her throat—"loved Michael out of *conspiring with the enemy*?"

"Everyone knows there's a fine line between love and hate. Besides, I read your tea leaves this morning, and there's definitely love in your immediate fu—"

"I didn't drink tea this morning."

Cherry's eyes went wide. "Then…they were my tea leaves I read. I'm the one who has a lover in her immediate future." She put a hand to her head and shot a panicked look around the cul-de-sac. "He could be anywhere. I can't let him see me like this." She whipped around and headed into the house.

"Wait, you forgot Roxy."

She glanced over her shoulder. "Go tinkle for Auntie Shay, Roxy Roo. Don't look at her," she ordered before tossing the booties to Shay and slamming the door.

"Don't lock..." Shay bowed her head at the sound of the lock engaging and caught a glimpse of her bare feet. She was about to turn and bang on the door when a blue Ford beater pulled in front of the Wests'.

A tall man in a black bomber jacket got out of the car and placed his arms on the roof to play with his phone. His dirty-blond hair and gaunt face reminded her of Eric Stewart, a man she'd once run cons with and helped put away fourteen months before.

With everything going on, it was a reminder she didn't need. She'd have to call Aidan Gallagher and find out what story the DEA had put out about her and if her cover had been blown. As far as she knew, the players were all still in jail, so that should make things easier.

The guy looked up from his phone and glanced her way. Obviously uncomfortable with having an audience, he straightened and gave her a hard-eyed stare.

There'd been a time when Shay would've taken that as a challenge to show him why she couldn't be intimidated. Now she just rolled her eyes and walked to get Roxy and... "Dammit, oh God, that's cold," she whined as her bare feet hit the frozen lawn.

Eric's look-alike snorted a contempt-filled laugh and

then walked around the hood of the car as a woman rushed out the front door.

Shay knew this because she'd turned to give *him* a hard-eyed stare. Instead her gaze narrowed on the woman who was obviously Teddy's mother. Shay wondered what it was with women running around half-naked this morning. Teddy's mom wore a ratty white robe over stretchy black boy shorts and a matching tank top. Unlike Shay, she'd thought to slip on a pair of fur-trimmed winter boots.

If not for her sallow skin, raccoon eyes, and smeared red lipstick, the woman would be attractive. She had dark, curly hair like Gabby and light blue eyes like Teddy, only the woman's were tired. She had an air about her that said she was in a fight with life and life was winning.

And maybe that explained her attraction to the man she raced across the front lawn toward. Shay knew down to her bones the guy was bad news. It had nothing to do with the beater car and the grungy clothes or the 'tude; some of the best people she knew had next to nothing. No, her instinct about this man came from years of running with the wrong crowd and from her time in prison.

Not your monkey, not your circus, she told herself. Then her conscience kicked her butt by flashing an image of Teddy kneeling on the kitchen floor last night with her baby sister in her arms. Shay swore under her breath and picked up Roxy.

Boots first and then an intervention with Teddy's mother, she decided, certain she'd either stick to the ground or lose a toe if she didn't get inside pronto. She sprinted to the door, trying to keep the whimpering to a minimum, and leaned on the bell.

"You better pray your mother hasn't moved on to fixing her hair or we'll be out here for two hours," she said to the shivering dog. Thinking in all likelihood that's exactly what Cherry was up to, Shay patted the pockets of her jeans for something to pick the lock. It was too bad she'd decided to fix the patio door last night instead of this morning.

"What the hell is this? This isn't the amount we agreed on."

Shay turned at the man's raised and angry voice to see him shove what looked like a fistful of bills at Teddy's mom and grab her hand. Shay put Roxy on the stoop and took off across the lawn.

"Let her go. Now," she called out in a voice she'd used in the prison's exercise yard, a little surprised it didn't work on him like it'd worked on the women in the pen. Then again, he didn't know her. He was about to, she thought when he twisted the woman's hand to get the bag of pills, making her cry out.

"Yeah, and what are you gonna do if I don't?" He rolled his eyes like Shay was as laughable as the threat in her voice and flipped her off. "Get lost and mind your own business. She's got my product."

His eyes narrowed as she kept coming, and he released Teddy's mom to turn and face Shay. He widened his stance, his expression cocky.

"It's okay. I'm fine." The woman gave Shay a nervous smile, closing her fingers over the baggie in her hand. "Gerry, just go. I'll square up with—"

"She's right, Gerry. You need to leave. And word of advice, don't come back," Shay said upon reaching them.

He moved into her, bumping against her with his chest, forcing her back a step.

"You heard me warn him to leave, didn't you?" she said to Teddy's mom, who gave a small, worried nod. "Good. I thought I made it clear. But just in case you didn't completely understand me…" She put her hands between them and shoved Gerry back three steps. "Consider this your last warning. Get in your car, drive away, and don't come around here again."

"Make me." He smirked as he once again got in her face.

"It'll be my pleasure." Shay smiled when he telegraphed his move. Just in case the neighbors were watching, she let him get in a punch, moving at the last minute so that it glanced off her jaw. "My two-year-old niece punches harder than you," she said, her smile fading at the nugget of truth in the statement.

She did have a niece. Only her sister had ensured Shay would never know her. It was too bad for Gerry that she'd mentioned the little girl. It reminded her of the meeting with her sister and served to feed Shay's temper.

Her movements contained and quick, she curved her right foot behind his ankles, jerking his feet out from under him at the same time she smashed him in the face with her forearm, ensuring that he fell backward and toppled like a tree, emitting a cry and a resounding thud when he hit the ground.

"Well, that was fun. Should we do it again?" she asked, looking down at him while inwardly praying he got up and went on his merry way. As far as fights go, it wasn't much of one, but it had served to take the edge off her temper, and the accompanying adrenaline rush was fading fast. Which meant the excruciating burn from her frozen feet was finally able to penetrate her senses. She gritted her teeth to hold back a moan of pain. If she didn't move this along, she'd be down there beside Gerry writhing and whimpering.

She turned to Teddy's mom, who was looking from Gerry groaning on the ground to Shay. Noting the movement of the curtain in the Wests' front window, Shay said, "We have an audience. Hand me the baggie and then get inside to your girls."

Clutching the pills to her chest, Teddy's mom stared at her. "No, you don't understand. I need them. Gerry, I promise, I'll find a way to get the rest of the money to you. I'll"—she averted her gaze from Shay and took a step toward the man working his way into a sitting position—"you know, like last time. Maybe we can work something out."

"You and Gerry aren't doing business anymore, lady. So unless you want me to take them from you, hand over the pills."

"Who do you think you are? You can't tell me—"

"Yeah, I can, and you know why?" She wrapped her fingers around the woman's wrist, exerting enough pressure to ensure she released the baggie. "Because you have two little girls who depend on you to be there for them, and if you keep doing what you're doing, you'll lose your kids."

"It's so easy for you to judge. You have no idea how hard my life is. No idea at all," she shouted tearfully at Shay before storming toward the house.

"Getting high isn't going to make it any easier, now, is it?" she said to the woman's retreating back and got a finger in response.

Okay, so really, who was Shay to judge? She had no idea what the woman was going through. But come on, you don't buy drugs out in the open for your kids and all the neighbors to see. And you don't bring trouble to your door.

Her uncle Charlie's middle name was trouble. He didn't do drugs, but booze and gambling brought a similar element to their door, not to mention the cons they ran. No doubt Colleen Gallagher's concerns about the Angel family had been similar to the ones Shay had for the Wests.

She didn't know where the thought had come from and immediately pushed it away. Just because she might understand the dead woman's motives didn't mean Colleen Gallagher had a right to do what she did.

Shay turned to Gerry, who was using the car's rusted fender to pull himself to his feet, and stuffed the baggie in his jacket pocket. "Next time I won't be so gentle. Stay away from her, Gerry."

* * *

Shay sat on the edge of the bathtub warming her feet in four inches of water. Standing at the sink in the small, bright white bathroom, Cherry heated towels with a blow-dryer. She'd Googled the best ways to warm up frozen feet. The towels were for Roxy, not Shay.

"Don't you worry, Roxy Roo. Mommy won't let Auntie Shay look after you again." Cherry addressed the shivering poodle in a voice that hurt Shay's teeth. High-pitched and childlike, Cherry saved it for special occasions, namely when both she and the dog felt Shay had messed up and put the animal in mortal jeopardy. Cherry and Roxy cast Shay the side-eye at almost the same time.

She held up her hands. "I've apologized five times, so the two of you need to get over it. And just FYI, I wasn't the one who locked the door." She didn't add that she'd been a little busy rescuing a woman from her slimeball drug dealer to worry about Roxy.

Making a fish face, Cherry leaned into the mirror and fluffed her now perfectly coiffed blond locks. "You don't have to remind me. I feel terrible as it is. But you understand, don't you, Roxy Roo? Poor Mommy hasn't gotten herself somethin' somethin' in"—Cherry fake sobbed, at least Shay thought she was faking—"five years. Five, Shaybae. Do you know how…" She winced. "Sorry, it's been what? Like ten for you? I don't know how you do it. Vibrators are great, but sometimes you just need a—"

"TMI."

Cherry angled her head to the side. "What do you mean, TMI?"

"My safe word, remember? I say TMI, and you stop talking. Immediately. No questions asked."

"Okay, okay, I forgot. It's just that you haven't used it in months."

"Well, I wasn't hanging with you twenty-four-seven like I am now."

"Believe me, I know, and you've just reminded me why you've got that whole bite-me attitude going on. For all our sakes, you need to get laid. And I'm going to get working on that as soon as we get to the Shaggy Dog."

"Salty Dog, and no…" She held up her hand to get Cherry's attention, gesturing for her to turn off the blow-dryer. She was almost positive someone was in the house. The air had cooled slightly, and she heard what sounded like the door being closed carefully and quietly.

Slowly removing her feet from the bathtub, Shay stood and wiped them dry on the bathmat, pressing a finger to her lips as she walked from the bathroom down the hall… "What do you think you're doing, kid? I could've shot you," she half-yelled at Teddy, angry that she'd gotten this far before Shay became aware of her presence. If it had been one of Costello's hit men, she, Cherry, and Roxy would be dead by now.

Women three times Teddy's age had been known to quake in fear at the voice Shay had just used on the teenager, a couple of men too. But the kid didn't even blink. She stood two feet from Shay wearing the same black-on-black outfit as last night: sneakers, jeans, and a sweatshirt. The only difference this morning was that she'd added a camel-colored padded vest with a fur-lined hood and carried a canvas backpack. But she wore that same surly look on her face, her upper lip rolled into a sneer.

Shay gave Teddy props for being able to pull it off. The kid wasn't as unfazed as she wanted her to believe. It took time and effort to get rid of a tell, and Teddy probably wasn't even aware she had one. The way the teenager was rubbing her thumb against the side of her forefinger told Shay she was nervous.

Seeing her trying so hard to act tough and cool broke Shay's heart. She couldn't help but see herself in Teddy at that age, not that she'd ever admit it to Cherry or Michael, who she knew had seen the resemblance too.

Cherry, who'd been peeking out into the hall with Roxy in her arms, made a *kid's got cajones* face, and ducked back in the bathroom, turning the blow-dryer setting to low. Presumably to give them the pretense of privacy while still being able to hear their conversation.

Relaxing her stance and losing the scared-straight tactics, Shay asked, "How did you get in? Did you pick the lock?" She'd been picking locks since she was twelve, so it wouldn't surprise her if the answer was yes.

"No. Charlie gave me a key."

Shay held out her hand. Until she knew what was going on with her uncle, she didn't want Teddy coming in and out whenever she pleased.

"It's not your house. It's Charlie's. I'll give him the key when he comes back. If he wants it. But he won't."

"You're real close to my uncle, aren't you?" Shay

hoped to God Charlie hadn't recruited Teddy for his cons. He'd told Shay he stopped the day she went to jail.

"Yeah, and I know all about you. You were in prison. You're a con."

She felt it, not a stab or the sharp twist of a knife, just a small pinch near her heart. Still, it hurt. Which surprised her. She thought she was tougher than that, her skin thicker. Maybe it was the sentiment she heard beneath the words—*you're worthless, no good, dirty*—that were responsible for the pain. "Ex."

The blow-dryer went quiet just before the sound of it being slammed on the counter echoed in the hall. Cherry stomped out of the bathroom, her face flushed. "Don't you ever let me hear you speak to her like that again, you got that, kid?"

Shay sighed. "Cherry, it's—"

"Oh no, she doesn't get to come in here talking to you like that after you froze your feet to protect her mother." She narrowed her eyes at Teddy while stabbing a finger in Shay's direction. "She's better than everyone in this town, and that includes you and me. You have no idea who she is; how much good she's done, the people she's saved, how many times she's risked her own life to help someone else."

She whirled on Shay. "You are one of the best people I know. You're my angel, Shaybae. Don't you listen to her. She's just a smartass kid who's taking the crap her mother doles out on her out on you." Cherry sniffed, making a flustered wipe at the tears tracking down her cheeks. "Now look what you've done, you, you little wannabe gangster. I have to redo my makeup."

Shay and Teddy stared after Cherry, who slammed the bathroom door. Teddy found her voice first. Lip curled, she snarled, "She's a real—"

"Good friend. Yeah, she is. One of the best. So do yourself a favor and don't say another word about my friend, unless it's—"

The bathroom door opened, and Cherry stood there with her hands pressed to her chest and a watery smile on her face. "Aww, Shaybae, I knew you loved me."

Shay rolled her eyes and waved her back into the bathroom. "Hurry up. I have to get to the pub. And you have to go to school." She practically felt the kid biting her tongue as she followed Shay to the front door. "So, what was so important that you walked into my home uninvited?"

And it was her home, though she'd never stake her claim to her uncle. Charlie had remortgaged the house to cover his gambling debts and had come close to losing it last year. Shay had used her savings to pay off his mortgage.

"My mom, she's not a druggie. She hurt her back at work, and she needs the pills, but the ones the doctor prescribes don't work anymore. They're too expensive."

"If she hurt her back on the job, she should be receiving compensation to help pay for her painkillers, Teddy."

"Yeah, right. I told you her boss is a tool. And no one at those compensation places cares about people like her anyway."

"People like her?"

Teddy fidgeted with the strap of her backpack. "She's a stripper." She glanced at Shay as though gauging her reaction to the news.

"So, she has the same right to compensation as anyone else. Tell her to talk to Cherry."

"Why?"

"She was an exotic dancer too." Knowing Charlie, he'd probably offered already, but Shay thought it couldn't hurt to try again. "I'll have a better idea once I spend some time at the pub today, but we might have an opening for your mom at the Salty Dog."

"He'd probably offered her a job already, and she turned him down. The money's too good at the club."

"Yeah, I've heard that too. But you're a smart kid, Teddy, so I'll give it to you straight. Something has to change, and change soon. Your mom keeps going the way that she is, the neighbors see the things that I'm pretty sure they do, your teachers at school too, and your family will end up on social services' radar. Trust me, Teddy, you don't want that to happen."

"I thought... You're not going to social services or the cops?"

"No. But you have to talk to your mom..." What was she doing? More than anyone, Shay knew what it was like to carry that kind of responsibility at such a young age. "Never mind. I'll talk to your mom, and we'll come up with a plan that works for all of you."

"Why would you do that? Why would you want to help us?"

"Maybe I don't want you to turn out like me, Teddy."

Chapter Eight

♥

At the *click*, *click*, *click* coming quickly down the hall toward the back office at the Salty Dog, Shay groaned in frustration. She'd recognize the sound of Cherry's thigh-high boots anywhere. Not surprising since she'd heard the exact same sound twenty times in the past four hours.

By the time Shay had searched the house from top to bottom for clues as to her uncle's whereabouts, it was noon when they arrived at the pub. Cherry had been barging into the office five times per hour, which broke down to one interruption every fifteen minutes. If the ensuing conversations—demands—lasted two minutes, Shay probably would've managed to get some work done. But Cherry took five minutes just getting herself organized to speak, a hair fluff here, a winning or in-gratiating smile there, and dependent on the audience, shoulders back and boobs thrust out.

The woman in question burst into the office wearing a body-hugging fuchsia sweater that today served as a dress. Cherry did a breathy little huff and puff while patting her exposed chest, and there was a lot of chest to pat courtesy of the lacy pink push-up bra that was also visible, and then moistened her lips before moving her hand to her hip, which she jutted out. "I need you out front like yesterday."

"I'll be right there," Shay said, even though she had no intention of leaving the office again. She couldn't afford to waste any more time checking out potential tea-leaf suitors.

Something didn't feel right about the whole Charlie going-off-to-track-down-her-sisters scenario. Rightly or wrongly, he blamed himself for Shay losing her sisters and for being put away. So would he want to find them to make amends? Definitely. Would he want to keep it from her in case his search didn't pan out? Absolutely.

He wouldn't want to get her hopes up just to have her disappointed again. He'd disappointed her plenty in the past. Still, despite being a recovering alcoholic, con, and gambler, the one thing she'd never doubted was his love for her. He'd tried his best, and maybe that's what he was doing again, but she couldn't shake the feeling there was something more going on. Tony's murder fed her suspicions.

At the snap of Cherry's fingers, Shay refocused on the woman. "Book it, Shaybae. Now."

"I'm not booking it, double-timing it, or jetting," she repeated Cherry's expression, including the two she'd used during her prior attempts.

"You don't understand. It's not like the other times. This is a desperate situation for reals. The guy that—"

"You know what, I just remembered, I did have a cup of tea this morning. So those were my tea leaves you read. The tea leaf gods are sending me the man of my dreams, not you. And since the men in my dreams typically turn into nightmares, I've decided I don't want anything to do with—"

Cherry's face fell, her glossy pink lips turning down. "I thought things were finally turning around for me. It's been so long since anything really good happened in my life, you know? And then you came along and rescued me and got me the job at Sterling and then you brought me home to Harmony Harbor with you. So this morning's news that I was finally going to find someone to love who would love me, too, well, that was just the pink icing on the red velvet cake. And to find out it was all a lie, I feel—"

Shay lightly banged her head on the desk. "Okay, okay, I was lying," she said, her voice muffled. "I had coffee. They were your tea leaves. He's the love of your life, not mine. I'm sure the tea leaf gods would send you only good guys, so go out there and procreate." She lifted her head and looked at Cherry. "Ignore the last part, but go dance or something with the guy. Have fun."

"No, I'm not doing anything with him. You said he's a dealer."

"Wait, what? Who are you talking about? I thought—"

"I'm talking about the for-reals desperate situation. The guy you beat up, he's sitting at the bar and asking questions about you," Cherry said.

She pushed back from the desk and stood up. "Why didn't you just say that in the first place?"

"I'm sure I did."

"Ah, no, you didn't." As Shay rounded the desk, Roxy gingerly placed a paw outside her princess bed beside the threadbare olive-green couch. Shay pointed a finger at the poodle. "You stay right where you are."

Charlie would croak if he walked in to see his dark and dingy office cluttered with pink chew toys, stuffed animals, a neon-pink satin bed, and puppy pads.

Cherry flounced past her. "Don't you listen to Auntie Shay, Roxie Roo. She's not as crusty as she pretends to be."

"Oh yeah, I am." And she was even crustier when she walked down the hall and past the Wenches and Mates bathrooms, named in keeping with the pub's pirate ship theme. The floors and walls were cedar and gave off a warm, fragrant scent. When it was busy, the woodsy aroma was overpowered by that of the soft pretzels and craft beer they were famous for.

Shay rounded the corner and spotted Gerry sitting at the bar. It was four o'clock on a Monday, so he wasn't hard to spot. They'd be busier around five when people dropped in for a beer before heading home.

Gerry hadn't spotted her yet. He was busy talking to Denise, who wore a peasant serving wench costume in green and burgundy the same as the rest of the female servers. Shay had been trying to get rid of the uniform for years, but her uncle was living out his pirate fantasies and there wasn't a chance she'd change his mind.

She nodded at two older men who sat at one of the

tables on barrels instead of chairs. Between each of the twenty tables were wooden wheels her uncle swore came from real pirate ships. Just like the cutlasses and swords that hung from the walls. One of the swords was reputed to have been William Gallagher's. Michael's grandfather many times over was rumored to have been a pirate. It's supposedly where the family's wealth had come from.

And where there wasn't a cutlass, sword, or rope, there were framed photos of Charlie and his staff dressed as famous pirates. To Shay's never-ending embarrassment, the photo of her as Grace O'Malley had a place of pride in the pub.

Denise looked over and lifted her chin at Shay. Gerry swiveled on the black leather barstool. His face paled, and he held up a hand. "I'm not here to cause trouble."

"You wouldn't be causing it for long if you were," she said as she rounded the bar. "Take a break if you want, Denise. I've got this."

Tall and buxom with her burgundy hair woven into a crown of braids on top of her head, the fiftysomething woman gave Shay a curt nod. Denise was her uncle's on-and-off-again girlfriend. She'd never been Shay's biggest fan. It was Charlie's fault. Her uncle didn't want a full-time girlfriend, so whenever Denise started pressuring him, he used Shay's supposed animosity toward Denise as an excuse. Shay actually liked the woman and had no opinion on their relationship whatsoever, which she'd told Denise on many occasions.

Shay picked up a towel and tossed it over the picture of herself as Grace O'Malley above the old-fashioned cash register. She turned to the man at the bar. "All right, Gerry, what are you doing here?"

He glanced around and then leaned toward her. "Me? What are you doing here? The cops, the DEA, they're all looking for you, lady. I had no idea who you were until I was telling my main man about this chick who broke my nose, and he started asking me questions about you. He got this shocked look on his face, and he says, "'Shit man, that was the Angel. You're lucky she didn't kill your sorry ass.'"

He held out his hands. "Swear to God, I wouldn't have come around if I'd known it was your territory. My man Eric, he says you're the best. You protected his ass from Keller, so whatever you need, I'm good for. But Costello ain't going to be happy if you start horning in on his business."

"Costello took over from Keller?" This was not good news. "I've been out of the country," she said, in case Gerry wondered why she wasn't in the know.

"Yeah, the guy's into everything now, drugs, extortion, strip clubs. Word is he's making a run on Libby's club." At Shay's blank look, he pointed to his nose. "Your neighbor."

"Right. The woman whose arm you were twisting hard enough to make her cry out."

"I know. I'm a jerk. But I can't be giving the stuff away for free. That's the second time Libby tried to stiff me. If Costello's guys found out, they'd be doing a lot worse. I never told though. I made up for it out of my own pocket. You don't screw Costello," Gerry said, swiveling on the barstool to lift his chin at the back room. "Something you should share with your uncle. Costello's been trying to get his poker machines in the Salty Dog. But Charlie won't have any of it."

"You sure about that?"

"Ah, yeah, Costello's trying to make inroads in Harmony Harbor. Charlie's getting the business owners riled up about it, getting them to take a stand against Costello. Not in his best interest to be doing that, if you know what I mean. Costello's a little off the wall. Doesn't help that his uncles will be out in a few weeks. Word on the street is they aren't happy with how he's been running the family business." He looked around again before lowering his voice when Denise began wiping down a table a few feet away. "You sure you should be here? I mean, far as I know, no one ratted you out, and it doesn't sound like the cops know who the woman was that night, still..."

It took everything she had not to let her fear show after what he'd said. Her gut was telling her this was most likely the reason Charlie had gone missing. "The cops don't have a clue who I am. But I didn't have a choice about coming back. My uncle's missing. There isn't any talk about him on the street, is there?"

"Not that I've heard. Then again, I didn't even know he was missing. I'll keep my ears open. Let you know if I hear anything."

"I'd appreciate it. And if I were you, I'd start looking for another line of work, Gerry. From what I hear, people don't live long doing what you do."

He swallowed audibly and slid off the barstool. "Are you telling me I'm dead unless I stop selling?"

"Pretty much."

"I...I don't understand. I'm just trying to help. Why would you threaten to kill me?"

"I..." She trailed off when a tall, silver-haired man entered the bar. He wore a black wool coat over a black suit, his bearing regal. She hadn't seen him in years. He worked for the Gallaghers, though Michael had always spoken about him as if he were more family than employee. And like the rest of the Gallagher clan, Jasper hadn't approved of her relationship with the heir apparent to his father's political career.

"Look, I'll do whatever you want me to, just... please don't kill me," Gerry pleaded, his voice rising above a frantic whisper.

At the quirk of Jasper's silver eyebrow, Shay briefly closed her eyes and counted to ten. It didn't help as much as the reminder that she no longer cared what the Gallaghers thought about her. She refocused on Gerry, who looked like he planned to go down on his knees to beg for her mercy. She leaned over the bar and fisted her hands in the front of his jacket, holding him in an upright position. "Don't be so dramatic. We're square. All I want you to do is keep your eyes and ears open."

"Okay, okay, I can do that. And I'll stay out of your territory. I'll cover for you with Costello. You can sell your dope wherever you want."

Great. No doubt Jasper was giving himself a mental high five at the proof they'd been right about her. And she couldn't defend herself without blowing her previous cover. It didn't matter. It wasn't like she and Michael were getting back together.

"I'm lying low, remember?" she said to Gerry as she let him go. "I'd advise you to do the same. Now get out of here." He gave a jerky nod and reached in his back pocket. "Don't worry about it. Your beer is on the house."

"Eric's right. You're like the bad guys' superhero. Glad you're on our side. Sorry," he said, bumping into Jasper as he turned to leave.

"What can I get for you?" Shay asked the older man as he approached, working to swallow a groan when she heard a familiar *click, click, click* coming their way.

As Cherry closed in on the bar, he said, "I was hoping to have a word with you, Ms. Angel."

Shay had to give him credit. There was no visible reaction on his face when he got an up-close-and-personal look at Cherry. "Sure, shoot." While holding his gaze, she covertly waved off Cherry. Tried to, she amended when the woman sidled up beside Jasper.

Cherry fluffed her hair, doing so in such a way that she thrust out her triple Ds. Then she fluttered her eyelashes while running the tip of her tongue over her lips—very, very slowly. "Well, hello, handsome," she said in a Marilyn Monroe voice.

Oh good God, Cherry thought Jasper was her tea-leaf suitor. Shay had to figure out a way to get rid of her.

Despite having a great poker face, she picked up on a definite hint of nerves in the quick uptick of Jasper's lips. "Miss." He nodded.

Cherry wrinkled her nose. "Oh, you're just so cute with that accent. Are you really as prim and proper as you sound?"

"Quite."

He had no idea what he'd just done. Converting him from prim and proper to wild and fun would be a challenge her friend couldn't resist. "Cherry, this is Jasper. He works for the *Gallaghers* at *Greystone Manor*," she stressed the two things that should give her friend pause since Shay had shared at least some of what had gone on in the past.

"Oh, nice," Cherry said, obviously not hearing a word Shay had said, her entire focus on Jasper. Smiling, Cherry pressed her body against his side and played with the hair at the nape of his neck. "Has anyone ever told you that you have the most amazing hair and eyes?"

Shay made a mental note to throw out every tea bag in the house, and in the pub.

"No." Jasper's voice came out an octave higher, and he cleared his throat. "No, I can't say that they have."

"Well you absolutely do, and I—"

Shay could see it happening right before her eyes. Jasper was going to have a coronary, and the Gallaghers would blame her. "Cherry," she snapped.

"What?" she snapped back, clearly perturbed at being interrupted.

"I need to speak with Jasper alone for a minute. It's probably time for you to take Roxy out for a walk anyway." She nudged her head in the direction of the office.

"No, I just took her out. But you go ahead and chat with Jaspy," she purred his name and hefted herself onto the barstool beside him. "I could listen to him talk all day."

Jasper quickly averted his gaze from Cherry.

Shay glanced at her friend to see why the older man's face had flushed. "Cherry." She gestured at her friend's sweater and mouthed, *Put on some pants.*

"You're such a prude. I'll be right back, and we'll get better acquainted, Jaspy." She gave the older man a lascivious wink before strutting away, hips swinging.

"Sorry about that," Shay said as she turned to take a bottle of Johnnie Walker off the glass shelf.

"You have nothing to apologize for, miss. But I'm afraid I do."

She poured two fingers of whiskey in a shot glass and placed it in front of the older man. "What do you have to apologize for?"

"Thank you," he said as he lifted the drink to his lips, surprising Shay by tossing it back. "Your uncle. I don't know if Master Michael told you or not, but I believe you have the right to know. I'm the one who gave Charlie the news about your sisters. I should have handled it better."

Gerry had basically confirmed her fears that Charlie hadn't gone in search of her sisters but was hiding (hopefully) from Danny Costello, so she wasn't quite sure how to respond to Jasper. But she appreciated he had the courage to face her and apologize. Still... "It's too bad no one thought to tell him years before. Or that Mrs. Gallagher didn't go to him with her concerns before turning us in to social services."

"Madame didn't intend for events to unfold as they did. She was concerned for your well-being. She didn't mean you harm. Am I correct in assuming you haven't read the papers I gave to your uncle?"

She nodded. "Charlie must have taken them with him. I've searched the house and his office and haven't found any evidence as to where or why he disappeared."

He angled his head, a silver eyebrow quirked as he studied her. "You don't believe he's gone in search of your sisters, do you?"

"I don't know why you'd think that. Right now it's the only lead I have."

He turned the shot glass between his long fingers. "No, I don't believe that's true. I think you have a very good idea what's happened to your uncle, Ms. Angel. And if that's the case, you should talk to Master Michael." He held her gaze with his piercing blue eyes. "You remind me of myself when I was younger, so trust me when I tell you that this is one battle you don't want to fight on your own."

Shay wondered if Jasper was suffering from some form of dementia. There was no way the dignified man sitting before her with his proper manners and sedate job had ever done or witnessed half of what she had.

His mouth twitched as though he knew what she was thinking. "Your judgments are colored by your own misconceptions and experiences, Ms. Angel. Rarely will someone allow you to see who they truly are. Whether you believe me or not, we are much more alike than you will ever know." He stood and reached in his back pocket, frowning as he began searching his other pockets for what she assumed was his wallet.

She was just about to tell him his drink was on the house when he gave her an amused smile. "It seems I should take my own advice."

Unsure what he was talking about, and worried he might actually be having cognitive problems, she was somewhat relieved when she looked up at a blast of cool, damp air from the open door to see Michael. He met her gaze over the heads of the older men he held the door open for.

"Exactly the point I've been trying to make," Jasper said when he caught Shay looking at Michael. "Give him a second chance. He deserves it, and so do you."

"Sorry, Jasper, but I'm beginning to question *your* judgment," she said, glancing over at the familiar *click, click, click* as Cherry walked over wearing a serving wench costume that had been altered to reveal a wide expanse of cleavage and leg. "That's not what I had in mind," Shay said.

Michael approached, hiding a smile behind his hand before nodding. "Shay. Nice costume, Cherry. What are you up to, Jeeves?"

"I stopped by for a libation. But I must be on my way now. Master Michael, Ms. Angel." He nodded and then turned to Cherry. "My wallet, miss."

Chapter Nine

♥

With her long hair pulled up in a high ponytail, Shay had her temper clearly on display. There was no concealing the angry flush coloring her gorgeous face or the glint of fire in her steel-gray eyes. So much for Michael's hope that she'd be in a better mood this afternoon than she had been this morning.

The irony didn't escape him. The only reason he wanted her in a good mood was so that he could question her and no doubt put her in a worse one. As if that made any sense at all. Only, when it came to Shay, it kind of did.

Judging by the way her arms were crossed over her black thermal Henley and the way she tapped the sexy high-heeled boot on the planked floor, she was definitely ticked off at her friend. In fact, he'd go so far as to say she'd crossed to the dark side of ticked.

Michael's hope that she wouldn't storm off before he got out half a sentence had just been obliterated. It didn't seem Shay could go a day without a Gallagher messing with her life.

But for her sake, and for his own, Michael really needed her to answer each and every one of his questions. Further investigation into the most recent victim's cell phone had revealed a threatening text sent by Charlie a few days before. A text that some might say—his partner for one—implicated Shay in the murder.

"So what you're trying to tell me is that you weren't all over Jasper because you thought he was your tea-leaf suitor; you were stealing his wallet to pay him back for"—Shay glanced at Michael and then averted her gaze—"the stuff we talked about last night?"

"Of course I didn't think he was my tea-leaf suitor. He's too ol—" Cherry pressed her lips together and opened her eyes wide, looking like she'd just stepped in something Roxy left behind. "Cute and...wiry to be my tea-leaf suitor. The pattern in my cup indicated a big man with muscles the size of my..." Her hands went to her chest.

Obviously knowing exactly where her friend was going with the comparison, Shay cut her off. "Whatever the reason you stole his wallet doesn't matter anymore, just that you won't do it again. You owe him an apology."

"Not until he apologizes to you first. You were very mean to my BFF when she was younger, Jaspy."

"Oh God, Cherry, no, don't—"

Cherry ignored Shay's frantic attempt to cut her off. "All you Gallaghers were, and it's time for you to own up to what you've done to the Angels, especially my Shaybae. Even you, Mikey. I know you've been trying to make amends, but have you said *sorry*? Like a heartfelt, down-on-your-knees apology said with feeling and—"

Michael glanced at Shay and winced. She'd gone from the dark side of ticked to apoplectic.

"That's it. You're done. I'm taking you home. Go. Now," she ordered her friend.

Cherry gasped. "I was just trying to stand up for you. Everyone thinks you're all tough and... Well, you are tough, but they don't understand you have feelings too."

"Ms. Cherry is right. We owe you an apology for the part—" Jasper broke off when he noticed the other woman shaking her head.

"It's not Ms. Cherry. It's Ms. Blossom. My name's Cherry Blossom."

Michael looked down at the planked floor in an effort to keep from laughing.

"It's a charming name," Jasper said with a straight face.

Barely able to contain the laughter rumbling in his chest, Michael thought he could take a few lessons from Jasper. The old man was good.

"Thank you. It's my stage name. My real name is Ethel Buckhead. I had it changed legally to Cherry Blossom ten years ago. My mother cried. But come on, do I look like an Ethel Buckhead to you?" She put out her hands and pushed out her chest.

"No, you most definitely do not," Jasper said with a hint of laughter in his voice.

At the heavy thud of a bottle landing on the bar, Michael glanced at Shay, who was now pouring herself a shot. She caught his eye as she tossed it back. He smiled at the thought of her friendship with Cherry. Shay was a loner who'd never gone out of her way to make friends. She wasn't a girly girl. She was strong, street-smart, and driven. His smile faded as he thought about what Cherry said. No one knew better than Michael that she was right. Underneath Shay's hardass demeanor was a loyal, generous, and thoughtful woman.

He wondered if Cherry was right about something else. In all these years, had he apologized to Shay? He was pretty sure that he had but was just as sure that he may have qualified it with "but you stole my car" or if he hadn't verbalized it there'd no doubt been a hint of defensiveness attached to the apology.

Holding Shay's gaze, he placed his hand over his heart and mouthed, *I'm sorry. For everything.*

As he mouthed the words, he knew that moments from now she'd wonder if he'd meant them for the past or the present. She rolled her eyes as if he were an idiot, but a second before she did, he thought he caught a hint of pleasure before she covered it with derision.

"Ms. Angel, on behalf of all of us at Greystone Manor, may I offer our sincerest apologies. I hope one day you come to understand why Madame did what she did and are able to forgive her. I know it would mean a lot to her if you did." Jasper gave his head a slight shake. "Your forgiveness *would have* meant a lot to her. But it would mean as much to both Kitty and myself, as we were the ones who decided your family were owed the truth. So perhaps you would accept an invitation to join us for tea one day. Just let us know which day works for—"

Cherry clapped. "How about tomorrow? Tomorrow would work for us, wouldn't it, Shaybae?"

Shay didn't answer her friend because she was staring at Michael, who'd blurted out a panicked, "No, that's not a good idea."

Cherry and Jasper frowned at him.

"It's just—" He rubbed the back of his neck that all of a sudden felt hot and sweaty. "Look, my mother's here for a few days, so it might be better to pick another time."

Shay poured herself another shot. Which wouldn't have been a big deal if the woman drank, but she didn't.

Jasper frowned. "I didn't see your mother. When did she arrive?"

"Early. She, uh, she's left my father." Who Michael had finally managed to get a hold of two hours before. His dad had no idea what was going on, nor did he seem inclined to beg his wife to come home. Logan and Connor had yet to return Michael's calls.

"Perhaps later in the week, then," Jasper said as he opened his wallet.

"Shot's on the house, Jasper. And thank you for the apology and invitation, but until Charlie is found..."

"I completely understand. And rest assured, I will do my part in finding your uncle."

A couple days before, Michael would've found the suggestion that Jasper had something to offer to the search amusing. He didn't anymore. Interestingly enough, Shay didn't laugh off his offer either.

Jasper said goodbye to the women and then took Michael by the arm. "A moment of your time, Master Michael."

"Sure," he said, curious as to what Jasper had to say. He followed the older man out the door and onto the sidewalk. They stood under the overhang, out of the icy drizzle. "What's up?"

"I have reason to believe Charlie hasn't gone looking for his nieces after all."

Michael had reached the same conclusion yesterday but hadn't wanted to admit it to himself. If Charlie had been searching for Shay's sisters, he would've taken her calls. There had to be a reason he wasn't, and the only reason Michael had come up with wasn't good.

"Why's that?" he asked Jasper, keeping his suspicions to himself.

"A conversation I heard earlier. Are you aware that the East Coast mob under the direction of Danny Costello has been trying to make inroads into Harmony Harbor?"

"I was aware Costello had been expanding his operations, but no, I wasn't aware they were making a move here."

"Well, as I understand it, Charlie had been spearheading the initiative to keep them out of town, and he wasn't quiet about it."

"You haven't had any problems at the manor, have you?"

"No, and I don't expect we shall," he said, giving Michael a chilling smile.

"There's more to you than any of us know, isn't there, Jeeves?"

"We all have our secrets, Master Michael." He glanced in the window of the Salty Dog. Shay, standing behind the bar with her hands on her narrow hips, appeared to be trying to give Cherry hell. *Trying* being the operative word. Cherry would go for a spin on the barstool every time Shay opened her mouth. Jasper smiled. "I believe Ms. Blossom will be good for Ms. Angel." He refocused on Michael. "You need to watch her closely."

He frowned. "Cherry?"

"Don't make me doubt my faith in you, my boy."

Michael laughed. "You sound like GG."

"Yes, well, her influence is still widely felt at the manor." He murmured something under his breath that Michael didn't quite catch, but it sounded like *More than you'll ever know.*

Before he had a chance to question him about the remark, Jasper said, "I believe that Ms. Angel has come to the same conclusion as you and I about her uncle's disappearance. And while I understand from Aidan that he's never come across anyone with Ms. Angel's abilities, I'm afraid those very same attributes will be her downfall in this instance. If she thinks Danny Costello has anything to do with Charlie's disappearance, she'll go after him, and she'll go after him alone. Because that woman"—he tapped the glass—"has never had anyone to depend on and has learned to fight her battles on her own. Show her that she can depend on you, Master Michael. Show her that, and you both might have a second chance." He patted Michael's shoulder before walking away. "She deserves one, and so do you."

There was nothing more Michael wanted than for Shay to trust him, but after he questioned her, he'd be the last person she'd turn to for help. If there'd been any way out of this, he'd have found it. The best he'd been able to do was get rid of his partner so that Michael was the one to question her and not James.

The federal branches of law enforcement shared information—and gossip—on a regular basis, so it wasn't surprising that word of Shay's undercover heroics had reached James's ears. As his partner knew, those attributes that Jasper so obviously admired, and for the most part Michael did too, could just as easily be used to wreak vengeance as justice.

Drawing in a fortifying breath, he opened the door to the bar. It had yet to fill up. No one had joined Cherry on the barstools, and she was evidently still doing her best to ignore Shay. A group of old-timers had pulled a couple of tables together at the other end of the pub near the stage.

Shay looked up from wiping down the bar as he approached, saying something to Cherry under her breath. He couldn't tell if she was disappointed or relieved that he hadn't left with Jasper. In the next fifteen minutes, there'd be no doubt as to how she'd feel.

Cherry popped off the barstool. "I told you exactly what your problem is this morning," she said to Shay over her shoulder. Then she stopped and her head swiveled like Linda Blair in *The Exorcist* and her heavily made-up eyes landed on Michael.

Shay looked about as freaked out as he felt. "Cherry, don't you dare—"

Cherry ignored Shay, who'd tossed the towel and was coming around the bar. "Just ignore her," Cherry said, looping her arm through his and fast-walking him toward the tables. "She's soooo crusty these days, but it's not her fault. The poor thing hasn't gotten lucky in ten years. Can you believe it? Ten years!"

"I swear to God, Cherry, I'm going to murder you. Don't listen to a word she says, Michael. The woman's a lunatic."

"I am not. I'm not the one threatening to *murder* their best friend, am I? Do you see what I have to live with, Mikey?" She sighed when Shay reached out and hauled them both to a stop. "Come on, you were friends with benefits before, and you really, really could use some benefits, Shaybae. What do you say, are you up for it, Mikey?"

"Yeah, what do you say, Mikey? Are you *up* for it?" a familiar voice asked from behind them.

Of all the pubs in town, he had to walk into this one. "James, what are you doing here? You were supposed to be talking to the medical examiner," Michael said to his partner.

"I talked to him on my way here. I had a feeling you might need me, partner. Ladies." James nodded at Shay, who still looked like she wanted to murder Cherry, who was staring at his partner like a starving woman presented with a five-course meal. Brow furrowed, James looked from Cherry to Michael. "She's not having a seizure, is she?"

Shay nudged her. "Snap out of it. You're scaring the man."

"It's him."

"Him, who?"

"You know. Him, him, my tea-leaf lover."

Shay rubbed a hand over her eyes and then blew out a breath. "Sorry, I'm Shay Angel, and this is Cherry. Why don't you grab a table, and I'll have someone come and take your order."

Cherry raised her hand to her hair, flicking it into Michael's eyes. "Sorry," she said, and then pushed out her chest and head in an odd move he supposed she might think was sexy. "Hello, I'm Cherry. Cherry Blossom," she said in a breathy voice.

"All right, Marilyn, let the men grab a table while you and I take Roxy for a walk."

Focused on James, Cherry waved off Shay. "You take her. Just be careful. She nearly let her freeze to death this morning," she added conspiratorially to James, who raised his eyebrows at Michael.

James then turned to Shay. "Ms. Angel, you sound like a dangerous woman. I've been here less than three minutes, and I've heard you threaten to murder your friend and hear you've nearly frozen her dog to death."

Shay's eyes narrowed. "You sound like you have something you want to say, *Special* Agent James. Go ahead, the floor is yours."

"Since you and Pretty Boy are such good *friends*, I think I'll let him do the honors of interrogating you."

Despite Michael's urge to drop-kick his partner, he stayed focused on Shay. If he hadn't been, he would've missed the quick flash of what looked to be betrayal before a resigned acceptance crossed her face.

Shay glanced toward a group of men as they entered the pub and took their places on the stools. "You and *Pretty Boy* will have to wait." She waved over an older woman with burgundy hair. "Denise will look after you, and I'll be with you when I can." Her voice was as cold as her beautiful, expressionless face. "Cherry, come give me a hand."

"But I..." Her eyes narrowed on Shay, and then she frowned at James and Michael. "I'm buying new tea leaves," she said, and stomped after Shay.

Michael debated going after Shay but could tell by her ramrod-straight back and angry stride that it wouldn't do him any good. "That was a bullshit move, James."

"So was you trying to ditch me," James said as he grabbed a seat at the closest table. "Right now, your ex-girlfriend is the closest thing we have to a suspect. So either you can do the job or you can't. It's no sweat off my nose. If you can't, I'll request your transfer to white-collar crimes as soon as we get back to HQ."

"Really? You want me gone so bad you're willing to railroad an innocent woman?"

James might skirt the rules and put a toe over the line every now and again, but he grew up in what some considered to be one of the worst neighborhoods in Boston and had no doubt seen his fair share of friends get the shaft because of where they lived and the color of their skin. James shifted uncomfortably on the barrel. "Come on, you saw the text."

"Yeah, and it's like we both read different ones. We can't actually verify that it was Charlie who sent the text because it was a burner phone, and even if it was his registered phone, there would be no way of knowing it came from him—"

"Geezus, you lawyers are all the same. Get to the freaking point."

"The point is, Charlie was scared. They're all scared, and none of them know who's out to get whom. So Charlie thinks Fast Eddie, our vic, offed Fat Tony—"

"Right, Fat Tony who we now know Suzy Sunshine used to call Uncle Tony."

Michael glanced at Shay behind the bar. "You didn't just call her Suzy Sunshine, did you?"

James chuckled. "Good one, right?" He shifted to look at Shay. "Seriously, man, that is one smoking-hot woman. I can see why you're still hung up on her, but you can't let your feelings mess with your head or your..." He gave Michael's lap a meaningful nod. "The bodies are starting to pile up, and this ain't over yet."

His partner made two very good points, and Michael looked away from the smoking-hot woman behind the bar. But not before she noticed and leveled him with a deadly glare.

"You see, that right there, that's some scary shit. That woman's fierce."

She was. And sadly, for Michael, that was one big turn-on. "She is, and everyone across three counties knows it. Which is why Charlie claimed Shay would hunt down whoever had Tony killed and ensure they suffered the same fate. He knew Fast Eddie would believe him. But I have no doubt Shay can provide us with an alibi."

He just needed to talk to her before she did because, according to the ME report, Fast Eddie was killed somewhere between midnight and three in the morning. And if Shay used Michael as an alibi, they both could have a problem if it came out she'd fired on a federal agent, who admittedly had broken into her house.

As to her *uncle* Tony, Michael planned to have a word with her about that too. She was making it difficult for him to protect her. He had a feeling that after tonight, he was going to have a hard time selling that he was actually trying to protect her.

"You better hope—" James broke off as the older woman with burgundy hair approached the table. "Denise, is it? I'm Special Agent James, and this is my partner Special Agent Gallagher. Would you mind answering a few questions for us?"

She glanced at the bar and then whispered, "It's about Shay threatening to kill Gerry Noles, isn't it? The man was shaking in his boots. I told Charlie he shouldn't let her work here, on account of her being an ex-con and all. But he wouldn't hear it. Terrible thing, guilt. It's like I always tell him, though, blood shows. Her parents, they were the real criminals. Low level, but they had ties to the higher-ups in the New England mob.

"Never wanted to say anything to Charlie, but I heard rumors Shay there's a hit woman. You ever seen her shoot a gun? Lordy." She nodded. "Wouldn't surprise me at all if she was."

James raised an eyebrow at Michael while smiling at the woman. "You've been very helpful, Denise. Very helpful indeed."

Chapter Ten

♥

Afraid of what she'd do or say if she stayed, Shay stormed from the bar and out the back door. It felt a little like she was running, and that bothered her almost as much as the accusation she thought she saw in Michael's eyes. She slid behind the wheel of her car and revved the engine, about to throw it in gear when Cherry grabbed the handle on the passenger door and wrenched it open.

"You forgot us," she grumbled as she put Roxy in the backseat and climbed in beside Shay, snapping on her seat belt.

"Sorry," she said, and hit the gas, turning onto South Shore Road with a squeal of tires.

"You don't have to worry about the FBI trying to frame you for murder; they're going to throw you in jail for recklessly endangering your best friend and her dog!" Cherry cried, clinging to the strap above the passenger window with both hands, her shiny black boots wedged against the dash.

Shay rolled her eyes. "Relax, I know what I'm doing. It's not as if I'm going a hundred..." She glanced at the speedometer and eased off the gas. "Sorry."

She should've calmed down before she got behind the wheel or punched something to get rid of her pent-up fury... and hurt. That was worse than the anger. No one would ever know how much it hurt that Michael thought her capable of murder. It didn't matter that he said his questions were simply standard operating procedure given Charlie's damning text; she'd seen the hint of doubt in his eyes.

She'd been surprised he'd been able to pierce her defenses. She supposed she shouldn't be. His opinion had always mattered to her. He'd made her want to change, to be better, to reinvent herself so that she fit in his world. If only she could go back and shake the girl she used to be. She'd tell her to run in the opposite direction when he first approached her on Main Street on that hot summer's day.

"It's okay. Roxy didn't even slide off the backseat," Cherry said, glancing over her shoulder as she let go of the strap and lowered her boots from the dash. "Maybe you should give up the security business to become a NASCAR driver. You've got the need for speed down, and the driving on two wheels when you take a corner. It was hair-raising in the moment, but even I can tell you have what it takes."

Shay felt like clunking her head on the steering wheel. All she wanted was an hour on her own to sort it all out. She wasn't used to having someone around twenty-four-seven, even if that someone was trying to be supportive. "I know what you're doing, and it's not necessary. I'm fine. I'm over it."

"You're not even the least bit worried they can build a case against you? Especially after what that Denise woman overheard? Agent Photoshop James even had me wondering if you'd done it. For a second, I mean. A nanosecond."

"So, is that why you stole his wallet?"

Cherry jerked, bumping her head against the window. "I didn't steal his wallet. He's the FBI. I don't mess with the FBI, even if he is my tea-leaf suitor and hot as—"

"You might want to check inside your corset."

"It's not a corset. It's a...I have his wallet." She whacked Shay with it. "Why did you let me steal it?"

"A six-foot-two rat with eyes of blue was interrogating me for murder. The same rat who's looking at my uncle for murder, too, so I'm sorry if all I wanted to do was get out of there."

"What am I going to do? I can't be sent to the big house for this. I'm not like you," Cherry said with a noticeable tremor in her voice.

"Relax, you're not going to jail. I'll drop you off and go back to the pub once the feds have left and make sure one of the staff finds the wallet." But first she'd go for a long drive. Alone. For at least two hours. It would give her time to come up with a plan as to how she was going to find Charlie and get out of this mess.

Cherry leaned across the console and hugged her. "You take such good care of me, Shaybae. I don't know what I'd do without you."

The temptation to hang her head and groan was there, but she fought against it, knowing her response would hurt Cherry's feelings. It wasn't easy, though. She practically broke out in a cold sweat at the thought that Cherry was so dependent on her. "If I don't figure out who's behind Tony's and Eddie's murders, you just might find out what it's like to live without me."

Cherry gasped, and then her eyes went wide. She frantically patted her chest.

"Okay, don't be so dramatic. I was just kidding." Kind of.

Pointing to her mouth, Cherry then grabbed her neck with both hands.

"Are you kidding me? You're choking?" Shay didn't wait for an answer and slammed on the brakes.

With a quick glance, she took in Cherry's bulging eyes and the purple tinge spreading across her flushed face and threw open the car door. She didn't look up at the sound of cars honking, tires squealing, doors slamming, or the smell of burned rubber as she raced around to the passenger side. Which might explain why she ran headlong into a man—a long, lean man who stood at least six-two, with a wide chest, strong hands, and a sexy, citrusy scent. She didn't need to look up to know he had eyes of blue.

"Are you okay? What's going on?"

"Cherry. Choking," she said, feeling panicked, and Shay didn't panic. *This is what happens when you let people into your life,* she thought, aggravated despite her fear.

At least Michael was levelheaded. He'd opened the

door and was talking to Cherry in a low, comforting voice while half-lifting her from the car. Shay wondered if his voice calmed Cherry half as much as it did her.

"Shay," he said, snapping her out of her daze, "hold the door open."

She frowned, wondering what he was talking about when she realized he'd wrapped his arms around Cherry to do the Heimlich maneuver, and the uneven road was causing the door to swing closed. She grabbed the edge of the window just before it hit them and heard the poodle whimpering in the backseat.

"It's okay, Roxy Roo. Mommy's going to be okay," Shay told the dog, then almost immediately rolled her eyes when what she'd said registered. Before Shay could wonder why she seemed to be channeling her friend, Cherry hacked up a lung. Whatever she was choking on flew out of her mouth to ping off the roof of Shay's car. Cherry coughed again and rubbed her chest, the blue tinge leaving her face.

Michael helped Cherry sit on the passenger seat to a smattering of applause from the drivers who'd gotten out of their vehicles to watch. Crouching at Cherry's feet, he pulled out his cell phone. "Anyone call nine-one-one?" he directed his question to the now-thinning crowd while those true-blue eyes of his moved over Shay like a hot caress.

True-blue eyes? A hot caress? What was she, a romance heroine? Less than twenty minutes ago, she'd wanted to punch his pretty face, and now she wanted to kiss those beautiful, sensual lips? She gave her head a slight shake to get rid of the thoughts that were making her hot on one hand and uncomfortable on the other. Then she realized what the problem was. It was a phenomenon common to doctors and cops. The adrenaline rush after a life-and-death situation.

Michael had saved Cherry, and Shay wanted to jump his bones. Completely normal reaction, she assured herself. Probably more so because the last time she had sex was ten years before, with him, and those memories had inconveniently come flooding back. *Good memories. Really, really good memories, and hot too. Burning hot.*

As her gaze moved over his chiseled profile, his broad shoulders and big hands, she couldn't help but wonder what it would be like to make love to the man he'd become.

The crowd's response to Michael's question pulled her from her messed-up thoughts. Their audience answered in the negative. The general consensus seemed to be that Michael had the situation under control. "I'd feel better if a doctor checked you out. I can call my cousin if you'd like."

"That's a really good idea. I'm feeling kind of weird."

Michael cocked his head, a hint of a smile touching his lips. "Shay, I was talking to Cherry."

"I know that. I meant I'm feeling weirded out about the whole thing. She needs to get her throat checked, and maybe her ribs. It looked like your arms were wrapped around her really, really tight and... Why are you both looking at me like that?"

"Aw, Shaybae, you were worried about me," Cherry wheezed.

"Of course I was worried. You nearly died in front of me. What were you choking on anyway?" Shay remembered the pinging sound and looked at the roof of her car. "Never mind. I can see it was a Jolly Rancher. A pink one. And you know how I know this? Because it made a dent in my roof." She sounded testy even to her own ears. Good, she was back to normal. No more of this emotional weirdness.

"What did you expect? Of course I'm going to choke on my Jolly Rancher when you tell me you have to find Fat Tony and Frisky Freddy's murderer before Mikey and Agent Photoshop send you back to prison."

"Shay...," Michael began as he slowly stood up, the wallet falling out of the car and landing at his feet. He picked it up, frowning as if it looked familiar, and then flipped it open. His beautiful mouth didn't look quite so sensuous with his lips flattened. "Would one of you like to explain what you're doing with Agent Photoshop's wallet?"

Cough. "Shay." *Hack.* "I think I." *Wheeze.* "Better go to the doctor. Hard time." *Cough.* "Breathing."

* * *

Michael sat in a chair at the clinic, his elbows resting on his knees as he watched Shay pace. She'd been worried, almost panicked, for her friend earlier. It was a side to Shay he'd never seen before, one that touched him and made him smile. She didn't often allow herself to be vulnerable. He imagined she was embarrassed and unhappy at just how much of herself she had revealed. He wasn't happy about her plans that Cherry had inadvertently revealed either. It was something he intended to talk to her about. And this time she wasn't going anywhere until they cleared some things up.

He straightened and pulled out his phone to text his cousin Finn, the doctor who was at that moment examining Cherry.

Hey buddy, do me a solid and keep your patient occupied for another twenty minutes.

Thirty seconds later, Finn responded:

Twenty? That's a joke, right?

No. I have some important business for the Bureau to take care of, and I can't have her interfering.

Would that important business have anything to do with a certain brunette prowling around my waiting room?

Yes, but that's not for public consumption. And that includes your brother.

What's it worth to you?

Name your price.

A night out with my wife. You babysit George.

You keep Cherry occupied for thirty minutes, and you've got a deal.

He was pretty sure he was getting the short end of the stick. He'd heard all about the precocious little girl. But having a half hour of uninterrupted time to straighten things out with Shay...priceless.

He got a thumbs-up in response and put his phone away. Shay glanced at him.

"Cherry's fine. Which you already know. She was faking so the two of you could come up with a story about the wallet on your way over here." With the number of times Cherry had looked around to see if he was still following behind in his Range Rover, he'd be surprised if she hadn't given herself whiplash.

"She was coughing and wheezing all over my car. There was no time to come up with a story. Besides, we didn't need one. A customer flagged me down on Main Street. He'd found the wallet in front of the pub. Near the door. To the left of the garbage can. I was going to return it once I dropped Cherry and Roxy off. Nothing's missing, so I don't know what the big deal is."

"One of the ways we can tell someone is lying is when they provide too much extraneous detail, like you just did. So why don't you give it another shot? Only this time try the truth."

"Fine. I took it. He was trying to make me sweat, so I thought I'd do the same to him."

Michael sat back and stretched out his legs, crossing

his arms and then his feet at the ankles before raising an eyebrow at her.

"Okay, but I'll warn you right now you don't have a shot at making this stick. Cherry's a kleptomaniac. When she gets nervous or upset, she steals things. Your partner made her nervous." She lifted a shoulder. "That's it, whole truth and nothing but the truth, so what are you going to do about it?"

"I called him on the way here and told him I went back after being unable to track you down, and he was gone but that he'd left his wallet. So, quid pro quo." He uncrossed his arms and patted the chair beside him. "Come here, I want to talk to you."

"Is that FBI speak for *interrogate you*? Because as much as I appreciate you not making a big deal over the wallet, I've met my quota for today, thanks. Next time, you can talk to my lawyer... What are you doing?" she said when he got up and walked toward her.

"If you won't come to me, I'll come to you." He moved into her and put his hands on her shoulders. She tensed beneath her black leather jacket. It was the dumbest thing he'd done in years. The last thing he ever should've allowed himself to do was get this close to her. Close enough to look deep into her silver eyes and smell the sweet scent of wildflowers. He couldn't smell the fragrance without thinking about her. Her scent alone had ruined what had the potential to be two amazing dates. He couldn't smell it without wanting her and her alone. The other women hadn't stood a chance. Still, he couldn't back away or release her.

She lowered her gaze from his as she brought her hands to his chest. "I can't do this."

"Can't do what?" His voice was gruffer than it should be, filled with too much want and need. Yet he couldn't say the words he wanted to or ask the questions that were on the tip of his tongue. Not yet. Not now. Not until this case was solved.

"What do you want from me, Michael?"

There it was again, that hint of vulnerability in her eyes. She sounded tired too. "I want to keep you safe. I want you to promise me you won't interfere with our investigation. And I want you to tell me everything you know about Danny Costello, Fat Tony, and Fast Eddie." And because the vulnerability had been erased, replaced by eyes shuttered in stone-cold defiance, he added, "Or as Cherry refers to him, Frisky Freddy."

As he'd intended, that got him a small laugh. What he hadn't intended was for her to move away from him to take a seat in one of the waiting room chairs.

"And while we're talking about names, do you think you can get her to stop calling me Mikey?" he asked as he took the seat one over from Shay to give her some space.

Her lips twitched as though trying not to smile but she wasn't able to keep the amusement from lighting up her eyes. "Would you prefer Pretty Boy?"

"You picked up on that, did you?"

"That and the tension. You and your partner don't get along?"

"Let's just say it's been interesting."

"That bad, huh?"

He shrugged and once again rested his elbows on his knees, glancing at her. "You don't have to worry about Oliver. He was just trying to rattle you. Other than the text, we have nothing to tie you to the murders."

"Right. Just motive and opportunity. Don't pretend my alibi would stand up in court. The jurors wouldn't believe Cherry. They'd think she was lying for me."

As much as it pained him to admit, she was right. "Why didn't you tell Oliver I was there last night?"

"And tell him that I'd fired on a federal agent? Yeah, I don't think so."

"A federal agent who'd broken into your home," he reminded her.

"Which I didn't report, and I fixed the lock, and we used to date. You could've had a key."

"I would never lie to protect myself if it meant hurting you, Shay."

She snorted a laugh. "You'd never lie period. You're a true white hat, Michael."

"You say that as if it's a bad thing."

She looked away. "It was, for us."

"Shay." He reached for her hand when she wouldn't look at him and gave it a gentle tug. "You need to tell me about your connection to Tony and anything you know about Eddie and the Costellos. I can't protect you if you're not straight with me."

She tilted her head to the side. "And what exactly do you think you're protecting me from? Do you actually believe I could shoot someone in cold blood?" Her eyes searched his face, and she nodded. "You do. Wow. I tried to convince myself that I was wrong. Guess I was right after all. There was a time I thought you knew me better than anyone else, Michael."

"I do, and I know if someone you loved was in danger, like your uncle, you would do whatever was necessary to protect them. Am I wrong?"

She made a noncommittal sound in her throat. "I didn't kill Eddie. I have no idea who he is or what his connection is to Charlie. My parents were small-time. I doubt they had any dealings with the Costellos. Their only connection would be through Tony." She told him about her relationship with the former Costello enforcer and the last time they'd had any contact. She'd been fond of the man, and no matter how hard she tried to hide it, Michael could see that his death upset her.

"I'm sorry about your friend. Everything pointed to him being out of the business for several years."

"Word in town is that Danny Costello was trying to get a toehold in Harmony Harbor. From what I hear, Charlie's been organizing the other bar owners both here and in Bridgeport to take a stand against Costello. Charlie can be a major pain in the butt when he wants to be, and he's vocal." She looked away again, and he gave her hand a comforting squeeze.

"We have nothing to indicate they've gotten to him, Shay. Or for that matter, that he had anything to do with Tony's and Eddie's murders. I promise I'll keep you in the loop, but I need you to promise to stay out of this."

She nodded. "Okay, I'll give you a few days. Any more than that—"

"How about we renegotiate on Thursday? I'll buy you a drink, and we can talk."

"I don't…Okay, so I don't drink *usually*," she said in response to his raised eyebrow.

"I figured today was an anomaly. Which was why I thought we'd go to Sweet Dreams Dairy Bar and have a s'more milkshake like we used to." Yes, it was cheesy, but he'd never enjoyed cheesy as much as he had with Shay.

"They closed a few years ago. Mr. Anderson got sick, and Mrs. Anderson lost interest after he was gone. None of the kids wanted to take over."

"That's too bad."

"Life moves on. Nothing stays the same."

"Some things never change," he said, wondering if she knew he wasn't talking about Sweet Dreams Dairy Bar.

Chapter Eleven

♥

The next morning, Shay woke up to Roxy sitting beside her bed, whining. "No, no way." She rolled over with every intention of ignoring the dog. Rather than fluffing her pillow into the shape she liked, she punched it. She hated mornings, and she really hated this one. She'd barely slept.

Every time she'd closed her eyes and started to nod off, Michael would pop in for a visit. In one dream, he'd put her in handcuffs before driving her back to prison, and in the next, he'd been representing her in court, defending her with his rapier wit and prodigious brain, winning her case, saving her from prison. The tug-of-war between good Michael and bad Michael continued in her head all night. It wasn't difficult to figure out why.

Good Michael had heroically saved Cherry both from immediate death and jail while bad Michael was digging deeper into Shay's and Charlie's lives, discovering things she didn't want him to know about her and her family. Asking her to stand down, to trust him to find her uncle, to go completely against her better judgment and leave their lives in his hands.

She lifted her head and punched her pillow again. "Cherry, Roxy has to go out," she called to her friend who'd been sleeping in Shay's sisters' bedroom.

"I need to sleep after my ordeal. Doctor's orders. You take her."

"I was standing right there. Finn said you were fine. Now get your butt out of bed. The fresh air will do you good."

"He was fine, wasn't he? I know he's married, but I think he might've been into me. He wasn't obvious about it or anything, but you don't keep someone locked in an examination room for half an hour after the exam unless you feel a little somethin' somethin' for them, right?"

Shay had her own theory about why Cherry's exam took so long, and he was six foot two with eyes of blue. Which admittedly could have described Michael's cousin, too, but he wasn't the one who'd orchestrated her alone time with Michael. It had been obvious from the men's silent exchanges that Special Agent Gallagher had put the good doctor up to it.

"I have no idea what Dr. Gallagher was thinking, but your dog looks like she's thinking about peeing in my room, and I swear to God, Cherry, if—" The doorbell rang, cutting off Shay midthreat. And it kept ringing, like someone was leaning on it. "It's eight flipping o'clock in the morning! Who in their right mind rings someone's doorbell at eight flipping o'clock in the flipping morning?"

Shay threw back the covers and stomped down the hall, glancing in her sisters' old bedroom to where Cherry lay in the double bed with her pink eye shades on, her pink satin pajama top visible above the white comforter, and her hands clasped peacefully with a beatific smile on her face. "You suck," Shay said before stomping down the hall to the front door.

"I love you too, Shaybae. No, you go with Auntie Shay, Roxy. She'll take you out for a tinkle."

"I'm not taking your dog for a tinkle!" she yelled at the same time she pulled open the door. On the other side of it stood her next door neighbors, Libby and Teddy, wearing matching sneers on their faces. Shay was just about to close the door on their ticked-off faces when Gabby stepped into view and gave her an angelic smile. Shay dragged in a deep breath while rubbing her fingers through her hair with the urge to tear it out right there. "Okay, so what brings you three to my door at eight in the flipping morning? No, no, that was not an invitation," she said as Libby and Teddy pushed their way inside.

Gabby stood in front of her in a pair of princess pajamas that were two sizes too small and stained with raspberry jam and orange juice. "Momma lost her job 'cause she don't have any medicine for her bad back."

Shay briefly closed her eyes, opening them to see Libby and her oldest daughter had crossed their arms and were staring at her with identical *what are you going to do about it?* looks on their faces.

"Roxy, come," Shay said, and without a word to the West family, she followed the dog outside. After calmly closing the door, she yelled at the top of her lungs. "Charlie, where the hell are you?" Roxy froze with a terrified look on her face. "Sorry, just go do your business. I'll be okay." She looked up at the sun peeking out from behind a fluffy cloud. The sullen weather of the past couple of days better suited her mood than what was starting out as a cheerful one.

She glanced at the Challenger, the sun's rays dancing on its sleek black frame. If she were in a fairy tale, the Hellcat would serve as her trusty black steed. Ready, willing, and able to save her from the nightmare she found herself in. All she had to do was go back inside, throw her clothes in a bag, grab her keys, and leave everyone in that house—all the demands and responsibilities—behind in a cloud of dust.

The door cracked open, and an arm appeared, wearing pink satin with a mug of what smelled like coffee. Shay sighed. "Thanks."

By the time Roxy had done her business and Shay had drunk half a cup of coffee, the Wests had made themselves at home in the dining room. Cherry came out of the galley-sized kitchen with a plate of toast in one hand and a box of cereal tucked under her arm. "All right, Teddy, first you're going to tell Shay what you saw last Tuesday night, and then we're going to figure out what to do about you, Libby. Don't worry, though— like I told you, Shay will take care of everything. She always does. Don't you, Shaybae?"

Shay went to drag in another calming breath but knew it was futile to search for calm at this moment. She clenched her teeth together to keep from swearing and walked toward the hutch in the corner, the chipped seashell-decorated lamp she'd found at a garage sale still gracing the top. Retrieving the extra white wooden chair from beside the hutch, she pulled it up to the round white table. She remembered the day she'd gone with her uncle to buy the furniture.

They'd been living with him for a year by then. She was eleven and going through a nesting phase, putting down roots, determined to make her uncle's bachelor pad a home for her and her sisters. Sometimes she wondered who she would've become if their family hadn't been torn apart the following year.

She turned the chair around and straddled it. "Okay, so what did you see, Teddy?"

The teenager glanced at her mother, who nodded. "I saw Charlie around ten-thirty like I told you and Agent Gallagher, but I saw him again, later." She hesitated, and Shay gave her a look of encouragement even though she instinctively knew she wasn't going to like what she was about to hear.

"When Mom's at work, I check the locks on the doors and windows before I go to bed."

Shay glanced at Libby, wondering how that made her feel. As a mother, it was her job to protect her daughters, not the other way around. Libby caught Shay looking at her and crossed her arms, her chin lifting.

Taking in their silent exchange, Teddy stopped talking.

Cherry, who'd returned with bowls, spoons, and a pitcher of milk, nodded at Teddy. "It's okay. Shay needs to know. She can protect you. She can protect all of us."

Shay bowed her head and rubbed her forehead before lifting her gaze to Teddy. "Someone came after him, didn't they?"

The young girl nodded. "A black car, a really expensive one, turned onto the street and turned off its headlights. Then it pulled into the driveway, and two men got out. They were big, and one of them had a gun."

"Jesus, kid, you went and warned Charlie, didn't you?" Admiration warred with fear for what might've happened to Teddy had the men seen her.

She gave a jerky nod. "Charlie pretends his hearing is fine, but it's not. I waited on our deck in the shadows, you know, to be sure they weren't going to come around to the back. When I heard the front doorbell, I ran over here and climbed in the window." She gave her mother a sheepish look and lifted a shoulder. "Charlie leaves it open in case I need anything."

"He gave you the key that night, didn't he?" Shay said.

"Yeah. When I found him, he was just sitting on one of the beds staring at some papers. He was acting all weird. I shook him and told him about the men. He snapped out of it then. We hid in the attic until they were gone."

Costello's men wouldn't have left like that, no matter what Teddy would have them believe. "They broke in, didn't they? Searched the house?"

Teddy swallowed and nodded, the fear she'd felt that night visible in her light blue eyes. Shay hoped that was enough to scare the kid straight. She was too brave for her own good. "They wrecked the place, pulling things apart, turning furniture over. I came back after school on Friday and cleaned it up."

"Did you notice anyone watching the house? No one came in to search a second time?"

"I saw the car Wednesday and Thursday, but they didn't come in. Me and Charlie put papers in the doors and window, so I'd be able to tell. He told me not to come back for a couple of days in case they did."

"All right, so what did Charlie do after you got out of the attic? Where did he go?"

"He said it was safer if I didn't know. He's okay, right?"

Maybe it was just wishful thinking on Shay's part, but she thought he was. "For now, he is. Has he called you? Did he give you a number where he could be reached?"

She shook her head. "He said you'd come. He said you'd come and help him."

A million deep breaths weren't going to alleviate the stress bubbles expanding in her chest. The only thing that would help was action. No matter what she promised Michael, Shay couldn't just sit by and do nothing.

Libby moved her coffee cup back and forth. "I'm really sorry about Charlie, but I've got bigger problems. Like no money coming in, thanks to you. Teddy says you told her you'd come up with a plan to help us, and I'm all ears. Plan away, lady."

"Seriously? You have bigger problems than my uncle? Lady, he has the East Coast mob after him. You don't get much bigger than that," she snapped at the woman, avoiding Teddy's and Gabby's anxious eyes. *Dammit, dammit, dammit*, she swore in her head. "All right, fine. Give me the name of your club and your boss, and I'll see what I can do."

"Shaybae, that's the thing. Her club, Pussy Cat East, has a new boss, *Danny Costello*, and her old boss, *Frisky Freddy*, was found dead the other day."

Shay smiled. "Well, Libby, it looks like today's your lucky day. I'm going to solve Charlie's problem and yours." She got up off the chair. "Let's get to work."

The four of them frowned at her. "What do you mean, work? I might not be the best mom on the planet, but I'm not putting my kids to work at the pub. They're not even allowed in the Salty Dog."

"Sure they are if they're with me, but that's not what I was talking about. You guys have ten hours to turn me into a stripper."

* * *

It was four-thirty on Tuesday afternoon and Michael had arrived home to find a note from his mother to come to the manor. Yes, his mother, who was still living with him. Michael had arranged to take his father to his favorite hole-in-the-wall diner near headquarters in hopes of getting to the bottom of his parents' marital problems. The only thing he'd come away with was the knowledge that both his parents were apparently happy with their current living arrangements. And either his brothers had moved and hadn't told him or they were avoiding his phone calls.

He opened the heavy door to Greystone Manor. "Hey, Jeeves, have you seen my mother? She said something about eating at the manor tonight." He was hoping to convince her to order takeout and eat at home.

He'd been gone since seven that morning and wanted to spend some time outside with Atticus. It was the first semi-decent day weather-wise since they'd moved into the cottage, and the sun would set in about half an hour.

Jasper grimaced.

The smile Michael had offered the older man upon entering the manor fell. "What is it?"

"It appears your mother has joined the Widows Club, Master Michael."

"My dad isn't dead."

"Yes, well, they've been known to bend the rules in certain circumstances. Take Ava and Lexi, for example. They were divorcées, not widows."

"Okay, so that aside, you know as well as I do that my mother's a... Well, she's a snob, Jeeves. She hates the manor, and all she's ever done is make fun of the Widows Club. She's my mother, and I love her, but you've gotta help me get her to go home. I don't want her to hurt you or Grams or anyone at the manor."

"We appreciate your concern, Master Michael, but we're old enough to look after ourselves. And your mother, surprisingly, has been quite genial. I'd go so far as to say she's a changed woman."

"Really? Well that's good to hear at least," Michael said, knowing he should be relieved, but something didn't feel right. He understood what Jasper was saying, though. He'd seen a change in Maura too. She'd been less strident and demanding with him.

"Yes, it is. But as to assisting you to get Maura to return to your father, I think that may prove to be bigger than us. We may require divine intervention." He looked at the black cat at his feet. "You know what I mean, don't you, Simon? Yes, you go off and let her know, won't you?" Jasper said as the cat slunk away.

Michael looked from the cat to Jasper. "Is there something you want to talk about? You're feeling okay, aren't you? No issues we should know about? You're as much a member of this family as anyone, Jeeves. I hope you know that and feel like you can come to any one of us at any time."

"That's most kind of you, Master Michael. And I do appreciate it. Rest assured, I'm well. But I'm afraid your mother has no intention of leaving until"—he clasped his hands behind his back and rocked on his polished black shoes—"you're happily married."

"What?"

"Yes, and I'm afraid it's even worse than you're imagining. She now has the Widows Club in her corner. They're gathering in the dining room as we speak... with the first two candidates."

"Candidates?"

"Matrimonial candidates."

Michael turned to leave.

Jasper stopped him with a hand on his shoulder. "Do yourself a favor and go along with them. They'll hunt you down if you don't, and you'll never know a moment's peace. Trust me, I've been watching them operate for years. I'll help you outmaneuver them."

"Michael darling, there you are. Come join us for tea."

He turned to see his mother and his grandmother standing arm and arm at the top of the stairs leading down into the dining room. He raised a hand and forced a smile for the two women he loved. Two women who just over a year before had barely been able to utter a civil word to each other. "I'll be right there. I'm just having a word with Jasper." Michael squinted at the poster sitting on a brass easel near Maura and Kitty. "Tell me that's not a picture of me."

"I wish I could, Master Michael. But it's an excellent photograph."

"I can't read what it says above the photo."

"Bachelor of the month. I'm afraid they're using it in all the manor's promotional material and social media accounts. If it makes you feel better, Sophie says it's been excellent publicity. We've never had so many hits."

He scowled at the man. "I can't tell you how much better that makes me feel, Jeeves."

"Quite. And I'm afraid the news only gets worse."

"How could it possibly get worse than this? My mother and grandmother are trying to auction me off to the highest bidder like a . . . like a piece of meat."

"Oh, I wasn't aware you knew about the auction."

"What auction?"

"You just said . . . Ah, I see, you were being facetious. Well, you have the dubious distinction of being February's bachelor of the month." At Michael's blank look, he continued. "The official month of love, the month when every single woman wants a man in her life."

"Why?"

Jasper sighed. "You're a highly intelligent man, Master Michael. But I must say your lack of knowledge about love and the fairer sex is somewhat shocking."

"No, it's your lack of knowledge of the modern woman, Jeeves. Maybe back in your day all women wanted was a man, but not now. Take Shay, for example. Do you really think she's sitting at home counting down the days to Valentine's Day and worrying she won't have a date or be in love by then? Yeah, I don't think so."

"You'd be surprised how little changes, Master Michael. And while Ms. Angel might not be actively seeking love, as Valentine's Day approaches, it will most definitely be on her mind. You should take advantage of that."

"Even if she showed the slightest interest in me, which she doesn't, I have to keep my distance until I figure out how deep she and Charlie are involved in my case. I can't let personal feelings get in the way of doing my job. This is my first case as an agent, and I don't want to blow it. I gave up a lot to get to where I am today."

"I suppose I shouldn't be surprised you're at a loss when it comes to love. After all, you did almost marry Ms. Adams."

"And why was I twelve hours shy of making the biggest mistake of my life? I see it's dawning on you now. My mother, Jeeves. My mother set me up with

Bethany, and I promised myself I'd never let her set me up again. So as much as you think I should just go along with them, I can't take the risk. Please apologize to everyone for me and tell them I got called into work."

As he walked down the pathway to his SUV, his cell phone rang. It was his partner. So maybe he hadn't lied after all.

"Pretty Boy, got any plans for tonight?"

"If I did, I can tell by your voice that you have every intention of ruining them. What's going on?"

"You know the club Fast Eddie managed, Pussy Cat East? Word on the street is that our favorite mobster has just taken it over, so I thought we'd check it out."

"You might want to curb your enthusiasm, James. You'll lose your cool card."

"Hey, I'm fine losing my cool card if I get to see me some T and A. And, Pretty Boy, wear one of your million-dollar suits. Women love that fancy rich-boy shit."

He reached in his pocket for an antacid. "You're trying to get me to transfer to white-collar crimes again, aren't you?"

Chapter Twelve

♥

Shay stood in the bathroom facing the empty white wall and not the mirror. Afraid she'd lose her ever-loving mind if she saw the end result of Cherry's makeover. They'd been in there an hour already.

"What are you two doing?" Libby yelled from the living room where she waited to oversee the dress rehearsal. It was hard to hear the woman over the Pussycat Dolls, who were belting out "Don't Cha" through the speakers.

Yeah, what are we still doing in here? Shay was about to ask Cherry, who was attacking her hair with a comb while Libby continued shouting over the Pussycat Dolls singing "hot like me."

"The new manager won't hire Shay until he sees her perform, and she still needs to work on her booty dancing and butt clasp."

Shay brought her hands to her face, about to do a face-palm, only to catch herself before it was too late. The last thing she wanted to do was draw Cherry's attention. As soon as her wannabe hairstylist had turned her attention to Shay's ponytail, Shay had discreetly pulled off the freshly applied fake eyelashes. She figured she'd be good if she didn't look directly at Cherry. At least in the fake eyelash department.

Everything else was far from good. Shay began second-guessing her decision to go undercover an hour after she'd made it. She'd initially worried that sending Libby in for the information put the mother of two at unnecessary risk, but that worry had diminished during their making-of-a-stripper session. The woman was a total hardass. But just as Shay was about to share her change of plans, Libby confessed that she hadn't exactly left the club peacefully, and the new management freaked her out.

So there went that plan, and Shay's next idea of going in as herself wasn't much better. As a former PI, she had plenty of experience questioning the employees and clients of any number of clubs...and they were notoriously closemouthed. She had no doubt that, if they knew anything, she'd get the information from them in a matter of days. Except as Teddy's story had only too clearly illustrated, time was running out for Charlie.

Cherry stuck her head out the open bathroom door. "Almost done. Come up with a stage name while you're waiting for us."

"I don't need a stage name. What I need is for you to stop teasing my hair. You should've left it in a ponytail. It's going to be annoying as hell when I'm strip—" The word got stuck in her throat, almost making her choke. "Dancing."

She couldn't believe she was actually going through with it. So far, she'd come up with two ways for her uncle to repay her—no more communicating with known criminals or sticking his nose in the mob's business, even if his intentions had been good. Personal experience had taught Shay not to get involved in anyone's business unless she was being paid to. This situation was precisely why she didn't.

Charlie was lucky she had no intention of stripping or he'd be unable to repay his debt to her in a million years. The only article of clothing she planned to remove was her leather jacket. Though the miniskirt Libby had loaned her was revealing enough.

"The whole point is to make every man, and possibly a woman or two, in that club so hot for you that they'll tell you whatever you want to know and be so enthralled with you they'll have no memory of what they told you or why. And, Shaybae, a ponytail says I get the job done—wham bam, thank you, ma'am—while this long, luxurious mane of beachy waves says I'm so good you'll never want to let me out of bed."

"Really? That's what my hair says?" Shay asked, her voice loaded with sarcasm and dread for the job ahead.

"See for yourself." And before Shay could stop her, Cherry turned her to face the mirror.

Huh, so her wannabe hairstylist was right. Shay's wild mane and sultry makeup said she had one thing on her mind and one thing only. Unless they happened to look into her eyes. If they did, they'd know that the promises of a good time were all a lie. She'd have to be careful to mask her true feelings. An almost impossible feat given how she felt about what she'd be doing and the men who watched.

Maybe she'd let the memories from yesterday come out to play. Her response to Michael's hands on her at the clinic, the heat of his body standing so close she smelled the citrusy scent of his cologne, and the way he looked...

She blinked, shocked by the emotions that accompanied the memories. She'd expected them to have been long gone by now. Last night she'd assumed they were simply a response to the drama and evidence of his heroics. The explanation for them today was more complicated and unwelcome.

"Whatever you're thinking about, stop thinking about it right now. Your mouth just flattened, and the edges turned down. Do this." Cherry moistened her lips with the tip of her tongue and then made a familiar fish face. She leaned so close to the mirror that Shay thought she intended to kiss it, and then Cherry's eyes went wide. "You took off the false eyelashes!"

"If the men are focusing on my eyes and not these"— she pointed to her boobs and butt—"then we've got a problem."

Cherry stepped back to take in the aforementioned body parts and got a not-particularly-flattering look on her face.

"Excuse me, I'm totally rocking my stripper outfit even if I don't want to be wearing it. Look at the muscle definition"—she posed her leg in Cherry's thigh-high black boots while looking down her half-zipped motorcycle jacket—"and abs. I'll guarantee none of Libby's dancer friends are as toned as me or as strong."

Cherry nodded but didn't look completely convinced. "I'm not sure that'll work in your favor at the club, Shaybae. No doubt those girls have more junk in their trunks and..." She cocked her head. "What are you, an A?"

She frowned down at her boobs in the black push-up bra. "What are you talking about? I'm a B."

Cherry gave her a *sure you are* smile and leaned out of the bathroom to yell, "Libby, get your pal Renee back on the line and tell her Cherry Blossom is making a surprise appearance tonight with her friend...Sugarlicious."

An hour later, Shay pulled Libby's white Ford Fiesta into the club's mostly empty parking lot. They'd decided the Fiesta would be less conspicuous than the Hellcat. Shay looked at the totally conspicuous woman sitting in the passenger seat beside her, who wore neon pink. It had been easier to just give in. Well, that's what Shay had told herself sixty minutes before. She wasn't so sure about that now.

"This is so exciting. I didn't realize until now how much I missed being onstage. It's the adulation, you know? The men screaming my name, throwing money at me, begging for private time with me and for a lap dance."

"No private anything, and that includes lap dances. No sitting on laps either. You stick close to me, and you do exactly what I say, when I say it."

"I have a better idea. You follow my lead on the

stage, and I'll follow yours when we're off it. Like when we're questioning the girls and bouncers and breaking into the manager's office."

"You're not breaking into his office. I am. You're going to distract the bouncers while keeping an eye out for Danny Costello." Libby had learned that Costello might be checking on his investment tonight. If he did, Shay wanted both her and Cherry off his radar. He didn't need to know she was investigating her uncle's disappearance. She thought her best chance of finding the information she needed was digging deeper into Fast Eddie. If she found a mutual acquaintance of Eddie and Tony who fit the profile, she might be able to get one step ahead of Costello's hit men and find her uncle at the same time. She cut off the voice in her head that said *If Charlie's even alive...*

Beside her, Cherry fluffed her hair and then adjusted her rhinestone-studded jacket that matched the micro-mini she'd paired with fishnet stockings and five-inch Lucite heels. "Okay, Sugar Tits, let's get this show on the road."

A pained sound emitted from Shay's mouth before she managed to choke out, "Sugarlicious."

"I know, that's what I said."

As Shay had learned in the past, it was no use wasting her breath arguing. She put a shoulder into the car door to push it open, shivering at the rush of cold, damp air. It smelled like exhaust fumes and the sea. The club was located on the highway, twenty minutes outside of Harmony Harbor on the way to Bridgeport.

Before Shay had the doors locked, Cherry bolted

across the parking lot swearing at the weather. "Be careful of the ice!" Shay yelled after her, finding it interesting to discover her friend could actually run when she wanted to. She'd have to keep that in mind for another time.

Teeth practically chattering when she entered the club, Shay took a moment to get her bearings. On either side of the main floor, there were shiny-topped black bars with purple padded fronts. The purple and black color scheme was carried throughout the club, from the barstools to the booths at the back of the space that were set up for table service. The club didn't open for another hour, so the main floor was empty save for a server and bartender, who offered Shay a chin lift.

Not wanting to appear suspicious, Shay returned his greeting while pretending to search through the black-studded purse Cherry had insisted she carry. Libby had drawn out the floor plan, so Shay knew there was a narrow hall on the other side of the bar to her right that led to the manager's office, but she felt better getting a feel for the place herself.

The main level was a horseshoe shape enclosed with a black railing that offered a view to the entertainment below. A large, lit square stage filled the center of the room on the lower level surrounded by comfortable black and purple pub chairs for the patrons. Overall, it was a step above most of the clubs she'd been in.

At the bottom of the curved staircase that led to the entertainment level, Cherry stood talking to one of the bouncers and spotted Shay. "Hurry up, they can't hold off the audition forever, Sugar—"

"Coming, coming right now," she cut Cherry off, trying to locate the security cameras as she made her way down the stairs. It wasn't something Libby had paid attention to.

"Benji, this is my good friend—" Cherry began once Shay joined them.

"Sugarlicious," she intervened, extending her hand. As she did, she wondered if the fortysomething, muscle-bound man with the scarred face and blond crew cut had picked up on her distaste for the name. It didn't appear to be the case. He was too busy checking her out.

"I know exactly what you're thinking, but don't write her off just because she's a little shy in the T and A department, Benji."

Shay crossed her arms and gave them both a *what the hell?* look.

The bouncer lifted a shoulder, and Cherry continued as if Shay wasn't staring her down. "I'm her mentor, after all, and you know I wouldn't put my stamp of approval on just anyone."

"Thing is, I don't really know you, Cherry...and your friend here seems a little on the scary side."

"Really? You're a bouncer, for crap sakes. How can you be afraid of me?"

Cherry gave her a *zip it* look and grabbed her by the arm. "Don't mind her. She's nervous, that's all. It's a lot of pressure to live up to, you know. But she'll blow Freaky Freddie away with her dance routine—just you wait and see. We'll go freshen up and be back in five." She began dragging Shay away.

The bouncer shot a pained look to what Shay knew was the smoked glass outer wall of the manager's office, which seemed to support Libby's theory that the manager could see them even if they couldn't see him. There was also a separate set of stairs that led to the office from the hall located off the dancers' dressing rooms. It's how Shay planned to get to the office unseen after their performance.

"Ah, Cherry, it's Friendly Freddie, and that's on account of him not being friendly at all, so maybe you should refrain from calling him anything other than Mr. Kozack," the bouncer said.

Shay glanced back at Benji as she followed Cherry to the dancers' changing rooms. "I hope he told you where the changing rooms are or he's going to wonder how we know where to go."

"Of course he did, and he told me something else too," Cherry said, looking inordinately pleased with herself, which worried Shay.

"Cherry, we talked about this. You don't ask questions unless I'm with you, and then you play off mine."

"I know, but I had a better idea. I told Benji that I was in the area paying a surprise visit to my boyfriend, Charlie Angel. No, no, wait. You'll see, it was a good idea," she interrupted Shay's groan. "I said how I was at loose ends on account of Charlie going out of town without letting me know, so I've been passing the time by mentoring you. And now that I've put my reputation on the line, you had better lose the attitude and get with the program."

Shay pulled her out of the way of a blonde with

bigger hair than Cherry, who was wearing less clothes and texting on her phone. Shay lowered her voice. "I told you I didn't want us on Costello's radar, and now you've put yourself directly there by saying you're dating my uncle."

"I know, I know, but here's the good news. Benji says he saw your uncle in here talking to Frisky Eddie the night he died."

Shay was too rattled by the news to remind her it was Fast Eddie, not Frisky Eddie. "He's positive it was Charlie?"

She nodded. "He said Charlie had been coming around regularly, and then they had a falling out or something. But they seemed buddy-buddy that night. They even left together. Good news, right? Now we know Charlie was still alive on Sunday."

"And was last seen in the company of a man who was murdered a few hours later."

"Oh, right, not so good news, then."

"For Charlie, no, but it is for me. The FBI mustn't know he was here that night. Michael would've said something." Shay looked over her shoulder. She couldn't see the manager's office from there, but she had a feeling it would be free of cameras, same as the secondary entryway. No doubt there were things going on at the Pussy Cat East that Fast Eddie hadn't wanted recorded. Namely things that went on in his office.

"So, did Benji seem upset about Fast Eddie's murder? Did he give any indication he thought my uncle was involved?"

"No, none. You could tell he liked Charlie, and his

old boss. I didn't get the impression he's a fan of the new one, though."

"Did he mention Costello?"

"No, but he's coming. I'm sure of it. Benji said we didn't have time to do a run-through before the audition because they were expecting a VIP tonight and—"

Shay heard the squeak of shoes on tile and put a hand on Cherry's arm.

"What's wrong? I don't hear anything."

"Give him a minute, and you will. Start walking," Shay said under her breath.

They only got a few yards when Benji called, "Geez, Cherry, I told you, you didn't have time to waste. Mr. Kozack is waiting for you to take the stage."

"You really are good, Shaybae. It's like you have bionic ears," Cherry whispered, and then turned to smile at Benji.

He thrust a whip at Shay. "Take it. I've been around long enough to see who's got it and who hasn't, and you don't got it, lady. So unless you want to embarrass Cherry, I figure you oughta play to your strengths. You look like you work out, and I don't mean no Pilates or yoga."

"MMA."

He grinned. "Totally would've called that. Okay, so work the pole." He rolled his eyes, she imagined in response to her stiffening. "Come on, this is a class joint. If you play the dominatrix onstage, no one's going to be expecting you to shake your thing. When you perform on the pole, Cherry will handle the stage routine."

"Like you said earlier, you don't know Cherry. So why are you really doing this?"

"Libby recommended you, so I figured you and her must be friends. How's she doing? She okay?"

Shay picked up on it right away. Benji cared about Libby. She might be able to work with that. "She could be better. She's out of a job and has two kids to support." She saved the best for last. "I think Kozack scared her."

A muscle flexed in his jaw, and his meaty hands balled into fists. "He's a scary guy. He's got a temper. It was time for her to quit."

"If he's so bad, why aren't you warning Cherry and me away?"

"Cherry's making a guest appearance, and I'm not worried about you. No ma'am, if anyone should be worried, I think it should be the customers . . . and maybe my boss?"

You're a smart man, Benji. Yes, you are. But she wasn't ready to share with him just yet. She'd watch him closely tonight. If they didn't get the information they needed on their own, he might prove to be an invaluable asset to have on the inside.

Cherry looped her arm through Benji's. "Your boss should definitely be worried, Benji, because this is—"

The rest of what Cherry was about to say was cut off by Shay bringing the whip down on the floor with a resounding *crack*.

Chapter Thirteen

♥

Black single-button Dolce and Gabbana suit with a white Eton multicolored button shirt...Very double-oh-seven, Pretty Boy. The suit was a good idea and so was leaving the five-o'clock shadow. Half the women in here mentally stripped you as soon as you walked in the club."

"And apparently that makes you happy. Though I'm not sure I understand why," Michael said as he joined his partner at the bar. He scanned the upper level of the Pussy Cat East for Danny Costello and his men.

"Because I don't have to do any work. I can sit back and take your leftovers. We should go to the clubs together more often." James nodded his thanks to the bartender and then grinned. "Time to check out the entertainment."

"Your self-restraint amazes me. And so does your girlie drink. What is that?"

"A Blue Hawaiian, and don't knock it till you try it. But you shouldn't. Only a man's man can pull it off," James said as he headed for the stairs.

"All right, He-Man, let's go check out the lower level. And please, don't embarrass me," Michael said, following behind.

James stopped on the third stair, turning to face him. "Ah, Pretty Boy, did you forget to tell me something?"

Michael was about to ask James what he was talking about when the announcer boomed, "And as a special treat, the Pussy Cat East is pleased to introduce our next dancers, none other than Cherry Blossom straight from Las Vegas and her protégé Sugarlicious."

Michael's hand tightened around the rail as Joe Cocker's "You Can Leave Your Hat On" came over the speakers. "Please tell me Sugarlicious isn't who I think it is."

It didn't take a genius to realize James wasn't going to answer Michael's question. He couldn't even if he wanted to; the man's tongue was practically touching the step below him.

It might have been better if it stayed that way, Michael thought when his partner regained his power of speech.

"Oh yeah, take it off, baby," James said, moving his shoulders to the music. He glanced back at Michael, who was still frozen on the top step weighing out the consequences of seeing a half-naked...fully naked?— good God, he hoped not—Shay.

If he'd thought he was over her, yesterday had provided ample evidence that wasn't the case. It's like the woman had imprinted herself on his heart and soul. So the idea of getting a full-on look at a grown-up version of the body he'd once worshipped wasn't exactly high on his bucket list. He wasn't a masochist, after all. And he didn't need any more reasons to lose sleep over her.

"Man, do I feel your pain. What did you do to lose her?"

"Nothing. It wasn't me; it was her." A half-truth, he supposed, since he'd been the one who allowed Maura to mess with his head. Listening to his mother, trusting her to have his best interests at heart, had been his first mistake. Not standing up for Shay had been the second and most damning.

Like his mother's lies, the pain over losing Shay had messed with his head. It was kind of sad to think that, even though he was older and wiser, not all that long ago he'd allowed his mother to manipulate his relationship with his ex. And Maura was up to her old tricks again.

"Here, you're gonna need this more than me." James reached back to hand his tropical blue drink to Michael.

Michael made the mistake of taking a restorative sip while watching the men whistling, cheering, and calling out to Cherry and Shay. But what the men were calling to Shay and their equally offensive hand gestures managed to penetrate his lingering shock, and his blood pressure skyrocketed. He had to look elsewhere before he had a heart attack or a brain aneurysm.

And because his rising blood pressure had obviously affected his ability to think straight, he looked at Shay. On the pole. Hanging upside down with her gorgeous inky black hair sweeping the stage. He might have been okay if he focused his attention there, although he wasn't sure if that was true or not. Even upside down, her flushed face was heart-stoppingly stunning.

But surprisingly the thought of his pounding head exploding didn't stop him. He allowed his gaze to travel over her creamy breasts being offered up to the drooling crowd by an enticing black bra. He touched his fingers to the side of his mouth. It wasn't the crowd drooling; it was him. As he self-consciously wiped the corner of his mouth, he dragged his gaze from her breasts to her sleek, toned torso. *Toned?* The woman had a six-pack. His hand went self-consciously to his own abs.

He would've been okay if he kept his attention on himself, but apparently he didn't care that the sight of her phenomenal body had already turned him into a lust-crazed, drooling idiot, so he let his gaze wander to the black leather micro miniskirt and her incredible, lean-muscled thighs that gripped the pole...Good God that was hot, so hot. She was hot. And the room suddenly felt hotter too. *Or maybe it's me,* he thought, and gulped down the Blue Hawaiian at the same time the facets of the diamond hanging around Shay's neck caught the light and his attention.

"What's she—" he began, and something wedged in his throat. He coughed, but the wedge didn't move. He coughed again, wheezing as he tried to get his partner's attention.

"What's your prob— Holy shit, are you choking?"

He nodded, pointing at his back while continuing to cough violently.

"Just a sec. Let me think." James rubbed his bald head, looking around while Michael choked to death.

"Okay, I remember now. You're not supposed to intervene if the person choking is coughing. So keep doing that. Keep coughing."

Glaring at James, Michael tried to pat his own back. He was just about at the point of throwing himself against the railing before he passed out when muscled arms came around him. The man lifted Michael off his feet a couple of times, and then a wedge of pineapple shot out of his mouth. There was a smattering of applause, a couple of *gross*es and a fair number of *eww*s. Afraid to see what Shay thought about it all, Michael turned to thank his rescuer.

He looked up, way up, because the man had to be at least seven foot five, and he was packing heat. And the only reason he would be was if he was part of Danny Costello's entourage. Michael extended his hand. "Thanks for helping me out."

"No problem. My boss wouldn't be happy if I let you die at his club." He confirmed Michael's initial impression, the man's accent identifying him as an Italian from Southie. He pointed at the stage. "Which one of the dancers made you choke?"

Michael made the mistake of looking at Shay, who twirled her way down the pole. If he thought she hadn't seen him, she cleared that up with her next move. Gray eyes narrowed on him, she picked up a whip and cracked it. Hard enough that several men in the audience jumped, including Michael.

Obviously there was a message that he wasn't picking up because she stared right at him, lifted her chin, and cracked the whip again. The only reason Michael could come up with for the action was that she didn't think he knew his rescuer was part of Costello's crew.

James distracted him from Shay by throwing an arm around Michael's shoulders. "You kidding? Look what the guy's drinking." He gave the other man a knowing grin. "Now, if you were onstage, that'd be another story. You should buy your hero a drink."

By the time Michael drained his third Blue Hawaiian at the upstairs bar, he'd come up with thirty creative ways to kill his partner. He might've come up with more if Luigi, Michael's savior, didn't just get the nod from one of his bodyguard pals. Michael turned to face the bar and ordered another drink. He didn't want either Costello or Kozack to get a look at him. At least not yet.

Luigi thought Michael was a lawyer of his brother's type. Actually, he thought he was Connor. Unable to give him one of his own business cards when he'd asked, Michael had given him his brother's. Something he should probably let Connor know. Though maybe the drinks were getting to him because he was seriously considering not telling him. It was either the drinks or the fact that his brother had yet to return his calls about their mother.

Luigi clapped Michael on the shoulder. "My time's not my own for the next few weeks, but I'll give you a call after things calm down and see if we can't get together again."

If things went as planned, Luigi would soon have more time on his hands than he'd bargained for. Aside from Luigi playing for the other team—both in his personal relationships and line of work—they had a lot in common. They cheered for the Red Sox and Bruins, liked classical music, and frequented the same restaurants in Boston.

Sadly for the investigation, that's pretty much all the information Michael got from him. Except a name that he hoped would end up being the break they needed. "Sounds good, my man. Thanks again."

They shared a manly handshake. "Anytime."

In the mirror behind the glass shelves, Michael watched Luigi join his buddies as his boss air-kissed Freddie Kozack goodbye. Danny Costello wore his thinning brown hair pulled back. His mustache was longer than his ponytail. The thirty-year-old Costello stood about five-ten and weighed just shy of two hundred pounds. No doubt some of that weight could be attributed to the gold chains he wore. Like Michael's partner, Costello was a fan of the flash. Like Michael's mother, he favored fur.

Michael lowered his eyes to his drink when the group of men passed behind him on their way to the exit. He held his breath as they stood and chatted for a moment more, praying they didn't head downstairs. He didn't want Costello anywhere near Shay. As Michael paid his tab, the mob boss and his crew took their leave, and Kozack headed down the curved staircase.

Michael followed behind at a respectable distance, searching the lower level for Shay as soon as he reached the stairs. She wasn't there, but his partner was. James had a prime seat, right at the front. He was currently taking advantage of the position to stuff some bills down a well-endowed woman's G-string.

Keeping an eye on Kozack, who was talking to one of the bouncers, Michael pulled out his cell phone. James sat near the speakers that were currently blasting Christina Aguilera's "Dirty" for the dancers onstage. He hoped his partner had his phone on vibrate, but Michael doubted he'd notice, as engrossed as he was in the ladies' performance.

Through all three tries, James continued dancing in his seat while cheering the women on. Just once, Michael would like to be wrong. And what he really wanted to be wrong about was a nagging feeling that Shay was up to something. The only reason for her to be here was to investigate the murders and Charlie's disappearance. It spoke to his level of concern, he supposed, that he wished he had an excuse to throw her in jail until this was over.

After a fourth attempt to reach his partner, Michael had no choice but to make his way through the rows of chairs to the stage. He needed someone to distract the bouncers while he went in search of Shay.

"Get out of the way! You're ruining the show."

"Buddy, take a seat!"

"Not cool, dude. Not cool."

"Sorry, I just have to get my friend." Michael bowed his head and then called out, "Friend! Friend! It's time to go." Okay, he knew he sounded like an idiot, but he couldn't risk calling his partner by name. They hadn't thought that far ahead.

Along with the men swearing, someone threw a fistful of peanuts at him and an ice cube. As a last resort, Michael picked up the peanuts and tossed one at his partner's head, hitting the dancer instead. "Sorry, ma'am, I—"

Before Michael knew what was happening, a bouncer had him in a chokehold while jerking his arm behind his back. "Wait, you got it all wrong. I wasn't throwing the peanuts at the dancer. I was just trying to get my friend's—" His voice was strained as he tried to explain.

"Save it for Mr. Kozack."

Not surprisingly, the commotion drew Michael's partner's attention. James came to his feet. "What's going on?"

"Stay out of it," the bouncer said to James, and then waved over another man. "Benji, handle that guy."

The fortysomething, muscle-bound guy with a blond crew cut walked over to deal with a loudly protesting James while Michael was roughly shoved back the way he'd come.

"It's okay, bro. I'm fine. Sit back down and enjoy the show," Michael called to his partner. To his way of thinking, the less attention they drew to themselves the better. James must have gotten the point he was trying to make because he settled down. Either that or he didn't want to miss the next performance.

"I'm not going to cause you any trouble, but legally you and your buddy are on shaky ground for using excessive force. So I'd suggest you let me go, and I'll be on my way," Michael said as the bouncer manhandled him down a hallway. The strong smell of perfume and cigars wafted through half-open doors. He caught a glimpse of Freddie Kozack in one of the rooms with two scantily clad women.

"Take it up with my boss," the bouncer said, tapping on the doorframe with his knuckles. "Mr. Kozack, sir, this is the guy who was throwing peanuts at the dancers. Do you want to talk to him here or in your office?"

"What's your problem? You don't like women? You like to hurt women?" Kozack, his hair obviously dyed black to match his handlebar mustache, asked as he joined them in the hall.

"No, I don't like to hurt women. The only person who was injured is me. Members of the audience were throwing peanuts and ice cubes. I went to throw one at the back of my friend's head to get his..." Michael trailed off.

At the other end of the hall, he spotted Cherry jumping up and down at the bottom of the stairs that led to Kozack's office. She was waving at him in a way that seemed to indicate, on threat of death, he wasn't supposed to let Kozack go to his office. Which meant Michael had discovered exactly what Shay was up to and where she was.

So in order to protect Shay, Michael did a one-eighty and went the suck-up route. "But these things happen, right? It was an innocent mistake, an accident. This is my favorite club. Tell me what you need me to do to make it right, and I'll fix it right here." He reached for his wallet. "Right on the spot. Then you can get back to the ladies."

"That's better. I like a reasonable man. Come on. We'll go to my office and have a drink. Work things out."

* * *

Michael crossed the club's parking lot with Shay yelling at him in a furious whisper, "You can apologize all you want. It doesn't change the outcome. You lost me the only opportunity I had to find information that might possibly save Charlie's life. Five more minutes and I would've found the files I was looking for. And not only did you blow my chance of getting information today, but you also blew my chance of getting back in that office. Kozack didn't buy my story that I wanted some one-on-one time with him to talk about my routine."

"You're damn lucky he didn't, Shay. You have no idea what that man's capable of," he whispered just as furiously back at her. Positive he was even more furious than she was and had even more reason to be.

She whipped around. "You don't have a clue, do you? I know better than you what that man's capable of. You're in over your head, Michael."

"What do you think I've been doing for the past eight years, Shay? Do you have any idea how many guys like Kozack and Costello I've put behind bars?"

"Well maybe you should've stuck with what you know. Because from what I saw tonight, you are going to get yourself killed."

"Okay, boys and girls, let's tone this down before you completely blow our covers," his partner cut in, angling his head at a man and woman who were leaving the club. "Listen, it's kinda cute how worried you two are about each other, but how about we all get a good night's sleep and talk about this tomorrow?" He glanced from Shay to Michael and shrugged. "All right, then. Catch you in the a.m., partner. Shay." He nodded and strolled over to his car.

Michael looked at her, really looked at her for the first time since the bouncers had hauled him into the manager's office. "He's right, isn't he? You're worried about me."

"No," she scoffed, and walked to a rusted-out white Ford Fiesta. She struggled for a minute to get the door open and then looked over at him and gave her head a slight, annoyed shake. "Fine. I'm worried about you. But really, what do you expect? I mean, I looked over from—"

"From where you were hanging half-naked on a pole, in front of at least sixty men yelling what they wanted you to take off next and what they wanted to do to you?" he said, walking to where she stood.

"I'm not half-naked."

He reached over and zipped up her leather jacket. "Maybe not now, but close enough before to be incredibly distracting."

"You weren't the only one who was distracted. I nearly fell off the pole when Costello's hired henchman started shaking you like a bottle of ketchup."

"What an attractive visual that is, thank you."

She rolled her eyes and got into the car before looking up at him. "You put yourself on Costello's and Kozack's radar tonight, Michael. This time tomorrow, they'll know who you are. They won't be happy you were snooping around without identifying yourself as a fed."

"Okay, I want you to think about what you just said. I'm a federal agent, and you are the niece of the man they're hunting and maybe even trying to frame for these murders. You were here tonight pretending to be someone you aren't and were also found alone in the manager's office. So tell me, Shay, which one of us would you go after first if you were Costello and Kozack?"

"They don't know who I am."

"You don't think they've been to the Salty Dog and seen the photograph of you? It's a little hard to miss."

"It doesn't matter. I barely recognized myself tonight."

"I'd recognize you anywhere. You're beautiful."

"Don't." She looked away, beeping the horn at Cherry, who was talking to one of the bouncers, and then turned the key to start the engine. Nothing happened. She did it again, and then again. It was completely dead. Shay must have figured out the same thing because when James pulled alongside them and rolled down the car window and offered a jump, she shook her head. "Thanks, but this car isn't going anywhere tonight, or anytime after that."

"Lock it up, and I'll drive you home," Michael said.

"She should probably drive you, partner. Those Blue Hawaiians can hit you when you least expect it, and you had a couple."

What James didn't know was that Michael had asked the bartender to hold off on the rum, curaçao, and vodka on the last two. But he didn't intend to share that information with either of them. There were things he wanted to ask Shay, and alone with nowhere for her to go presented the perfect opportunity to do so.

Shay leaned on the horn.

"Coming! Don't leave without me!" Cherry called, running across the parking lot.

He had no idea how, but he'd managed to forget that Cherry would need a ride, too. Still, the opportunity was too good to pass up, so he had to think of something…"Hey, James, you mind driving Cherry to Shay's place? I only have room for one." The three of them looked at him. "Of course, I normally have room for more, but Atticus was sick in the backseat this morning, and I didn't have time to clean it up."

Cherry didn't wait for an invitation from his partner. She opened the passenger door and got into James's car. He noticed his partner didn't complain about adding another hour to his drive. He'd been looking at Shay's friend differently since her performance. Shay locked up the Ford Fiesta and then went to open the back door of his partner's car.

"What? You're going to leave me stranded? I can't drive myself home."

"You've got money. Call a cab," Shay said.

He leaned into her. "And you're wearing my engagement ring. So you either come with me and talk to me about it alone or I talk to you about it here, with an audience."

Chapter Fourteen

♥

I don't know why you're making such a big deal about me wearing the engagement ring," Shay said to Michael from behind the wheel of his Range Rover. Before he had a chance to respond, she shifted from reverse to drive and shot out of the parking lot. Straight into oncoming traffic.

"Shay, watch out for..." He trailed off, his heart in his throat as she expertly avoided being creamed by another speeding SUV.

With his hand still gripping the door and his foot pressed on the floor as if he could somehow miraculously slow the vehicle down, Michael said, "Obviously the ring is a big deal to you or you wouldn't be trying to kill me."

"Being aggressive will save you. Being cautious, that's what'll kill you."

"No doubt you'll live to be a hundred and ten, then." He relaxed when the speedometer needle inched down toward a more reasonable speed. "I'm taking it that your life lesson only refers to driving; otherwise you would've been applauding my efforts at the club."

She glanced at him, a smile tipping up the corner of her mouth. "So, you actually choked on purpose to cozy up to Costello's hired henchman and disrupted the dancer's performance so the bouncers would haul you to Kozack's office?"

He ignored everything else but the part that would get him an answer to his earlier question. "I choked because you took my breath away, and——"

She laughed. "Either you're easily impressed or you don't get out to many strip clubs. Kozack was going to fire me even before he found me in his office."

"Neither is true, but you didn't let me finish. As incredible as you looked doing what you were doing on that pole, I choked because I saw the engagement ring on the chain around your neck."

He leaned across the console and slid his hand beneath her leather jacket. Her skin was like satin, and he could smell her warm, floral scent. The temptation to press his face to the tender spot between her shoulder and neck almost overwhelmed him. It was one of his favorite places to kiss her. One of her favorite places to be kissed. Her breath caught on a quick inhalation as he hooked a finger around the white-gold chain and gently tugged until the diamond ring appeared.

She glanced at the ring now lying on his palm, lifted her gaze to his, and then refocused on the road with a shrug. "I haven't found an honest dealer yet. And it's not like I can leave it in my dresser drawer. It's safer on me."

"There's a thing called a safe-deposit box. And if you're afraid the bank will get held up, you could put it in the safe at the Salty Dog. No one in their right mind would try to hold up the pub with you there. Please tell me you have it insured at least." He caught the wince just before she blanked her expression. "Are you kidding me?" he groaned. "That ring is worth—"

"You know what? It's mine now, not yours. So stop worrying about it." She tugged the ring from his hand, rubbing the stone between her fingers before tucking it beneath her jacket.

The action proved what he'd already known—the ring meant something to her. No matter how much he wanted to believe it had to do with her feelings for him, he didn't understand how that could be. He'd given it to another woman after all. But something told him he needed to push her to get to the truth. "You've had the ring for more than a year, Shay. I can't believe you haven't found someone to sell it to in all that time. Why are you really keeping it? I wouldn't have given you a diamond like that, you know. If I'd asked you to marry me, that's not the ring I would've chosen."

Bethany had picked out the ring on a shopping trip with her girlfriends. All he'd done was pay the exorbitant price. He'd balked at first. The idea of buying a ring that could feed at least ten families for a year rankled. But like he'd done with Bethany from almost the beginning, he'd given in.

"I know. That's why I keep it. I keep it to remind me of the woman you were going to marry. A woman from your world, not mine."

It was an old argument, one he'd grown tired of. But the fact that she'd made it gave him hope. She must feel something for him if she kept the ring as a reminder of why she shouldn't. He wanted to take her left hand in his and rub his thumb over the finger he once wanted his ring to sit upon. Instead, he said, "I have your ring, Shay. I've had it since the night we made love at the inn at Driftwood Cove."

"Don't. You're supposed to be a straight arrow, honest to a fault. Yet you're lying to me now. You have to be. We'd only been together a few weeks before we went to the inn."

He lifted a shoulder. "As crazy and maybe a little pathetic as it sounds, it's true."

"You bought me a ring?"

"No, it was given to me by GG." He imagined Shay's opinion of his great-grandmother hadn't changed since they last spoke, so he quickly moved on to the next part of the story. "It was her mother's, who'd been given it by her mother. I knew the moment I saw the ring that it was meant to be yours. GG said her mother was strong, like the warriors of old. She'd suffered the loss of a child, and their farm when her husband, GG's father, broke his back, yet she never gave up or let herself become bitter."

"Please. Don't say any more."

There was a small break in her voice, her fingers clenching and unclenching on the steering wheel. But in case they were wrong about Charlie and Michael was put in the unforgivable position of arresting her uncle, he couldn't do as Shay asked. She had to know just how much she meant…how much she'd once meant to him. "The ring's still beautiful after generations of wear. If anything, it's grown more so with age. It's solid and true, and steeped in history. It represents family, love, loyalty, and ties that bind forever. It represents everything I wanted to give to you."

Her eyes didn't stray from the road, her lips pressed in a firm line that looked almost painful. He now understood what the saying *the silence was deafening* meant. It was heavy, weighted with memories and sadness. It felt like a funeral, the final death knell of their once relationship.

He took her hand, brought it to his mouth, and gently pressed his lips to her palm. "I'm sorry I never got that chance. I thought we might get another one at Christmas, but you never showed. I waited for you at the bandstand, you know? Even after you didn't take my calls for months, I still went there and waited, for hours." He gave a self-conscious laugh. "I never did know when to give up, did I?"

"I'm sorry. When I made the promise, I planned to keep it. I really did. I thought maybe we'd have a second chance too. But then things happened, and I knew it was best for both of us if we just left things the way they were."

He thought about the things she'd said over the past few days. Her move to Vegas. Her reaction to his news about her sisters. "Something happened ten months ago to change your mind. What was it?"

"It's not important."

"It is to me."

Maybe she felt like she owed him something for his embarrassingly long wait at the bandstand on Christmas Day, because she relented. "I found my sisters. After years of dead ends and false leads, I finally found them, and they wanted nothing to do with me and Charlie." She shrugged as if it didn't bother her. He knew better. "It's not their fault. They'd moved on to lives with a mother and father, siblings too. Their adoptive families were ones they could be proud of; good, churchgoing people with stable careers, respected by their communities. The perfect American families."

She rubbed her hands on the steering wheel, and he thought maybe she was finished. He opened his mouth to tell her how sorry he was, how much his heart broke for her, but she surprised him by continuing. "I didn't blame them, but still, it was hard to hear they wanted nothing to do with us. Ever since we were separated, I thought about the day we'd be together again as a family, that moment when I finally found them and what it would be like."

She gave a small laugh. "It didn't exactly go according to plan. Charlotte, the baby, she's Donna now and has a two-year-old of her own. Her husband owns a tech company and does well. She's involved in charity work. I guess because Lanie was older, they let her keep her name. You'd like her; she's a lawyer. Graduated top of her class. Her father's a congressman. Her siblings are involved in politics too. She was engaged when I saw her. She'd be married now."

He wanted to hold her and take away the hurt in her

voice. He wanted to track down her sisters and beg them to call her, to tell her that it had all been a mistake, that they missed her as much as she missed them, that they'd thought about her every day like she'd thought about them. "It's their loss. They don't know what they're missing not having you in their lives."

"Right, an ex-con who's suspected of murder and God knows what else by the FBI, and an uncle who's either running from the mob or running with them."

"Stop. You're letting the past, your past, define you. You were a kid, Shay. You made a mistake, and it's time to let it go before it ruins your future."

"Maybe it already has."

"That's bullshit, and you know it."

"Do I? You guys wouldn't be looking at me for this if I didn't have a record."

"Sorry to disappoint you, babe, but yeah, we would, because your uncle pointed the finger directly at you," he snapped, and then took a moment to calm himself before he said something he couldn't take back.

She loved Charlie. The old man was the only family she had left, and Michael wasn't about to make things worse by telling her exactly where to lay the blame for everything she'd endured. "I shouldn't have snapped at you. I'm sorry. I don't like hearing you put yourself down."

"It doesn't bother me, so it shouldn't bother you." She took the turnoff to Harmony Harbor. "Are you okay to drive back from my place? Or should I drop you off and walk home?"

This wasn't how he'd hoped the night would end.

Obviously, he should've kept his opinions to himself. "It's fine. I...Hang on a sec," he said when his cell phone rang. "Hey, Jasper, what's up?"

"I don't wish to disturb your evening, but I think it would be best for you to come home immediately, Master Michael."

"I'm almost there. What's going on? What's wrong?"

"It appears someone left the door to the cottage open, and Atticus is gone. Liam, Griffin, and I have been searching the area for the past half hour and haven't found any sign of him," he said, referring to Michael's cousins, Finn's and Aidan's brothers. Both men were highly trained in search and rescue. Liam was a firefighter, and Griffin was a former Navy SEAL now with the Coast Guard. The fact they hadn't been able to find Atticus yet worried him.

"I'm ten minutes out."

"Michael, what is it?" Shay asked when he disconnected.

"Atticus. He's missing."

* * *

Shay held the flashlight on Michael as he took off his coat to wrap around Atticus. They'd been searching through the woods across from the cottage for the past thirty minutes when Michael thought he heard something. While he called for the dog, Shay and Jasper had listened for any sound. A few minutes ago, they'd heard a low, mournful howl, which led them to where they were now, a small creek bed.

"Is he okay?" Shay asked Michael from where she stood on the bank.

"Just cold, wet, exhausted, and completely disoriented, I think," he said as he crouched to lift the dog in his arms. He staggered a little as he rose to his feet. Not surprisingly since Atticus was the size of a small horse and weighed at least a hundred and twenty pounds.

After their earlier conversation on the way here, the last thing she should be doing is touching the man, but she couldn't seem to help herself and gave Michael's arm a comforting rub when he made it up the embankment. He'd been beside himself with worry over his dog, and that touched her. He'd touched her earlier too.

If she closed her eyes, she could still feel the weight of his hand against her skin. It wasn't the only place he touched her, though. She might've been safer if it had been. But his words went deeper. His confession that he'd waited for her at the bandstand for hours, and his talk about a ring had touched deep down to her very soul.

This tall, handsome man, with his money and manners, loved deeply and faithfully. He was kind and gentle. And right now, all his love and attention were focused on his dog. "And what about you? How are you doing?" she asked.

"Wet, cold, and immensely relieved," he admitted.

"As are we all, Master Michael. I've let your cousins know that Atticus has been found. I've also taken the liberty of ordering a GPS tracker. You gave us a fright," the older man said to the dog, the telling sheen in his eyes quickly blinked away. "I'll let everyone at the manor know all has ended well. Perhaps it would be best if I told your mother that you and Atticus aren't up for a visit this evening and to drop by in the morning."

"Thanks, Jeeves. I can always count on you," he said, stumbling on the loose rocks.

"Would you like some help? I can...Okay," Shay said, trying, but not able, to hold back a laugh. "It wasn't a shot at your manhood, you know. I just thought we could take turns."

"Was that supposed to make me feel better?"

"You've done it now, miss. He was always competitive. He won't take a break now."

"That's ridiculous. Michael. You're cold and wet, and Atticus must weigh close to a hundred and twenty pounds."

"One forty."

"All right, forget the macho act. You can't carry him all the way to the cottage. You'll strain your back. Why don't you put him down and see if he can walk? I'm sure—"

"He's been lost and alone for almost two hours, and he can barely see, Shay. I'm not putting him down."

She stared after him as he strode ahead of them. "What does he think he's doing?"

"At any other time, I might say proving a point. But I believe his worry for Atticus outweighs anything else at the moment. He wants to get him inside and warmed up as soon as possible."

"Atticus is the size of a horse and wearing a fur coat. As well as Michael's coat. I'm sure he'll be fine."

"Perhaps it would be best if you kept those thoughts

to yourself, at least for tonight. Master Michael has always been protective of Atticus, but even more so now that the dog is going blind."

"I guess I shouldn't be surprised he pampers Atticus. He always struck me as the overindulgent type."

"Yes, he is that, and sometimes to his detriment."

They caught up with Michael ten minutes later as he walked up the path to the white cottage.

"You're crazy and stubborn, you know that?" Shay said as she moved around him to open the screen door. "Would you just put the dog down?"

"You can tell you're not an animal lover," he muttered, the strain evident on his face. The dog *still* in his arms.

"Who says I'm not? Atticus likes me, and so does Roxy. Mostly." She followed him inside. She'd been here twice when they were younger. It hadn't changed much. The high white pine ceilings gave the space a light and airy feel. The back opened to an enclosed porch with views of the ocean and the tip of Starlight Pointe, where a lighthouse stood watch.

A nautical theme was carried throughout the cottage, from the porch to the large kitchen and living room of the open floor plan. The stark white walls were offset by ocean-blue focal walls at either end, blue-and-white-striped wallpaper framing the row of windows at the back.

The overlarge furniture had obviously been purchased for comfort and durability, not show, as it had stood the test of time and three boys. Although here and there she could pick out Maura Gallagher's influence.

Like the white baby grand piano in the corner and the expensive artwork on the large wall above the leather sectional.

Just enough to remind Maura's family of her presence, Shay supposed. As far as she knew, Michael's mother, unlike her sons, had never liked to spend time here.

"Master Michael, your teeth are chattering. Put Atticus down and grab a hot shower. I'm sure Ms. Angel wouldn't mind towel-drying Atticus while you do." When she hesitated, Jasper said, "I'd stay, but there are a few things I need to take care of at the manor."

She looked at Michael and Atticus and didn't think she'd ever seen a more forlorn-looking pair. "You two are pathetic," she said, unzipping her boots and leaving them on the mat by the door. "Put him down right now, Michael, and go have a shower."

"I'm not leaving him alone with you. He's just been through a traumatic experience, and you're yelling at him, and at me too. Do you always have to be such a hardass?"

"All right, then, I'll just leave you two to work it out," Jasper said, and backed out the door.

"Oh my God, he's a dog." She stomped over to take Atticus from Michael's arms, nearly collapsing under the weight when she did.

Michael grinned.

She gave him a clenched teeth smile in return and then weaved her way across the room to the doggy bed under the window. If not for the challenge in Michael's eyes, she would've put Atticus down. The man must

have arms and legs of steel and more fortitude and
stamina than she'd ever imagined. At the thought, her
mind went to an extremely dangerous place. A place in
which she tested the strength of his arms and legs and
his fortitude and stamina... in bed, naked.

"No, don't put him in his bed."

She turned, sweat beginning to bead on her forehead,
her knees about to buckle. "Why not?"

"Because..." He angled his head. "Are you all right?
You look a little flushed."

"Fine. I admit it. You're stronger than me and in better shape. Happy now?" she said, setting Atticus gently
on his feet. "How that's even possible, I have no idea.
Now before your dog gets in his bed and you give me
grief, tell me what... Yes, I'm happy to see you too,"
she said when Atticus gave her a chin-to-nose lick.

Michael walked over with a worn comforter in his
hand and crouched to tuck the well-loved quilt in the
dog's bed. "I don't know what it is about her, boy.
She's cranky, bossy, and demanding, yet we keep coming back for more," he said as he rose to his feet.

"I'm not cranky, or bossy. I'm—" The rest of what
she was about to say left her head when his strong
hand slid under her hair and curved around her neck.
She stared up at him, into those vibrant blue eyes that
seemed to be looking at her with both amusement and
exasperation. As he slowly bent his head, he murmured,
"I'm going to kiss you now, okay?"

"Why do you want to kiss me? You just said I'm
cranky, bossy, and demanding." There was a touch of
nerves in her voice, along with irritation. But, of their

own volition, her hands slid up his damp white shirt that gave her a toe-curling view of his well-defined chest beneath. Her fingers came to rest on his broad shoulders, smoothing the damp fabric of his ruined suit coat before clasping behind his neck. It felt familiar and wildly different at the same time.

He gave her a slow smile as his hands moved to her waist. They were heavy and warm as they drew her firmly against him. "You are cranky, bossy, and demanding. You're also exasperating and frustrating." His fingers tightened, holding her in place as she went to pull away. "*But* you stayed and helped me look for Atticus, and despite wearing next to nothing and killer heels, you never complained. Not when the branch slapped you in the face, or when you tripped over the log, or when you leaned on the tree and water cascaded from the leaves, soaking you and making your makeup run."

She curled her fingers into the fabric of his jacket, refusing to give in to the urge to wipe off the mascara that must be running down her face. Her worries about what she must look like with her ruined makeup and wet hair disappeared the moment he said, "And no matter how much you try to hide it with your cranky-ass act, you were worried about me and my dog."

"For a smart man who was once purportedly the best prosecutor in the state, you're not doing a very good job convincing me to let you kiss me, you know."

"No?"

"No, and stop looking amused. It makes your eyes bluer and crinkles the corners and makes you look older and sexier."

"I better stop, then."

"Yes, stop talking and kiss me so you can shower and I can towel-dry your dog."

He threw back his head and laughed, and as the deep, rich sound washed over her, she couldn't help but remember all the good times they'd had. And like the branch and the cascading water of earlier tonight, the truth she'd been denying for what felt like forever hit her. She'd missed being with this man, being held by him, and, if he eventually stopped laughing, being kissed by him.

But then when he did stop laughing, she found herself wishing that he hadn't. It was the emotion that darkened his eyes. She knew what it was; she'd seen it before. Every time he'd looked at her that long ago summer. "Don't," she pleaded, unprepared for this now.

His expression softened, and he lifted his hands to cup her face. "I wish it was that easy, but it's not. Don't you get it, Angel? I love you when you're a bossy, moody, demanding, exasperating, infuriating pain in the butt. I love every part of you, and as hard as I've tried to forget you, I've never been able to. And I'm terrified that by kissing you right now, I'll be doomed forever, frozen here in this room, in this moment, unable to move on. I'll be alone, just me and my dog. But I need to kiss you like I need air to breathe. So please, don't say no; say yes."

She knew if she said yes to him right now, she was saying yes to more than a kiss. She was saying yes to the promise of them. She'd broken her promise to him once before. She'd never break another one. Not after what he'd just said.

A battle between yes and no raged inside her. The last thing she wanted to do was hurt him, and that's why she had to protect him. Even if it was from himself, even if it was the hardest thing she'd ever done.

He hadn't thought this through. His job and the respect of his colleagues and family would all be on the line if they got involved. Her uncle was a suspect, and so was she.

Just as she opened her mouth to try and explain why they couldn't do this, at least not right now, there was a knock on the door.

Maybe because he'd seen the answer in her eyes before she uttered the word, his smile faded just a little. "Saved by the butler," he murmured, the disappointment she heard in his voice proof that he knew what she'd been about to say.

She touched his arm as he went to step away. "I'm sorry."

Chapter Fifteen

♥

While trying to come to terms with how badly he'd crashed and burned with Shay, Michael opened the door to find Jasper standing on the back deck with a conspiratorial curve to his lips and a picnic basket no doubt filled with a romantic late-night snack.

"I thought you and Ms. Angel would enjoy..." He looked from Michael to Shay, and the matchmaking gleam in his eyes turned to one of frustrated concern. "All right, off you go and have your showers while I see to Atticus. Ms. Angel, you can take the one in the master," Jasper ordered in a voice that dared them to refuse as he marched into the cottage and set the picnic basket on the coffee table.

Fully expecting Shay to refuse, Michael remained by the door to see her out. Instead, she shocked him by nodding and heading to his parents' bedroom. It didn't take long for his shock to become understanding.

It happened while he stood under a fine spray of hot water in the shower. The entire night began playing in his head: Shay dancing, seeing the ring, interrupting her in Kozack's office, the drive here, searching for Atticus, finding him… The mental film clip came to a grinding halt, frozen on Shay at the precise moment her fingers brushed his arm and she apologized, pity and tenderness clearly stamped on her beautiful face. The only reason Shay had done as Jasper ordered was to make sure Michael was okay.

He stepped out of the shower and made his way to the change of clothes on his bed, toweling his hair dry as he did. At the distant sound of the shower in his parents' bedroom, he considered stalling, not sure he wanted to face Shay or what he should say. If Jasper hadn't gone to the trouble of making them a late-night snack, Michael might've turned on the shower and sat on his bed until he heard the front door close behind her.

Instead, he got dressed and then walked out of the bedroom to the great room, glancing at Atticus, who was trying to get comfortable in his bed, at Jasper putting the final touches to his romantic dinner, doing his utmost to ensure Michael got a second shot at love.

And there it was, he thought with a smile; he didn't have to search for something positive in the night. He was a lucky man indeed. His family would always be there for him. In case he backslid a bit when he thought about Shay, he'd remind himself he'd escaped an even more dire fate. She hadn't kissed him. So maybe he'd be able to move on after all.

"Everything's good here, Jeeves. Thanks for going to all that trouble. A romantic dinner is exactly what's needed to turn things around. I'd be lost if I didn't have you in my corner," Michael said, lying through his teeth that a beautifully laid-out antipasto platter accompanied by a baguette and an assortment of miniature cheesecakes could change the outcome of the evening. But he wasn't about to let the older man know his efforts were for naught. Given the way Jasper angled his head to study him, it's possible Michael had overplayed his hand.

Under the intent gaze of the man who'd been watching him since he was a boy, Michael forced himself to release any sign of tension from his face and body and relaxed on the piano bench. He wore an untucked white shirt over his faded blue jeans and took his time rolling the sleeves to his elbows. Then he crossed his bare feet at the ankles and lightly danced his fingers over the piano keys.

He glanced at Jasper, noting the other man's tension fading too. Atticus made a contented noise, settling deeper in his bed. Music comforted his dog as much as it did Michael.

"I think 'Killing Me Softly' would set the mood nicely," the older man suggested, referring to the well-known favorite of Michael's great-grandmother. Michael indulged him, thinking the song an appropriate choice, as Shay had indeed killed him softly. If tonight had gone differently, he'd be playing John Legend's "All of Me" instead.

"You're very good at this romance stuff, Jasper. One would almost think you had some practice," Michael teased while continuing to play. Despite their objections, or more specifically his grandmother's, he was pretty sure Jasper and Kitty were romantically involved.

"Truth be told, I've had rather a lot of practice," Jasper said as he bent to retrieve a candle from the table and then walked over to place it on the piano. "I believe a little extra ambience is called for." He moved toward the opposite wall. "And you'll be pleased to know you don't have to worry about your mother arriving unannounced. She's afraid you're upset with her for leaving the door open after retrieving her luggage."

"I am." His mother was the reason Atticus had gotten out earlier. Information Jasper had quietly imparted to Michael as they searched the woods. Maura had been upset that Michael had left without meeting the women she and the Widows Club had chosen for him. As punishment, she moved from the cottage to the manor.

Little did she know that, in his eyes, that was more reward than punishment. He didn't plan on enlightening her. "Have you found out why she's..." The lights went out, and he looked around, thinking a breaker must have blown, when he twigged where Jasper was standing. "You know, I think that might be a little much. Maybe you should turn the lights back on, Jeeves."

"I think it's rather perfect myself." He smiled. "Here's Ms. Angel now."

Michael looked to where Shay stood frozen just outside the master bedroom door, her gaze taking in the feast laid out on the table, the mood lighting, and him at the piano. She'd changed into clothes Jasper must have dug up for her—a red hooded Harvard sweatshirt of Michael's and a matching pair of track pants. Wearing too-big clothes and with her face freshly scrubbed, she didn't look much older than the day they'd first met. His heart tripped at the thought, and his fingers hit a discordant note. Knowing how things would turn out between them, he wasn't sure he should've tracked her down that long-ago summer's day on Main Street.

"Well, I shall take my leave. No one likes a third wheel," Jasper said with a smile, and then went to give Atticus a pat goodbye. "Unless that third wheel is a dog."

Afraid Shay would reveal the truth of the situation, Michael opened his mouth to stave off a response from her. Only he was too late.

"Everything looks great, Jasper. Very...romantic."

Michael narrowed his eyes at her, unable to tell if the hitch he'd heard in her voice was a small laugh of amusement or one of horror. However, when Jasper smiled, looking inordinately pleased with himself, it didn't matter.

Shay walked over to the table and picked up the bottle of wine and two glasses. "You sure you won't stay and have a drink with us?"

"No, thank you, miss. I have a cup of cocoa and a biscuit awaiting my return."

Noting the man's smile, Michael said, "Are you sure that's all you have waiting for you?"

"I don't know what you're talking about, Master Michael. Enjoy the rest of your evening."

"What was that about?" Shay asked after they thanked Jasper once again and said good night.

He sighed, suddenly tired and thinking it might've been best if she left. He didn't relish the idea of telling her that in Jasper's mind they were steps away from the altar. Lifting his hands from the keys, he was about to stand up when she joined him on the bench. "What are you doing?" he asked, his surprise evident in his voice.

"Maybe I'm reading this wrong. Did you not want me here?"

As much as he didn't want to share with her Jasper's hopes and dreams for their future, he didn't want to rehash what his had been. He'd already embarrassed himself enough for one night. "If you were paying any attention at all earlier, you wouldn't have to ask. And if you don't mind, I'd prefer not to talk about it anymore."

She lifted a shoulder and offered him a glass. "Wine?"

He looked from the glass to her. "What are you doing?"

"Seducing you. Is it working?" She laughed. "I always thought the expression 'their jaw dropped' was stupid. How can a jaw drop, right? Guess it's true after all."

He picked up his jaw from the floor. "Just twenty minutes ago..." He pointed to the spot where they'd been standing and then shook his head. "I'm lost. What happened between *I'm sorry* and *Seducing you*?"

She poured him a glass of wine. "Play for me. Please."

"Thanks," he murmured, holding her gaze as he took

a sip and then placed the glass on top of the piano. With the look in her eyes and the way her warm body pressed against him, hope surged through him as fast as the dry cabernet. He played a different song than he would've had the night gone the way he'd hoped. Though he wasn't about to complain, not with Shay still here by his side.

"What's the song?"

"'Like There's No Yesterday' by Mark Wills." The lyrics spoke to his hope for Shay. He might not know what this was about, but he knew that for her to get the life she deserved, even if that life didn't include him, she had to find a way to get over her past and heal her wounds. He wanted her to dance like there was no yesterday.

She nudged him. "Sing it for me."

"You're mixing me up with my cousins. The Harmony Harbor Gallaghers sing, the Summer Gallaghers play." Michael played the piano, his brother Logan the guitar, and Connor the sax.

"You used to sing for me."

"All right," he agreed. Even though his voice wasn't anywhere close to being as good as his cousins, he could carry a tune without making animals cry. Atticus actually seemed to like when he sang. Shay had too.

"I'm not broken, you know? Or alone."

He didn't look at her, just kept singing and playing, and maybe praying, just a little, that the lyrics would stay with her over the next few days. Toward the end of the song, he glanced at her. Her head was bent as she contemplated the wine in her glass. There was a stillness about her that bothered him, and he questioned his choice of song. Maybe he was pushing too hard.

Her head came up when he began playing another song, their song. Sarah McLachlan's "Angel." She smiled at him, and he nodded, raising his eyebrows. It was the one song she'd sing with him. Sometimes.

She leaned down to put her glass on the floor and then straightened. "I just want to listen to you," she said, and put her arms around his waist, resting her head on his shoulder.

It got to him more than it should, and the next words came out gruff, laden with emotion. "I don't know if I can do this, Shay," he told her honestly. "I want you too badly to just be friends. I'm sorry. Maybe in a few months from now, I'll—"

"I don't want to be just friends," she said, and placed a hand on his jaw, bringing his face around to hers, and then she kissed him. Softly, tentatively, as if unsure of his response. He kissed her back, savoring the feel of her soft, pliant lips beneath his. He'd been waiting so long for this moment that he didn't want to rush it. It was hard to hold back, but he did and pulled away. He needed answers first. "Why now?"

She groaned. "You're such a lawyer."

"Agent."

"That too." He slid back to swing his right leg over the bench. Then he leaned forward to wrap his hands around her calves, drawing her closer. He held her gaze as he placed her left leg over his right and then her right leg over his left. Moving his hands to her butt, he drew her snug against him.

She released a small, gratifying moan, and he gave her behind a gentle squeeze. She closed her eyes and moved against him like she was performing at the club. He wouldn't last long if she kept it up, and right now he wanted to last all night.

He brought his hands to her face and kissed her, giving her a taste of how much he wanted her, how much he'd missed her, and then he pulled back once more.

"Oh, come on, that's not fair."

He could tell her a couple of other things that weren't fair, but right now he just wanted the answer to his earlier question. "Why now?"

"Can't we just go to bed, make love, and then talk?"

"Wow, I had no idea I was getting lucky tonight. I thought the most I could hope for was a kiss, and even that looked doubtful an hour ago."

She released an irritated sigh and went to move away.

He gave her behind a firm squeeze and kept her exactly where she was. "You're not moving an inch until I get some answers, babe. And then the only place you're going is my bed."

She tilted her head to the side, a slow smile lifting her lips that still glistened from his kiss. "Yeah?"

"Yeah, so tell me why the sudden change of heart. You seemed pretty definite before."

"Cherry called. She was worried that I wasn't home yet, and when I told her where I was"—she made a face—"she said she wasn't letting me in unless I got some somethin' somethin.' Her words, not mine."

"I kinda figured that." Disappointed and a little ticked at the reason for her sudden desire to jump his bones, he moved his hands to his forehead and rubbed as though that would take care of his frustration.

She removed his hands from his face to put them around her neck, and then she put hers around his. "I'm not doing a very good job of this. Cherry telling me I need to get laid because I'm supposedly off-the-charts cranky has nothing to do with...Okay, so it might have a little something to do with me still being here. But it was more what she said after she said I needed to get laid because I'm off-the-charts cranky."

"Until you've finished your explanation, could you maybe stop talking about getting laid? It makes it a little hard to stay focused."

"Oh, and what about when I do this?" she said, and moved her hips.

He lifted his hands from around her neck and placed them on her hips. "I'm not sure which is worse. Maybe you should do it again..."

"No, I think you need to hear what I have to say, so there's no misunderstandings the morning after."

He stilled and lifted his gaze to hers. "I'm beginning to think talking is overrated."

"When you asked to kiss me earlier, it felt like you were asking for more. Like by kissing you, I was promising that we were back together again. Like we went from zero to a hundred with nothing in between. I didn't want to break another promise to you. I *won't*

break another promise to you. You deserve better."
She stroked his damp hair from his forehead as her
eyes roamed his face. "I haven't felt for any man, or
wanted any man, the way I feel for and want you,
Michael. But we were young, and I'm worried how
we feel about each other, or how we think we feel
about each other, isn't real. It's just unresolved feelings from the past."

"Shay, what I feel—"

She placed a finger on his lips. "Let me finish. I've
changed, and so have you. And there are so many reasons, really good reasons, why we shouldn't be together. Why we won't work. Like your job, and me
being a suspect, and my uncle being on the run. I guess,
I'm..." She looked away and gave her head a slight
shake.

"You're afraid." He kissed her fingers and smiled at
the scowl on her face. "You can still be strong and be
afraid. In fact, Atticus and I had this exact conversation just the other morning. So I'll tell you what I told
him. Everyone's afraid. It's what you do with your fear
that matters. It seems to me that by not giving us a second chance because you're afraid is more like running
away. And that's not you, Shay. You face your fears
head-on."

She bit back a smile. "So, you and Atticus...Do you
have these types of conversations all the time?"

"Often enough. Is that a problem?"

"No, as long as you don't think he'll have a problem
with me being around."

"If that means you're going to give his owner another

shot, I'm sure he wouldn't have a problem with it. Are you?"

"Yeah, but I'm not making any promises. Are you good with that?"

"I'm good with that *for now*. As long as we agree to revisit it in the next few days. Agreed?"

"Uh, no, that's way too soon."

"Sometimes you just know. And it's not like we've just met. How about Valentine's Day? That gives you a whole ten days."

"If we find Charlie by then, okay. We'll talk about promises and commitments then. Now can we talk about sex?"

"We've talked enough. I think we should get to the good stuff." He kissed her while scooping his hands under her backside and lifting her into his arms. He broke the kiss to blow out the candle on the piano, and then the ones on the coffee table. "We can grab something to eat later. I think it's important we deal with your cranky issue first."

"We might not be eating until morning, then, because, according to Cherry, I'm really, really cranky."

"I might just have to call in sick."

* * *

Shay startled awake. It took a moment for her to realize where she was. She smiled at the weight and the warmth of the man behind her. His arm, even in sleep, held her tucked against him. She wondered if he'd moved and that's what woke her up. She heard something outside the closed bedroom door and raised herself on an elbow, glancing toward the door. The navy drapes over the bedroom window blocked out any light, and it took a moment for her eyes to adjust.

There was a low grunt from Michael, and then warm lips pressed against her bare shoulder. "It's early. Go back to sleep."

"I heard something."

"You could hear a pin drop. It's probably just Atticus getting a drink of water." He lifted his arm, pressed a button, and the face of his watch lit up. "It's seven." He yawned and dragged a hand down his handsome face before rolling her into his arms. Burying his face in the crook between her neck and shoulder, he kissed the sensitive spot, making her squirm. "You know, this is the first morning I haven't wanted to get out of bed in I don't know how long."

She placed her hand on the back of his head, running her fingers through his thick, dark hair before pressing his face back to where it had been. "Maybe you could stay a few minutes—"

There was a knock on the door, and it cracked open. "Michael, what were you thinking leaving all the food out? Michael?" The door opened wide to reveal Maura Gallagher.

Shay's heart slowed, its beat languid, her brain and body either unwilling or unable to respond to her commands. She knew she had to do something but had no idea what to do or how to do it.

"What are you still doing in bed? You're always up at six. I wanted to talk to you about yesterday's little misunderstanding," his mother continued, and Michael snapped out of his frozen state. He grabbed the covers and was about to push Shay beneath them when his mother's eyes, apparently adjusting to the lack of light, went wide. "You! Michael, what were you thinking letting that...that thief into your bed? You're an FBI agent. You'll lose your job over her, and then where will you be? Get her out of here! Get her out of my home now!"

Chapter Sixteen

♥

Shay unlocked the door of her uncle's office at the Salty Dog and opened it an inch. Teased blond hair and a squinty eye filled the crack. Shay sighed. "I'm warning you, Cherry. He better be gone this time."

Michael had arrived at the bar fifteen minutes ago. No doubt to make a case in his mother's defense, a defense Shay had no interest in hearing. So she'd locked herself in her uncle's office to avoid having to.

Moments ago, Cherry, who was apparently on Michael's side, had said she needed to speak to her, and Shay had trustingly opened the door to the man who'd made her forget a hard-won life lesson: Protect yourself because no one else will.

Cherry pushed open the door. "Yes, the poor man is gone, dragging his broken heart behind him."

"Don't be so dramatic. He's fine. And how do I know he's fine, you ask?"

"No, I didn't ask," Cherry huffed, and walked past Shay to the other end of the office, where she flopped down on the olive-green couch.

Shay ignored the woman while doing her best to convince herself she was right. She wasn't a hardass, and she hadn't broken Michael's heart or another promise. "I know he's fine because it took him more than nine hours to track me down after his mother unceremoniously kicked me out of his bed this morning, and then—"

"Because the man is an FBI agent and has his priorities straight. Important things like keeping your butt out of prison and your uncle safe from the mob. Plus, he called you at least twenty times during the day, but would you snap out of your woe-is-me snit long enough to pick up the phone? No, of course not."

"Whose friend are you anyway?"

"Yours, and I'm trying very hard to help you get the wonderful life you deserve. A life with an amazing man who loves you, friends who care about you, and a family too. And you keep screwing it up."

"I didn't ask you to fix my life, so stop trying. I like it just the way it is. No, scratch that, I like the way my life used to be... two years ago." Before her sisters rejected her and Michael gave her a glimpse of what a future with him might look like and made her believe for one brief and shining moment that it was possible. And then his mother had once again shown her that Shay Angel didn't deserve a happily-ever-after, especially one with Michael.

"Are you forgetting who you talked to last night before you got it on with tall, dark, and delicious? Me. You were talking to me. And do you know what I heard? I'll tell you. I heard a woman in love. A woman who needed her best friend to say 'Hell yeah, you deserve a happy life. Go out there and grab your Prince Charming and make both of your dreams come true.'"

"No, you told me to get, you know, and I got it. So I'm good." It'd been so good, so flipping amazing, and now it was going to be awful because she remembered what she was missing.

"What? For another ten years?"

Shay's phone rang. She glanced at the screen and declined the call. And then she did what she hadn't been able to ten months ago—she blocked Michael's number.

"You're sabotaging yourself, you know? You don't believe you deserve to be happy, so every time you get close"—Cherry brought her hands together in a thunderous clap—"you do something to ruin it."

"It's not me. It's God, the universe, karma, whatever you want to call it. I did what you said. I opened up to Michael. I told him the truth. And we had an incredible night. It was the kind of night they write songs about, and then history repeated itself. His mother ranted about how I'd ruin his future, how she couldn't die knowing he wasn't with someone good and decent, a woman who has the ability to make his life happy instead of ruining it. And you know who Michael went to first? His mother.

"And you know who Michael defended to me? Begged me to just give him some time to make her see reason? His mother. The woman who did everything in her power to have me locked up for the rest of my life because I made the mistake of loving her son. A man I would never, not in a million years, be good enough for in the eyes of her and the world." Shay looked away, resting her face in her hand while surreptitiously catching a tear on the tip of her finger.

Seconds later, she found herself enveloped in a powder-scented hug. "You leave it to me, Shaybae. I'll fix everything. I promise."

"Thanks, but it can't be fixed. It's over. We were over years before, and I should've had the sense to leave it at that. I knew better." She did, and usually that would be enough to stop her from doing something stupid. But she'd never been able to play it smart where Michael was concerned. The scientists were right; love really did make you stupid.

"I know it feels like that right now, but you wait and see. Your BFF will take care— What?" Cherry yelled, nearly blowing out Shay's eardrum in the process.

The door opened, and Denise stuck her burgundy head inside and gave them a purse-lipped look. "Julia Landon is here to see you. She's head of the Harmony Harbor Business Development Committee. She's probably here looking for donations. Word of advice, you better not squander your uncle's hard-earned money. He wouldn't like it."

"Word of advice to you, Witchy Poo, if I was the boss and not Shay, your ass would be cash." She shrugged when Shay stared at her. "Well, it's something like that. And I'm just speaking the truth. You should fire her after what she said to Agent James. Either that or take her out back and off her."

Denise gasped, her face turning white as she stumbled into the hall and then ran down it.

"You did that on purpose, didn't you?"

"Yep, now I can take Witchy Poo's place, and Libby can take mine."

"Interesting. I didn't realize you had any managerial experience or were working here in the first place."

"Today was my first day on the job. But you'll see, I'm a fast learner. I'm so good, I had a premonition we were going to need someone for tonight, and Libby will be arriving any minute now." She reached around Shay and started clearing off her desk.

"What are you doing?"

"Teddy and Gabby are coming too. They need a place to do their homework." Cherry waved her off. "Shoo, go talk to the business committee woman. I'll be there in a minute."

Shay looked from Cherry to her desk and realized what her *BFF* was up to. She grabbed her cell phone. "Don't even think about getting involved in this. It's over. Done. *Finis.*"

"Sure. *Arrivederci.* Over. Trust me, I know."

Shay made an aggravated sound in her throat. The woman was going to drive her to drink. But Cherry was right about Denise; she had to go. Charlie could hire her back when he came home. Her uncle, that's what she needed to focus on. Not Denise and definitely not Michael and his mother.

A woman with long, dark hair; sparkling, violet eyes; and a hundred-watt smile popped off the stool when Shay reached the bar. "Hi, you must be Shay. I'm Julia. I own Books and Beans."

"She writes mommy porn too," Gerry said from behind the bar, waggling his eyebrows. Shay crossed her arms, and his grin faded. He cleared his throat. "Not porn, books mommies"—Shay angled her head to the side—"girls"—she raised an eyebrow—"women like to read."

"Enlightened men too. My fiancé reads my books. And FYI, Gerry, they're romance, not porn. Which means you should be reading them too. They might help with that little problem you were telling me about."

"Yeah, well, okay, I'll do that." He wiped his flushed, perspiring face with a bar towel. "Uh, boss, Julia wants a mermaid cocktail. I'm not sure what's in it. I just got hired this morning," he said to Julia. "Shay punched me in the face the other day, and I had a come-to-Jesus moment. Like she said, if I didn't change my ways, I was going to meet my maker before my time."

"Okay, let's not tell every customer that story, Gerry. Don't make me regret hiring you." She'd regretted it at least five times already today. She reached across the bar for a pad and pen and wrote out the drink's ingredients. "You sure you want one of these now? They're pretty potent," she said to Julia.

"I thought I'd do a taste test with my girlfriends. I'm having a mermaid-themed wedding in July."

"Cool. Congrats. Denise told me you're the chair of the business committee?"

"I am. You know Denise quit, right? She told everyone you'd taken a contract out on her. I'm sure no one believed her, though."

"Why would they, right?" Gerry said, measuring out

the spiced rum. "Shay doesn't need to put out a hit on anyone. She just kills them herself."

Shay couldn't figure out if it was the town or the bar, but she couldn't remember dealing with so many quirky people in her life. Unless she factored in her time in prison. "So, Julia, what can I do for you?"

"Well, first you can promise not to kill me." The woman laughed. "I'm just teasing. I know who you are. My fiancé is Aidan Gallagher."

"Right, okay, so why don't we go over here and chat?" Shay jerked her thumb at an empty table far enough away that they wouldn't be heard. "Sorry," she said once they were seated on the barrels. "I have to keep my contract work for the DEA on the down low. No one around here knows I was undercover then."

"Don't worry, my lips are sealed." Julia smiled and made a zip-it motion with her fingers before saying, "I'd love to interview you sometime. You'd make the perfect heroine for one of my books."

That might work well since Shay wouldn't be having sex in real life for the foreseeable future, and from the sounds of it, she'd be having plenty between the pages of Julia's books. Maybe she'd even get a happily-ever-after too. The thought surprised and annoyed her. Obviously, Michael had put the idea in her head. It wasn't one she'd ever had as a teenager or adult.

Then, as though to make a liar out of her, an inconvenient memory came to mind. It had been their first Christmas living with Charlie and their first Christmas without their parents. Charlie had spoiled them rotten. He must have cleared the toy store of everything princess related, from toys to dolls to clothes to books. It was like someone had thrown pink glitter over the living room, and Shay had loved it.

"Only if you have time, though. I know you're busy," Julia said, breaking the prolonged silence.

"Sorry. Yeah, I can make some time for you once my uncle's back. I'll be sticking around for a week or so after he's home." She hadn't been idle while she'd been hiding out in Charlie's office today. She'd scoured his files and computer for a name, for someone who was connected to Tony and Eddie. When she'd come up empty, she'd read every article published on the New England mob, writing down the names of anyone who had some connection to the Costello family. Her next step was to investigate each and every one, after she tracked down her uncle's best friend. Her messages were piling up on Don's voice mail. His second wife had recently left him and didn't care whether he was alive or dead.

Julia drew her from her thoughts. "I have a confession to make," the other woman said. "I'm the one who told Aidan and his cousin Michael that I saw Jasper with Charlie last Tuesday night. I hope I didn't make things worse for you and your uncle."

"Don't worry about it. It's a small town. No doubt someone else saw them and would've eventually come forward." She thought of Teddy and realized she hadn't told Michael what the teenager said. Shay wasn't exactly in a sharing mood now.

At the familiar *click, click, click*, she looked over

to see Cherry approaching with Julia's drink, and Shay covered her face.

"This is really good," Cherry said around the straw. Taking one last sip before handing the drink to Julia, Cherry pulled out a barrel to sit. "Hi, I'm Cherry Blossom, the new manager of this fine establishment."

"Perfect, just the person I wanted to talk to," Julia said as the two women shook hands.

Cherry gave Shay a smug smile. "I guess my reputation precedes me."

"I don't know how—you've been manager for less than ten minutes," Shay said, wondering why Cherry was perfect to talk to and not her.

Cherry waved her off. "Don't listen to Shay. Tell me what I can do for you, Julia."

"As I'm sure you're well aware, V-Day is fast approaching."

Okay, so now Shay knew why Julia had chosen Cherry over her. It was probably obvious that Shay wasn't a hearts-and-flowers kind of girl.

"Ugh. V-Day is right. I'd rather have a venereal disease than have to spend another one alone. That's the one day I'm guaranteed to hear from my mother. As if I don't feel bad enough that I'm dateless on the most romantic night of the year, she manages to make me feel worse than I already do."

"That's it! Oh, I like you, Cherry. We're going to get along just great. You too, Shay." Julia smiled and patted Shay's hand. "Anyway, I was talking to my friends who own businesses in town, and a couple of them were bemoaning the approach of Cupid's birthday. So we decided to shake things up this year. Having a man in your life is lovely—I adore mine—but come on, we don't need one to have fun and celebrate love. Why can't we celebrate the love of our friends, family, or our pets? And that's where the Salty Dog comes in. We were hoping you'd be willing to host a singles' V-Day party."

"Yes! It's just what the pub needs to liven things up. I'm planning to make some big changes around here," Cherry shared with Julia, ignoring Shay's *what the hell?* stare.

"Yay! This is so exciting. We'll probably have some competition from the manor, but once the auction is over, the single ladies in town will be eager for a diversion."

Cherry leaned in, elbows on the table, hands cupping her chin. "What's our competition doing? Maybe we can get some ideas."

"I doubt you'll be able to compete. They're auctioning off the bachelor of the month, Michael Gallagher. He probably has no idea, but the auction is just a ruse. His mother and the Widows Club are looking for his perfect match. I heard from Sophie—she's Greystone's manager—that women have been crashing the manor's website signing up for the auction. I don't blame them. He's an FBI agent, and don't tell Aidan, but the man is double-oh-seven hot. He has this chill vibe and—"

"He's hot all right. Just ask Shay—she knows," Cherry cut off Julia in a ticked-off voice. "And he's already found his perfect match. Her."

Julia's eyes went wide. "You and Michael are together? Aidan never said anything." She sighed. "I don't know why I'm surprised. Guys never really talk about this kind of stuff, do they?" She glanced over her shoulder as two women entered the bar and waved. "Over here. Gerry, two more mermaids... Wait, do you guys want one too?"

The conversation changed so fast that Shay thought it best to let the comment about Michael go, especially with Cherry sitting right there, poised to argue and no doubt make incredibly embarrassing and inappropriate comments. "I should get back to work. Thanks for the offer, though," Shay said, and stood up. "Cherry." She nudged her head. There's no way she was leaving her alone with Julia and her friends.

"No, please stay. I want you to meet my friends." Julia stood up. "We'll just move another couple of barrels over, if that's okay?"

"Of course, it is. Gerry, make that four mermaids," Cherry called out as she stood to help Julia, but not before giving Shay a light elbow to the ribs on her way by and whispering, "You sit back down right now or I'll tell them all your secrets."

"Trust me, you do not want to take that tack with me."

Cherry rolled her eyes and then turned a wide smile on the two women who approached the table. "Hello, ladies. Welcome to the Salty Dog. If you're friends of Julia, you're friends of ours."

Oh God, she should've known what Cherry was up to. If she couldn't give Shay a man to love, she was going to give her more friends. Lots and lots of friends. Shay cringed at a vivid mental image of hordes of women clamoring for her attention and time. Why couldn't Cherry get it through her head that Shay was happy just the way she was?

A woman with perfectly styled shoulder-length auburn hair and pale green eyes frowned at Shay. There was something vaguely familiar about her, but when she opened her mouth and a husky voice with a sultry Southern accent came out, Shay was sure they'd never met before. Until the woman pressed a hand to her chest. "Shay. Shay Angel. I wasn't expecting to see you."

Beside Shay, Cherry stiffened. No doubt, like Shay, she was anticipating the friends thing going downhill fast from here on out. In Cherry's book, the woman already had two strikes against her. One, she wore a pale pink coat and Burberry pink and gray checked scarf that screamed classy Southern belle. And two, she obviously had money. Factor in that, from her shocked expression, Shay assumed she'd heard she'd done time. If that was the case, this wasn't going to end well. She had to get Cherry out of there now.

"Yeah, that's me. We'll leave you to—" She bowed her head and swore under her breath when Cherry's hand went to her hip, her upper body moving in a *You wanna piece of me? I'll give you a piece of me* threatening stance.

"What's that supposed to mean? Do you not think she's good enough for you because she did time?"

Shay stifled a groan at the same time grabbing Cherry by the arm. "Sorry, she started sampling the product earlier than usual. Drinks are on the house. No," she said when Cherry got a stubborn look on her face and opened her mouth.

"Wait, don't leave," the woman said, reaching for Shay. "I wasn't being rude. Don't you remember me?"

"Sorry, no, should I?"

"Now I'm offended. Shay, it's me, Jenna Bell. We used to be best friends."

Cherry snorted a laugh. "Yeah, right. You're a little too shishy poo poo for my Shaybae, if you know what I mean." Cherry mimed drinking a cup of tea with her pinky raised.

The elegant blonde standing beside Jenna laughed and extended her hand. "You probably don't remember me either, Shay. I'm Arianna Bell. My sister Serena and I own the wedding shop, Tie the Knot, on Main Street."

Jenna stood smiling beside her sister, but Shay had witnessed a small shadow crossing her face. For some reason, it appeared her sister had hurt her feelings. Which, sadly, Shay was not the only one to notice.

Cherry frowned, looking from one sister to the other. "So, what's up with you two?"

Jenna looked like she'd just been caught running naked down Main Street. "Nothing, why?"

Cherry frowned. "Well, you sound like you grew up in the South, and she sounds like she grew up here."

"Jenna's mother married our father. They moved to Charleston when…" She glanced at Jenna. "How old were you, twelve?"

"Yes, twelve." Jenna nodded, her smile strained, but it became less so when she looked at Shay. "Which is why you probably don't remember me."

Jenna's sister laughed, and it wasn't a particularly nice laugh. "Right, like it doesn't have anything to do with you losing thirty pounds of baby fat"—she made air quotes around the word *baby*—"and Daddy paying a small fortune to have your nose and teeth fixed."

"Look, here comes Gerry with our drinks and pretzels. You guys are going to love the Blue Mermaids and the garlic cheese pretzels," Julia said in an overly enthusiastic voice. "Sit down, sit down. Jenna, sit beside Shay so you can catch up." She patted the barrel beside her. "Arianna, you sit here."

Cherry helped Jenna off with her coat, glancing at Shay as she did. Shay knew Cherry well enough to read the silent message in her eyes. *Are you taking that biatch out, or am I?*

Great, another member to add to Shay's merry band of misfits. She gave Cherry a *relax, I've got this* look. At about the same time she did, she remembered who Jenna was. It wasn't a surprise that Shay hadn't been able to easily access the memory, and it had nothing to do with the changes to Jenna's appearance that her stepsister had so unkindly pointed out, despite being sort of true.

Jenna had been a good friend to Shay, one of the best she'd ever had, really. Though she wouldn't hurt Cherry by sharing that little tidbit. Shay and Jenna had pretty much been inseparable, and then her friend had moved away...two weeks before social services arrived at Charlie's door. By the time they'd released Shay back to Charlie's care, months' worth of letters had piled up on her bed. Jenna had written her every day.

"I'm sorry I never wrote you back. It wasn't a great time," Shay admitted.

Jenna reached over and gently squeezed Shay's hand. "I know. I got worried when I didn't hear from you and made my mother call your uncle. He told us what happened. I would've kept writing, but..." She glanced at her sister and lowered her voice. "My mom died nine months after we moved."

"I'm sorry. She was a sweet lady."

"She was, wasn't she? Remember how she'd bring us to high tea at the manor? We'd pretend we were princesses visiting the castle, and we were going to marry a Gallagher prince."

Cherry, who'd just taken a sip of her Blue Mermaid, choked on the drink.

Heat rose to Shay's cheeks, and she quickly changed the subject, at the same time shooting Cherry a *don't even* look. "So, what brings you back to Harmony Harbor?"

Jenna gave her a dimpled smile and held up her hand. "I finally found my prince."

"Whoa, he must be a real one," Cherry said, grabbing Jenna's hand, practically salivating over the pink diamond.

"He certainly is." Jenna glanced at her sister, who was rolling her eyes, and then said to Shay, "We're getting married in June at Greystone Manor." Her mouth fell open, and she pressed a hand to her chest. "You can be my bridesmaid! It'll be just like we talked about when we were little girls. It'll be wonderful." She clasped her hands in prayer. "Please, please say yes."

"Of course she will," Cherry said, throwing an arm around Shay's shoulders. "Who knows? If she gets her head out of her butt, you two could have a double wedding."

Shay stopped paying attention to the women's conversation when she spotted movement from the other end of the pub. Charlie's best friend, the man she'd been intent on tracking down, had found her instead. He peeked out from the back hall, around the edge of the wall, motioning to her with a frantic wave. She gave him an almost imperceptible nod as she glanced around the bar and came to her feet.

As soon as she got inside the office, she locked the door and then turned to Don. He was sitting slumped in the chair across from the desk, rubbing his hands over his face.

Afraid he was about to tell her Charlie was dead, she slowly lowered herself onto the chair behind the desk. She stayed quiet, giving herself time as much as him. Two minutes later, she couldn't hold out any longer; she had to know. "What's happened, Don? Where's Charlie?"

He lowered his hands from his face. He looked like he hadn't slept in a week. "No clue. He says it's safer that way."

She let go of the arms of the chair. There were gouges left by her fingernails in the leather. "When was the last time you saw him?"

"Yesterday. I dropped off some food and cash at a park. I've been doing it every couple days since he took off."

"Okay." She nodded, feeling tension release that she hadn't even known she'd been carrying around. "Okay, that's good. But, Don, it might've been nice if you'd let me know. I've left at least thirty messages on your phone."

"Lost it that first day we were on the run. I'm not cut out for this sort of thing." He pulled a burner phone from his pocket. "Charlie said I've gotta get rid of this one. He's paranoid."

"It's kept him alive so far. Do you have a number for him? I need to reach him."

He shook his head. "No, that's why I'm here. He wants you to go back to Vegas. He doesn't want you hurt on account of him, Shay. He'd never forgive himself if the FBI puts you away. He knows they're looking at you for the murders."

"I'm not leaving. When's your next meet? I'm coming with you."

"There isn't going to be one. Charlie says Costello's men made me. He wants me to go into hiding too. Only I don't know where to go."

"Don't worry, I'll take care of it. There's a room above the pub. You'll be safe, and I'll be able to keep an eye on you. But you have to do exactly what I say, Don."

"I will. Charlie's not going to be happy, though."

"He'll have to deal with it. I'm not going anywhere until this is over." She leaned back in the chair, trying to figure out her next steps.

"You're a good girl, Shay. Charlie's real proud of you. He thinks of you as a daughter, you know. He may not be a great role model, but he loves you something fierce."

She nodded, unable to speak. Afraid she might cry if she did.

Don leaned across the desk to pat her hand. "He'll come home in one piece, darlin'. Charlie's real good at hiding. He's had lots of practice. No one will find him unless he wants them to."

Chapter Seventeen

♥

There was trouble afoot at the manor in the form of a big-haired, buxom blond woman wearing hot pink from head to toe. She'd been on the prowl for the last hour. And speaking as an expert snooper herself, Colleen knew how to identify whether someone was snooping, curious, or lost. She'd seen her fair share of curious and lost hotel guests and tourists over the years.

It was one of the consequences of living in a mansion that had been built to be the exact replica of a medieval castle and all that entailed, including turrets and towers and stained-glass windows. Every stick of furniture, the chandeliers and wall sconces, the oriental rugs, and decorative pieces were all antiques—both authentic and replicas. There were even secret panels in some of the rooms that led to passageways and tunnels in the basement.

Decades before they'd been overrun by treasure hunters, but the rumors of buried treasure had eventually died away. If she remembered correctly, and she was prone to remembering incorrectly or not being able to remember at all, it was her son Ronan who'd squelched the rumors.

The big-haired woman was definitely of the snooping variety. Only ten minutes before, Colleen had caught her with her ear pressed to the closed library door where Maura and Kitty were interviewing potential matches for Michael. It was somewhat surreal for Colleen to see the two frenemies working together. Now that they had a common goal of seeing Michael wed, they were bosom buddies.

She looked back at the library but the buxom blonde was gone. Kitty and Maura were in the hall seeing off one of Michael's matrimonial candidates. Sadly for the young woman, it didn't look like she'd made the cut.

And it certainly wouldn't bode well for Maura and Kitty if Michael knew what they were up to. It hadn't taken long for them to come to the conclusion that he wouldn't agree to date the women they'd chosen for him so they'd gotten creative. The money raised at the auction would be split between Michael's two favorite charities. Second Chance Inc., an organization that helped to reintegrate ex-convicts back into society, and the Steppingstone Foundation, which provided programs for underserved students so that they stood a better chance of going to college.

The contenders in the matchmaking war, and it did indeed qualify as a war since the entire Widows Club was involved and had their own candidates in the running, would have an advantage in the auction, as the older women would be funding their candidates' bids. For the charities, it was a win-win situation. Not so for the matchmakers of Harmony Harbor. Some of whom stood a good chance of going broke.

Maura ushered the forlorn-looking woman to the entryway while Kitty hurried another woman, who'd been waiting in the wings, into the library. Colleen checked the hall and study for the blonde. There was still no sign of her. When Maura returned to the library, Colleen followed her inside.

"Maura, this is Serena Bell," Kitty said of the attractive thirtysomething woman sitting in the leather wingback chair in front of the window. "She and her sister, Arianna, own Tie the Knot, a fabulous bridal shop in town. Arianna's an incredibly talented wedding dress designer. Olivia's hoping to convince them to expand into wedding planning. Olivia is Finn's wife, you know. They're expecting sometime in May, and he wants her to cut back on her workload," Kitty explained to Maura, who had no interest in any member of the Gallagher family save her own. Which she proved by sighing.

Colleen angled her head with a frown. She could've sworn she heard an echo of Maura's sigh coming from behind her. She turned. The walls of the library, right up to the third story, were covered with dark oak shelves lined with books—some priceless first editions and some timeworn favorites. A brass ladder on wheels granted access to the books on the first and second levels, while a narrow oak walk circled the perimeter of the third.

Odd, the ladder was off-kilter. It looked like...
Colleen gasped at the sight of pink fabric poking out
from between a row of books. She walked through the
bookshelf and through the buxom blonde on the other
side. Colleen shivered like she always did when she
walked through a live human being. Not that she'd
walked through any dead ones.

The sensation was as disconcerting as always, however, not as disconcerting as discovering there was a
hidden panel in the library. Though she had to admit,
there was a possibility she'd known about it and forgotten.

She studied the woman who had her eye pressed
to a small opening and wondered how she'd known
about the hidey-hole. To Colleen's mind, there were
two possibilities. One: that the lady in pink was another spy sent by the developer who wanted to buy the
manor. Or two: that the woman had panicked at the
sound of Serena and Kitty adjourning to the study and
fell into it by accident.

Colleen was betting on the latter. She prayed to the
good Lord and the Holy Ghost that was the case. She
didn't think she could withstand another fight with the
developer.

She shuddered as she once again walked through the
woman and into the library. Given her ghostly limitations, she needed Simon's help to gain Jasper's attention. She glanced at the three women before walking
through the door and out into the hall. Serena appeared
to be having more luck than the previous candidate. Little did the woman know what she was up against.

Colleen was determined that Michael and Shay be granted a second chance at love, and Kitty and Maura had nothing on her in the matchmaking department. Especially when Colleen's ghostly talents were cooperating. "Simon," she called as she made her way to the entryway and came upon Jasper greeting Colleen's great-grandson instead.

"Welcome back, Master Michael. I trust you made some headway in your investigation?"

As Colleen had gathered from listening in on Kitty and Jasper's conversations, her great-grandson had been out of town following up on a promising lead as well as interviewing the six members of the Costellos' old guard. She'd kept in close proximity of Kitty and Jasper after learning about the debacle with Maura yesterday morning. She imagined Michael was anxious to get home to Atticus and to make things right with Shay.

"Not as much as we'd hoped, I'm afraid, Jeeves."

"And with Ms. Angel? Any news to report there?"

"I'm afraid I'm striking out on all ends. She still won't take my calls. I'll head over to the pub after I've spent a few hours with Atticus. Cherry's making sure Shay's at work."

Jasper looked around. "I'm sure I saw Ms. Blossom here not long ago. She was passing out flyers to a business she and Ms. West have recently begun. Strippercise with the North Shore Pole Dancers."

Colleen thought about the woman in the library and smiled, relieved. It looked like she wasn't alone in her bid to get Michael and Shay back together again. Too bad Ms. Blossom couldn't see her or hear her.

"You're sure it's just Cherry and Libby? There was no mention of Shay?"

"Not that I'm aware of, which is something to be thankful for. Your mother and Ms. Blossom had a run-in. Maura collected the flyers and threw them out while sharing her opinion of the business and exotic dancers with Ms. Blossom."

"I didn't see any ambulances or squad cars when I pulled in, so I'm taking it a fight didn't break out?"

"It might have if your grandmother hadn't intervened. She signed herself and the Widows Club up for an introductory lesson."

"You look pleased with the outcome," Michael teased with a grin.

"I am, as should you be. If Ms. Blossom puts down roots in Harmony Harbor, I'd take that to mean Ms. Angel will think of doing the same."

"Which won't be much use to me if I can't get her to talk to me."

"I have no doubt that you'll be able to convince Ms. Angel to give you a second chance. After all, you've never had a shortage of charm and were always able to talk your way out of any situation as a boy. I believe our immediate concern is why your mother has moved into the manor. And how we can get her and your father back together. She's interviewing future brides for you as we speak, Master Michael."

Colleen thought it interesting that Jasper didn't mention that Kitty was doing the same.

Her old friend continued despite Michael's groan. "And not that I wish to remind you, but I hardly see Ms.

Angel wanting to renew your relationship with Maura in town."

"Thanks, Jeeves. I could've done without the reminder. But you're right, and maybe if my dad would open up and my brothers would take the time to respond to their messages, we could come up with a workable plan."

"I have some good news on that end. It's why I asked you to stop by before you went home. Master Logan should be arriving any moment now. His plane landed in Boston two hours ago. Master Connor is at the bar awaiting your arrival. I should warn you, though, he's had a rather distressing day."

"He can get in line. The past two days haven't exactly been a cakewalk for me. I should probably go home first and decompress before I talk to him. I'll take Atticus for a walk and then—"

"I've just returned from taking him out. Simon remained to keep him company. I believe Atticus thinks the cat is actually a dog."

Colleen smiled, pleased that Simon had taken her lecture to be kind to Atticus to heart. At times, the black cat acted as uppity as any lord of the manor, but underneath he was a good soul. She cocked her head at the thought, wondering if Simon did indeed possess a soul...a human soul. It was something Colleen had considered of late. Cats were smart, but Simon had passed smart a long way back.

Connor came into view in the grand hall and ended any further ruminating on the matter. The lad paced in front of the stone fireplace with his phone pressed to his ear. Like his brother Michael, he wore a black bespoke suit, the glint of what was no doubt an expensive watch on his wrist, and equally expensive brown shoes. With their similar height and build, dark hair, and bright blue Gallagher eyes, Michael and Connor could pass for twins. But that's where the similarities ended.

A high-powered attorney with a passion for all things expensive, including fast cars and even faster women, Connor reminded Colleen most of his father. Like his son, Sean liked the good life. They were equally addicted to power and control, and just as stubborn to boot. Although as the years passed, Sean had mellowed as much as his ambition. Something that Colleen imagined hadn't gone over well with his social-climbing wife.

"Maura," Colleen murmured as a thought passed through her brain so fast that it left only a faded shadow of memory behind. It had something to do with when Sean first met Maura.

Colleen had the feeling that, if she just remembered what it was, she'd have the key to solving the couple's marital problems. Though for the life of her, she didn't know why she'd want to. She'd never thought Maura and Sean belonged together. She straightened. *Bejaysus, maybe they didn't*. Maybe her grandson's true love was out there waiting for him, and Colleen had written her name in her book. Somehow, she had to get Jasper to look up Sean and Maura's stories in *The Secret Keeper of Harmony Harbor*. After all, it wasn't just her great-grandchildren's lives she had to straighten out before she could take the magic carpet ride to the Pearly Gates.

The medieval door leading into the manor creaked open, and she was greeted by a sight she hadn't seen in years. Of course, she had seen Logan when he'd come to her funeral, but she'd been living betwixt and between then.

"You ninny, where do you think you're living now?" she asked herself. The point was legitimate, but she'd been in a spectral state for fifteen months now, so she wasn't as out of sorts as she'd been in the beginning.

Yes, she realized she was having the conversation with herself. It's what happened when you were straddling the land of the living and of the dead with only a cat to hear you. A cat who might very well be a human spirit trapped in a feline form.

"Master Logan, welcome home," Jasper said, clapping Colleen's great-grandson on the back. Michael greeted his big brother warmly, giving him one of those manly hugs the younger set were so fond of. Logan, the oldest of Sean and Maura's boys, reminded Colleen of his uncle Colin. The strong, quiet type, steady and dependable. Always willing to step up and step in. The lad had a true warrior's spirit that she imagined served him well as a Secret Service agent.

As did his size. He was brawnier and taller than his brothers but just as handsome with his Gallagher blue eyes and the strong jaw they all shared. With his black hair cut military short, he had a commanding air about him.

"You," a deep voice cut through the happy reunion,

"have some explaining to do, baby brother." Connor walked toward them, briefly stopping to greet his older brother before turning on Michael.

"What are you talking—"

"I just had an interesting conversation with a man named Luigi, a man who, if I'm not mistaken, thinks I'm you and also thinks I'm into him. Anything you'd like to share?"

"Sorry, I meant to call. Then again, you probably wouldn't have picked up anyway." Michael glanced at Jasper and his brothers, who were staring at him with mouths agape. Colleen had a feeling her jaw had dropped too. "It's not what you think. Even though I have no idea why you'd think I was in the closet. If I was gay, you guys would've been the first to know. I'm working a case. Luigi is a bodyguard for Danny Costello."

"That's you trying to be funny, right? You are not seriously telling me you gave my contact information to a member of the East Coast mob?"

"What are you worried about, bro? You get guys like that not-guilty verdicts every day of the week. No one's going to come after you." Logan winked at Michael. He'd always looked out for his baby brother, even though Michael was probably the last person they had to look out for. *In the brains department at least,* Colleen reminded herself. He'd never been much of a fighter. "Come on. I'll drop my bags in my room and meet you two at the bar, and you can tell me what's going on with Mom and Dad."

"Join your brothers, Master Logan. I'll take your

bags to the tower room. By the way, I've been keeping up with news from Merradien and hear congratulations are in order. Your brother was awarded the Medal of Honor by His Royal Highness for saving the princess's life," Jasper informed Logan's brothers proudly. The assignment her great-grandson had just left was located in a small principality bordered by Spain and France.

Both men congratulated their brother, Michael with an almost jovial smile on his face. "This is perfect. Are you thinking what I'm thinking, Jeeves?"

"I know exactly what you're thinking, Master Michael. And although the idea holds merit, it's not fair to throw your brother under the bus when he's just come home."

"No one's throwing me under the bus, and just so we're clear, I start my assignment in Washington in ten days. I'm here to figure out what to do with Mom and Dad, that's all."

"All right. What about you? You didn't happen to fall in love in the past week, did you?" Michael asked Connor as the four men walked down the steps to the great room.

Connor laughed. "Why would I do that?" Then he cocked his head to study Michael. "You sound desperate. What's going on?"

"Mom has decided now that she doesn't have Dad to manage, she's going to manage me. And apparently what I need most in my life is a wife."

His brothers backed away from him like he had something contagious.

"Jeeves, I think I'll stay with Uncle Colin for a couple of days. I haven't seen him for a while. It'd be great to catch up," Logan said, reaching for his bags.

Connor pushed back his sleeve to glance at his watch. "Would you look at the time? I have an appointment I can't be late for. Call me before you leave, Logan. We'll go out for a drink."

Michael's objection to his brothers' excuses was interrupted by an explosive *boom* that reverberated throughout the manor. Michael and Logan reacted almost immediately. Once they'd ensured no one had been injured, they raced for the door, Michael drawing his weapon. "Jasper, keep everyone inside."

If Colleen's heart was still beating, it would've stopped the moment she watched her great-grandsons run out the door. Telling Jasper to keep everyone inside was like waving a red flag in front of a bull when it came to Connor. Always one for the action, he tore off after his brothers.

"Now where the Sam Hill do you think you're going?" Colleen called after Jasper. Of course he didn't answer, not only because he couldn't hear her but also because he was already out the door. She supposed she didn't blame him. She would've done the same had she been able, but she was tied to the manor. Though perhaps that was no longer the case, she thought, and tried to walk through the dark, medieval door. She bounced off it instead. There was no help for it; she'd just have to find a guest room with a view of the parking lot.

She was about to head for the grand staircase or catch a ride in the elevator when the door burst open. "Now,

Master Connor, I'm sure your insurance will cover the damage."

"Damage, Jeeves? A bomb just blew my one-day-old Lamborghini to smithereens. Or I should say, the mob blew up my car because they thought my brother was me."

Chapter Eighteen

♥

Two hours after the explosion, feeling like she'd had quite enough excitement for one day, Colleen retired to the quiet of the library.

She loved her great-grandsons to distraction. However, for the safety of her family and guests, she was tempted to send them packing. How she planned to do that, she had no idea. It wasn't easy to scare off an FBI agent, a Secret Service agent, and an attorney who'd dealt with a long list of unsavory clients over the years. Colleen was proud of the jobs all her to-serve-and-protect great-grandsons did, but there were times, like this, that she wished they'd chosen nice, boring careers. Careers that didn't have the East Coast mob blowing up her great-grandson's brand-new Lamborghini in the parking lot of her family estate.

To be fair, Michael's investigation might not have anything at all to do with the car bombing. It's possible this Luigi man who'd called Connor wasn't involved. Though to hear Connor tell it, Michael might as well have planted the bomb himself. Colleen supposed the lad had a point. After all, Michael had dragged his brother into the investigation by using his name.

While questioning his brother's theory, Michael threw out several of his own. His suggestions ranged from the possibility that Connor's disgruntled clients were involved to the women his brother had loved and left carrying out an act of vengeance. Until Michael ticked off the names of the many women, Colleen had been unaware Connor was a serial dater.

Deep, aggravated voices came through the vents. Her great-grandsons were still arguing across the hall in the study. Par for the course, she supposed, when you put a former prosecutor and a defense attorney in the same room. Every few minutes, Logan tried to inject some level of calm into the conversation.

"Good luck with that, laddie," Colleen murmured as she took a seat in the wingback chair by the window. She was just about to close her eyes to rest after the events of the day when she heard a scraping sound and then a low *thunk*. As cold night air tickled the back of her neck and the smell of spring and garden soil wafted past her nostrils, she straightened and turned, releasing a shocked gasp at the sight that greeted her.

A black baseball hat worn low on her head, Shay Angel pushed up the window. Something caught the girl's attention, and she glanced over her shoulder. "What do you think you're doing? I told you to wait in the car."

"I can't. The place is crawling with cops, and they keep shooting me suspicious looks like I might have had something to do with that burned-out car in the lot. I feel safer here with you."

"Fine. Crouch behind the tree and don't make a... What are your hands doing on my butt?"

Colleen leaned around to see the buxom blonde from earlier. "I thought you could use a boost," the woman said.

"I'm perfectly capable of doing this on my own. All I have to do is reach through the window"—Shay grunted a little as she stretched out her arm to do just that—"and put the phone on the table."

"But that's not where Michael's mother left it. She left it on the chair."

Maura's phone? What the bejaysus had Shay's friend been up to earlier?

"It doesn't matter as long as she finds it. And no one finds it on you. I'm not fooling around anymore, Cherry. I'm calling Dr. Gallagher to get a referral for you first thing in the morning."

The woman did a dance with her hands. "I forgot to tell you. He and his wife are expecting. The nerve of him hitting on me when he has a pregnant wife at home!"

"The man wasn't hitting on you. I told you, Michael was the reason Finn kept you locked in the examination room. So forget about it and stop talking about it. All we need is for someone to hear you. Trust me, the last thing you want to do is make trouble for the Gallaghers."

"You're still bitter, aren't you, girlie? I can't say I blame you, though I had hoped, when you learned I was the reason that social services allowed you to remain with your uncle, that you would be able to forgive me. I promised your case worker that I would keep an eye on you. As best as I could, I fulfilled that promise." Until that fateful day that long-ago summer.

A pained expression came over the blonde's face. "And because of me taking the phone, you're breaking into their castle. I'm sorry. But his mother was going on and on about one of her favorite candidates for Michael's wife, and I got upset. You know what happens when I get upset. I can't help myself; I just pick things up. You'd be upset too. I mean, the woman's beautiful, a veterinarian, and heir to her family's dog food fortune. How are you supposed to compete with this?" Shay's friend said, patting down the pockets of her bright pink, bejeweled jacket. "Maura had a picture of her on her phone, and I snapped a pic of it with mine."

"It doesn't matter."

"You might be able to fool your friend with your calm and cool voice, but you can't fool me. Don't you worry, though; you've got me on your side."

Jasper too, Colleen imagined.

The blonde emitted a panicked gasp, and Shay glanced over her shoulder. "What?"

"My phone! I don't have my phone!"

"Relax, it's probably in the car."

"No, I think"—she hooked her arms on the windowsill to pull herself up—"it's over there. It must have fallen out of my pocket when I was making my getaway earlier."

* * *

"You know what? I'm done arguing with you, Connor. I've left a message with Luigi telling him I'd mistakenly given him my lawyer's business card and not my own," Michael said. "So, if there's a chance they're behind the car bombing, which, as I repeatedly told you, I highly doubt, that should be enough to get them to back off. By this time tomorrow, they'll know exactly who I am and how far we're into their business."

If the prison grapevine hadn't already spread the word, Michael and his partner had decided it was time to rattle Costello and see what shook out. They were both tired of wasting time.

He could tell by the expression on his brother's face that he wasn't prepared to let it go. Connor would never admit that there was a chance he'd brought this on himself. While Michael was 99 percent sure that he had. The car bomb didn't fit the Costellos' MO.

"No, we're not done, baby brother. Not by a long shot. There's—" Connor began, only to turn with Michael and Logan as their mother walked into the study.

"Enough of this squabbling. It's been ages since we've all been together as a family, and I won't have you waste another moment of it fighting. I've had the kitchen prepare all your favorites to welcome you home, Logan. I hope you're hungry, darling."

Michael smiled as his mother looked up at her oldest son, her face practically glowing with pride. Michael was sure from the expression on her face that Maura knew all about Logan's heroic royal rescue and was plotting ways to snag her oldest a princess bride, and that left Michael feeling more positive and hopeful about his own love life than he had been in the past couple of days.

If his mother was focused on making a royal match for Logan, she'd leave Michael alone to patch things up with Shay. In his heart, he knew they didn't stand much of a chance with his mother hanging around to remind Shay of their past. Not to mention Maura's almost rabid obsession with finding him a suitable bride.

There were only two ways Michael could see out of the situation. Either he got his mom to patch up things with their dad or he made sure Maura went to Washington with Logan. Since he loved and admired his brother, Michael went with option number one. "Shouldn't we wait for Dad?" he asked, pulling out his cell phone. "I'll give him a call. See how far out—"

"Put your phone away. I didn't invite your father. I didn't want him encroaching on my time with my sons. He's done it enough over the years. If you boys want to see him, you can do so on your own time."

Okay, so Operation Reconciliation was out. He didn't have the luxury of time where his relationship with Shay was concerned, and it was beginning to look like getting his parents back together would take weeks. He took in the hard set of his mother's features. Maybe months.

"Mom, is there something else going on? Something you're not telling us? Because Dad seemed as surprised as we are that you left him. And just as surprised that you're here. You always hated the manor," Logan said. There was no judgment in his brother's voice, just a genuine concern for their mother. Logan was the favorite son for a reason. Which was why Michael didn't feel guilty for what he was about to do. His oldest brother was better equipped to handle Maura than Michael and Connor were.

Michael stuck his phone in the pocket of his suit coat as he gave his mother a commiserating smile at the same time avoiding Logan's narrowed gaze. "She didn't have anywhere else to go, did you, Mom? But now that you're home, she doesn't have to stick around here anymore. She can help you get settled in Washington, bro."

"I have a better idea," Connor said. "Why don't you take Mom to Merradien and introduce her to the royal family? I'll pay for the entire trip. I'll send you first class and put you up in the best hotel. You know what, I'll send you to Paris first. You look like you could use a holiday, Mom. You too, big brother."

Michael glanced at Connor as he made his generous offer. He supposed he shouldn't be surprised that, despite being ticked, his brother was joining forces with him. Like Michael, Connor had a vested interest in getting their mother out of town before she turned her matchmaking sights on him.

There was something about his brother's comment that teased a memory. It had to do with the morning his mother had found Shay in his bed. There'd been something she said that had given him pause. Every word she spewed in her hate-filled rage took him aback, but there was something else she said that he couldn't remember. And for a guy who had a pretty good memory, that was annoying. In his defense, he'd been half-awake, furious on Shay's behalf, and a little embarrassed too. It would come to him eventually, he knew. It always did.

"Connor's right, Mom. You don't look like yourself. You're pale, and you seem more tired than usual." He didn't add she hadn't been acting like herself either. Sure, the matchmaking wasn't completely out of character, but she was being nicer to Jeeves and Kitty, taking their feelings into consideration rather than bulldozing over them. It was an odd and somewhat worrisome development.

"I don't know what you're talking about. I'm perfectly fine. If I look pale and tired, it's because I've been losing sleep over you and that…that Angel woman." His mother sniffed and lifted her chin. "You boys need to talk to your brother. Especially you, Connor. You're a lawyer. Tell him what he's risking being involved with an ex-con."

"Ah, Mom, are you forgetting I was an ADA before I became an agent? I don't need my brother advising me on my love life with Shay." He didn't think it was the time to enlighten his mother to the fact that Shay being an ex-con didn't create a problem so much as her insinuating herself into his case did. And then there was the chance that her uncle might be more involved than they knew. Now, that would create a problem, one he hadn't been allowing himself to think about.

"Wait a minute. If you're involved with Shay, why are you bachelor of the month? And why are Grams and Mom searching for your future wife?"

Michael gave Connor a look like the one his mother

had recently given him, one that said *I used to think you were so smart*.

"He's not involved with her," his mother scoffed. "He was in... He slept with her, that's all."

"And you know this how?" Logan asked with an edge in his voice. His oldest brother had been out of the country when everything went down with Shay, but he hadn't been happy when he'd heard about it later. Neither had Connor.

"It doesn't matter. All that matters is that Michael stays away from her. I expect you boys to talk to him about it. He's your baby brother, after all. It's your job to protect him."

"Oh, God, Mother, not this again. If anyone needs protection, it's Shay. And she could probably make a case that she needs protection from us."

"Mom, I'm warning you. Stay out of this and leave Shay alone. Michael's old enough and smart enough to know—" Logan began before Connor cut him off.

"What do you mean she needs to be protected from us?"

Michael told them what GG had done and how difficult losing her sisters had been for Shay. He hoped in sharing the story that his mother would be more compassionate toward her.

"I don't want to rain on your parade, but between what GG did to her family and what Mom did to her, you can kiss a relationship with the woman goodbye," Connor said.

Just as Michael was about to tell his brother that he was wrong, a thunderous crash came from the direction of the library, followed by a high-pitched scream. Michael and his brothers ran out of the study to what sounded like a waterfall of books hitting the floor.

Logan reached the door first. He rattled the knob. "I can't get in. It's locked."

"I have the key, Master Logan," Jasper said, striding down the hall toward them. As they gave the older man room, Simon, the black cat, sat down at Jasper's feet and *meowed* loudly.

Connor rubbed his arms. "Anyone else feel a draft?"

Logan nodded. "I do. Someone must've left the window in the library open. It's probably why the books fell."

They found out moments later that wasn't the case at all. "It's not what it looks like," Shay said from where she helped Cherry out the window.

If his mother hadn't chosen to step into the library at that exact second, things might have gone differently. He knew for a fact they would've gone much better if Shay had let Cherry fall out the window instead of helping her.

"Those are first editions! Stop her, she's trying to steal them! Jasper, don't just stand there! Call the police."

"I wasn't stealing anything. Cherry, not a word. Just go. I'll handle this," Shay said, trying to pry her friend's fingers from the ledge. But Cherry wasn't having it. She hauled herself back through the window, her butt in the air.

"Mom, just calm down. Shay wasn't stealing anything. I invited her here," Michael said, casting Shay an apologetic glance. She wouldn't look at him. Though it was possible she didn't hear him over Cherry creatively cursing out his mother.

"Really? And this is how she dresses to come to dinner at the manor? Like a thief? Do not try to protect her, Michael. She'll just make a fool of you like she did all those years before."

"That's enough, Mother. Logan." Michael nudged his head at his mother in hopes that his big brother would get her out of there.

"I would suggest you refrain from attacking Ms. Angel, Mother. In my opinion, she could make a very strong case against you and the Gallaghers."

"What are you talking about, Connor?" his mother snapped.

"I guess you weren't listening when Michael told us that GG was the reason social services removed Ms. Angel and her sisters from her uncle's care, indirectly depriving her of a relationship with her sisters even to this day. And I'm sure you don't need me to remind you what you did, Mother." Connor walked over to Shay and helped Cherry off the floor. "If you'd like to take my family to court, I'd be more than happy to represent you, Ms. Angel. Pro bono." He held Michael's gaze as he smiled and offered Shay his arm. "Why don't we talk about it over drinks?"

* * *

Approximately twenty-four hours after she'd turned down Connor's offer of representation, Shay had a feeling she might be needing his help after all. Standing outside Two-Face Terry's run-down apartment, she glanced around the dimly lit hall. Terry was the last man on her list who fit Tony's and Eddie's profile. The other four hadn't panned out. She knocked on the door for a second time, silently urging Terry to answer. She didn't have time to waste. She'd been playing cat and mouse with Michael and his partner for the better part of the day.

Twenty minutes ago, she'd had a close call. They'd entered the pool hall just as she'd been about to leave. She'd escaped out the back door without them seeing her. She had a feeling they'd hear about her visit, though. The owner hadn't exactly been happy with her nosing around.

"Come on, Terry," she murmured, pressing her ear to the door. She heard what sounded like the TV in the background and nothing more. Taking another look around the hall, she stuck her gloved hand in her pocket and withdrew her lock kit. It took her less than a minute to pick the piece-of-crap lock.

She brushed a hand over her damp brow. She shouldn't be sweating. But she was, and she knew why. She couldn't shake the feeling that something wasn't right. She'd been fighting it from the moment she approached the old building on Boston's south side.

As she eased the door open, a familiar smell slapped her in the face. Blood. Death. She was too late. But how late was she really? It hadn't happened that long ago if the lingering smell of gunpowder was anything to go by. No one had come out of the building when she approached. No one had passed her on the stairs. It stood to reason the killer could still be inside.

Would he have heard her open the door? The TV was loud enough that it probably muffled the sound. It didn't matter. Despite the danger, she was tired of the game. She wanted her uncle out of hiding, and she wanted to stop Costello before he implicated Shay or Charlie any deeper in his crimes.

She withdrew her gun from under her jacket. The worn linoleum floor creaked under her boot as she stepped inside and carefully closed the door. There were splotches of water on the floor. Whoever had killed Terry had kept their boots on. It was snowing… Down the hall a drawer closed, stopping her mid-thought. She wasn't alone.

Ducking into the bathroom off the narrow hall, she bent to undo her boots. Another drawer closed, louder this time. He was getting frustrated. She wondered what he was looking for. Sliding off her boots, she used the bathroom mirror to check the hall. It was empty. She tiptoed from the bathroom, listening intently as she did. Her back to the wall, she inched her way slowly and carefully to the living room. The man she knew from his picture to be Terry Boyle lay facedown on the blue carpet.

There wasn't much chance he was alive; still, she had to check. At the rattle of hangers from the room to her right, she hurried to his side. Crouching while keeping an eye on the doorway, she lightly pressed two fingers to Terry's neck. No pulse, but there was a phone clutched in his hand. She freed it from his death grip at the same time a man cursed and what sounded like a fist hit the wall.

Shay searched the room for the best vantage point for a surprise attack. A phone rang. Her heart bumped against her ribs, and she powered off Terry's cell.

"No, the guy offed himself before I could get anything out of him. There's no sign Angel has been here." Shay's head jerked up. She dug her phone from her pocket and pressed Record. "Who knows, maybe your uncle got to him."

There was a long pause. She tiptoed across the room. Holding her breath, she peeked through the crack in the door. The man looked out a window, his back to her. Even from behind, there was no mistaking who he was—the man who saved Michael from choking at Pussy Cat East. She darted past the door and pressed her back against the wall.

"Yeah, I already did that. It'll look like Angel organized to meet with Two Face a few minutes ago. Timing works. Yeah, yeah, I'll text a threat from him to Terry's phone, mention the niece coming after him. The guys are tracking her down. Word is she's not in Vegas. They'll check the house and bar again."

Shay's heart dropped to her feet. No matter how much she wanted this guy, she couldn't waste time. She had to get back to Harmony Harbor to protect Cherry, Libby, and the kids. She didn't want them anywhere around when Costello's goon searched Charlie's house and the Salty Dog. Shay inched toward the edge of the wall. She was positive he still stood at the window with his back to her. She would've heard the rustle of clothing, the sound of his boots. Pocketing the phone, she wrapped both hands around her gun and then once again darted past the doorway. Only this time she kept going, tiptoeing backward to the bathroom with her gun aimed at the bedroom.

He was on the move. She made it to the bathroom doorway at the same time the toe of his black boot crossed the bedroom's threshold. He was still on the phone.

Heart pounding in her ears, she scooped up her boots and made a dash for the front door only to freeze when he said, "Say again. Freddie's sure he's a fed? Michael Gallagher? You're positive?" He grunted a couple of times and then said, "I don't want any part of that, boss. I'm not taking out a couple of feds. Nope, no way."

Shay stepped to where he could see her. "Down on your knees, and say goodbye to your boss."

Chapter Nineteen

♥

I've got a bad feeling about this. You sure the guy told you to meet him here?" Michael asked his partner as he leaned over the steering wheel to clear the fogged windshield. The snow had been falling for the past few hours, blanketing the surrounding trees and the nearly empty parking lot. Snowflakes swirled under a pool of golden light from the lone working lamppost.

"Yeah, I plugged it in the GPS when he was setting up the meet. Relax, he probably just got delayed by the weather. It's a freakin' blizzard out there, or haven't you noticed?"

Michael dug his phone from his pocket instead of reminding his partner that they'd made it from Boston in under forty-five minutes. James had gotten the call from a long-time snitch just as they were leaving the pool hall. The guy had information on Danny Costello and Pussy Cat East. They'd been waiting for almost an hour. Admittedly, road conditions had steadily worsened since they'd turned off the highway.

Still, despite sitting snug and warm inside his Range

Rover, Michael couldn't shake the cold dread lying heavy in his belly. Maybe it had something to do with the location of the meet... and the memories.

They were waiting outside a combination gas station and corner store in the middle of nowhere. A nowhere Michael was familiar with, as he'd been here before. The gas station was located fifteen minutes off the highway, up the road from Driftwood Cove and the inn where he'd spent the best night of his life and his worst morning.

He'd been doing his damnedest not to think about Shay. It just made him angry, frustrated too. She was messing with their case. Not to mention making them look like Keystone Cops. Everywhere they went, the people they questioned had already been interrogated by a hot, dark-haired woman driving an equally hot set of wheels. She'd been one step ahead of them all day. Sticking her nose where it didn't belong and putting herself squarely on Costello's radar.

His brother's offer of representation last night wouldn't help her in this case. Michael's mouth twisted at the memory. He'd tried to talk to her, but his mother wouldn't back off and neither would Cherry. Connor had just made it worse trying to stick it to Michael for his perceived guilt in the car bombing. Nothing had gone according to plan. Apparently today wasn't going to be much better.

In the rearview mirror, Michael watched as a black Lincoln Navigator crawled down the country road with a charcoal Mercedes following close behind. He had a feeling he'd been overly optimistic. Today was about to get much, much worse.

"We've got company, and I'm pretty sure they're not here for gas," he said to his partner, who looked over his shoulder and muttered a blistering curse.

As though to prove Michael right, and he really wished they hadn't, the Navigator backed into the entrance to the parking lot and the Mercedes idled in the exit, effectively blocking them in. Michael pushed back his coat and pulled out his sidearm.

"I've got no cell reception. Try yours," James said while looking over his shoulder and withdrawing his gun.

Michael tried his phone. "Nothing." His gaze went back to the rearview mirror and then to the gas tanks and the corner store. There were at least three people that he knew of inside.

"Son of... We've got a man from each vehicle coming our way."

And they had more firepower than Michael and his partner. Michael leaned across the console to unlock the glove compartment and remove a second piece. "If we're lucky, someone inside the corner store is calling 911."

James bent at the waist and lifted his pant leg to reveal another gun. "Hate to break it to you, but they're not going to get here fast enough. Please tell me this baby is outfitted in armor."

"Wish I could." He'd been offered the upgrade but turned it down. He'd never been threatened or shot at as an ADA and couldn't justify the cost. The first thing he planned to do once this was over was have the SUV retrofitted. If they made it out of this alive.

At the thought, images of Shay and Atticus from

the other night were followed by flashes of special moments with his brothers, parents, and extended family. He pushed them back. There was no time for sentimentality and emotion. What he needed to do was evaluate the situation calmly and rationally.

They were outgunned and outmanned, and he had no doubt Costello's cars were armored. And the men running in a crouch across the parking lot with AK-47s in their hands wouldn't care about the people in the gas station. There was only one option available to them. "Hang on, partner. We're going for a ride."

Michael revved the engine and threw the gear into reverse. "Get down," he yelled when the *rat-a-tat-tat* of gunfire filled the night air, bullets shattering the back windshield. Michael braked, jerked the wheel hard to the right, and hit the gas. The SUV spun out, sending up an arc of snow before he got the vehicle under control, aiming it directly at the Mercedes. He was counting on them moving, but if they didn't, he'd ram the back end of the vehicle until he either put them out of commission or made it around them.

At the rush of cold air and snow whipping around in the SUV, Michael took his eyes off the faint glow of red through the blizzard to glance at his partner, who was half-hanging out the window. "Get back in here before I ram the car and you fly out."

"He's gonna try to shoot out the tires," James yelled over the roar of the engine and the howling wind, gesturing to the gunmen on the right before he took aim and got off a couple shots of his own.

Michael couldn't tell if James had hit the gunman or

not. He had other things to worry about, like the Navigator's headlights turning in their direction from the other end of the lot and the *rat-a-tat-tat* of the second gunman's bullets hitting uncomfortably close to the gas tank.

"Hang on, we're going off—" A round of bullets smashed into the driver's-side window, cutting him off. He ducked just in time, glass shattering all around him. Shards of the window stuck in his hands and head, a trickle of something warm running down his cheek.

He slammed the SUV into reverse at the same time James fell back against the seat. "There's a trail leading into the woods at the back of the gas station. I'll get us in as deep as I can, and then we'll—" Michael began as he powered up the passenger-side window and braked hard. His partner's gun hit the floor. Michael's gaze jerked to James. His face was pale and tight with pain. He'd been hit. "How bad?"

James shifted and winced. "It's not a flesh wound, I can tell that much."

"Don't move around. Put pressure on it and breathe slow and easy. I'll have you out of here in..." He trailed off at the sight of a sleek black car flying through a wall of snow to land between Michael's SUV and the Navigator.

James gave a strained laugh. "Looks like we've been saved by an Angel, partner."

Michael stared, stunned, as the Hellcat spun in a graceful arc and came to a stop. Both the driver's-side and passenger's windows went down and automatic gunfire rent the air on all sides. Costello's men cried out and dropped to the ground at almost the same time. The Navigator and Mercedes peeled away. In the distance came the welcome sound of sirens.

The doors of the Hellcat opened, and Shay stepped out of the driver's side, Luigi the passenger side.

"Okay, now that I wasn't expecting," James said.

Michael didn't answer, his gaze locked on the woman dressed in black walking through the swirling snow toward him. She was beautiful, capable, strong, a hero, and he didn't know when he'd ever been more angry or relieved.

* * *

Shay couldn't read Michael's expression as he walked to where she leaned against the coffee counter. No doubt some of the emotion she saw on his face was concern for his partner, who'd left by ambulance twenty minutes earlier, and probably some for her too. He wouldn't be happy she'd put herself at risk. He had no idea just how far she would go to protect him or how angry she was at him for almost getting himself killed. She didn't know what she would've done if she'd lost him.

Even when she wasn't with him for all those years and never thought in a million more that she would be again, she'd taken comfort in knowing that he was out there living and loving and doing good things.

"Sorry to keep you waiting. I had to get their statements." Michael nodded at Jim, the owner of the gas station, and his two customers. "I need yours, too, but it's going to take some time. I thought we'd just head to the inn."

"Inn?" There was only one inn she knew of in the area, and it was one she'd promised herself never to set foot in again. She'd buried the memories of that night and the next morning, and the last thing she wanted to do was dig them up.

"Everything's shut down, Shay. Other than emergency vehicles, they're not letting anyone out on the roads or highway."

"I'll drive. You flash your badge, and we're good." She wanted to get back to Harmony Harbor to check on Cherry, Libby, and the kids. She'd called to warn them to stay away from the pub and the house. They promised they would, but still...

"Look, I don't know how you even made it here in one piece, but you're not going out in that again."

"So what, you're planning on walking to the inn?"

"Jim has a snowmobile he said I can borrow. And I'm not going alone. You're coming with me. Don't argue, or I'll arrest you right here."

She struggled to breathe. She couldn't get air in or push it out. It was like everything inside her had frozen, and the room started to spin.

Strong, warm fingers linked with hers and gently squeezed as her breath wheezed in and out, in and out. The dizziness passed. "I'm sorry, Shay. I shouldn't have said that. I was...We need to talk. I need you to listen. If tonight showed me anything, it was that none of us know how long we've got." He glanced around. The men were talking to one of the local cops. Michael ducked his head to whisper in her ear, "Don't make me tell you here. I want you in my arms when I try to convince you we deserve a second chance. When I tell you I've never been more grateful and relieved or angry and terrified to see you." He gently nipped her earlobe. "Please, come with me to the inn. Stay with me tonight."

He had no idea those same emotions were still thrumming through her. She wanted to kiss him and shake him and yell at him all at the same time. "Fine. As long as you let me drive."

"You're lucky I have a healthy sense of self-esteem. Some men might find your need to be in control all the time emasculating."

"It has nothing to do with control. You just drive too slow."

Michael gave her a look and then went to wrap things up with the locals. Fifteen minutes later they were on their way. Less than ten minutes later, she parked the snowmobile at the side of the old-fashioned blue clapboard inn.

"You know, you won't lose your superhero card if you go the speed limit," Michael grumbled as he got off the snowmobile.

She kept her smile under wraps as she took off her helmet. "Sorry, we must have passed the signs when you were yelling at me to slow down. You're a terrible backseat driver, you know."

"I wasn't yelling at *you*. I had to yell to be heard over the roar of the engine as you drove down an incredibly narrow path at full throttle, in the dead of night, in a blizzard," he said as he walked to the steps that led to the white wraparound porch.

As much as she was teasing him, he was teasing her. She could hear the hint of amusement and admiration in his voice. That was the thing that made Michael different from the men she'd dated over the past five years, and the reason why they'd never made it to first base; he wasn't intimidated by her. He didn't want to change her. He liked who she was. He was confident with a strong sense of self. When he was younger, those qualities had come across as arrogance, but now he was just good in his own skin.

For some reason, she wanted to let him know how much she loved that about him, how much she respected the man he'd become. Maybe she wanted to tell him how she felt about him because she'd come so close to losing him. He would've died without knowing he was it for her.

She walked up behind him and wrapped her arms around his waist, pressing her cheek to the wet wool of his black coat. "Thanks for not dying tonight." She closed her eyes. That's not what she meant to say.

He turned in her arms and wrapped his around her, his eyes crinkled with warmth and humor. "Thank you for saving the day, and for loving me enough to put your life on the line for me. I'd do it for you, too, you know. But I have a feeling I'll never get the chance."

"God, I hope not," she said, and shivered as much with cold as at the thought of him risking his life for hers.

He laughed and then gave her a quick kiss. "Come

on, you're freezing, and I'm freezing. We'll get the key from Mrs. Jaworski and beg her for some food."

She drew back. "Mrs. Jaworski still owns the place?"

"That's what Jim said. She was in her midfifties when we used to come here. She's not that old."

"Right." She looked around, trying to come up with an excuse not to make a trip to the inn's reception desk. "You go ahead. I wanna move the snowmobile to a more sheltered location."

"Leave it. I'll do it later."

"No, I..." She looked up at him. "I don't want to face Mrs. Jaworski tonight, okay? I haven't seen her since the trial."

"Don't keep doing this to yourself, babe. Mrs. Jaworski would love to see you. She—"

"Please."

"Okay. I won't be long." He jogged up the stairs.

"Michael," she called after him.

He turned. His gaze roamed her face, and then he nodded. "I'll make sure we get another room."

Shay sat on a bench tucked in a corner of the deck. Like the small cove with its driftwood-littered beach now covered in snow, she was somewhat sheltered from the gale-force winds coming off the Atlantic. But there weren't enough walls, external or internal, to completely protect her from either the elements or her memories. Michael was right; in many ways she was her own worst enemy. She'd allowed what she'd done to define her.

She thought of herself as an ex-con, someone who wasn't worthy of love or respect, someone who was less than. But the truth of it was, that if her life hadn't been interrupted, if she hadn't gone to prison, she might have been sucked deeper into Charlie's world. Even if she hadn't been put away, eventually his mother would have come between them. The guy he used to be would've caved to the pressure, and then where would Shay have been?

Certainly she wouldn't have developed the skills that made it possible for her to protect Michael and his partner today. Nor would she have gotten her degrees. Degrees, she reminded herself, that were going to waste. She'd let fear win. Her master's in social work wouldn't provide the income she'd felt compelled to strive for in a bid to protect herself from being put away again. But Ray Sterling had proven to her that sometimes even money wasn't enough to keep you out of jail.

She looked over at the sound of a door closing and heavy footfalls coming her way. Michael smiled as he rounded the corner, a key and a bag of what smelled like fried chicken in his hand. Her stomach tightened in anticipation. Whether in response to the food or Michael, she wasn't sure. Even cold, wet, and slightly battered, the man looked as delectable as the chicken smelled. And if the blizzard kept up, they could be stranded here for a week.

If Charlie wasn't out there somewhere, she couldn't think of anything she'd like better. The thought surprised her. For years, she wouldn't let herself think about the Inn at Driftwood Cove, let alone throwing caution to the wind, burying the hurts of the past, and finally going after what she wanted.

Apparently tonight had been the turning point, the thing that sent her on a path to Michael and love. Knowing Costello had ordered a hit on him, not knowing if she'd get to him on time, seeing him in the middle of a shoot-out, terrified that she might lose him, had made her realize that nothing else mattered but the man who was looking at her with love in his staggering blue eyes.

"Ready?" He held up the bag and key.

She smiled. "You have no idea how ready I am."

He helped her off the bench and wrapped his arm around her shoulders. "That sounded like it was about more than getting a room and something to eat."

"It was. It was about us. I love you, Michael. I never stopped. I don't think we would've made it, though, even if I hadn't stolen your car and gone to jail. I'm sorry about that, by the way. I'm not sure I've ever said that to you." She remembered him saying he was sorry to her at the pub and how much it had meant to her.

"It was never about the car. It was about waking up after the best night of my life to find you gone. To realize that you didn't trust me or love me enough to tell me what was going on."

"I guess we didn't know back then that we had something worth fighting for."

"I did. I just didn't know how to fight for you. I do now." He stopped in front of a door at the end of the long porch.

Shay blinked at the plaque on the door. "It's the honeymoon suite."

He turned the key with a grin. "Which means it has

a Jacuzzi. Even better, Mrs. Jaworski says it's looking like we might be stuck here for a few days."

Michael drew her into the room with him and set down the bag and key on the desk before drawing her into his arms. "I know you're worried about Charlie, but Costello doesn't have him. Luigi would've told you if they did. And I would've gotten it out of his buddies before they took them away. Charlie's smart. All he needs to do is lie low for the next few days. We've got them, babe. Thanks to you, Luigi's agreed to provide state's evidence in exchange for immunity."

"I know, but you have to bring it to the DA, and then a judge has to sign off on it before you can make a move against Danny. You said so yourself that it could take days."

"And it probably will. But there's nothing we can do about that now, so let's take the win. We're here, and we're together, and we have fried chicken and a Jacuzzi."

"And a really big bed."

Chapter Twenty

♥

I hope the manor's liability insurance is up to date," Colleen said to Simon as they watched Jasper secure the pole to both the ceiling and the floor in the main sitting room after the ballroom had proved impractical.

Shay's friend Cherry had insisted they hold the Widows Club introductory Strippercise class at the manor instead of the Salty Dog. Colleen overheard Cherry tell Jasper it was on account of the mob looking for Shay.

At least the woman had the good sense not to say it loud enough for Maura to hear. Colleen's granddaughter-in-law had been on a tear since she'd caught Shay in the library. It'd gotten worse last night when Aidan came by to let them know Michael had been involved in an incident near Driftwood Cove, an incident that Shay had been involved in too.

Aidan couldn't give them details, only to say the couple was fine and riding out the blizzard together at the Inn at Driftwood Cove. Maura had been in a right state after that. It was a good thing Logan had been here to calm his mother down and confiscate her car keys.

Colleen had sent up a prayer of thanks last night. This was exactly what Michael and Shay needed, time alone.

"Oh, Jaspy, that looks perfect," Cherry said as she walked into the sitting room with her partner Libby, and Libby's two children, Teddy and Gabby, the youngest of whom carried a pink poodle. School had been canceled for the day. The two women were dressed in stretchy bra tops and boy shorts. Libby's had a leopard print, and Cherry's were, not surprisingly, electric pink with rhinestones.

"I might've taken up pole dancing myself if it came with a guarantee my stomach would look like theirs...Holy Mary Mother of God, what were they thinking?" Colleen said when Kitty strolled in with her best friend and fellow member of the Widows Club, Rosa DiRossi. They wore high-heeled boots and black Lycra dresses that skimmed their thighs.

Jasper had turned to address Cherry, and his eyes went wide. He opened his mouth as though speaking but no words came out. Unless Colleen had suddenly lost her hearing. "Is he saying anything, Simon?"

But Simon had left her side to wind himself around Cherry's and Libby's long, toned legs. She should've known she'd lose his attention. He was a leg man.

Logan walked in with Atticus by his side. He took one look at his grandmother and Rosa, said *Jesus* under his breath, and then turned around and walked out.

"Hey you, handsome, get back here," Libby called.

"Mom," Teddy said, like only an embarrassed teenager could, drawing Colleen's attention to the pretty girl with the long dark hair and attitude. As her gaze moved from Teddy to the little girl at her side, Colleen was shocked to find light blue eyes locked on hers.

Colleen touched her chest. "Can you see me, little one?" she asked Gabby, working to ensure her expression was as genial as possible so as not to frighten the child.

The little girl gave her a hesitant nod, looking about as though to gauge whether she alone could see Colleen. Simon lifted his head and stared at the child. "You're a canny lad, aren't you?" she said to the cat.

Jasper, as though picking up on something, too, drew his gaze from Kitty to glance from Simon to the little girl.

This was it, exactly what Colleen had been praying for. Now that Michael and Shay were well on their way to happily-ever-after, Colleen wanted to seal the deal by ensuring that Shay received a copy of the page in her memoir that Jasper and Kitty had clearly forgotten to give Charlie. If they were going to try and correct the wrongs on her behalf, the least they could do was get it right. Shay needed to know that, in the end, Colleen had tried to make amends by intervening on her behalf with social services.

"I need your help, little one," Colleen said to Gabby, whose mother had gone off in search of Logan with Teddy and Cherry following after her. Kitty and Rosa weren't paying any attention to anyone. They were busy examining the pole. Colleen hoped that's where their focus remained. The last thing she wanted to endure was another attempt at a ghostorcism.

Colleen got up from the chair and walked to within a few feet of the child so that she stood between Gabby and Jasper. "Tell him"—she pointed at Jasper—"That GG says he forgot a page for Shay."

"GG says you—"

Jasper shot a look at Kitty, who was helping Rosa get her leg up and around the pole. "*Morane a mi*, not so high," Rosa exhorted, making the sign of the cross.

Looking relieved that the women hadn't heard the little girl, Jasper passed through Colleen as she frantically waved her arms. "No, child. Whisper it in his ear."

Gabby put down the poodle and crooked a finger at Jasper, who obediently crouched in front of the little girl. He nodded, frowned, then nodded again, and said something quietly to the child. Gabby smiled at Colleen and made a zip-it motion with her fingers at the same time Rosa fell off the pole.

"You see, that's exactly why we need you and your muscles," Libby said to Logan as she dragged him into the sitting room. Cherry and Jasper hurried to Rosa's aid while Kitty frantically assured her friend it had been an accident.

Logan, looking uncomfortable, turned as several more members of the Widows Club arrived. "You've got plenty of spotters now," he said with a *thank God* expression on his face.

"Yes, but none of them are as gorgeous as you. You know, I—"

"Mom!" Teddy groaned.

Logan raised a hand to get Jasper's attention. "Jeeves, you got a sec?"

Now what was that about? Colleen wondered. Thinking her great-grandson might have news to share about either his mother or Michael, Colleen followed him. He waited outside the sitting room for Jasper, glancing around as though something had gone missing. He stepped away to visually search the great room.

"Atticus," he called to the wolfhound, who was sniffing around two men at the bar.

"You'll have to retrieve him yourself, Master Logan. His vision is rapidly deteriorating," Jasper said when he joined them.

"You and Michael are spoiling him. He can hear better than you and I combined, Jeeves. Come here, boy," he called, offering an apology to the men at the bar, who barely spared him a passing glance.

Jasper pursed his lips. "I think perhaps I should take him for his walk, Master Logan."

"Yeah, okay. I want to head over to the police station and talk to Aidan, see if he needs another set of eyes on the pub and Shay and her uncle's place."

"You're a fine man, Logan my boy, that you are. You belong here, you know. And once I've ensured your brother and Shay have found their happily-ever-after, you're next, laddie. Though I may have to dust off my matchmaking cap. The woman I had chosen for you has gone and gotten herself engaged. And wouldn't you know it, she's getting married at the manor. Oh well, in the end it might be for the best. I think her family had a secret, a big one at that. I may have exposed it...or maybe I didn't. I can't be sure anymore."

Colleen had been so busy having a conversation with

herself that Jasper and Logan had already gone about
their business. As she drew her gaze from their retreating backs, she caught the two men at the bar watching
them intently. She took in their dark clothing and shifty
eyes, and it hit her who they were. The mob had come
to the manor.

"Simon! Come quick!" she called into the sitting
room. As though recognizing the panic in her voice, Simon didn't saunter as he was wont to do. He hightailed
it out of there so fast he was but a blur, the pink poodle
chasing after him. "Jasper. Get Jasper, Simon. Trouble
has come to Greystone."

When the manor door closed after Logan, Jasper, and
Atticus, the older of the two men gave his companion a
nod. The tall, skinny one got up and headed to the door.
Colleen knew right away what he was about. He was
standing guard. They'd drawn the conclusion that without the presence of Logan and Jasper to protect them,
the women wouldn't put up a fight.

"Little do you know what you're up against, laddie,"
she murmured as the older man headed across the grand
hall. Colleen hurried to Gabby's side and crouched in
front of the little girl. "Close the door and bar it, child.
Get Teddy to help you. The men looking for Shay,
they've come to the manor. Don't you worry, though.
I'll take care of them, but I need help. Go now."

Gabby ran to where her sister sat in the corner on
her phone, whispered in her ear, and pointed at Colleen.
Teddy laughed and shook her head. Colleen glanced out
the open door. The man was coming their way. Quickly,
she knelt beside the coffee table. Centering all her en-

ergy on her hand, she slowly closed it around the coffee cup. She didn't cheer when her hand wrapped around the ceramic and held firm. She stayed focused, concentrating on lifting the cup off the table. She caught sight of Teddy gaping as the cup hung in midair. Colleen's focus broke, and the cup fell, coffee spilling onto the oriental rug.

Teddy raced to the door with her sister and slammed it shut. "Gabby!" She pointed at the buffet table, both of them hurrying to each grab an end, struggling to carry it to the door.

The women in the room finally took notice and asked what they were doing. Gabby whispered something to Teddy. The teenager nodded, then said, "There's a man out there. I think it's the guy who was after Charlie. The one who's looking for Shay."

Libby gasped. "Cherry, they're gonna use you to draw her out."

Cherry goggled at the woman. "I never thought of that. I thought they were coming after me because I told them at the club I was Charlie's girlfriend."

"You what?" Libby shrieked, slapping a hand over her mouth when there was a loud knock on the door. Several of the Widows Club gasped and leaned back on their heels.

As Libby ran to grab her daughters, Rosa said, "Cherry, get on the pole. Not too high. Ladies, gather around like she's teaching you. Kitty, wait until I say okay, and then open the door."

"You want me to let him in? Are you crazy?"

Rosa walked to the fireplace and grabbed the brass

poker, slapping it lightly on her open palm. "You don't think I can deal with one measly wise guy? Eh, my father, he was a made man, a member of the Cosa Nostra."

"You always said Marco was telling tall tales when he talked about his great-grandfather," Kitty whispered as she moved the table out of the way with Rosa's help.

"Telling tales out of school, more like." Waving at Kitty to answer the loud banging on the door, Rosa flattened her back against the dark-paneled wall.

"I'll be right with you," Kitty said, rubbing her palms on her dress. She mouthed, *Be careful* to Rosa, her eyes worried as she looked at her old friend, and then she opened the door. "Hello, can I help you?"

"Yeah, I'm looking for someone," he said, roughly moving Kitty aside to swagger into the room. "Charlie Angel's broad. Anyone know—" *Whoomph*. Rosa brought the poker down on his back.

He fell face-first on the floor, and a gun went off. Obviously he'd been holding his weapon in the pocket of his black coat and involuntarily pulled the trigger. His leg jerked, and smoke came out of the sole of his black shoe. It looked like he'd shot himself in the foot.

Worried his partner had heard the gunshot and would come running, Colleen waved to get Gabby's attention. She mouthed that the man had a partner and that he'd been stationed at the door. The little girl passed along the information to her sister, who sighed. No doubt wondering how she was supposed to share the news. "I think he has a partner," she blurted. "He wouldn't come alone."

"I bet he's guarding the door," Gabby added.

Apparently seeing their friend take out a wise guy had triggered the competitive nature—and confidence—of the Widows Club. Picking up weaponry in the form of vases and fireplace tools, the women set off. Rosa reached into the unconscious man's pocket and carefully removed the gun. "Kitty, sit on him and make sure he doesn't move," Rosa said, and marched off after her friends, looking entirely too comfortable with the gun in her hand.

* * *

Standing in the gas station's parking lot under a red and purple sky, Michael placed his hands on either side of Shay, trapping her between him and her car. "Come on, stay and wait for my rental with me. Jim said he'd look after your car like it's his own. I promise, we'll come get it as soon as the snow starts to melt."

"Michael, I'm fine."

"Yeah, I know exactly how fine you are, which is why I don't want to let you go." He leaned in to nuzzle her neck, his lips warm and teasing. "We can have at least another hour alone together. I'll take you for dinner at the diner you like outside of town."

She curled her hands into his coat and went up on her toes to kiss him. She only meant it to be a quick kiss, but Michael had other ideas, which she would've been on board with if they hadn't just received disturbing news from the manor.

As reluctant as she was to break the kiss, she did. "Are you forgetting Cherry was almost kidnapped a

couple hours ago? I have to check on her, Libby, and the
kids." The phone lines were still down, but Aidan had
gotten in touch with the county sheriff, who'd delivered
the news, at the same time informing them the highway had reopened. No doubt hoping to be done with his
messenger duties once and for all.

"Of course you do, because you don't trust my
cousins, brother, and the entire Harmony Harbor police
force to protect them as well as you."

Okay, so he had a point. Not that she'd admit it to
him. "We just spent nearly twenty-four hours together,
and you're acting as if you'll never see me again."

"It's happened before."

"Now who can't let go of the past?" She leaned in
and kissed the underside of his jaw, inhaling his warm,
spicy sent. "I love you. I'll see you and Atticus later
tonight."

He opened the car door for her. "I'm holding you to
that. But listen, if you're going to the pub, I want you to
call me. I'll go with you."

"I thought you were going to headquarters after you
stopped by the hospital to see Oliver." The sheriff had
also delivered news that Michael's partner was having
surgery on his shoulder today.

"I should be back in town around nine. I figured
you'd be checking in around then anyway."

"I probably won't get to the pub before then, but if
I do—" she began as she slid behind the wheel, her attention drawn to a cell phone on the passenger seat. It
wasn't hers. She frowned, leaning over to pick it up.
She felt a panicked cry working its way up from the

base of her throat. She swallowed hard. Instinctively, she dropped the phone and turned her body to block the photo of Charlie from Michael's view. She cleared her throat, forcing a smile. "I-I'll check with HHPD."

"You okay? You got pale all of a sudden."

"Just cold," she said, telling him the truth, but not the whole truth. It wasn't what she should be telling him, and she knew it.

"You sure it's not something more? You know you can tell me anything. I—"

"I just want this to be over. They're coming after people who matter to me. It needs to end."

"And it will. It's almost over, babe." He crouched beside the open car door and gave her knee a gentle squeeze. "You have to trust me to take care of this, okay? You take care of yourself, Cherry, Libby, and the kids, and I'll deal with Costello and his crew. I need you to promise me that your involvement in this is done, Shay. I'm not fooling around."

"I know. I know." She nodded, her words strained as she struggled to keep from blurting out the truth. She had to know what she was dealing with first. She'd tell him, she promised herself. She would. She'd tell him once she got the lay of the land.

He curved his hand around her neck and drew her mouth to his. "I love you," he said as he brushed his lips over hers. "Trust me to have your back and Charlie's. I won't let you down. I'll never let you down again."

The only person who could save her uncle was her. She knew the minds of criminals better than Michael did, better than his colleagues did. She should; she'd been one. And in her heart, she knew that's who she would always be.

"I love you," she whispered, her throat thick with unshed tears. She hated the tears, hated that he'd broken down her walls and found the woman she might've been. They'd done this to her. All of them: Michael, her uncle, Cherry, Teddy, Gabby, and Libby. They made her soft and vulnerable. They made her weak. She pulled back. "I've gotta go."

"I'll see you tonight, right?"

No. "Yeah."

Chapter Twenty-One

♥

Michael stood in the parking lot, hands in the pockets of his black coat as he watched Shay's taillights disappear from view. It felt like the last time, only then she'd driven away in *his* car and not her own. He hadn't been awake or been given the opportunity to kiss her goodbye or beg her to stay. She probably wondered what was going on, wondered when he'd turned into a needy guy, pretty much begging her to stay. The thing was, he hadn't been able to shake the feeling that something was going down today and they'd end up in the same place they had ten years before.

Moments ago, he'd discovered he hadn't been wrong. The sense of impending doom that had been hanging over him all morning, the worry he assumed was because of their past, had proven not to be misplaced anxiety after all.

He'd seen the phone on the passenger seat of her car, caught a glimpse of Charlie's photo when she picked up the cell. Michael had given her plenty of opportunity to come clean. It didn't take a genius to know why he hadn't confronted her. He was afraid he knew what her answer would be. That was the problem with knowing the woman he loved as well as he knew himself.

He raised his right hand, rubbing his fingers over his chest in an attempt to soothe the burning ache. With his other hand, he felt around in his pocket for the antacids he always carried with him and realized he hadn't replaced the empty pack last week. He hadn't needed them since Shay came back in his life.

"Michael." He turned to see Jim, the gas station owner, waving him over. "Landline's working. The boys say cell service is back online too."

Michael wondered if Shay knew. Even now was she on the phone to Costello? Torn between wanting to do his job and wanting to protect her, Michael tightened his fingers around the phone in his pocket.

"Dammit, Shay," he muttered, his anger a living, breathing thing. How did she not get that he'd open a vein for her? God knew it felt like she'd opened one in him, that he was bleeding out right here in the parking lot.

He knew the moment he asked if he'd see her tonight that she was lying to him. She'd made her decision. He wasn't going to see her again. And if he did, odds were she'd either be dead, lying in a hospital bed, or on the other side of a two-way mirror.

* * *

"What are you doing here?" Cherry said. "If we saw the lights, so will Costello's men. Come on, you have to get out of here." She strode across Shay's bedroom and grabbed her arm.

"Trust me, they're not going to come looking for me. You should go, though. It's safer for you to stay with Libby and the kids until this is over." Unable to look at the other woman, Shay shook her arm free to finish stuffing her clothes in her knapsack.

Cherry sat on the edge of the bed, reaching up to brush Shay's hair over her shoulder. She gasped. "You've been crying. What is it? What happened?"

She rubbed her face. "No, I haven't been crying. I just…There's things going on I can't talk to you about. I've gotta get out of—"

"What things? I'm your BFF. You can't not talk to me about things. You have to tell me everything. And why are you packing?" She shot off the bed and got in Shay's face. "Stop and talk, because this right here"— she circled Shay's knapsack with her finger—"this is not happening. You are not running because things get hard."

A harsh laugh scraped from Shay's throat. "Me? Run when things get hard? Who took care of the Sterlings? Who took care of you in the alley that night, of Ace and his gang? I don't run when things get tough, Cherry. I stay and fight."

"That's not the things I'm talking about. I'm talking about the things that *you* have a hard time dealing with. Like letting people help you, letting people love you and care about you. Real important stuff like letting yourself be vulnerable and leaning on someone else for a change. Trusting that we will do our best to never let you down. We're not going anywhere, Shay. No one can make us leave you."

"Don't. I can't deal with this right now, Cherry."

"You have no choice. You are going to screw up the best—"

"They've got Charlie! They've got my uncle, and they've beaten the crap out of him." She grabbed the phone off her bed. "Look for yourself. It's all there in Technicolor and Dolby sound. Every last punch and kick, him screaming and begging for them to stop. Him calling out for..." She sat on the edge of the bed and drew her hand across her leaking eyes and nose. "They want a trade, me for him, and that's...that's what I'm doing."

Once they had her, she was fairly certain they'd use her to get Michael to revoke Luigi's immunity. Without Luigi's testimony, they didn't have enough to put Costello away. Sooner or later, the FBI would get the evidence they needed. Only it wouldn't be soon enough for her uncle.

"No, you can't." Cherry knelt on the floor in front of her, tears rolling down her face. "You and me, we know men like Costello. They're not going to let you go, and they won't let Charlie go either. Whatever they promised you is a lie."

"I have to try. He has to know that I tried. I won't let him think I abandoned him. I won't let him die by himself. I won't."

"We'll call Michael. He'll know what to do. They

can look at the video. They'll see things we don't. They'll find him."

"I can't. I can't take the risk. They told me they'll kill Charlie if I go to the FBI or police. They threatened Michael. They threatened everyone...everyone that I love," she said, feeling the anger rise up inside her. It was a relief. For the past two hours, all she'd felt was helpless and alone.

"They won't know. I can go talk to Michael. No one will suspect a thing. Or we can go to his brother Logan. He's still in town. Or his cousin Aidan, the detective at HHPD, we can talk to him."

"She can't talk to anyone. They'll know. They've got people on the inside." They turned to see Libby leaning against the doorjamb.

"You can't know—" Cherry began before Shay cut her off.

"Yes, she does. And she knows where they have Charlie, don't you, Libby? It's Benji, isn't it? He called you," she said, referring to the bouncer with the crew cut at Pussy Cat East.

She gave a quick nod, anxiously twisting her hands. "I swear to you, he had no idea what was going on, Shay. He wants no part of it."

"Then tell him to go to the cops or the FBI," Cherry challenged.

"They'll kill him. Now that Luigi has agreed to turn state's evidence, they're desperate. They have nothing to lose." She looked at Shay. "Will you help him? When you go get Charlie, can you get him out too? I'll go with you. I'll do whatever you tell me to."

They all froze when Shay's cell phone rang. She closed her eyes. It was Michael. She waited until the call went to voice mail and picked it up, torn between wanting to hear his voice and not wanting to hear what he said.

"You should listen to his message. Maybe he's called to tell you they know where Charlie is," Cherry said.

Or maybe he was going to tell her how much he loved her again and reassure her that this would be over soon, that they'd finally get the happily-ever-after they deserved. He didn't know that Shay and Charlie didn't get happily-ever-afters. "I can't."

Cherry picked up the phone, putting his message on speaker before Shay could stop her. When Michael's deep voice came over the line, she couldn't bring herself to end the call.

"Shay, I'm putting my job on the line telling you this. I saw the cell phone and the photo of Charlie in your car so I know that you've most likely been in contact with Costello or his men by now. We know they have him, and we will find him. Let us do our job. If you get involved in any way, you're going to make it harder for me to protect you from prosecution. At the very least, they will charge you with obstruction."

He paused and drew in a ragged breath, his voice quieter, the frustration and anger clearly audible when next he spoke. "They got to Luigi, Shay. He's dead. He can't back your story. There's evidence that puts you at Two Face's apartment along with what they planted. I love—"

Cherry took the phone off speaker and handed it to

Shay. She brought the phone to her ear. "—you. I honestly don't think you have any idea how much. But I can't keep doing this. You either trust me or you don't. And I can't be with a woman who doesn't. A woman who won't open up to me and let me in. So if you go after him on your own, we're done. Don't do it, babe. Don't do it to—"

The phone beeped, cutting him off. The message had gone on too long, but it was clear enough. They were over.

"What are you going to do?" Cherry looked resigned as she asked the question, as if she already knew. Libby looked anxious yet hopeful. Both women knew her. Michael did too. He knew what she was going to do, which meant he'd have someone watching her.

There was a knock at the front door, and the two women jumped. Shay started down the hall. "Relax. They're not coming to get me. I've already arranged the meet."

Cherry and Libby followed her. "But what about Benji?" Libby asked.

"I'll do what I can. You should go home, be with your girls."

"I don't want them around until this is over. After what happened at the manor today, I'm not taking any chances. They're staying with a friend in Rhode Island."

"Good call," Shay said as she opened the door. "Jasper, hi."

"Miss, may I come in? Hello, ladies," he said as Shay

opened the door wide, and he stepped inside. His gaze moved over the three of them. "Have I come at a bad time?"

Before Shay could stop her, Cherry threw herself into Jasper's arms and cried all over his overcoat, spilling her guts and Shay's secrets. Shay bowed her head and shut the door, preparing for Jasper to make his disapproval known and try to change her mind. Because even though she'd barely had any time at all, Cherry managed to cover pretty much everything. Including—and for someone who hadn't heard the rest of the call, she'd done a good job connecting the dots—that if Shay capitulated to Costello's demands, her relationship with Michael was over.

"There, there, miss." Jasper patted Cherry's back and guided her to a chair in the living room. No sooner had he gotten her settled then Libby threw herself at him and blubbered Benji's sorry tale.

Shay sighed and walked over to the couch. She stretched out and covered her eyes with her arm, listening to Jasper comfort Libby. There was a part of Shay, one that she didn't want to acknowledge, that wished someone would comfort her like that. But what was there to say? She could only see one way for this to end.

She'd either get her uncle out of this alive or they'd both be dead before the night was over. Whatever happened, their life here was over. They couldn't stay in Harmony Harbor. The mob would always be after them. They'd have to go into hiding.

In the limited time that she'd had, Shay had prepared

as best she could. She wasn't sure if they'd stand up in court, but she'd drawn up papers leaving the house to Cherry and the management of the Salty Dog to Cherry and Libby. The car was packed and gassed, and Shay had close to eighty grand on hand.

The first thing she'd done after talking to Costello was pawn the Harry Winston Belle engagement ring. She'd felt naked without it hanging close to her heart. It seemed silly after Michael had told her he never would have chosen the ring for her; still, it had felt like she carried something of him with her.

She fingered the ring that now hung around her neck. She wondered if he'd ever know she was the one who'd taken it. She'd stopped by the cottage on her way back from the pawnshop. She'd only meant to take something small, maybe a cuff link or an old school ring, just a tiny memento to wear close to her heart. And then she saw it. The ring his great-grandmother had given him. The one he'd talked about that night. He'd said it was meant for her. She didn't want him to give it to anyone else.

"Shaybae, Jasper asked you a question."

She raised her arm. "Sorry, I must've been out of it. What was it that you asked, Jasper?"

"How long do we have before Costello is expecting you to turn yourself over?"

She frowned and sat up, a niggle of worry scratching at her mind when she caught Cherry's and Libby's expressions. They looked...relieved. Maybe even a little gleeful. "Why?"

Cherry pressed her hands together, prayer-like. "Be-

cause Jasper has a plan. We're going to get Charlie and
Benji out of there without anyone the wiser and without you risking your life. And if no one's the wiser,
that means Michael will never know you broke your
promise to him."

"Yes to all of the above but the last. I highly recom-
mend you tell Master Michael the truth, miss. Over the
years, I've learned it has a way of coming out. Speaking of which"—he reached in his coat and pulled out a
folded piece of paper—"as you will see, Madame tried
to make amends." He handed it to her.

She looked up after reading the paper. It seemed
like maybe she owed Michael's great-grandmother an
apology and her thanks. She'd been trying to help.
And as Shay knew, no matter how well intentioned,
sometimes when you intervened, things went bad.
"Thank you for this and for your offer to help, but
I don't want to put anyone else in danger. I do have
a plan. I'm not going in there intending to sacrifice
myself for Charlie."

"I'm glad to hear it. But I'm afraid you're outvoted.
This is not just about you and Charlie anymore. This is
about our town, my home, and my family. They tried to
kill Master Michael, they came to the manor and put the
people I love in harm's way. I won't let them get away
with it."

* * *

They were dressed in black from head to toe with cam-
ouflage stripes on their faces. Cherry had added the

stripes on the way to Pussy Cat East. It was a little hard to escape her when they were seat-belted in.

"Benji left the delivery door open. It leads through the kitchen. As soon as I send him the coded text, he'll make sure it's empty. Once we're in, he'll text us to let us know the best way to reach Charlie. He says they're moving him, but he was still in Kozack's office ten minutes ago."

They crouched in the woods behind the club. Pussy Cat East was closed because of the blizzard. At least that was the excuse they were using. There were two black vans in the lot, as well as a familiar Mercedes and Navigator. Shay handed Cherry and Libby the Tasers. Shay didn't plan on letting them close to anyone or letting anyone close to them, but if things went south, she didn't want them defenseless either.

"Be careful with those things; they're not toys. And remember, the first thing you grab is their gun, then shove the gag in their mouth and zip tie their hands like we practiced," she whispered, repeating the same instructions she'd given them at least five times before, only this time she didn't demonstrate on their prone bodies.

Jasper's head jerked up at the same time she heard the men's voices. They were shooting the breeze while sharing a joint. Fifty more feet and they'd see them. They walked over to the Mercedes, checking out something on the vehicle. Shay glanced at Jasper. He nodded. Go time.

Jasper was as quiet and as fast as she was. As they approached, the moon peeked from behind a cloud, and one of the men caught their reflection in the glass. Shay rushed forward to give him a roundhouse kick to the head. He staggered but didn't go down. A one-two punch to his face took care of that. She caught him before he hit the ground, lowering him carefully. As she gagged and zip tied him, she smiled at Jasper, who was doing the same to his man. "Nice ax kick."

"Excellent roundhouse."

From behind them came a guttural laugh. "Yeah, real nice, Bruce Lee and Jackie Chan. Now stand up and come with— *Ah-ah-ah*." His body spasmed as he fell to the ground.

Cherry and Libby stood over him arguing. "I said I was going to do it."

"No, I did."

"Weapon, gag, zip tie," Shay reminded them.

"Then trunk," Jasper added.

It took them ten minutes just to roll the men in the trunks of the Navigator and Mercedes, and then Shay and Jasper had to put two more men out of commission at the loading dock. Shay didn't want to say anything to Libby, but she was worried that either Benji was a plant or he'd been found out. Her concerns were proven wrong when he met them in the empty kitchen. And then he proved what Shay had believed from the first night they met correct. Benji was in love with Libby.

"Libby, what are you doing here?" He rounded on Shay. "Why did you bring her? She's a mother with two kids."

"Yeah, two kids who were in that room when

Costello's men came to the manor. It's not right, Benji. What they're doing isn't right," Libby said.

"Look, Benji, I know you're worried about her. But trust me, Libby can hold her own. Now we're wasting time. Is Charlie still in Kozack's office?"

"Yeah." He wouldn't meet her eyes.

"What is it?" Afraid to ask the question that was on the tip of her tongue.

"He's alive, but Costello and two of his men are in there. They've been working him over. It's not pretty."

Three men. She could take three men no problem.

"Shay." A hand on her arm stopped her forward motion. "Remember the plan. We go together. We draw them out one at a time," Jasper said.

Benji stood out in the hall as they made their way to the dressing rooms. They didn't run into anyone. Jasper ducked into the changing room closest to the back stairs and pushed over a mirror. As it crashed to the floor, they got in position. Overhead, they heard the sound of the office door opening, and then one of Costello's men banged down the stairs. "What the hell?" he said upon entering the dressing room.

He noticed Shay just before she slammed a fist into his face. She sighed when he went down. She needed someone to put up a fight. The next man they drew out of the office went down just as easy.

But five minutes later when she kicked in the door of Kozack's office, she got her wish. Benji had miscounted. Kozack, Costello, and two other men were in the office. One of the men had a gun to her uncle's

head. From behind her, a bullet whizzed past. The
man who held the gun on Charlie let out a shocked
cry and dropped to the floor, dead. Then—*bang!*—so
was the other man who went to take his place. She
hadn't taken the shot, either one. She turned, trying
to come to terms with what had just happened. From
somewhere in the club, she heard yelling and a stam-
pede of booted feet.

Costello swore. "Don't even think about moving,"
she said, holding her gun on him as she moved to her
uncle's side.

"Ah, ah, ah." Kozack jerked as he crumpled to the
ground, the gun in his hand going off. The bullet hit
Costello, and he toppled over, bringing down a table
with him.

FBI agents poured into the room, weapons drawn.
"On the floor. Now."

Shay looked around as she slowly lowered herself
to the floor, relieved. Jasper was nowhere to be found.
"They had nothing to do with it. He's a bouncer, and
they're dancers. All they're guilty of is trying to help
my uncle. It's all on me, no one else."

* * *

Without looking at Shay, Michael nodded at his brother
Connor and left the interrogation room at FBI headquarters. Connor pulled out the chair and sat beside her at
the table. His brilliant white smile was more flash than
reassurance. Though the warmth and compassion in his
eyes made up for it.

Michael's gaze had been condemning and Arctic cold. He'd looked right through her. She still felt the chill deep down in her bones. She wished there was something she could say that would make him understand. But she wasn't sure she completely understood why she hadn't been able to find another way herself. Why she'd destroyed the best thing that had ever happened to her.

She glanced at the mirror across from her, wondering if Michael stood behind it. She rubbed her nails, focusing on cleaning off specks of her uncle's blood. She didn't want to hear what Michael's brother and the two agents were saying about the charges. If she did, she was afraid she wouldn't be able to hide her fear at the thought of being locked away again.

She swallowed the bile that burned her throat, blinking back the moisture gathering in her eyes to refocus on her hands. They were sweaty, yet she was shivering. The reaction struck her as odd. The room was hot, not cold. She wondered if they'd turned up the heat to purposely make her sweat. No, she was sweating because, no matter how much she tried to pretend she didn't hear them, she did. Ten years to life? Had she heard that right? The room started to spin.

The glass on the opposite wall shuddered, and moments later, Michael strode into the room. He threw his badge on the table, pushed back his jacket, and withdrew his gun from the holster, laying it alongside his shield. "Let the record show I'm taking over as Ms. Angel's attorney."

"Are you kidding me? You got me to come down

here at two in the morning to represent Shay, and now you're firing me?"

"You were going to plead her out. She's innocent. And the only deal we're taking is one that clears her of all charges. A commendation for bravery for her role in saving my life and my partner's might be nice too."

Chapter Twenty-Two

♥

The vibrations of the cell phone on the arm of the chair sounded overly loud in the quiet of her uncle's hospital room at North Shore General. Shay didn't need to look at the screen to know who it was; she'd been expecting his call. Michael's meeting with the FBI's lawyers and his former boss took place that morning. His goal was to save her from going to trial.

She picked up the phone, a noticeable tremble in her fingers, and bowed her head. Taking a deep breath, she forced her lips to curve in the hope that's what he'd hear in her voice, a hopeful smile and not fear. "How did it go?"

Hi. She should've opened with *hi.* Told him she missed him, told him how sorry she was that this was how they ended up. Begged him to let her make it up to him, to give her a second chance.

"Better than I'd hoped. It's over, Shay. You've been cleared of all charges." His smooth, deep voice was as sexy as ever, but it no longer felt like his strong, elegant fingers were reaching through the phone line to touch and caress her. There was an underlying coolness in his voice, a chilly politeness that said his walls were up and she didn't stand a chance of getting through them.

Which might've been why she wasn't cheering at the top of her lungs and dancing around the room at his life-altering news. "I don't know what to say, Michael. Thank you doesn't begin to cover what I owe you. I—"

He cleared his throat. "It's the least I could do. You saved my life, and my partner's. I'm sorry I couldn't get them to budge on the commendation."

"It doesn't matter. All I care about is . . ." The *you* got stuck in her throat. He didn't want to hear it, and she didn't think she could take him telling her that today of all days. ". . . that you're alive. I wish you'd let me pay you. Or take you out for—"

"It's not necessary. I have to go. Take care of yourself, Shay."

"Michael, I—" She stared at the buzzing phone. She hadn't needed millions of dollars or influence and power after all. Michael had been her get-out-of-jail-free card. And he'd paid a steep price. One she could never repay, nor, as he'd just proven, would he let her try. She'd paid a price too. He'd obviously meant what he'd said the other night. They were done.

Sounding like he was in pain, her uncle grunted and batted at the covers. He'd been in and out of consciousness for the past few days. The doctors were hopeful he'd make a full recovery, though. Despite his age and his bad habits, the man had the constitution of a horse.

His eyelids fluttered open. "Shay," he said, his voice gravelly and weak.

There was an alertness in his blue gaze that hadn't been there for days. "It's me, Uncle Charlie. You're in the hospital, but you're going to be fine."

"Costello? Kozack?"

"They won't hurt you or anyone else anymore. They're in jail. Well, Costello will be once he's released from the hospital. Kozack accidently shot him."

"Ha! Good on the bastard." He pushed himself up and grimaced.

"Here, let me help you."

He waved her off. "I've got it. I'm not an invalid, you—" He gasped in pain as he reached back for a pillow.

"You're a stubborn old man, you know that? You have to start letting people help you." She huffed a silent laugh. She was one to talk. It was obvious who she'd picked up that particular trait from. Lucky for her, Jasper, Cherry, and Libby had been as stubborn as she was. And Michael . . . She gave her head a slight shake, pushing thoughts of him away. Charlie was going to be okay, and she'd be here to take care of him and not in jail. She had to focus on that.

Gently, she slid an arm behind her uncle's back while sliding another pillow into place. "How did you get involved in all of it?" she asked as she eased him onto the pillows, carefully fluffing them.

"Danny's uncle Sal. Tony introduced us years before Sal was put away. We used to play cards. When Danny started making a run on the bars in town, I went to see Sal. It was a you-scratch-my-back-I'll-scratch-yours kind of deal. But then Costello had Tony killed. I wasn't going to let him get away with it. I knew Eddie and Freddie too. I tried to warn them, but I was too late."

"How did Costello's men finally catch you?"

"You were on their radar. I wanted to warn you. I came home. They must have been looking for you and caught me instead."

"Next time, call me."

"I tried. I got a new phone, forgot to transfer your number from the old one, and couldn't remember it. I tried your place in Vegas and your office. I left messages." He rubbed his eyes and tried to hide a yawn.

"We'll talk some more later. Right now you need your rest. Do you want some water?"

He nodded. She held the cup for him. He took a few sips from the straw and then leaned back against the pillows, clearly exhausted. "What about the other two, the two that did this to me? They were going to shoot me, you know. Just before you got there."

She put the cup down on the bed tray. "I didn't think you knew I was there."

He moved his hand. "I was in and out. Memories are a bit fuzzy. Know you didn't shoot them, though. I saw a man, behind you. He was the one who shot them."

The only man behind her had been Jasper. She hadn't been a hundred percent certain it was him, but Charlie just confirmed what she'd suspected. So the older man wasn't just proficient in martial arts; he was an expert marksman as well. The shots were too difficult and too accurate for him not to be. "I don't know who it was, but I'm grateful to them."

"Could've sworn it was Jasper."

"From Greystone Manor?" she asked, playing stupid.

He grunted, his voice almost a snarl. "They owe us. The whole lot of them owe us. And not only for what they did to you all those years ago. They stole your sisters from us too. Surprised, are you? So was I. I found out just before the Costello thing blew up in my face. The old lady, Colleen, she called social services on us. But we can find your sisters now. I have their—"

She'd ignore his comment about her sisters. If he pushed, she'd pretend she couldn't find them. He'd eventually give up. If he didn't, she'd have no choice but to tell him the truth. She wouldn't let him hear it from her sisters.

"Uncle Charlie, the Gallaghers don't owe us anymore. They've more than paid their debt." She wished she could confirm it was Jasper who'd saved his life— twice—but didn't think that was her story to tell. Instead, she told her uncle that Colleen was the reason she'd been allowed to return to his care all those years ago, and how Michael's cousins and older brother had taken shifts keeping an eye on the house and the pub, how Michael had given up his job to defend her and had saved her from going to prison again.

"I've spent a good long while nursing my hatred of the Gallaghers. It won't be easy letting it go. I knew Michael was a good one, though."

"Uh-huh, that's why you tried to shoot him the Christmas before last."

"I was just having some fun. We worked things out; · you know that. Where is he? I want to thank him for

looking out for my girl." He gave a gravelly laugh.
"Guess you're his girl now. That mean you'll be sticking around?"

"I'll always be your girl, Uncle Charlie." She kissed
his grizzled cheek. "Now rest. I have to check on...the
pub." She eliminated *the Valentine's Day setup* from
the sentence. She didn't want to give him a coronary on
top of his other injuries.

* * *

"Thanks for coming, Victoria. I appreciate you making
a house call." Michael held open the door to the cottage
for the attractive blond veterinarian.

"Anytime. I'm just sorry to be the bearer of bad
news. But trust me, in no time at all he'll adjust to the
loss of both his vision and hearing. So will you. I'll send
you some links to articles you might find helpful," she
offered, and then gave him a self-deprecating smile. "I
guess I better go change for the auction. I don't know
who'd be more disappointed if I showed up looking like
this, my mother or yours."

He tried to hold back a grimace but must not have
been successful at hiding his feelings because Victoria
laughed. "Just keep reminding yourself it's for a good
cause. That's what I do." She gave his arm a commiserating pat. "Don't worry. With both our mothers'
financial backing, there's no way anyone can afford to
outbid me, so you're safe. We'll come back here, order Chinese, hang out with Atticus, and then we'll call
it a night. If you want, we can pretend we're dating for

a month to make them happy and then have a friendly breakup."

"Wait, so you don't want to marry me?"

She didn't even try to hide her distaste at the suggestion. "No, I'm in a relationship. My partner would kill me if she knew what I was doing, but you understand, don't you? Your mother's just like mine."

After the particularly crappy few days he'd had, it looked like things might be turning around. First, getting Shay cleared of the charges, and now this. "Listen, if someone outbids you, and your mother and mine fold, keep bidding. I'll cover it."

"Perfect." Her brow furrowed. "You're a great guy. If I was straight, I would totally be willing to spend half my trust fund to hook up with you. How is it that you're still available?"

"Thanks, and it's a long story."

"And not a happy one by the looks of you. I'm sorry, and I was sorry to hear about your mom too. I hope it's not as serious as she—"

Okay, that didn't sound like she was talking about his parents splitting up. "I'm not sure I know what you mean. Are you talking about my parents—"

She got an *oh, crap* look on her face. "Yes, of course that's what I was talking about. Hopefully it'll all work out. I better run. See you at the auction!" She hurried to her truck.

Logan ran up the path beside the cottage. Jogging on the spot, he checked his pulse while returning Victoria's wave. "She left in a hurry. What did you say to scare her away?"

"It's not what I said, it's what she said. Is there something going on with Mom that I don't know about?"

Logan shrugged. "She's been pretty happy the past few days on account of you resigning from the FBI, and she was even happier to learn you and Shay are done. But she's acting weird this morning. She asked Jasper to move her out of the tower room. She said something about it being haunted and that she didn't get any sleep last night."

"None of that sounds like what Victoria was talking about. Are you staying out here or coming inside?"

"Are you in a better mood than you have been for the past few days?"

"The auction is in three hours, so what do you think?"

"I'll pass on the invite. But as your big brother, I'm going to give you a word of advice—get your head out of your ass and talk to Shay. Anyone can see that you love her. Why torture yourself? And us."

"You're right, I do. I'll never love anyone like I love Shay. It wouldn't be easy, but if she asked, I eventually would've forgiven her for not listening to me and rescuing her uncle and putting herself at risk because that's who she is. Her bravery and her strength, they're just two of the many reasons I love her. But she didn't ask. She's always the one to walk away. I've finally realized I love her more than she loves me."

"Did you ever think she just has a hard time showing it? She hasn't exactly had great role models in her life."

"I've thought of that. But if she really loved me, she

would've put up a fight. She fights for everyone else, just not us."

"You know what, you're right. You deserve some-one who will fight as hard for you as you fought for her. I hope you find that someone, baby bro. But don't worry if you don't. I'm sure Mom will."

"I know you and Connor think this whole matchmak-ing thing is hilarious, but just wait until she sets her sights on one of you."

"The way things are looking, we're safe for at least another year."

* * *

It looked like Cupid had taken over the Salty Dog. There wasn't an inch of the bar that hadn't been pinki-fied, glitterfied, or heartified. Including the topless bar-tender who wore a bow tie with sparkly red hearts. "Gerry, would you put on a shirt, please?"

"Sorry, no can do. The boss says this is tonight's uniform. For the men at least," he said, shaking the cocktail maker in time to Bruno Mars's "Just the Way You Are."

"Gerry, I am the boss."

"Sure, you are. How about a Valentini?"

She opened her mouth and then closed it. Some-where in the bar Cherry was calling, "Next!" Shay fol-lowed the sound of her voice and then wished she hadn't. There was a row of shirtless older men, several of whom were friends of her uncle waiting in line. "What do you think you're doing?" she asked when she reached Cherry, who was at that moment spraying Shay's uncle's best friend with a fake tan.

Cherry leaned back on the sky-high heels of her boots to whisper, "They're not what you'd call buff, so I thought I'd give them a little help. Everything looks better tanned."

"No, everything would look better covered up. With a shirt. Don," she said to her uncle's best friend. "Put that phone down now. No pictures, do you hear me? That goes for all of you. If Charlie hears about this from anyone, you'll answer to me."

"Why don't you go have a pink champagne Jell-O shot or try one of the desserts from Truly Scrumptious? The cherry chocolate chip brownies are to die for, and they'll put you in a better mood," Cherry said.

"The red velvet blossoms are real good too," Don said.

"So is the sweetheart martini."

"We are going to make a killing tonight, Shaybae. Just you wait and see. Oh, you're on at seven."

"On what? Behind the bar, you mean?"

"No, Libby's working the bar with Gerry. You're working the pole."

Several of the men sounded like they were choking, and two of them were definitely laughing.

"She's joking," Shay said to the men in line, and under her breath to Cherry, "Please tell me you're not advertising that there'll be strippers performing tonight."

"Exotic dancers," she corrected while continuing to spray Don, and then she looked toward the door and her mouth fell open. She turned to Shay and nailed her with the spray tan. "Sorry, sorry," she blurted, distractedly wiping at the front of Shay's white shirt. "Finn's wife is here. Do you think she heard about him locking me in the examination room with him?"

The line of men turned to look at the attractive and very obviously pregnant blonde, who entered the bar with two other women. "He didn't. They weren't locked in the examination room together. She's joking. Tell them you're joking," Shay said to Cherry.

"I'm joking." She tugged on Shay's arm. "They're coming this way, and Kitty Gallagher and Rosa DiRossi just arrived too."

Shay didn't get a chance to respond or to wonder what was going on. "Shay, I'm Olivia Gallagher." The blonde extended her hand with a warm smile. "And you probably know my sisters-in-law Ava and Sophie." She gestured to the attractive dark-haired women, who Shay remembered from growing up in Harmony Harbor.

"Hi, yeah, I do." She smiled at Ava and Sophie and shook Olivia's hand. "Nice to meet you. This is my friend Cherry."

They'd just finished the introductions when Kitty and Rosa reached them and took Shay by either arm. "You can't have her, she's ours."

"I'm your what?"

"Our golden ticket," Rosa said.

"*Nonna*, she has no idea what you're talking about," Sophie said to her grandmother before looking at Shay. "The Widows Club has a bet on tonight's auction. They've all sponsored candidates, and if theirs wins the date with Michael, they win the bet."

"No, well, yes, but there's much more at stake than two hundred dollars—that's the prize for our candidate winning," Kitty explained to Shay. "What we want is the grand prize, the title of Matchmaker of the Year."

"Nice. Okay. I wish I could help you out but—"

Cherry cut off Shay. "How do you win the title?"

"Michael has to not only go on a date with your candidate, but he also has to marry her."

"You better pick someone else if you want to win," Shay said. The bar had suddenly gotten hot and her heart was beating a little too fast. She couldn't think of Michael dating someone else, let alone marrying them, without feeling like she was going to throw up.

"But we thought you loved him?" Michael's grandmother said, looking confused.

"She does, and she's now officially your candidate," Cherry said to Kitty and Rosa, handing Don the spray tan and shooing the older men on their way.

"Our candidate," Olivia corrected. "That's why we're here."

"No, we're here because our husbands and Logan sent us. They want you to put Michael out of his misery," Sophie said.

"I wish I could help. I really do. But Michael made it clear we were over. He doesn't want me anymore. If you don't believe me, ask him yourself."

"What about you? Do you love him?"

* * *

"Ms. Angel, this is a surprise," Jasper said from where he stood at the entrance to the tastefully decorated ballroom wearing a black suit. Unlike the Salty Dog, it was the audience that provided the color and glitter.

"I know. I'm surprised too." She looked behind her. "I seemed to have lost my entourage. Do you know what I'm supposed to do?"

He held out his arm. "I'd be delighted to escort you to a seat. The festivities have already begun, but lucky for you, I have one available at the front. And may I say you look beautiful tonight."

"Really? I was afraid to look in the mirror." She glanced down at the body-hugging, low-cut red dress and black heels with red bottoms that she wore.

As soon as she'd agreed to come, the women dragged her down the street to Tie the Knot, where Jenna and Arianna awaited her. While Cherry did her hair and makeup, the other women hunted for her outfit, and Jenna gave her a pep talk. Her childhood best friend assured Shay that Michael was her one, which Shay knew. At least she knew he was hers. In a matter of minutes, she'd know if she was his.

"Trust me, you do," Jasper assured her over the women who started clapping and cheering. Several stood up and whistled. "And I believe I'm not the only one who thinks so." He smiled and lifted his chin at the stage.

She'd avoided looking in that direction. From the women's reactions, she knew Michael was there. As soon as she saw his face, she'd know. She'd never been more terrified to look at someone in her life. At Jasper's careful nudge, she slowly lifted her gaze.

No wonder the women were going nuts, was her first thought. Michael looked like he belonged on the cover of *People* magazine's Sexiest Man Alive issue. He wore a black tux that fit his tall, well-built frame to perfection. The collar of the white shirt unbuttoned, his hands resting loosely in the pockets of his pants, he was the picture of easy elegance and supreme confidence.

She raised her eyes to a face that had inspired her to dream of a life bigger than the one she'd thought she deserved. Michael's impossibly blue eyes locked with hers, and she held her breath for so long the room began to spin. And then his eyes filled with an emotion that took away her breath and her fears, and she sagged against Jasper. She'd never been more relieved in her life. Or at least she had been until she caught a glimpse of Michael's mother to the right of the stage.

"Don't worry, miss. I have it on good authority Maura has seen the light."

Shay didn't have time to contemplate Jasper's comment. He settled her in a chair in the front row beside an attractive blonde.

The woman smiled and offered her hand. "Victoria." She leaned in to whisper, "I saw the way you two just looked at each other so I want you to know, if I didn't have to do this, I wouldn't. No hard feelings, but Michael and I have an understanding. For tonight and the next month, he's mine, and then he's all yours."

Stunned, Shay was still staring openmouthed at the blonde when the bidding began, which meant by the time she recovered from her shock, the bidding was already at twenty grand. Twenty grand? Were they flipping insane?

"All right, ladies, let's open our pocketbooks a little wider," the auctioneer said. "Remember, not only do you get a *night* with our delectable bachelor, the money raised here tonight goes to Michael's favorite charities. Second Chance Inc., an organization that helps to reintegrate ex-convicts back into society, and the Steppingstone Foundation, which provides programs for underserved students so that they have a better chance of going to college."

Shay didn't think she could love Michael any more, but upon hearing that he supported Second Chance Inc., she jumped to her feet. "Eighty thousand dollars."

She had a moment of satisfaction when the women around her fell quiet in shock. However, Michael's mother ensured Shay's satisfaction didn't last any longer than a moment.

Maura Gallagher grabbed a paddle and shot to her feet. "A hundred thousand dollars."

"For God's sake, Mom, you can't buy a date with me. I'm your son."

She held up a finger to silence him and walked to Shay. "Do you love my son?"

"Do you think I'd be standing here, looking like this"—she gestured at her outfit, made-up face, and out-to-there hair—"and offering to spend eighty thousand dollars just to get five minutes alone with him if I didn't?"

Maura gave her a pointed stare.

Shay sighed. Obviously, the only way to satisfy

Michael's mother was for Shay to bare her soul right here in front of half of Harmony Harbor. "I've never loved anyone as much as I love your son, and I never will. I've spent the last ten years trying to make something of myself, trying to be someone who deserved someone like him. I know in your eyes, I never will be—"

She hadn't realized Michael had come down off the stage until he took her hands in his. "You have been and will always be the best woman for me. I don't care what anyone else thinks. You're it for me." He looked at his mother. "I love you, Mom. But don't make me choose between you and Shay because I'll choose her. Every single time."

"I wasn't planning to make you choose, Michael. But I am your mother, and I want you to be with someone who loves you even more than I do. I believe you do, Shay, so you can have my date with my son. And while I know it can never be enough, as an apology for the pain I caused you all those years ago, I will be making out the check to Second Chance Inc. in your name. I hope it will go to someone who has shown the same strength and commitment as you have into turning your life around."

Shay offered Michael's mother her hand. "Thank you."

Kitty stood up. "Michael, darling, I don't want to rush you, but you are eventually going to ask Shay to marry you, aren't you?"

"Yes, Grams, I am. Would you like me to do it now?"

"Yes, please. We have a title on the line, you see."

Michael looked down at Shay. "If I leave for a minute to get your ring, you promise to be here when I get back?"

"They'd have to drag me away. But you don't have to leave," she said, self-consciously tugging the chain from under her dress. "I, um, pawned the other ring you gave me, and I wanted something of you with me when I left town, so I kind of took this." She held up his great-grandmother's ring. "You did say you were going to give it to me..."

He went down on bended knee. "Shay Angel, you didn't need a piece of me. You've always had all of me."

Olivia Davenport has finally gotten her life back together. But her past catches up to her when Olivia learns that she's now guardian of her ex's young daughter. With her world spinning, she doesn't have time for her new next door neighbor, no matter how handsome he is.

An excerpt from *Primrose Lane* follows.

Available now

Finn Gallagher stood on the garden path calling after the willowy redhead running after his dog. "Dana, don't chase him! He thinks you want to play!"

If he wasn't concerned about Miller getting lost in the woods because some crazy woman wouldn't listen, Finn might take the time to figure out what it said about Dana Templeton that she was gardening in a pink shirt and a pair of khaki slacks stuffed into beige rubber boots decorated with pink flowers. He thought it was seriously weird that someone coordinated their wardrobe to dig in the dirt.

She whipped around, the pink floppy hat falling off her head. If he didn't know better, it appeared her shoulder-length red hair was about to do the same.

"You don't understand. He has my gardening gloves!"

"Good God, woman, I'll buy you another pair! Just stop running after him." He blew out an annoyed breath when she ignored him and continued to sprint down the path. He didn't know what ticked him off more—that she wouldn't listen to him or that he now had to chase after her and his dog.

"It's okay. Don't strain your leg, Finn. I'll go," his sister-in-law offered.

Huh, he didn't think anything could have ticked him off more than Dana and his inability to run like he used to, but his sister-in-law had just proved him wrong.

He started after Dana. "Thanks, but I've got this. I'm not an invalid, you know," he said to Sophie. Then realizing he was being hypersensitive, he added over his shoulder, "My overprotective baby brother would have my head if he knew I let you run a five-mile marathon when you're pregnant and not feeling well. Go home and put your feet up, have a nap."

Sophie called after him, sounding a little sheepish, "It was just an excuse. I'm feeling fine. I didn't want Kitty and Tina to know we're having an early Mother's Day celebration with Rosa today."

Their grandmothers had a long-standing feud. He didn't know what it was about or if they'd just taken up where their DiRossi and Gallagher ancestors had left off. According to local folklore, the original feud had started sometime in the seventeen hundreds. Apparently his grandmother had started this one by insisting that Sophie's mother, Tina, stay at the manor. A move that was guaranteed to tick off Rosa, who wasn't exactly her former daughter-in-law's number one fan.

"I've got your back, but you might want to…" He lifted his chin at the dark-haired woman crouched on the path picking up the flowerpots that Miller had bowled over. Because he wasn't paying attention,

Finn's foot landed awkwardly on the uneven woodland trail. His pained grimace turned into an eye roll when he heard Miller's playful bark and Dana's panicked cries for his dog to stop before he dies.

Talk about a drama queen. Then again, maybe it was a reaction to whatever drug she was on. She might be delusional, but she was also fast. He was running full-out…He shook his head at his assessment.

His full-out was equivalent to someone jogging. Finn ignored the voice in his head that said he had to accept his limitations, that he was lucky to have survived the rebels' attack. The voice sounded a lot like his old man's.

Finn grimaced, and this time it wasn't due to the twisting pain in his leg. It was because Sophie was right; the family wouldn't be happy about him leaving. Grams, never one to let the grass grow under her feet, as his great-grandmother Colleen used to say, had already come up with what she seemed to believe was a winning strategy.

First, she and her fellow members of the Widows Club had decided he should take over for Doc Bishop, the local family physician, who was retiring next week. Not that it was going to happen, because the last thing Finn wanted was to move back home and have his every move dissected, discussed, and evaluated.

He loved his family, but really, what thirty-four-year-old guy would subject himself to 24/7 surveillance and interference? Grams had proven him right when she suggested Dana would make a wonderful wife. *Wife?* He barely knew the woman. But he'd seen and heard enough to know that she wasn't his type, even when she wasn't wasted.

Up ahead, he caught a glimpse of pink through the trees. They were closing in on the footbridge that arched over the tide pools. The bridge connected the estate to the windswept spit of land his oldest brother, Griff, a former Navy SEAL, had recently purchased. Griff and his wife, Sophie's cousin, were renovating the lighthouse.

They'd be back in a few days from their honeymoon...and he'd break the news he was leaving the next day. He'd put off telling his family. Mostly because he hated goodbyes. And it was tough to hold his ground in the face of their sorrow. He hoped none of them cried. Tears got to him every time. There was a part of him that wanted to sneak off in the middle of the night without saying goodbye.

"Miller, stop this instant!"

The image of what his family would do to him if he left without saying goodbye faded at the sound of Dana's voice. Her tone was all proper and superior. He thought of it as her high-society voice. Come to think of it, that might have been the reason he'd taken an almost instant dislike to Dana.

It wasn't her fault. She reminded him of Amber, a woman he'd dated while doing his residency. Amber and her mother, who lunched and raised funds for the hospital like the rest of their moneyed friends. Women who had no idea how the other half lived and had no interest in knowing. The only thing they were concerned about was their social standing, having a wing named after the family, and the preferential treatment they felt they were entitled to due to their connections and their husband's or daddy's bank accounts.

But even if Dana were his type, the last thing Finn wanted was a wife. He didn't do long-term relationships. He liked his women fun and fleeting. Did he have issues? Sure he did, and he'd made friends with his issues years before. And if his grandmother thought that was going to change anytime soon, she was as delusional as the woman she was trying to set him up with. The one who was currently on her knees and elbows, her backside in the air, playing tug-of-war with Miller.

Now, Finn might not have any interest in the woman, but he had to admit she had one great-looking ass. He wondered how he'd failed to notice that. Probably because her conservative wardrobe was classy and not sexy or the least bit revealing. He couldn't help but wonder what else she'd been hiding, because that was one sweet...

As though his matchmaking grandmother could see that particular thought bubble over his head, Finn quickly burst it by reminding himself that Dana was the reason for the persistent throb in his leg.

He limped to the small hill in the clearing where the tug-of-war continued. Miller was winning, and Dana was...Oh hell, she was sobbing. "Please, I don't want you to die. Please let me have the glove."

"Hey, come on, don't cry. Miller isn't going to die because he ate your garden glove." He had to work to keep the sarcasm from his voice. Beige with pink flowers, the glove matched her gardening outfit to a T. His leg screaming in protest as he crouched beside her, he bit back a curse and rested a hand on her shoulder. "Seriously, if you saw what he eats, you wouldn't be worried about a little—"

She looked up at him, a tear slipping from eyes that almost looked black. "No, you don't understand. The glove came in contact with a monkshood leaf. They're highly poisonous." A sob broke in her voice. "Does…does he look dizzy or confused to you?"

The slivers of bright blue that ringed her dilated pupils reminded him that he was dealing with a woman whose feelings and thoughts may not exactly be grounded in reality.

"Let go of the glove, okay? I'll handle it from here." He spoke to her in low, soothing tones, smiling to let her know he wasn't mad and everything was good.

Her eyes narrowed. "I am not high, so don't speak to me like I am. If you want to save your dog, call a vet and then pry his mouth open while I get the glove." She tossed him her phone.

He felt bad that she'd obviously overheard his conversation with Sophie, but her clipped and proper tone took his guilt down a notch or two. And maybe because it did, and his kneecap felt like it was tearing through his skin, he said, "Your dilated pupils and glazed eyes say you're high and so does the way you're enunciating your words. You're trying not to slur. And FYI, I'm a doctor, and"—he pointed at the dog—"Miller is not dying." He swore under his breath when the retriever rolled on his back and pretended to be dead. It's a trick they'd taught him when he was a puppy. But he only did it when Finn or his brothers used the word *dead* or when they shot him with their fingers.

Finn only had a moment to wonder whether Miller was confused by the word *dying* or the hand gesture before Olivia threw herself at the dog. It looked like she was about to give Miller mouth-to-mouth. Finn had to admit that his opinion of her went up a couple of notches at that.

But it went down when she turned on him. "What is wrong with you? Don't just sit there—do something. Call the vet, do chest compressions, just do something!" she cried, tears sliding down her cheeks.

Finn sighed, leaned over, and picked up the infamous glove Miller had dropped when he rolled over. "Miller, buddy, go fetch," Finn said, pretending to throw the glove.

Miller rolled over so fast that he took out Dana. Finn assumed it was either because her rubber boots slid on the grass or because her balance was impaired due to the fact that she was high.

She lay flat on her back, blinking, and then slowly turned her head to look at him. "He's not dying?"

He bit back a smile. She looked pretty cute lying there, and he wasn't going to kick her when she was down. With a hint of pink tinting her pale cheeks, it was obvious she was embarrassed for overreacting. Miller had galloped toward the white wooden footbridge in search of the elusive glove, snuffling the patches of clover. Before he gave up and came back, Finn examined the glove, lifting it to his nose. "It smells like—"

She made a grab for the glove. "No, don't, there

could still be— Oh!" she gasped, and began rolling down the hill.

He stared at her, kind of in shock and then positive that she'd realize all she had to do was put out a hand or a foot and stop her downward momentum. But no, apparently, she was just going to roll right on down the hill and into the—

"Dana!" he yelled, lunging in an effort to reach her. At the same time he made a grab for her, she lifted her head, and his fingers got tangled in her hair. Figuring the pain of him tearing a hunk of hair from her scalp would be worse than her landing in the tide pool, he was about to let go when she jerked away, leaving him holding an entire head of hair. He didn't have time to wonder why she was wearing a wig because at that moment he realized *he* was in trouble.

Dana's jarring movement had not only left him holding a fistful of red hair, but it'd also thrown him completely off balance. Over his grunts of pain as he repeatedly rolled over his bad leg, he heard a splash and a shriek. Then a *whoomph* when he landed on top of her in the tide pool.

It was a surprisingly soft landing. Her boringly expensive wardrobe did a good job of concealing not only a nicely rounded backside, but some other intriguing curves as well. And for the first time—since they were practically nose to nose—he noticed her features were softer than he expected.

Her creamy skin was flawless, the defined bow of her full upper lip sexy, and her blue eyes...were not blue. Well, the left one was but the right one was brown.

Okay, that was a little weird; he could have sworn...He didn't have time to contemplate why the woman was in disguise because, at that moment, she made a funny sound in her throat.

After a quick visual search ensured that she wasn't outwardly injured or lying on a rock, he realized he was probably responsible for her distress. He wasn't exactly a lightweight. "Sorry, just give me a sec, and I'll get—" He bit down a pained groan. His leg had locked. He wasn't sure how to break it to Dana that they might be stuck in this position for a while. He looked over his shoulder to see Miller sitting at the top of the hill with his head cocked as if to say, *Stupid humans.*

"Hurry! There's something biting...Ow!" Dana yelped, pushing against Finn's chest while trying to move out from under him.

His brain flashed a warning: *Do not react to the soft, tantalizing body parts rubbing against you.* The warning proved unnecessary when her knee slammed into his. Hers was sharp and bony, and his had only recently recovered from knee surgery. "Dammit, woman, are you trying to ensure I never walk again?" he asked through clenched teeth as he let go of her wig to grab his leg.

"Sorry, I'm so sorry. I didn't mean to hurt you. But you really need to get off me. Something bit me and...," she babbled, and then howled, "Ow!"

"I'm trying, and it's probably a minnow. So could you just relax and stop yelling in my ear?" he shouted, and then felt bad for doing so because, for all he knew, she was hallucinating.

"You don't have to be so cross. It's not my fault something is biting me."

Cross? Seriously, who talked like that? Oh right, she did. Somehow, despite lying in a pool of stagnant water, she still managed to pull off her superior act. He supposed he was being unfair. She'd never been anything but nice to him.

Unfair or not, Dana was the reason they were currently in the position they were in. And if the crippling pain in his leg was any indication, she had more than likely set his recovery back by a couple of weeks. So maybe he was *cross* after all. Because she'd just ensured he wouldn't be leaving Harmony Harbor next week as he had planned.

He scowled down at her as he admitted the embarrassing truth. "My leg locked. Just give me a minute."

A flash of panic and then frustration crossed her face, but both were quickly replaced with sympathy. He'd prefer the frustration, which obviously he wasn't going to get now. He shouldn't have opened his big mouth.

"I'm so sorry. Let me see if I can just move..." She wrapped her arms around him and bit her bottom lip to stifle an *ouch* from what he imagined was another nip from her pal the minnow.

At that moment, he kind of envied the minnow. Just a normal guy reaction, he assured himself. It had nothing to do with... She lifted her hips, and he stifled a groan. Good God, he had to get off her. "Miller! Come on, boy. Come play." He hoped Dana didn't pick up on the desperation in his voice.

It didn't seem like she noticed, or maybe she did and

thought it would be fun to torture him, because she kept lifting her hips while yelling, "Get off me. Oh, please get off me."

As Miller galloped to their rescue, latching on to the back of Finn's shirt with his teeth to drag him off Dana, he realized she'd been saying *it*. And he knew this because when she jumped from the tide pool and began dancing in a circle, she cried, "Get it off me. Please, get it off me."

He winced. It wasn't a minnow after all. She had a green crab clinging to her backside.

About the Author

Debbie Mason is the *USA Today* bestselling author of the Christmas, Colorado, and Harmony Harbor series. Her books have been praised for their "likable characters, clever dialogue and juicy plots" (*RT Book Reviews*). When she isn't writing or reading, Debbie enjoys spending time with her very own real-life hero, three wonderful children, and two adorable grand-babies, in Ontario, Canada.

You can learn more at:
AuthorDebbieMason.com
Twitter @AuthorDebMason
Facebook.com/DebbieMasonBooks/

Melissa Portman is fighting a losing battle when it comes to saving her grandmother's bookstore—and selling the historic building may be her only option. Yet when a handsome stranger wanders in one day, she wonders if her very own fairy tale is just beginning…

A bonus story from *USA Today* bestselling author Hope Ramsay follows.

Chapter One

♥

Jefferson Talbert-Lyndon turned up his jacket collar and hunkered down in an easy chair by the front window of Bean There Done That, the trendy coffee shop in downtown Shenandoah Falls, Virginia.

He fired up his tablet, connected to the coffee shop's Internet, and scanned the headlines from the *Washington Post* and several cable news networks. Things had not improved since he'd left New York a week ago.

Jeff was still being pilloried by the president's political party for a series of articles he'd written for *New York, New York* about Joanna Tyrell-Durand, the nominee for the Supreme Court, and her husband's and brother's illegal lobbying on behalf of various oil and gas interests.

Jeff's stories had relied on information from Val Charonneau, a well-known climate-change advocate and one of Jeff's longtime friends. But it turned out Val's source of information, which included printouts of several damning e-mails, was the unreliable Helena Tyrell, the nominee's soon-to-be-ex sister-in-law.

So what had appeared to be a career-making scoop had turned into the blunder of the century, featuring a philandering husband and a vengeful wife. The embarrassment reached critical mass last week when Brendan Tyrell filed a defamation suit against *New York, New York,* and on the same day, Jeff's father, Thomas Lyndon, the US ambassador to Japan, issued a statement saying that Jeff was a lifelong screwup who had no business trying to be a journalist.

Jeff had resigned from the magazine the next day and headed out here to the wilderness of the Blue Ridge Mountains in order to escape the carnage he'd unloosed on himself and his career.

He turned his tablet off. He needed to move on. But toward what?

If he wasn't a journalist and a writer, then who was he? The man his mother wanted him to become? The CEO of the Talbert Foundation?

He couldn't think of anything he wanted to do less than managing his family's money.

He returned his gaze to the picturesque town beyond the window. Despite the chilly spring rain, the town reminded him of a Norman Rockwell painting. The wrought-iron light posts lining Liberty Avenue were hung with American flags, in honor of the upcoming Memorial Day celebrations. Several of the storefronts were draped in red, white, and blue bunting.

His eye was drawn to the store across the street— a used bookshop called Secondhand Prose—which wasn't draped or decorated. Instead, like independent bookshops everywhere, this one had flyers for upcoming community events and a large orange "Help Wanted" sign taped to its front windows. The store reminded him of his favorite bookshop in Park Slope. He found himself smiling.

Until his gaze snapped to the dark-haired woman dressed in a blue raincoat and carrying a blue umbrella, standing at the corner in front of the shop.

What the hell was Aunt Pam doing in downtown Shenandoah Falls on a rainy Friday morning? Her husband, Mark Lyndon, was a US senator. Didn't they live in DC most of the time?

Oh, wait, the Senate had probably adjourned yesterday because of the holiday. Crap. He'd lost track of time up in his cabin. This was bad.

Aunt Pam was the only member of the Lyndon family, besides his father, who would recognize him on sight. Pam was the only family member who had remained a friend after his mom and dad's messy divorce. Although Jeff had a bunch of Lyndon cousins, he'd never met most of them. He'd visited the family compound at Charlotte's Grove only once in his life, when he was fourteen. That year Dad had been posted in Washington instead of someplace foreign.

Aunt Pam crossed the street and swept into the coffee shop as only Aunt Pam could—like she owned the place.

Jeff leaned his elbow on the table and planted his face in his hand. He stroked the patchy, one-week's growth of scruff on his face. He didn't have a lot of faith in his disguise.

He needed to get out of here. If Pam knew he was

hiding out in Dad's fishing cabin, she'd tell Mom, and Mom would come running. Even worse, Pam would invite him to stay at Charlotte's Grove. Jeff couldn't think of anything more excruciating, especially after what Dad had done to him last week. Jeff might have Lyndon in his hyphenated name, but he'd never, ever been a member of Dad's family.

Jeff waited until Pam's attention was focused on the barista behind the counter. It was now or never.

He stood and scooted out the front door, then loped across Liberty Avenue, but had to wait for the traffic on Church Street before he could cross. The rain pelted him as he waited for the light to change.

Pam must have ordered black coffee because she came out of the coffee shop when he was halfway across Church Street.

He needed to hide. Now. He headed for the used bookstore, collar up, head down. A little jingle bell rang as he pushed through the front door.

Jeff loved the way old bookstores smelled, and this bookshop had a lot of old books on its shelves that gave the place the aroma of bookbinder's glue and dry paper.

Jeff turned toward the window, intent on Pam's whereabouts, and discovered a cat tree, complete with a cat, sitting in the front window. The cat was gray and regarded Jeff with a pair of cool, amber eyes.

"Hello," he said in his most cat-friendly voice as he ducked down and glanced through the dusty window. Where was Pam going?

The cat arched its back and hissed.

"Shhh," he hissed back at the cat. Oh, good. Pam had gone into the real estate office across the way.

The cat growled.

"Sorry," Jeff said as he backed away.

He ought to leave the store, but the thought of going back to the solitary cabin on a rainy day left him slightly depressed. Besides, the only good reading material up there was a complete set of Hardy Boys mysteries, and he'd already been so desperate for entertainment that he'd plowed through all of them.

He had planned to download some reading material at the coffee shop, but Pam had put the kibosh on that. And now the coffee shop was officially off-limits. Maybe he should rethink. Maybe he should hunt down Val and wring his neck.

Or maybe he should just buy a couple of books.

He spent the next twenty minutes browsing the store. He selected four books on various aspects of American history, a couple of John Grisham novels that he found in a box in a dusty corner, and a clothbound edition of *Walden* that was shelved with a bunch of philosophy.

He'd been thinking a lot about Henry David Thoreau. Thoreau had spent years living alone and off the grid. Maybe the long-dead author had some tips for surviving cabin life.

Jeff headed for the checkout, where he stumbled over a second cat—a long-haired calico—intent on winding itself around his ankles. This one was like a puffball with legs. Jeff put his books on the counter and scooped the animal into his arms.

It settled, purring like the engine of his vintage

Porsche 911—the car he'd reluctantly left in Brooklyn.
He'd "borrowed" Mom's Land Rover from its garage
at the house on the Hudson. He'd left a note so Mom
wouldn't worry, but she would worry anyway.

He stood there a moment, stroking the cat, waiting
for someone to arrive at the checkout, when he realized
that he'd been browsing for almost half an hour without
seeing another soul.

"Hello?" he called.

Crickets. The silence was almost deafening.

"Is anyone here?" He shouted a little louder this
time.

Footsteps sounded from the back of the store, and
a moment later a girl appeared, heading slowly in his
direction with her face buried in a paperback. Dark,
horn-rimmed glasses perched on her nose. Thick, curly
chestnut hair tumbled around her narrow face like an
untamed mane. She wore a T-shirt with a vintage book
illustration of Cinderella under a faded orange plaid
flannel shirt and rust-colored skintight jeans that
showed her slender figure.

She looked up with a puckish smile. "Hello," she
said. "I heard you the first time. But I was at a particularly good part of the story." She closed the book,
marking the place with her finger.

He had to return the smile. "What are you reading?"
he asked.

The girl's pale cheeks colored. "Oh, just a paperback," she said in an I-just-got-caught-with-my-hand-
in-the-cookie-jar voice. She hid the book behind her
back.

Then, with catlike grace of her own, she climbed over the box of books that blocked her path to the cash register and quickly transferred the secret novel to a shelf under the counter where he couldn't see it.

"I'm sorry about the mess," she said in a rush, her face growing pinker still. "The books are from a large estate sale, and I haven't gotten around to cataloging and shelving them all."

No doubt because she'd been spending her time reading paperback novels. What had she been reading? Mystery, suspense, *Fifty Shades of Grey*? He warmed at the thought.

Her eyes were the dark blue color of a fall sky, and the moment their gazes connected, he revised his estimation of her. She wasn't just some girl in colorful clothing. She was older than he'd first thought, and behind those smart-girl glasses, she was stunningly beautiful.

Awareness jolted him right behind his navel.

He had all day with nothing to do. A crazy, halfway desperate idea popped into his head. "I saw the sign in the window," he said as he gazed at the disorder around the checkout. "Guess you need some help, huh?"

She tilted her chin up a fraction. One eyebrow arched. "Do you know someone who loves books and is willing to work for nothing?" She had a low, sexy voice that did something strange and hot to his insides, while it erased his better judgment.

He rested his hip against the counter and, forgetting all about his recent troubles, he said, "How about me?"

* * *

Melissa Portman almost laughed in the man's face. He was most definitely not the teenager Grammy had been searching for when she'd put the "Help Wanted" sign in the window three months ago.

He was a grown man, probably her age or a little older, in his late twenties or early thirties. He wore clothes that branded him as someone who came from way, way out of town: a brown tweed jacket with elbow patches, a striped button-down shirt, and a pair of skinny jeans that showed off his muscular thighs. All in all, he gave the impression of a hot college professor.

He also had dark, soulful brown eyes, too-long black hair that curled over his forehead like a sensitive poet's, and a well-groomed scruff of beard that Melissa found way too attractive for her own good. To top it all off, he held Hugo in his arms like a man who knew something about cats. In fact, just watching his long fingers stroke the cat was vaguely erotic.

No question about it. He was delicious eye candy. And she wasn't stupid enough to believe that he needed a job. The guy was flirting.

Wow, that hadn't happened in, like, forever.

She arched her eyebrow the way Grammy used to when faced with the utterly absurd and said, "You want to work here? Really?" She invested her voice with just the right tone of skepticism.

His mouth quirked and exposed adorable laugh lines that peeked through his *GQ*-style stubble. "Really," he said. "I appreciate literature."

His voice was low, deep, and had just the right hint of tease in it—like he might be calling her out for the book she'd hidden beneath the counter. Had he seen the title? She hoped not.

"Seriously," he said, "I'm interested in the job."

"It's minimum wage," she said.

"How much is that? I'm new around here."

No kidding. "Seven twenty-five an hour." She managed to say this with a straight face.

The professor's eyebrows lowered. "That's not very much, is it?"

Obviously Mr. Professor had been spending all his time in ivory towers or something. "Right," she said, nodding. "And that's why we only hire high school students. You're a little old for that."

He continued to stroke Hugo as he gazed at her out of those impossibly hot brown eyes. "I know, but I need the work. I recently lost my job."

Something in the set of his broad shoulders suggested that he was telling the truth, even if he was flirting at the same time. A momentary pang of sympathy swelled inside Melissa. She was in the same boat. She'd given up a good job with the Fairfax County Public Schools in order to take care of Grammy, and now she'd be out a full-time teaching job until next September. She didn't know how she'd pay her bills.

Unless she sold the historic building that housed Secondhand Prose. The Lyndons were willing to pay a fortune for it—enough to pay all of Melissa's bills, cover the property taxes, and give her something left over to invest. But selling out to the Lyndons was the last thing Melissa wanted to do. In her heart of hearts, she wanted to keep Secondhand Prose's doors open, which was just silly, wishful thinking.

"I could be very helpful," Mr. Professor said, breaking through Melissa's financial worries. "I'm good at organizing things, and I have other experience and qualifications that could be valuable to you."

She eyed the cat and then his handsome face. "Aside from charming killer cats?"

His mouth twitched again. "I'm an avid reader."

She rolled her eyes. "Aren't we all? But really, there is no job."

"But the sign. And you're clearly short—"

"The sign has been there for a while. My grandmother put it up before she died. I'm sorry, but there's no job available here."

"Oh. I'm so sorry about your grandmother."

For an uncomfortable moment, their gazes caught, and the kindness and concern in his eyes surprised her. "Grammy was pretty old," Melissa said, her voice barely hiding the sorrow that had hollowed out her insides. "So let me ring these books up for you, okay?"

Melissa picked up the books he'd laid on the counter while Mr. Hottie Professor continued to lean his hip into the counter, his mere presence disturbing the atmosphere and making Melissa adolescently self-conscious.

"That'll be twenty-five dollars for the books," she said in her best customer-service voice. She expected him to hand over a credit card, but instead the guy pulled out a money clip that held a big wad of bills. He sure wasn't a professor, not carrying cash like that.

He had to thumb through several hundred-dollar bills to find a five and a twenty. So who was he? She was suddenly dying to know.

He put Hugo down, but the damn cat continued to circle his legs. "Nice cat," he said.

"His name is Hugo—well, his full name is Victor Hugo—and he's not friendly."

"Could have fooled me."

The cat meowed as if he knew they were talking about him. What was Hugo up to? He never made friends with strangers.

She handed the guy his bag. "So, where are you staying?" she asked, hoping she might prolong this conversation and get his name, e-mail address, or even his profile on Match.com.

He took his bag and broke eye contact. "I love your store. Next time I'm going to make friends with the cat in the window."

"Ha. I don't think so. Dickens is half wild."

"I already figured that out. Have a nice day."

And with that the guy turned and strolled down the aisle toward the door, looking amazingly like the hero in the romance novel she'd been reading when he'd first arrived.

Chapter Two

♥

At six o'clock Melissa locked up the store and headed down Liberty Avenue with *The Lonesome Cowboy* tucked into her purse. She took her usual spot at the lunch counter and ordered the meat loaf blue-plate special and a glass of iced tea.

She'd been there for about ten minutes when Gracie Teague, the diner's owner and chief waitress, leaned over the counter, casting a shadow on page 183 of Melissa's book. "So what's it tonight, English aristocrats or down-home cowboys?" she asked.

"Cowboys," Melissa said, blinking up from the page. Gracie and Mom had been best friends in high school; maybe that's why Gracie had nominated herself as Melissa's keeper. Even before Grammy died, Gracie had been a fixture in Melissa's life. Their relationship started that summer when Mom and Dad had dropped Melissa off with Grammy while they'd pursued their lifetime dream of buying a sailboat and sailing from the Caribbean up the East Coast.

Even as an eight-year-old Melissa had loved books,

but an eight-year-old wasn't patient enough to spend a whole day in a bookstore. So she'd come down to the diner and hung out with Gracie. Then the news had come that Mom and Dad had perished in a storm. The death of her parents had changed Melissa's life forever while simultaneously cementing her relationship with Gracie.

Gracie had attended Melissa's high school graduation. Gracie had made her prom dress. Gracie had driven Melissa down to Charlottesville to help her set up her freshman dorm room at the University of Virginia. Gracie had fed her ice cream when she'd broken up with Chris. And in the last three weeks, since Grammy had died, Gracie had provided the blue-plate special free of charge.

Gracie also made no bones about the fact that she intended to dance at Melissa's wedding—someday soon.

She gazed down at Melissa's book and shook her head. "Girl, it's Friday night, and here you are perched on your stool like you have been every night since Harriet died. You need to stop with the books and go find yourself a real man."

"I don't think so. I tried that once, and you know how it turned out. Besides, book boyfriends are much easier, and you don't have to clean up after them."

Gracie snorted. "You wouldn't clean up after anyone anyway."

Melissa nodded. "That's probably true. I love my dust bunnies. They're way sweeter than Grammy's cats."

"Exactly my point. You're too young to settle into

the role of crazy cat-lady spinster. You should sell out, hon, and go somewhere exotic where rich, handsome bachelors hang out in droves."

Melissa gave Gracie one of Grammy's evil-eyed looks. "I could say the same for you."

"I don't have cats, and I don't want to sell out."

"So?"

"I guess you have a point," Gracie said as she scanned the diner, which had exactly one other customer this evening.

Several chain restaurants had opened up at the new strip mall down near the highway interchange. The new competition had siphoned off a lot of Gracie's evening business. Just like the online book retailers had siphoned off a lot of Secondhand Prose's business.

"I think I need to change my menu," Gracie continued on a long, sorrowful sigh.

"I like your menu just the way it is. People will get tired of the chain restaurants. I'm sure of it."

Gracie could give a look as well as she could take one. "Melissa, you are so stuck in your rut you can't even see the road in front of you anymore."

Melissa shrugged this off and turned back to her book.

Gracie freshened her tea, rang up the other customer, and returned to the lunch counter, where she sat down with a copy of *People* magazine. They sat together reading for a few minutes before Gracie asked, "Do you think he got her pregnant?"

"Huh?" Melissa looked up from her book, which just happened to have a plot line involving a secret baby. She was momentarily confused. "Who got pregnant?"

"Mia Paquet."

"Mia Paquet's pregnant? That's good news, if it makes her retire from reality television."

"Don't be superior, Melissa. A lot of people liked her in that show about Vegas pole dancers."

"So someone knocked her up?" Melissa glanced at Gracie's magazine. A big color photo of Mia Paquet and her cleavage dominated the page. A small black-and-white inset showed the reality star on the arm of some ridiculously cute guy wearing a tux and a bad-boy smile.

"Not just someone," Gracie said. "Daniel Lyndon."

"Oh, for crying out loud. Which Lyndon is he?"

"One of Charles's boys. Dropped out of college and seems to be intent on blowing his trust fund out in California."

"Give it a rest, Gracie. The Lyndons are not the saints and martyrs you seem to think they are."

"Danny is just young and misguided. He'll come around."

"If he got Mia Paquet pregnant, I certainly hope he marries her."

"I do, too. But you know how things go in Hollywood."

"Whatever." Melissa went back to reading.

"I'm much more worried about David," Gracie said, smoothing back her outrageously bright red hair.

When Gracie got on the subject of the Lyndons, she was like a pit bull with a bone. Melissa put her finger down at her place in the book and looked up again.

"He's not moving on with his life, bless his heart. He needs to find love again," Gracie continued.

Melissa closed her book. If she wanted to finish *The Lonesome Cowboy,* she would have to leave the diner. "Okay, I can see how David needs to move on, but please don't put me on your list of possible mates for him, okay? I mean, I feel for the guy. I knew Shelly a little bit. She used to come in the store all the time with Willow Petersen and buy romances by the dozens."

"See?" Gracie said. "You and David's late wife are a lot alike."

"No, we weren't. She was all about being a nice wife and fitting in with the Lyndon family's plans for David's political career. Can you see me doing that? Ever?"

"You could learn…"

"Gracie, please. I don't like Pam Lyndon, and I'm not interested in her son."

"Only because your grandmother carried a grudge. You know it's time to lay that to rest with her, don't you?"

"I guess."

"And you could do worse than hooking up with a Lyndon. If David isn't the one for you, he's got four or five cousins. They're all handsome as the devil."

Melissa ground her teeth. "Gracie, stop. I don't want anything to do with any of the Lyndons. Period. End of subject."

But of course it wasn't the end of the subject, because the way things were shaping up, she would be selling the Lyndons the one thing she held most dear.

Chapter Three

♥

Mr. Hottie Professor made Melissa's Tuesday when he returned to Secondhand Prose. He walked through the door and almost bowled Melissa over in the front aisle, where she was shelving a few books on military history. In fact, she would have toppled right over if the guy hadn't snagged her shoulders and steadied her.

"Oh, hi," she said, taking a step back and shrugging off his touch, which had sent an electric shock down her backbone that woke up her girl parts. They had been dead to her for such a long time that she hardly even remembered she had them.

And now suddenly there they were, awake and aware and...well...aroused.

Whoa, wait one sec. She was not about to let her hormones take a dive into insanity. This guy was more than merely handsome. He was like Chris—an intellectual. And Chris was just the latest in a long line of attractive, brainy boyfriends, all of whom had broken her heart.

Mr. Professor looked utterly tempting today in his skinny jeans, oxford cloth button-down, and a blue tweed sweater. The guy definitely had the urban casual vibe going for him—the kind that took a sizable clothing budget to achieve.

"Hi," she said. "How did you enjoy the Thoreau?"

"To be honest, it sucked."

"You didn't like *Walden*, really?" She blurted the words in surprise. He looked exactly like the type of guy who would not only enjoy Thoreau, but make a big deal of discussing it.

"No, I didn't. It doesn't work as a manual for living off the grid in the twenty-first century. And Thoreau is kind of preachy. I mean, it's depressing to discover that I'm living a life of quiet desperation caused by the weight of my personal possessions."

"Only if you're the type of person who values material things."

"I know. And that's why I'm here. I have a plan to improve myself."

"You do?" she asked. Was he flirting or trying to have a book discussion, or maybe both?

"Yes. I came to volunteer," he said.

"Volunteer?"

"Yeah. You need help, and I'm here to lend a hand."

"Doing what?" Several things came to mind, none of them involving books, unless he might consider reading poetry to her. Robert Browning would be perfect. She took another step back.

"I'm here to do whatever it is you need me to do. And I don't need the seven twenty-five an hour. According to Thoreau, working for nothing is more enlightening than working for peanuts."

He took another step forward, invading her space with impunity. He plucked the books from her hand.

"Ah," he said, studying their spines, "these are military history, so they get shelved here, right?"

She found herself nodding.

"By title or author?"

"Author."

He turned and started shelving the books.

"Look, you can't just—"

"What? Give you some help?" He finished shelving the books and turned back toward her.

"Um, I can't pay you."

"I know. And I have a plan for that, too. See, I've been trying to follow in Thoreau's footsteps—staying in a cabin that's way off the grid—but I've discovered that I can't survive without Internet. So I thought maybe we could work out an arrangement, you know? I'll give you a few hours a day doing whatever, and in return you can let me set up my laptop somewhere and borrow your Internet."

Something didn't add up. The guys who lived in those remote cabins usually wore camo vests or fishing shirts, not urban-hip tweed sweaters. She cleared her throat and tried to sound tough and decisive. "Uh, thanks, but I told you I don't need help."

"Then why do you keep the 'Help Wanted' poster on the front door?"

She shrugged, and they stood staring at each other for a long moment.

"Look," he finally said on a long breath, his eyes going even more soulful, "the truth is I'm a writer and—"

"Wait a sec. You're a writer?" Now she understood the tweeds and the bulky sweaters and the Byronic hair and her fatal attraction. She loved writers. They were, in her opinion, practically gods. And here stood a particularly handsome specimen, right in the middle of her bookstore.

He nodded. "Yeah, I am a writer, and I—"

"Oh my God. What's your name?"

* * *

Damn. What now? If the bookshop girl stayed abreast of current events, she'd recognize his name, and he damn sure didn't want to have a discussion of his failings as a journalist. He also didn't want her blabbing her mouth around town. He just wanted something to occupy his time while he considered what he was going to do with the rest of his life. He'd discovered that brooding about the future, while spending endless days utterly alone in a cabin, was murder on his psyche.

He would have to lie.

"I'm not famous," he said. "I'm not even published."

"Oh," Melissa said in a disappointed tone.

He stuck out his hand. "I'm Jeff Talbert. Author in the making." This was only a half-truth. Like every journalist worth his salt, Jeff was sure he had a novel in him somewhere. He'd been talking about writing a book for years, but he'd done nothing about actually starting it.

He studied her face, waiting to see if she bought any of this, especially the abridged version of his Jefferson

Talbert-Lyndon byline. She seemed to take him utterly at face value.

She took his hand, her palm warm and soft. "I'm Melissa Portman," she said. "I inherited this store from my grandmother."

"And I'm here to help you shelve books in return for borrowing your Internet. Oh, and I also intend to make friends with your demon cat."

Melissa let go of a long breath. "I've told you, I don't need help. And forget about Dickens. He doesn't like people."

"I find that hard to believe."

She cocked her head, and Jeff swore her cheeks colored. She looked a lot like the vintage book illustration of Snow White on her pink T-shirt—pale skin, a round face with rosy cheeks, and a dark cloud of hair pulled away from her face with a plaid hairband. Her skinny jeans were green and hugged her curves, and she wasn't wearing any socks with her red Converse low-top lace-ups.

She eyed him from behind her black glasses, one eyebrow arched. "I'm not kidding. Dickens is a crazy cat. Don't try to pet him. You'll draw back a bloody nub."

"Okay. I'll stay away from the cats." He took another step forward in the narrow aisle, forcing her to retreat again. "I'll just head over to the checkout and start sorting the piles of books over there."

"I told you already, I don't need or want your help," Melissa said, crossing her arms over her Snow White T-shirt. She looked bad-ass, in a colorfully hip way.

He ignored her and simply took another step forward
and then eased his way around her, brushing against her
in the process. She smelled great, like a field of wildflowers.

He headed for the checkout, where he picked up the
book on top of one lopsided pile—a hardback edition
of *Robinson Crusoe*. "This is fiction," he said, laying
the book aside and picking up the next one, a reference
book on how to knit. "This goes in the how-to, reference area."

He laid that one down to start another subpile, then
glanced over his shoulder. The adorable Melissa Portman still had her arms crossed, only now there was a big
rumple across her brow. He wanted to erase those lines.

"How am I doing so far?" he asked.

"I don't need your help."

"Of course you do." He turned away and sorted several more books, while Melissa's gaze burned a hole in
his back between his shoulder blades.

The standoff lasted several minutes until Dickens,
the demon cat, jumped down from his throne in the window and padded toward Jeff, his amber eyes dilated,
his tail erect, ears perked. The body language seemed
friendly enough, but Jeff could only see the cat out of
the corner of his eye.

Jeff had had plenty of experience with feral cats in
his day, so he avoided direct eye contact. He'd learned
just about everything anyone ever needed to know
about wild cats during his visits to Grandmother
Talbert—a woman lovingly referred to as the Crazy Cat
Lady on the Hudson.

So he braced for the cat to pounce, with claws extended.

But the attack never came. Instead Dickens gave a friendly sounding meow and then pussyfooted up against Jeff and gave him a little head butt that was a cat's classic request for attention.

He squatted down slowly and let Dickens get a good sniff of him before he carefully and gently rubbed his hands from the cat's head to his tail. The animal arched its hind end up to press against his touch.

Dickens's eyes closed to slits, and he started to purr as Jeff settled in to scratch him liberally behind his ears. When Jeff took his hand away, the cat moved forward and leaned his forehead against Jeff's knee.

He picked Dickens up and settled him in his arms. Then he turned toward Melissa. "See, I told you I would make friends with your cat."

Melissa's eyes had grown wide behind her glasses. "I'm seeing it, but I don't believe it," she said. "What are you, some kind of cat whisperer?"

Chapter Four

♥

When Dickens came down from his tree and allowed Jeff to pick him up, Melissa had no choice, really, but to let Jeff stay and volunteer.

She relented for Dickens's sake. Since Grammy's death, Dickens had occupied the cat tree in the window almost twenty-four-seven, allowing no one to touch him, hardly eating, and leaving his perch only for litter-box calls.

She told herself that letting Jeff volunteer was about the cat, but having Jeff shelve the books that Grammy had purchased before she died gave Melissa a big dose of hope in a situation that was utterly hopeless. Having someone else around the store eased the loneliness that had settled into the deepest recesses of her heart.

Still, it was a fantasy, this idea of fixing up the store. She needed to end the charade. Tomorrow she would make an appointment with Walter Braden, the Realtor in town who handled commercial real estate sales. He'd already called a few times to let her know that the Lyndons were anxious to make an offer on the building Grammy had owned for sixty years.

But Melissa's resolve disappeared on Wednesday morning, when Jeff showed up on her doorstep bright and early bearing gifts: a new, expensive-looking coffeemaker for the back room, a bag of cat treats for Hugo, and a catnip mouse for Dickens, who came down from his tree and played with it for a solid hour.

"So what's on today's agenda?" Jeff asked after he'd set up the coffeemaker and brewed the first pot of the day. Why the man didn't just get his coffee across the street was a mystery. But once she took her first sip of coffee from his new machine, she had to admit that the guy knew how to brew a good cup of coffee. Obviously Jeff was a master at winning lonely cat ladies over.

Plus she had a weakness for guys who wore tweed jackets...and formfitting white T-shirts and jeans, which was Wednesday's outfit.

Yup, he was as yummy as the coffee.

"Let's get the boxes behind the counter cleaned up and shelved," she said, casting aside her resolution about calling Walter Braden.

They went to work hauling books around the store while she attempted to give him the third degree. But he was slippery. Their conversations always left something to be desired.

"Where are you staying?" she asked.

"Up on the ridge." No specific address. And the Blue Ridge ran right through the middle of the state. Saying you were living in the Blue Ridge Mountains wasn't very informative.

"Where are you from?" she asked as they tidied up the history section.

"New York." Of course he was from New York. She could hear it in his accent.

"State? City?"

"Both." He was a master of the one-syllable response.

"Where did you learn to handle cats?" she asked as they reorganized the fiction department.

"My grandmother. She was a cat lady."

Two sentences. She was on a roll. "Mine too."

"I figured."

And that was the end of that conversation, unless she wanted to tell him all about Grammy, and at the moment conversations about Grammy tended to become overly emotional. She wasn't ready for Jeff to see her cry. And besides, she really ought to be calling Walter about selling the place. Tomorrow.

But on Thursday she forgot all about calling Walter. She'd had trouble sleeping that night, and she was all prepared with a bunch of book-related questions. Jeff seemed to know his literature.

So as they started dusting every inch of the store, she asked him if he'd ever read any Jack Kerouac. It was just the first question on her list of sneaky ones designed to see if he was a literature snob, like Chris.

He gave her a look from the measureless dark of his eyes. "Is that a trick question?"

Damn, he was onto her. "How could a simple question about a book be a trick question? Have you read *On the Road*?"

"Have you?"

"Of course I have."

"Did you read it because you thought it was hip?"

She blinked at him because the truth was she had read it because Chris had told her she needed to read it in order to be well rounded. She had not particularly enjoyed the book.

Jeff smiled before she could respond. "Don't worry. I won't tell the in crowd that you didn't much like it. The problem with reading Kerouac today is that everyone thinks he's cool, when the truth is, he was just the writer guy, you know, the dude with the journal keeping notes on the crazy stuff his friends did."

"I'm not worried about what people think," she said. "So, are you like him? I mean, are you the writer guy who keeps a journal and chronicles the crazy stuff your friends do?"

His smile faded. "No. Not really. But I have a question for you."

"Okay." She wasn't sure she wanted to be on the receiving end of any questions.

"What were you reading that day when I came in the store the first time?"

Oh, crap. She wasn't about to tell him she'd been reading a romance novel. How pathetic would that be? So she thought fast and lied. *"Oliver Twist."*

His mouth turned up adorably. He didn't believe her. "Good book. I wholeheartedly believe that we should all ask for more."

And that was the end of her attempt at using book talk to discover his secrets. It was, however, the beginning of several long conversations about the classics, where she discovered that Jeff Talbert had actually read Jane Eyre. He'd hated every minute of it, but he'd read it in high school.

He'd also read *The Call of the Wild* and *The Last of the Mohicans*. Those books he'd liked. She wasn't surprised.

All that book talk was tantalizing. So when Thursday came to a close, she took a leap and asked, "So, uh, you want to go down to the Jaybird for a drink or something?"

He gave her a soulful brown-eyed look and shook his head. "No. Maybe some other time." And then he left the store, but not before he glanced out the window as if checking to see who might be out there on the sidewalk, watching.

* * *

He should stop. Now. Going to Secondhand Prose on a daily basis was a dumb idea. Even though the store wasn't exactly the type of place Pam would frequent, he still risked being seen. He'd learned from the grapevine that Aunt Pam didn't spend much time with Uncle Mark in DC. She stayed at Charlotte's Grove and managed things. What things she managed were not precisely clear, but it wasn't unusual for Aunt Pam to be seen on Liberty Avenue shopping or visiting with merchants.

Maybe he should book a flight to the Bahamas or something.

He jettisoned the idea. For some reason, helping

Melissa clean and organize her grandmother's bookstore had become the thing he wanted to do right now. It filled his days. It gave him purpose.

And maybe he was accomplishing something important—pulling Melissa out of her funk. She may not have shed a tear or said a word, but Melissa was grieving for her Grammy. Working to clean and organize the place seemed to have given her a purpose, too.

She obviously loved that store and wanted to keep it open. But she didn't have enough customers. That kept him up at night, worrying. And worrying about how to save Secondhand Prose seemed way more productive than worrying about his lost career in journalism.

So, despite his better judgment, he returned to the shop on Friday with a bag filled with color-coded adhesive tags.

"We're going to change your pricing system," he announced as he came through the door and gave Dickens a long head scratch.

"Why would we do that?" Melissa asked.

She must have been anticipating his arrival this morning, since she was standing in the history section at the front of the store, but she didn't seem to be shelving books or doing anything at all, except waiting for him. Today she greeted him wearing a bright yellow *Hansel and Gretel* T-shirt with red jeans.

He warmed at his first sight of her. What was she going to do today? Yesterday's book discussions had been way more fun than Wednesday's third degree. Last night she'd even asked him out for a drink. Saying no had been hard, but he needed to figure out where the

Jaybird Café was located and whether Aunt Pam was a regular customer.

Scoping the place out was on his to-do list. But until he could fully define safe, Pam-free zones, he was sticking to his plan of mostly hiding out at Dad's cabin or here at the bookstore, where no one ever shopped.

"Change is good for the soul," he said, knowing full well that Secondhand Prose didn't really need a change in its pricing system. It basically needed a total makeover and an influx of lots of cash. Not to mention advertising and new merchandise. But she would probably get all freaked out if he said any of that. And besides, saying stuff like that might be offensive. After all, the bookshop had been owned and managed by Melissa's grandmother, and Melissa hadn't said one thing to suggest that she wanted to change things around here.

In fact, Melissa was resistant to change. Which was to be expected. So small steps were called for.

"I've got colored adhesive tags. I figure we could group books and price them accordingly. Like all hardbound books at one price and all mass-market paperbacks at another."

"Uh, well, we sort of do that already."

"Yeah, but you have to handwrite a price sticker for every book in the store. Wouldn't it be easier to post signs with the color codes and then just put colored dots on each book?"

She nodded. "I guess, but it's a lot of work to do that for books that already have prices on them."

He shrugged. "I know, but I don't have anything better to do."

So he got to work, and before noon came around, Melissa was helping him while they had a lively discussion of *The Catcher in the Rye, The Color Purple,* and Ayn Rand's political philosophy.

When Friday came to a close, he didn't want to leave, but he didn't dare ask her out for a drink. So he reluctantly headed back up the ridge, but before he was out of cell phone range, his phone vibrated. It was his father, calling all the way from Japan.

He pulled the Land Rover over to the side of the road and punched the talk button on his phone. "Hello, Dad," he said.

"Where the hell are you?"

Jeff said nothing.

"Don't pull the silent treatment on me. Your mother is about to call the police and proclaim that you've been kidnapped."

He sighed. "I told her I was going away for a while. She knows I haven't been kidnapped."

"That's debatable. She's hysterical."

"You know, she wouldn't be hysterical if you hadn't allowed the White House to issue that statement in which you said I had no business being a journalist. I think that ticked her off. It sure ticked me off."

"Well, that's too bad. Because it's the truth. Go home, Jeff. Go manage your mother's money. She has so much of it, I doubt that you could screw things up the way you've screwed up the Durand nomination. But whatever you do, stay out of journalism and stay out of politics. Because you sure didn't inherit any of the Lyndon smarts when it comes to those things."

That was it. He'd had enough. "Ambassador Lyndon," he said in a tight voice, "I'm happy to comply with your request that I take myself out of the family. Tomorrow I'll be calling my lawyers and starting the formal process of removing your last name from mine." He pressed the disconnect button and sat there for several minutes breathing hard while his fury subsided. He hated his father. The feeling was clearly mutual.

He probably ought to move out of Dad's cabin. But what the heck. The guy was in Japan, and Jeff had the key. Besides, leaving Shenandoah Falls was the last thing he wanted to do right now.

* * *

On Saturday Melissa found herself anticipating Jeff's arrival, and the moment the front door opened with a jingle, she and Dickens had almost the same reaction. The cat sat up and meowed plaintively until Jeff stopped and gave him a good scratch behind the ears and told him what a beautiful feline he was. Melissa got hot and bothered just watching him stroke the cat.

Hugo wasn't about to let Dickens get all the attention. He waddled out from his lair in the back and demanded equal time. Jeff lavished praise on him, too, allowing Melissa to appreciate Jeff's manly but gentle hands, with their long, patrician fingers.

Once Jeff satisfied the cats, he turned and strolled past her toward the back room and the coffeemaker. "Can I interest you in a cup of hazelnut coffee, light on the cream, heavy on the sugar?"

He pulled a package of coffee and a coffee grinder from the sack he was carrying. "I stopped at the store on the way in."

Wow. He'd been listening when she'd said that hazelnut coffee was her favorite. Boy, he was kind of terrific, wasn't he?

He disappeared into the back room and emerged several minutes later with a mug of coffee, made exactly the way she liked it. She was ready to melt right in front of him. Where had this guy come from and why was he here?

"So what's it going to be today?" he asked.

The coffee warmed her hand. The spark in his brown eyes warmed up every other part of her. "I don't know, Jeff," she said. "I told you I didn't need help. Why don't you tell me what I need?"

He grinned. "How about I fix the ladder?" He gestured to the floor-to-ceiling shelves along the northwest wall. "Then you could use the upper bookshelves again."

"I can't even remember the last time we had access to those shelves. I'm pretty sure the ladder is long gone."

"Actually, I found it in the back room when I was tidying up."

She was tempted to tell him to forget the ladder. She could use someone to tidy up the small apartment above the bookstore where she was living. But she held her tongue. She didn't want him to know what a slob she was. Her inability to keep things neat and tidy had been a serious bone of contention between her and Chris. "It's missing some pieces, I think," she said instead.

"Is it? Let's figure out what it needs and get it working again." He strolled past her, leaving his yummy scent—soap, coffee, and cedar—behind.

She settled into a comfy chair behind the checkout and watched him work. Today he was channeling his inner lumbersexual. His beard was impeccably groomed, and he wore a plaid flannel shirt and a chest-hugging black T-shirt. He'd left his skinny black jeans behind this morning and instead he wore a pair of faded blue ones that were almost threadbare in the seat and the knees.

Yummy.

He'd been impressive with his colored dots, but when he pulled out the old toolbox from the back room, along with the pieces of the broken library ladder, the show definitely took an erotic turn. What was it about a man in a flannel shirt and faded jeans using a screwdriver?

It took him two trips to the hardware store for parts, but by noon he had the ladder rolling along the rails the way it had when Melissa was eight years old and had first come to live with Grammy.

He was using the ladder to reorganize the books in the children's area, near the back of the store, when the front door opened, jingling the bell. Pamela Lyndon—who Grammy always referred to as the Duchess of Charlotte's Grove—came gliding into the store wearing a designer dress in her signature shade of pale blue.

The duchess got about two steps into the bookshop

before Dickens arched his back, fluffed out his fur, and yowled at her in a way that could only be called blood-curdling.

Several things happened in quick succession after this.

First the duchess said, "Goodness!" and retreated a step, clutching her purse in front of her like a shield. "Shoo, kitty," she said in a totally ineffective voice.

Second Jeff, who was up on the ladder shelving fiction on the highest shelf, turned toward the cat and said several X-rated words. He must have thrown his weight to one side, because the ladder's rail (which he apparently hadn't checked earlier in the day) detached from the bookshelf. The ladder unexpectedly pivoted and slammed Jeff into the back wall of the store.

And that's when the unthinkable happened.

A long time ago, when the store had been more successful, Grammy had put up a bunch of coat hooks on the back wall, where she'd hung merchandise for kids. The coat hooks were empty at the moment. But when Jeff slammed against the wall, somehow his slightly threadbare jeans got snagged, so when the ladder pivoted again, Jeff didn't pivot with it. Instead, he was left behind, hanging there on the wall for a moment, suspended by the seat of his pants.

That didn't last very long. There was an audible *riiiiippp* as his jeans split. Jeff came down, dumped unceremoniously onto Melissa's favorite beanbag chair. His pants stayed put, snarled in the coat hook, his legs still caught in them.

"Good God," the duchess said.

Which was totally an understatement, because Jeff had started his day without underwear.

Melissa was momentarily stunned by the view, which probably explained why she was a little late in coming to Jeff's aid. But that was okay because the beanbag chair had cushioned his fall. He shucked off his shoes, disentangled his legs, and covered his private parts with those manly hands of his.

Even so, the view was stirring. Especially when he stood up and streaked into the back room, slamming the door behind his incredibly hot backside.

Chapter Five

♥

Damn.

It was bad losing his pants. Although he still wasn't sure exactly how that had happened. One moment he'd been up on the ladder, and the next he'd been stuck to the wall and then falling.

A flush of embarrassment heated his body from head to toe. This was his penance for not doing his laundry. Although he had to admit he didn't mind Melissa seeing his junk, and in the nanosecond before he covered himself, she'd certainly been looking. With interest.

Being half naked in Melissa's presence didn't suck. Not so much with Aunt Pam though.

Why the hell was Pam here? Of all the places in Shenandoah Falls, this was the last place he'd ever expected his aunt to visit. Had she recognized him?

He eased the door open a crack, just large enough to see the checkout counter where Pam and Melissa were talking.

"So, Melissa," Pam said in her Tennessee drawl, "I see you've been making improvements. I'm so glad.

Maybe my visit is well timed." She cleared her throat, then glanced toward the scene of his disrobing. "Who was that man?"

He tensed. Pam would figure it out if Melissa said his name.

"Just the new helper," Melissa said, thank God.

"Uh-huh." Pam paused for a long moment as she swept her gaze over the store's interior before turning back toward Melissa. "Darlin', I know your grandmother had a blind spot about some things. But we both know her determination never to mortgage this property was old-fashioned."

"She had her reasons," Melissa said, crossing her arms over the *Sleeping Beauty* T-shirt she was wearing today.

"Well, yes, I suppose she did. But look, we need your help. The Town Council and the Liberty Avenue Property Owners Association have agreed to move forward with a request for a block grant to revitalize the historic structures downtown. That means we need every property owner between Lord Fairfax Highway and Sixth Street to agree to a special assessment that will provide the matching funds for the project."

"Every property owner? That means the Lyndon Companies and me, right? And when you say a special assessment, you mean a special tax, don't you?" Melissa sounded downright belligerent. Her body language said it all. She didn't like Aunt Pam.

Pam spoke again. "It's true that the Lyndon Companies owns more buildings than anyone else, but there are a total of five additional landowners, including yourself. And an assessment is not a tax."

"Oh, okay, how is it different?"

"To begin with, it's voluntary. But those who chip in will get matching funds to renovate their storefronts. By participating, you'll save a lot of money on the storefront renovations needed to get this building listed on the historic register. And, darlin', this building is worthy of that honor."

"I would love to see this building on the historic register, Mrs. Lyndon. But I can't afford your assessment without a mortgage. And if I mortgage the place, I'll probably have to close the store and find a more lucrative tenant."

"Darlin', that doesn't sound terrible to me. You could make money on this building. And while I know this is a difficult time for you, I really need your support. The deadline to submit our application is June fifteenth. That's just three weeks away. We'll have a better chance of winning this grant if we have unanimous participation."

"I need to think about it," Melissa said.

Aunt Pam leaned over the checkout, her body language aggressive. "In a few days you'll be officially in arrears on your property taxes. At that time the county will start proceedings to foreclose on this property, and Lyndon Properties is ready, willing, and able to buy this building. We'd prefer to pay full price if you're willing to sell. But you could finance this, Melissa, and make a lot of money. Rick Sharp down at the bank is ready to help you with the financing, and I know Walter Braden would help you find a well-paying commercial tenant."

"I need to think about it," Melissa repeated as she uncrossed her arms and stood toe to toe with Pam, staring her down.

Pam stepped back. "All right. I understand. But you don't have much time left, you hear?" She turned and headed toward the door. Dickens hissed at her on her way out.

* * *

Melissa was shaking when the bell above the door finally jangled and Pam Lyndon left the store. The time had come to make a decision. And, unfortunately, the decision would require her to close Secondhand Prose. Forever.

Her eyes filled with tears as she studied Dickens. "Maybe Jeff will take you," she whispered, then blew out a long breath. She stood there for a moment, collecting herself and wiping her cheeks.

When she'd regained control, she headed toward the back of the store to examine the damaged pants; then she headed toward the back room.

"Hey, are you okay in there?" she asked through the door.

"I'm good," Jeff replied. His voice eased her jangled nerves and soothed her aching heart. Just the sound of him calmed her down.

"I just checked your jeans. They're beyond repair."

Silence greeted her from the other side of the door, and her momentary melancholy was replaced by something else. It might be fun to open the door and have a good look at him. It would definitely distract her from her problems.

"Guess I picked the wrong day to go commando, huh?" he finally said. "Truth is, I need to do some laundry."

"Do you do laundry?"

"What does that mean?"

"Oh, nothing. It's just that your wardrobe is always so..."

"What?"

"I don't know. Together. I figured you took everything to the dry cleaner's."

"Well, yeah, I do."

"There's a good dry cleaner on South Third Street. Just sayin'."

"Thanks. But that doesn't exactly solve my current problem. Got any ideas?"

Melissa had a few, but they were all bad ones. The best thing would be to get him some pants so her libido would go back to sleep.

"Okay, look, hang loose..." She paused a moment because these words brought an image to her mind that was X-rated. "Uh...um, maybe that was the wrong choice of words. Just wait there for a minute, and I'll get you a pair of pants."

She checked the size of the shredded jeans and then headed down the street to the Haggle Shop, the local consignment store, where she scoured the rack for a pair of jeans with a thirty-four-inch waist and a thirty-six inseam.

The Haggle Shop had lots of cool vintage stuff, but

you never knew what you'd find there, and the selection of guys' pants in a thirty-six inseam was limited to four pairs of ugly beige khakis and one pair of cool argyle golf pants in kelly green and pastel yellow.

* * *

The pants were loud. And fun. Wearing them was like being invited into Melissa's slightly weird, totally unique world of fashion. He opened the door to find her standing there with a naughty gleam in her too-blue eyes.

"I like the pants," he said. "I'm thinking I need more color in my life." He took a step forward. This time she didn't retreat, and he caught a whiff of her scent: a mountain meadow.

"Look, Melissa, I overheard what that woman said." He touched her shoulder, and she pressed herself in to his hand. Just like a cat hunting for a good scratch.

"I've been trying to tell you that the bookstore is a lost cause," she said. "I have to put it up for sale. I'm scheduling an appointment with Walter from Braden Realty on Monday." Melissa's voice was full of defeat.

His heart stumbled. "Won't that play right into that woman's hand?" His words came out in a rush.

"Maybe. But it's got to be done. Jeff, I'm sorry. I've been sitting here for a few weeks, unable to make a decision. That's why I left the 'Help Wanted' sign on the door. And then you arrived, and I got all caught up in the ridiculous fantasy that maybe I could keep the store going. But I can't. Taxes are due, and I have to mortgage the place to pay them. But I can't make mortgage payments by selling used books. There just isn't enough income in it." Her voice wobbled as she spoke, and then her eyes filled with tears.

He took her big black glasses off her face and pulled her into his arms. "It's okay. Just let it out. I'm thinking maybe you haven't even let yourself cry for your grandmother."

She didn't cry. But she leaned against him like Hugo did when he wanted attention. Jeff stroked the back of her head, her curly hair gliding under his palms, igniting a deep yearning. He had to admit the truth. It wasn't so much the bookstore that had him coming here every day as it was Melissa. He wanted to protect her. He wanted to be the comic book hero who swoops in and saves the world and gets the hot girl at the same time.

And why the hell not? He didn't need any superpowers to fix this problem. Money would do the trick, and if Jeff had anything, it was money—a gigantic and bothersome trust fund that made people think he didn't have any ambition or drive. A mother with so much money she needed someone to manage it all. Money was a big pain in the neck for Jeff, but it could solve all of Melissa's problems.

He could fix this for her and thwart Aunt Pam's plans at the same time. He just needed one day to make the arrangements.

Like changing his name, it would be the ultimate statement of rebellion.

* * *

Oh God. She was in Jeff's arms, and it felt like heaven, leaning up against his hard, male body. A girl could get used to leaning on a guy like Jeff. He was steady. Dependable. Sweet. Considerate. And he dressed well.

Also, his lips were warm and soft where they rested against her forehead. She wanted him to do something naughty with those lips.

She tilted her head, hoping he would get the message that she wanted to be kissed. He was all blurry since she wasn't wearing her glasses, so she couldn't read his expression. Was he just being kind? That would be so frustrating.

She wanted more from him than help with the store. The store was irrelevant. It had to be closed and the building had to be sold.

And just like that she made the decision she'd been putting off. She would sell out, and she would stop waiting around for life to begin.

Today was the first day of the rest of her life, and she was going to seize control of it. Jeff Talbert might not be a forever love, but he was a nice guy and she was alone in the world. Besides, she'd been living like a nun for too long.

"So," she said, letting her voice drop into the husky range. "The store is closed tomorrow. You want to do something fun? I could take you up to the falls. It's a fun hike. Or are you opposed to long walks in the woods?"

"Are you asking me out on a date?"

"Uh, yeah, I guess."

"You guess? You don't know?"

Damn. The man was impossible.

"Yes, I'm asking you out on a date. Tomorrow."

She must have frowned at him or something because he started stroking her forehead with his thumb. The touch was comforting and arousing all at once. The cats loved it when he rubbed his thumb over their foreheads. Now she understood. She didn't purr, but her body definitely started to rev itself up for more. In fact, she closed her eyes and made a little moan of pleasure.

That obviously did it for him. He stopped stroking her, settled his hands on her hips, and pulled her in tight against his chest and thighs and all his other hard manly parts. His lips went back to her temple, but this time he kissed his way down the side of her face, over her cheek to the corner of her mouth. She moved into the kiss and opened up for him.

When their tongues finally met, she threw her arms around his neck and pulled him into the kiss. He was a virtuoso at this dance of tongues, doling out something sweet, carnal, mysterious, and addictive.

But when one of his hands left her hip and moved up toward her breast, she inadvertently stiffened. It happened like a reflex. She might fantasize about no-strings sex, but she was abysmally bad at actually having it. Her underlying caution always reared its head.

Damn.

And wouldn't you know it? Jeff was such a gentleman that he backed away a little. "Not okay?" he asked.

What was she supposed to do now? It was all so awkward. So she said nothing, even though she really wanted him to go back to kissing her and maybe even touching her.

Instead he relaxed his grip and put her in a safer zone without actually letting her go. "So," he said in a rough voice, "I'd love to take a hike with you up to the falls."

Oh, good. She'd have a second chance to get this right. "Great," she said.

"Cool," he replied. "Why don't we meet at Gracie's Diner for brunch or something?"

No, no, no. She backed out of his embrace. "Uh, no, not Gracie's. Let's meet at the Old Laurel Chapel. In the parking lot. At nine o'clock."

"The Old Laurel Chapel?"

"It's off Morgan Avenue, just north of State Road 606. There's a little gravel parking lot there and access to the Appalachian Trail, which connects to the trail that leads to the falls."

"What about brunch?"

"I'll pack a picnic."

There was a beat of silence before he said, "Are you ashamed to be seen in public with me?"

"Oh, no, that's not it. You see Gracie is..." Her shoulders tensed and her voice stumbled.

"Gracie's what?"

"A busybody." And so much more. Gracie would grill Jeff because she saw it as her purpose in life to find Melissa the right husband, and Jeff was probably not that guy even if his kisses were amazing. He was probably just a guy passing through, looking for some fun.

"Oh, I see. Good thinking. I don't want any gossip," he said. Which seemed odd for a guy from out of town. But she let it slide.

Chapter Six

♥

Melissa hardly slept a wink. She kept replaying the kiss in her mind, not to mention that moment when Jeff had scooted, butt-naked, into the back room. Hot. So hot.

She gave up trying to sleep at six a.m., when she got up and took a frigid shower, threw on some clothes, and headed to the Food Lion for the picnic stuff and a box of condoms.

Buying them was like burning the bridges to her past. Deciding to have a little fun with Jeff had become an important part of letting go of the store and moving on with her life.

A few hours later, with a backpack full of sandwiches and other goodies, she pulled off Morgan Avenue into the patchy gravel lot by the Old Laurel Chapel.

The stone ruin hadn't seen a congregation in more than a hundred years, and it had been sadly neglected during that time. Its roof had all but fallen in, leaving behind four stone walls with empty vaulted windows.

Today the mountain laurel surrounding the building was
in full, glorious bloom, edging the cemetery and dotting
the woods with its pale pink blossoms.

Jeff hadn't arrived yet, so Melissa left her car and
strolled through the ancient graveyard, where many of
the headstones bore the surname of Lyndon or
McNeil—families who had helped to found Shenandoah Falls almost three centuries ago.

The sound of tires crunching on gravel had her raising her head in time to see Jeff pull a late-model Land
Rover into the lot. With a car like that, he wasn't hurting
for money. But what did he do for a living besides being
an unpublished author? Where did he come from? Why
was he here?

Maybe she'd learn the answers today. Or maybe
not. She'd decided that it didn't matter. Today was
about not grieving, and not worrying, and just having
a little bit of fun.

"Hey," she called, and waved. "I'm over here."

He locked his car and strolled toward her, wearing
a pair of jeans and a black body-hugging T-shirt that
showed off his shoulders and the wide, muscular expanse of his chest.

"Sorry I'm late," he said. "I had a few phone calls I
needed to make. One of them took a while."

"Business?" she asked in a leading tone.

"No, just a personal call. Family stuff." He turned
away from her to inspect the church. "Wow. That looks
like it's been here three hundred years."

"So, you have a family?" she asked, ignoring his
comments about the chapel.

"Yeah. A mother in New York. She's kind of over-bearing and overprotective."

"Ah."

She wanted him to elaborate. Instead, he turned his gaze on her and then pulled her into a hot, sexy kiss that fogged her glasses and her brain. She wrapped her hands around the back of his head, running her fingers through his too-long hair, and tried to eat him up.

The kiss might have led to other things, but they were interrupted by a little girl who came skipping out of the woods like Little Red Riding Hood with a wicker basket on her arm. She wasn't wearing a red cloak, but her hair was certainly red. And tangled.

The child skidded to a noisy stop before she said, "Oh!"

Jeff and Melissa jumped apart like guilty teenagers caught in the act.

"Hello," the girl said.

Melissa adjusted her glasses. Oh, great. Nothing like being caught in the clinches by a Lyndon. The girl was Natalie, David Lyndon's daughter. A moment later Natalie's grandmother, Poppy Marchand, appeared at the forest's edge. Poppy was in her sixties, and Laurel Chapel was on the grounds of Eagle Hill Manor, which Poppy owned. Technically, Melissa and Jeff were trespassing.

Poppy eyed Melissa and then shifted her gaze to Jeff, where it remained for a long moment. "Hello," she said.

"Uh, hi, Mrs. Marchand. Good morning," Melissa said in a rush. "We're taking the shortcut to the Appalachian Trail. Is it okay to leave our cars in the lot?" She pointed with her thumb over her shoulder.

"You hiking up to the falls?" Poppy asked.

"Yeah."

"Nice day for it. The laurel is lovely this time of year. It's no problem about the cars. No one ever comes up here anymore." Poppy paused for a moment as she continued to study Jeff. "Do I know you? Have you visited Eagle Hill Manor before?"

"No. I'm sure we've never met."

Poppy nodded. "I guess not. But you look very familiar for some reason."

Natalie tugged at Poppy's hand. "C'mon, Grammy, let's go." She pulled Poppy toward the old church. "Let's play princess, 'kay?"

"Y'all have a nice hike," Poppy said as the girl pulled her up the steps and into the ruined chapel.

"Let's go," Melissa said, pulling Jeff in the opposite direction. "There's a short path here that connects with the Appalachian Trail. We'll walk that for a couple of miles and then take the turnoff for the falls."

They found the main trail without much trouble, and Jeff took the lead as the ground began to rise. About half a mile before they reached the turnoff for the falls, they came to a break in the forest's cover that provided a view up a rise to a grand Georgian-style brick mansion. The house stood atop the hill, with the Blue Ridge Mountains at its back and its grand portico facing the Shenandoah Valley.

Jeff stopped in his tracks and stared at the house for a long, silent moment.

Melissa played tour guide. "That's Charlotte's Grove," she said. "The house you see was built after the Revolution. But the original cabin—"

"Save the history lesson. I know all about Charlotte's Grove."

"You do?"

"That's where the Lyndons live. The people who want to buy your store." There was no mistaking the enmity in his voice.

The big concrete bunker she'd built around her heart cracked a little bit. Jeff Talbert was on her side. She had an ally. "Yeah, they are. But the store has to be sold, you know."

He turned on her, his dark eyes suddenly intense. "No, it doesn't."

She laughed. "Jeff, it does. And I've finally made up my mind about it. So let's not talk about the store. Let's just have a fun day in the woods, okay?"

* * *

The sky got into Melissa's blue eyes somehow, and for a moment Jeff lost himself in that deep, limitless color. Looking into her eyes was almost like free-falling. He took her shoulders and drew her forward for another hard, needy kiss on her soft, open lips.

She tasted like the outdoors. Like springtime. He should have planned this better. He should have brought a couple of blankets. Maybe some condoms. She was sending up all kinds of signals that he was receiving loud and clear.

No. Just. No.

Not here, within sight of Charlotte's Grove. And not with her wearing that T-shirt with a truly gruesome illustration of innocent Little Red Riding Hood and a menacing wolf. Where did she get these T-shirts anyway? From the Brothers Grimm Department Store?

He broke the kiss. He owed her the truth about his background or he was no better than that ogling wolf on her T-shirt. He ought to say something right now, but that would ruin everything he'd put in motion yesterday afternoon. He needed one more day before he told her the truth. Once his plans were fully in place, he could tell her about his father, and she'd know right away whose side he was on.

She gazed up at him as wide-eyed as ever, even behind those glasses of hers, so innocent, so beautiful. She'd certainly found a place in his heart.

"Okay, you've got it. Today we'll pretend the Lyndons don't exist," he said.

"That sounds like the perfect plan," she said.

He gave her a quick kiss on the cheek and headed up the trail at a brisk pace, even though the path began to ascend steeply. By the time they arrived at the turnoff for the falls trail, Melissa was wheezing behind him. He turned. "I'm sorry. You should have told me to slow down."

"No, it's okay. I'm out of shape," she said on a puff of air. "This is what happens when you spend too much time in a beanbag chair reading genre fiction."

He laughed. "So you admit that you read genre fiction?"

She shrugged. "Yeah."

"So, what were you reading that day when I first came into the store and bought the Thoreau?"

She eyed him warily. "I'm not telling."

"Afraid to lose your credentials as a discerning reader?"

She laughed. "You're funny." She pointed to the trail that led off to the right. "C'mon. Let's go, but maybe a little slower. The falls are only two more miles."

The trail went up sharply for more than a mile, while the rushing sound of a fast-moving stream met their ears. Then, abruptly, the path narrowed and headed downhill through lichen-covered rocks to a patch of sandy beach at the edge of a fast-moving freestone creek—Liberty Run.

Upstream, the run cascaded down a twenty-five-foot fall, sending water droplets into the air and filling the forest with its powerful roar. Eons of flowing water had cut a plunge pool at the base of the waterfall surrounded by tumbled rocks of various sizes.

They stood for a moment, under a canopy of red oaks and yellow poplars, interspersed with the occasional hemlock. It was green here. Green rocks, green canopy. Even the run had a brown-green tinge to it, created by the tannins in the water.

"It's magical here, isn't it?" he said.

"Magical?" Melissa stepped up onto the first stone of a rocky staircase that led to the top of the falls. She didn't climb all the way. Instead she sat down and started taking off her hiking shoes.

"Look around. Can't you imagine wood elves living here? Or maybe fairies?" he asked.

She cocked her head. "Have you been reading Tolkien on the sly?"

He laughed. "No. I haven't. I don't even like fantasy. It's just that this place seems enchanted somehow."

"Well, I've been up here to the falls at least a hundred times, and it's usually just like this. No fairies or elves. But you will encounter snakes and bugs. I can also attest that the falls are ghost-free. I know this because I spent one cold, wet night up here hoping to see Elakala's ghost."

"Who's Elakala?"

"She's supposed to have been an Iroquois princess whose father insisted that she marry the wealthy son of a rival chieftain. But Elakala loved a poor brave who didn't have much in the way of worldly goods. So on her wedding day she sneaked away and threw herself off the falls." Melissa gazed up at the cascades. "I find it hard to believe that she could actually accomplish that feat, to tell you the truth, since the water doesn't drop straight down. Some have speculated that she drowned herself in the plunge pool, which is also unlikely.

"Of course, you know how these Native American legends go. Every waterfall has a similar legend, and wherever there's a story of tragic death, there's also a ghost. And the legend grows bigger every time some foolish boy dives into the pool and comes up with a Native American relic."

"People dive for relics? Really?"

She stood up and scrunched her toes in the sand by the river's edge. "You'd be surprised by some of the stuff people have brought up from the bottom of the pool. Mostly junk, but every once in a while you find something cool."

"Oh." He took off the backpack and set it down on one of the rocks by the pool.

"To tell you the truth, teenage boys dive in the pool because it has the reputation of being dangerous. And also boys will be boys," she said, rolling her eyes in a way that was clearly a challenge.

"And that means...?"

"Every girl who grew up here in Jefferson County knows a boy who tried to impress her by diving into the pool, looking for Native American relics. It's a macho thing."

"Are you daring me to dive in the pool?"

"No. I wouldn't do any such thing," she said. He didn't believe her for one minute. Like every female, she gave off two messages at the same time. One with her words and another one with her gaze and her body.

Oh, yeah, her body. He hadn't forgotten about the feel of her hips beneath his hands or the pleasure of standing that close to her. Yeah, he had designs on her body, but he wanted her admiration, too.

Just then a purely adolescent idea popped into his brain. He didn't stop to think it through. He simply shucked his shoes, pulled his T-shirt over his head, and dropped trou. He streaked across the sandy beach and took a deep breath.

"Oh my God, no, Jeff. The water is—"

He didn't hear the rest of her admonition before the water closed over his head. Holy God, it was freezing cold. But then again, it was only May. The summer hadn't yet warmed the water, which was also dark and murky.

He frog kicked down, fighting the stream's current, until he reached the rocky riverbed. The pool wasn't all that deep—maybe eight or nine feet—but he was totally blind. He felt along the bottom, encountering mostly round river rocks and scree. But one of the stones had an oddly flat shape. He palmed it, and with lungs burning, he pushed off the bottom.

* * *

Melissa stood by the water's edge with her heart pounding in her ears. Her racing pulse had more to do with the magnificent sight of Jeff's naked bod than her fear for his safety, although this time of year the water was pretty cold. Good thing she'd brought a blanket and some beach towels. Not to mention the box of condoms.

Which just might come in handy after all.

She was pondering what came next when his head popped up above the water. He wore a big grin, like he'd proved something to someone. Such a guy.

"Guess you just discovered that it's probably too cold to go diving for relics this time of year." These were not exactly the first words her heart wanted to say. But they were what came out when she let her brain take over.

"I found something," he said as he swam toward her.

"You found something?" Her heart, already beating hard, began to race now in anticipation of him reaching the shallow water. Full-frontal nudity worked for her.

Although she had to remind herself not to be disappointed. The water was probably no more than fifty-five degrees.

He stood up, water sluicing down his chest and abs and... other parts. He held out his treasure in his open palm, but Melissa's gaze was locked on his family jewels.

He seemed unaffected by her intimate study. "It's an arrowhead. Who knew?"

"What?" Her brain was starting to work again, sort of.

He raised his head and seemed to notice for the first time that she was totally ogling him.

"Enjoying the view?" He gave her a wolfish, predatory grin.

"Yes, I am, as a matter of fact."

He took a step forward. She stepped back. "Uh, look, um, you're all wet. And..."

Oh, bad move on her part, because he lunged and caught her in his cold, wet embrace. An embrace that immediately kindled an undeniable heat inside her.

"I could throw you in," he whispered in her ear, setting off hot, freezing shivers.

"Uh, please don't. I didn't bring a change of clothes."

"Oh, well, we can make sure your clothes don't get wet."

That was probably a challenge, but she wasn't getting naked to go swimming. She had other ideas in mind. So she wrapped her arms more tightly around his neck, pressed her mouth against his, and gave him a hungry kiss. Taking charge of it this time made her feel powerful, especially when Jeff let out a small, inarticulate growl and then kissed his way down her throat to a spot right by her earlobe that more or less set her on fire.

She tilted her head and let him have access to the sensitive flesh, groaning out loud while she snaked her hands up through his wet hair and pulled him closer, losing her glasses in the process.

Who knew where they fell? She didn't care as the world went out of focus, especially, a moment later, when Jeff snaked his hand under her T-shirt and cupped her breast. Blood pounded in her ears in a rhythm that echoed the rush of the stream at their feet.

"You're beautiful," he whispered wetly against her neck, and she drank him up like it was happy hour at the Jaybird Café and Music Hall and the margaritas were half price. She let him touch her, and she touched him right back, running her hands over the muscles of his chest and then down his spine, cupping his hard backside. And suddenly standing there was not nearly enough. She wanted to feel the weight of him. On her. In her.

"There's a blanket in the backpack," she whispered against the stubble on his chin. She was kissing her way down his neck when she spoke.

"You brought a blanket? Why?"

"We needed a place to sit. You know, for the picnic." She murmured the words across his collarbone. She was planning to take her mouth even lower, but he tilted her head up. His face was almost in focus even without her glasses. But it didn't matter because she closed her eyes while she was kissing him. Plus he smelled really good. She buried her nose in his skin and took a deep breath.

"You're a genius." His words rumbled in his chest. "Don't go anywhere. I'll be back."

He took his body and his fabulous smell away for a moment, leaving her standing there blind and almost deaf and totally dumb.

"Uh, wait," he said from across the beach. "You brought more than a blanket."

She didn't even blush when he started laughing. "I think we're going to be here for a while."

Thank goodness he returned a moment later, spreading the blanket on the sand and tossing himself and the box of condoms down onto it. Then he leaned back on his elbows, the condoms right beside him.

Even all blurry, a naked Jeff made her burn. So hot that she needed to take off her clothes. Now.

She pulled her T-shirt over her head and shucked out of her jeans with a little flourish, turned on by the fact that he was watching her every move. When she finally joined him on the blanket, he grabbed her by the shoulders and tilted her back. "You're killing me," he said in a gruff voice right before he covered her body with his own.

Finally they were skin to skin, chest to breast, sex to sex, heart to heart.

Chapter Seven

♥

Good God. She had actually carried through with her crazy plan to have sex with Jeff Talbert. In public, no less. She had wanted to be brave, but she'd never truly believed she could be *that* brave.

But why not? Jeff was delicious and erotic. And...well...lots of things that her heart shouldn't be thinking right now. Hearts had no business doing the thinking anyway. Brains were much better for that sort of thing.

She wanted more, but he hadn't invited her back to his cabin. She hadn't invited him up to the apartment above the bookstore either. But that was only because the apartment needed a total spring cleaning.

Knowing Jeff, he'd take one look at it and feel the need to reorganize before they could get naked. So she spent Sunday afternoon scrubbing her bathroom, straightening the living room, hosing down the kitchen, and putting fresh sheets on the bed.

Her mind was preoccupied reliving those moments by the plunge pool. But as evening approached, it wandered and became fixated on her phone. She expected him to call. She wanted him to call. In fact, she was stupidly hoping he would call so she could invite him over for a pizza or something else, with the emphasis on the something else.

Maybe she should call him? She was being brave, after all. She was taking charge. She was about to do just that when the doorbell at the back entrance to the apartment rang, sending her heart racing. She sprang to the door, threw it open . . .

And found her BFFs, Courtney Wallace and Arwen Jacobs, standing there looking concerned and positively grave.

"Uh, hi," Melissa said.

"Hi," Courtney answered, peeking around Melissa's shoulder at the freshly dusted surfaces in her living room. "Expecting company?"

"Uh, no. Come on in."

"No," Courtney said. "We're making an intervention."

"And taking you to the Jaybird for drinks and dinner," Arwen added.

"And we want to know who the hell this new guy is. Gracie called us both this afternoon. Apparently the Liberty Avenue Merchants Association has taken note that you've hired someone to redo Secondhand Prose. They've informed Gracie of this because, you know, Gracie is their fearless leader," Courtney said.

"And this afternoon Poppy Marchand came into the diner and told Gracie that she'd seen you this morning up at the Old Laurel Chapel, holding hands with someone," said Arwen.

Melissa's face began to burn.

Courtney turned toward Arwen. "Note the red face. The clean apartment. The fact that she's wearing a pair of common, ordinary blue jeans and a shirt that doesn't have one of those fairy-tale illustrations all over it. This is serious."

Arwen nodded. "Who is he?"

The answer to that question was so complex Melissa didn't even know where to start. So she changed the subject. "You know," she said, grabbing her purse from the hook beside the door, "margaritas sound great. Let's go."

Ten minutes later they strolled into the Jaybird Café and Music Hall, located in an old warehouse on the south side of town. Juni Petersen, whose family owned the Jaybird, had reserved a corner table in the back for Melissa and her friends, proving that Juni was also in on this intervention—a big problem, because if Juni knew about Jeff, then everyone would know about him by tomorrow morning.

The margaritas were also waiting for them when they arrived.

Melissa sank into a hard-backed chair and snagged her drink. She took a healthy swallow, the salt and sweet bursting on her tongue, just as Courtney said, "All right, we want all the details. Pippa Custis apparently told Gracie that your new assistant is 'the bomb.'"

Melissa put down her drink. "The bomb, really?"

"Well, you know, Pippa is sixty, and she's trying to be cool. She thinks he's cute."

"Is he?" Arwen asked.

"C'mon, guys, he's just a guy." Melissa turned away. "Who's singing tonight?"

"Earth to Melissa, it's Sunday, remember? Karaoke night."

"Oh, uh, yeah." Melissa's insides broiled. A girl in her situation—having just gotten all sweaty with a guy she didn't know that well—needed time for reflection, not the third degree from her friends. How much of what had happened today was plain garden-variety lust? And how much was something else?

Her heart said there was something else there, but her heart was so notoriously wrong about stuff like this. She probably shouldn't have done what she did today. It was foolish. Reckless even.

Oh, but it had felt like heaven.

"Oh my God, she's got a dreamy look on her face," Arwen said.

Courtney touched Melissa's hand where it rested on the table. "We're concerned about you. We all know about the financial mess your grandmother left you. So when it gets around town that you've hired some guy no one knows to help you fix up the store, it's natural for us to worry. Who is this guy? Where is he from? What kind of business plan have you come up with to deal with the mess Harriet left you?"

Melissa picked up her drink and drained it in several long gulps, but chugging her drink didn't make her friends disappear.

Oh hell. She wasn't going to be able to keep this secret. But she needed more fortification before she spilled the beans. She waggled her glass at Rory Ahearn, the bartender, indicating another round for all.

"Coming right up, luv," he said in his sexy Irish accent.

"You're stalling," Courtney said.

"Okay, it all started last week, with Hugo."

"Hugo? The cat?" Arwen's big brown eyes widened.

"Is there anyone else in my life named Hugo?" Melissa said.

"What does the cat have to do with this guy you've hired?" Courtney demanded.

"Last Friday a guy walked into the store, picked up Hugo, and bought a copy of *Walden*."

"No way," they said in unison.

"Yes way. He held Hugo for a long while, and the cat actually purred."

Juni Petersen overheard this because she was delivering their drinks. "Someone made friends with Hugo? Really?" she asked.

"Uh, yeah." Melissa snatched up her drink and took a big gulp.

"Who?" Juni asked.

"A guy. And it's not just Hugo. Dickens likes him, too."

There was a moment of silence around the table. Dickens didn't like anyone. It was a well-known fact.

"Oh," Juni said, "that's a sign for sure." She cocked her head and gave Melissa a goofy stare.

Meanwhile Courtney and Arwen nodded like a couple of bobblehead dolls. It was totally annoying the way her friends believed the stuff Juni said. Juni was into crystals and manifesting and reading people's auras.

"Okay, Melissa, stop beating around the bush," Courtney said. "We need a name."

"His name is Jeff Talbert."

"And..." Courtney pressed, as if she were cross-examining Melissa.

"And what?" Melissa said.

"And what else do you know about him?"

"Not much." Except he knew how to kiss, and he knew how to touch, and for a little while he'd made her believe there was a way to salvage the bookstore.

"And you hired him anyway?" Courtney asked. "What is he? A librarian? A contractor? An interior designer? What?"

Oh, crap. She searched for a handy lie and came up empty. "I didn't hire him," she finally admitted.

"You didn't?" Juni and her BFFs said more or less in unison.

She chugged down her second margarita. The tequila was starting to make her face feel a little numb. "He's a writer. Well, he's an unpublished writer who doesn't seem to do much writing. But, anyway, he just sort of volunteered to help. For free. But he's good at sorting books and color-coding price tags. Plus, he's widely read."

"He *volunteered*?" Arwen said this in a voice loud enough so that half a dozen other Jaybird patrons turned and stared.

Courtney leaned forward with real concern on her face. "Are you out of your mind? Don't you realize this guy could be a serial murderer, or a rapist, or something? You don't know anything about this guy."

Melissa didn't know if Jeff was a serial murderer, but he sure wasn't a rapist. That was good, wasn't it?

Arwen pulled her iPhone from her purse. "Let's just Google his name and see what comes up, okay?" Her thumbs got busy in an impressive way.

"Hmm, interesting. There are at least three Jeffrey Talberts who are professors, but they're—"

"No way. That's totally awesome." Melissa got all warm and gooey inside as she grabbed Arwen's phone. "Lemme see."

The letdown was kind of momentous when the first photo—of Professor Jeffrey Talbert—was a balding guy in his late fifties. The next photo wasn't much better. Melissa's pulse kicked up as she continued to scroll through half a dozen Jeffrey Talberts, none of whom was younger than forty-five.

And then, finally, there he was. Only she almost didn't recognize him. The photo was a professional studio head shot, and Jeff was wearing a dark, conservative suit jacket and a red tie. His face was clean-shaven, and his hair was a whole lot shorter.

"That's him," she said with a wistful sigh as she pointed to his photo.

Arwen snatched her phone away. Her thumbs got busy again, and then suddenly she said, "Oh my God, I can't believe it."

"What? Is he really a professor, because he dresses like—"

"No, honey, unfortunately not." She tilted her phone so both Melissa and Courtney could see the screen. This time it was a photo of Jeff wearing a tuxedo with a blond bombshell on his arm. Jealousy pricked Melissa from the inside. Oh boy, she was an idiot.

"His full legal name is Jefferson Talbert-Lyndon. That should strike a familiar chord since the *New York Times*, the *Washington Post*, the *Wall Street Journal*, and every cable news network known to man have been dragging him through the mud for the last three weeks. Honey, he's a journalist. And he's also Nina Talbert's sole heir. When she kicks the bucket, he gets her billions."

"What? Did you say Lyndon?" Melissa was confused. The margaritas had fogged her brain.

"Lemme see that," Courtney said, grabbing the phone out of Arwen's hand. "Oh my God. Melissa, he *is* a Lyndon."

"What?" Melissa's brain was having trouble processing her friends' words.

"He's that guy on the news. You know, the one who wrote that article that everyone is screaming about. About the Supreme Court."

Melissa shook her head. She had no idea what Courtney was talking about. She'd been hiding out in the store these last few weeks, reading genre fiction and letting the world pass her by. She wasn't up on current events.

"Honey, the Lyndon family is in a snit about him," Arwen said. "He's Pam Lyndon's nephew, and my boss at Lyndon, Lyndon & Kopp is his uncle. You didn't know this? He didn't tell you?"

"Well, at least he's not a serial killer," Courtney said brightly. "We can be thankful for that, even if he is a lying douche bag."

"A filthy rich and unbelievably cute douche bag," Arwen added.

How could this be? The duchess had been in the store yesterday and hadn't acknowledged Jeff at all. Why? Surely she'd recognized him, even if he hadn't been wearing pants.

And why hadn't he been honest about Pam? She'd told him everything. Trusted him. And he'd been lying from the start.

Melissa sank her head to the table and *thunk*ed it a couple of times before the swearing started. The profanity didn't last all that long, because her vocabulary of bad words was limited, and also by the time she started to repeat herself, her throat had closed up, her eyes had overflowed, and talking had become impossible.

Chapter Eight

♥

Secondhand Prose wasn't open on Mondays, but Jeff found himself standing on the sidewalk staring through the windows. Dickens was keeping watch on his cat tree as always, but the place was dark.

He pounded on the door because he desperately needed to talk to Melissa and she'd been ignoring his phone messages and texts. He was just about to channel Stanley Kowalski, the character in *A Streetcar Named Desire* who stood outside the window and yelled his wife's name for all to hear, when a diminutive, fiftysomething woman wearing a big, brown tweed sweater tapped him on the shoulder and said, "You know, if you would just read the sign on the door, you'd realize the store isn't open today."

"I know that," he said as civilly as he could manage, considering his current state of mind. Why the hell was Melissa avoiding him? Yesterday had been amazing. Had he screwed up somehow? *Damn*.

"Good. I'm glad you can read," the woman said with a nod. "And since the store is closed, it doesn't make any sense to be pounding on the door. You're disturbing my beginning knitters class." She waved in the direction of the adjacent storefront with the sign over the door that said EWE AND ME FINE YARNS AND KNITTING SUPPLIES. The women of the aforementioned knitting class were gathered around the yarn shop's window, trying to watch their instructor do battle with him.

"Do you know where I can find Melissa Portman?" he asked.

"I know who you are," the woman said. "And so does Melissa."

It was like the woman had just dumped a bucket of ice water over his head. "What?"

"You're Jefferson Talbert-Lyndon. And I heard at the Merchants Association meeting this morning that you lied to Melissa about your name and background. And everyone wants to know why."

The woman shook her finger in his direction as she continued. "Shame on you, lying to a nice girl like Melissa. What were you up to? Softening her up so that Pam Lyndon could buy her out on the cheap?"

The scorn in the woman's voice shamed him. "No. You have it all wrong."

"I don't believe you."

The knitting instructor gave him a cold stare that he was all too familiar with. He'd seen that look in his editor's eyes at the moment when George had lost faith in him, when the tide of public opinion had turned against him.

If the merchants were gossiping like this, then it

wouldn't be long before his father's family heard all about it. And then things would get much, much worse.

He needed to do something fast if he ever wanted to regain Melissa's trust.

And not just talk. Talk was cheap, and apologies at this point would fall flat.

And not just writing a check. He'd already done that, and Melissa would be finding out about it soon. But paying her taxes had been easy, too. All it took was money—and not even a lot of it. For him, money might as well grow on trees. He had more than he'd ever be able to spend in several lifetimes. Money could buy a lot, but it couldn't buy trust and it couldn't buy love.

If he wanted Melissa in his life—and he did—he would have to earn back her trust. And then he might be lucky enough to earn her love, too.

* * *

Fifteen minutes later a maid ushered Jeff into Charlotte's Grove and left him waiting in a sitting room right off the main foyer. He'd visited Charlotte's Grove only once in his life, and his memories of the place were vague—just a sense of formality that left him cold. He'd expected the historic house to be filled with museum-quality Georgian furniture, but the room he was led to seemed surprisingly contemporary, with a couch and two well-used wing chairs.

"Oh my God, Jeff, I'm so glad you turned up." Aunt Pam entered the room from the hallway dressed for a day in the garden, in a pair of slacks and a long-sleeve cotton T-shirt that was slightly dirty. Her hair was pulled back in a haphazard ponytail, and she wasn't wearing makeup.

She hurried across the wide-plank wood floor and gave Jeff a fierce, motherly hug. She smelled of the garden. Like roses or lavender or something.

"I've called your mother," she said as she let him go. "She's so relieved. Honestly, Jeff, you should have called her. Where on earth have you been? And when did you grow a beard?"

Jeff steeled his resolve. He'd seen Aunt Pam in action; she certainly hadn't been this sweet to Melissa on Saturday. He took a step back. "I've been staying at Dad's fishing cabin, and I grew a beard so you wouldn't recognize me."

"But—"

"Look, Aunt Pam, I'm not here to reconnect with the family. I'm here to issue an ultimatum."

"What on earth...? About what?" A little V of puzzlement formed on her forehead.

"About Melissa Portman and Secondhand Prose."

The frown morphed into an expression of utter astonishment. "What in the...? Oh my goodness, you're the man who fell off the ladder." She chuckled. "I'm afraid I wasn't looking at your face that day."

His humiliation was utterly complete. But he wasn't going to let it get the best of him. It was well past time to go on the offensive.

"Yeah, I admit I managed to get disrobed by a coat hook. But that's beside the point. I'm here to let you know that I've paid Melissa's taxes. So you won't be getting your hands on that building."

"Oh, that's wonderful news, Jeff. I'm so pleased. I've been worried about Melissa. I know it's hard to let go of that bookstore, but once she realizes she can make money leasing out the space, I know she'll come around."

Wait a sec. What the hell was Pam saying? That she didn't want the building? That she cared about Melissa's future? "Wait. I'm confused. You don't want her building?"

"Well, if she wants to sell it, I'm ready to buy it. But I'd rather see her join the rest of the property owners and participate in our downtown restoration project."

He stood there for a moment trying to figure out which Pam Lyndon was the real one, the woman who had threatened Melissa on Saturday or this sweet Southern lady.

"Sit down, Jeff. Lidia will bring us some tea, and we'll talk. I can see you're upset. But, truly, if you've paid her taxes, then that's good news." Her drawl was suddenly thick as a brick.

"I don't want any tea or talk, Aunt Pam. What I want is for you to call Melissa Portman and tell her you're sorry for the way you threatened her. I want you to make it clear that there is no truth to the rumors flying around town that you used me to soften her up so she'd sell out."

"What? Why are people saying that?"

"I don't really understand, except that when I introduced myself to her, I dropped the Lyndon from my last name. But now everyone in town thinks I lied because of some nefarious plan you set in motion. Honestly, you need to do some fence mending with some of the Liberty Avenue merchants."

Pam continued to look at him as if he'd blown in from Mars. "Why on earth did you drop the Lyndon from your last name?"

"Because I don't want anything to do with any of you, my father most of all. And just so we're clear, I've asked my attorney to begin the process of legally changing my name to Jefferson Talbert."

"Well, that's just ridiculous," she said. "Even if you change your name, you'll still be family. Don't let Tom manipulate you, darlin'. We all know your father is a dick."

"What?" Her words left him breathless.

"You heard me. He's an idiot and a...Well, I've already used language I shouldn't have used, but in Thomas's case, it fits the bill. Thomas obviously hasn't said it recently, or maybe ever, but, Jeff, we're all so very proud of you."

Before he could collect himself, Pam stood up. "Wait right there, darlin'. Don't run away again, please. There's something you need to hear."

She left the room, and he started pacing. Had she even heard what he had to say? He didn't think so. Damn. He came to rest in front of a big window with old glass that gave a slightly wobbly view of the outside.

"Jeff?" an oddly familiar masculine voice said from behind him. Was his father here?

He turned. No. Not Dad. Uncle Mark.

The senator stood beside one of the comfortable easy chairs, wearing a pair of jeans and a golf shirt. The Senate was obviously not in session today.

"I'm so glad you came to find us," he said, resting his hand on the chair back. "Pam says you've been staying up at the fishing cabin. That's probably the last place any of us would have looked for you." He chuckled, his brown eyes dancing with some kind of merriment that eluded Jeff.

"What is it you want, Uncle Mark? I've already told Aunt—"

"I want to talk to you. First of all, I want you to know that the entire family was shocked by Tom's public statements about your story."

Jeff said nothing. His life had suddenly become theater of the absurd.

"I see I've surprised you," Uncle Mark said.

Jeff shrugged. "I don't give a flying fart what the family thinks about anything, really. I'm only here because Aunt Pam has gotten the Liberty Avenue merchants in an uproar. And they all think I'm part of some weird plan that she has to take over the real estate downtown. And, really, the only problem here is that I decided to drop the Lyndon from my name. And, you know, I'm not ever going to use that name again."

The senator's shoulders sagged a little. "I understand. And as for your aunt, she can sometimes be like a steamroller. I'll see what I can do to smooth things over with the merchants. It won't be the first time."

"Thanks. That's all I want. I'll be going now." Jeff

turned and headed toward the door, but the senator blocked his way.

"Son," Uncle Mark said, "you have every right to be furious with your father. We're all furious with him. Family comes before politics, and Tom forgot that. So I just want you to think this through. If you want to strike back at your father, then you need to help me kill this nomination."

It took a moment for Uncle Mark's words to make it past Jeff's anger. "Wait a sec. Are you saying you believe the story I wrote about Joanna Durand?"

"Of course I do. Durand's family has a reputation for bending the rules when it comes to oil and gas. And her husband has more lobbying clients than a dog has fleas. I'm sure her husband and brother have been up to no good, and I could use your help in putting the kibosh on this nomination.

"By the way, I'm saying this, not as your uncle but as a member of the Senate Judiciary Committee. Her confirmation hearing is set for this coming Thursday, and I have every intention of giving her a hard time."

"Oh." The adrenaline in Jeff's body began to dissipate.

Mark Lyndon continued. "I'm not letting Joanna Durand's nomination get out of committee. So, I'd like you to give my chief of staff a call and help him hunt down the smoking gun that will simultaneously clear your name and sink this nomination for good and all."

Jeff stood there frozen. He hadn't expected this. Not in a million years. "Okay, I'll help, of course, but—"

"Son, if you want to change your last name, go right ahead and do it. No one could blame you. But it won't change anything as far as I'm concerned, and I suspect you'll discover that resigning from the Lyndon family is a whole lot harder than you might expect."

Chapter Nine

♥

Hugo jumped on Melissa's bed and settled on her pillow, purring like a finely tuned engine. That was unusual, since the cat hadn't been upstairs since Grammy died. And never, in all the cat's twelve years on the planet, had he ever jumped up on Melissa's bed. So why had he chosen this morning, when her head was pounding like nobody's business?

She batted the cat away and pulled the pillow over her head, hoping that would quiet the pounding. But the cat meowed loudly and then opened his claws on her shoulder.

She sat up. Her stomach lurched as she groped for her glasses. She should never have had the third margarita. The world came into focus as she settled her glasses on her nose. She picked up her cell phone and checked the time. It was well past noon.

So much for getting an early start on the rest of her life. She had barely enough time to take a shower before her one o'clock meeting with Walter Braden. She was about to put the phone down when she noticed that she had new voice mail messages—twelve, in fact—all from Jeff. She'd missed his calls last night because she'd inadvertently left her cell phone at home.

Damn.

She listened to his voice mail. He'd actually called last night to invite her up to his cabin. And then he'd called again in the morning to invite her to breakfast.

Double damn.

Maybe she should return his calls.

No. He needed to come to her. Most definitely. And in the meantime, she needed to take a shower and move on with her life.

She got up, fed the cats, made some coffee, but instead of taking a shower, she called Walter and rescheduled her appointment for the next day. Then she set up her laptop on the kitchen table and started searching Jeff's name. Wow. He had lied about a lot of things, starting with the fact that he was, really and truly, a published writer.

An hour later she was still sitting there reading Jeff's articles—not just the one on Joanna Durand, but a dozen others. The man was a talented writer with a knack for writing profiles of the rich and famous. She was totally engrossed when someone tapped on her back door. Her heart took flight. Maybe Jeff had come to explain himself.

But it wasn't Jeff.

Gracie Teague stood on her landing wearing her waitress uniform and a determined expression. She didn't wait to be invited in. She just took the territory like General Patton rolling over France.

"I brought you a bacon and egg sandwich and some serious advice." She plunked a sandwich wrapped in wax paper onto the kitchen table and eyed the computer, the empty bag of M&M's, and the wastebasket filled with used tissues. "I should have come sooner."

"I'm all right. Really. I didn't make my appointment with Walter Braden, but I did reschedule for tomorrow. I've decided to take your advice and sell out, take the proceeds after taxes and find a beach somewhere with hot, gorgeous, rich men."

She'd expected Gracie to be overjoyed with this news, but instead her mother's BFF frowned. "You will do no such thing," she said. "Sit down. I have something you need to hear."

Melissa sat, and Gracie took the other chair. "There was an emergency meeting of the Liberty Avenue Merchants Association at oh dark thirty this morning. You know how everyone loved Harriet. And everyone remembers you as a little girl, and we're all just a little overprotective of you, I guess. So this Jefferson Lyndon situation has gotten everyone into an uproar. Half the shop owners think Pam Lyndon sent that man to soften you up. To convince you to sell out."

"But—"

Gracie held up a hand. "I know, hon. Why would a man help you fix up the store if he'd been sent to convince you that keeping it going was pointless?"

Melissa nodded. "Exactly."

"Well, not everyone is as logical as you and I. Anyway," Gracie said with a little gleam in her eye, "at the meeting this morning, some of the merchants took up a collection to help you with your taxes. It's not much, but we figured it might be enough to buy you some time. I was nominated to go down to the county clerk's office to make a payment on your behalf. But when I got there, I found out that someone had already paid your taxes in full."

"What?"

"That's right. Paid in full first thing this morning, just an hour before I got there. The clerk wouldn't tell me who. She said it was a privacy matter or something. As if there's any privacy in a town as small as Shenandoah Falls."

"You think Jeff paid my taxes?" The weight in Melissa's chest began to lift.

"That would be my guess. Now, why would a man do a thing like that?"

Melissa tried to think of a good business reason and drew a blank. "Because he believes in independent bookstores?" It was lame.

"Or maybe he believes in you?" Gracie said, covering one of Melissa's hands with hers.

Melissa's eyes filled up, but this time the tears weren't angry. "And I believe in him, Gracie," she whispered, her lips trembling. "I've been sitting here reading the things he's written, and I can't help myself. I think what he wrote in that story about the Durand nomination is true. I think he ran away from New York because even his father refused to stand by him."

"You know," Gracie said, "if my daddy had publicly disavowed me, I think I might return the favor. You know, by dropping the hyphenated part of my last name."

"Really? Because now that I'm sober and I've read his story and the reaction to it, I've come to the same conclusion."

Just then Dickens jumped up on the kitchen table, sat down facing Melissa, and proceeded to meow at her as if he were scolding her or something. Hugo followed suit, only he yowled in a way that was practically mournful.

"Mercy," Gracie said. "I've never seen them do anything like that before."

Melissa got up from the table. "It's a sign, Gracie. They've been trying to tell me for days that Jeff belongs here. I just wasn't listening."

* * *

Melissa called Walter Braden back and canceled her meeting. Without a tax bill looming over her, maybe she could make a go of keeping Secondhand Prose alive, saving Hugo and Dickens's home, and preserving a little piece of Grammy for a while.

And all because of Jeff, who had walked into her store and insisted on fixing it up. Not because he was paid to do it. Not because she'd asked him to do it. But because he had simply belonged there.

The cats knew it. And now Melissa did, too.

She needed to talk to him, so she decided the ball wasn't in his court after all. The ball was in hers. She texted him.

Melissa: *We need to talk. Where are you?*

Jeff: *I'm just leaving Charlotte's Grove. Expect an apology call from Pam. I'll be at the store in ten minutes.*

Melissa: *No, not here. Too many busybodies. Where's your cabin?*

Jeff: *:)*

His emoticon was followed by an address in the Blue Ridge off Scottish Heights Road. She told him she'd meet him there in twenty minutes.

The cabin turned out to be high up on the ridge off a dirt road. Jeff certainly hadn't been exaggerating when he'd said that he'd been living back in the woods.

It was an old place, built years before people had started putting up luxury vacation homes in the area. Its weathered logs and rustic stone chimney looked as if they'd been there for a century. It sat in a clearing, nestled between two gigantic oaks, on a ledge that provided a commanding view westward toward the Shenandoah Valley and the Allegheny Mountains beyond.

Jeff was waiting for her, sitting in an Adirondack chair on the covered porch. He stood up as she pulled her VW in behind his shiny Land Rover, and he was right there when she got out of the car.

"Let me explain," he said before she had a chance to say one word of the speech she'd been rehearsing in her head. "I never—"

"You didn't tell me the truth," she blurted.

"I'm sorry. I didn't mean to mislead you. I just—"

"I know you didn't. I get it. If I had a father who issued public statements about me, I'd want to divorce

him, too. But you could have told me that. You could
have trusted me."

Jeff's gaze intensified, his brown eyes full of emotion. "Are you telling me that you actually understand
why I didn't give you my full name?"

"Well, duh. I read what your father said about you.
And it was brutal. But more important, it was just
wrong. I spent a lot of time today reading some of the
things you've written for *New York, New York*. They
were wonderful articles, Jeff. You have a gift for words.
So what he said was just not true. You're a writer—a
really good one. But the thing is, you should have been
honest with me from the start."

He let go of a long breath and closed his eyes for a
moment. "I'm sorry I wasn't honest, but I didn't know
you at first. And then... Well, I wanted to take care of
your taxes before I said anything. Please tell me you
never believed that crap that's going around town about
how Pam used me to set you up, because that's just not
true."

"Of course I don't believe that. If that was your purpose, you had a funny way of going about it. All that
dusting and organizing and color coding. It didn't make
it easier to decide to sell the place, you know."

"You aren't going to sell it, are you? I'd hate to see
that bookshop go out of business."

Tears filled her eyes, and a lump the size of a peach
stone swelled in her throat. She shook her head. "I never
wanted to sell. I just had to."

He took her by the shoulders and pulled her right
into his arms. Her head hit his strong, steady shoulder,

and she leaned on him like she'd never leaned on anyone in her life. The emotions she'd been denying finally found their way to the surface. She had to take off her glasses when the tears came. She cried for Grammy and her parents. She cried because, standing there in the circle of Jeff's arms, she didn't feel alone anymore. And finally, she cried because she didn't have to close her store.

He held her tight, stroked her head, and gave her a place to stand, a place to be. Leaning on him was like coming home.

When the tears had run their course, she tilted her head up, but it was no use. She couldn't see him because her vision was still smeared with tears. But it was all right, because he came toward her and started kissing away the tears that had run down her cheeks.

She started laughing then, which was weird because her heart had swelled to the point where breathing had become difficult. He ignored her laugh and continued to dispense little kisses all along her cheeks and over to her ear, where he whispered, "Listen to me, Melissa, for just one minute. I went up to Charlotte's Grove, and I told Mark and Pam Lyndon that I was changing my name. I've already taken the first steps to do that legally. I also told Pam that she needed to call you to apologize for the way she acted the other day."

She pushed him back and gazed into his eyes. He was a complete blur, but that didn't matter. "You told Pam Lyndon she needed to apologize? Oh my God, I don't think anyone has ever told Pam Lyndon that in her entire life."

He laughed a little and put his forehead against hers. "Well, there's a first time for everything."

They stood like that for a long moment as the tension of the last few days melted away. "So, I have a million questions," Melissa said.

"About what?"

"About you, Jeff. I want to know everything. I want to know what your favorite color is and what you like for breakfast, and lunch, and dinner. And which vegetable makes you want to yak. I want to know your birthday and the worst and best Christmas present you ever got. I want to know it all because, damn it, I crave your body, and when that happens, it means my heart is automatically involved. You know? I don't do the whole friends-with-benefits thing well. So if that's all this is, I'll just get in my car and go now, okay?"

She was prepared to have her heart crushed when he said, "Brussels sprouts."

"What?"

"I hate brussels sprouts. How about you?"

She took in a deep breath filled with the woodsy scent of him. "It's cauliflower that makes me want to hurl. And, for the record, my birthday is the sixteenth of March."

"Really? Mine's on the seventeenth. Next year we should throw a big party."

Next year. She closed her eyes and rested her head against his chest. His arms were still around her. She was safe here. She'd always be safe here. She may have met him only days ago, but he was "the One."

"I have something to seal this moment," he said,

moving back a little bit. "I intended to present it to you last night. But you didn't answer my calls."

"I was getting drunk with the girls. Bad move on my part."

He laughed. "Put on your glasses."

She snagged them from her jeans pocket where she'd put them right before her crying jag. She slipped them on just in time to see him pull something from his pocket.

He held it out to her, nestled in his palm. "It's the arrowhead," he said. "Yesterday I bought a rawhide shoelace and made a necklace out of it. When I get a chance, I intend to take it to a jeweler for a proper gold chain. I thought you might like a little memento of our first time." He gave her a salacious grin. "Turn around. Let me put it on you."

She turned, and he pulled her hair aside and then fastened the necklace at her nape. He pressed his lips to the spot right below her ear, and she groaned out loud.

"Our first time, huh? That implies there will be a second time," she said.

"Yeah. And many, many more, I hope." And then he did the most romantic thing ever. He lifted her into his arms and carried her over the threshold of his cabin.

Epilogue

♥

Three Months Later

Melissa was manning the checkout at Secondhand Prose and reading a murder mystery when the front door jangled. She looked up in time to see Jeff strolling through the door, carrying a cardboard box that looked as if it had come from an online bookseller.

Both cats immediately arrived on the scene and tried to trip him as he headed in Melissa's direction.

"Hey, you guys, give me a break," he said as he stepped over the felines with admirable grace—grace that hadn't yet failed to warm Melissa's insides.

"I bring gifts," he said, putting the carton on the counter and leaning across it to give her a kiss that left them both a little breathless.

"Hmm, nice. I like your gifts," she said.

He laughed. "I was talking about this," he said, nudging the box.

"This looks like a box of books," she said. "From the competition."

"Ah, but this isn't just any box of books. Look inside."

She opened the carton, and right on the top was a large-format paperback book titled *A Child's Book of Stories*. "Oh, how beautiful!" Melissa said in a rush as she opened the book and started browsing through. "I love Jessie Wilcox Smith's illustrations. She's my favorite illustrator of all time."

"Yes, I know. That was one of the first things I learned about you. All those fairy-tale T-shirts."

She looked up from the book and gave him another kiss.

"There's another book in the box," Jeff said after a very long, hot moment.

"Another Jessie Wilcox Smith book?"

"No, it's a hardbound copy of *Grimm's Complete Fairy Tales*."

She put her paperback on the counter and pulled the second book from the box. It was one of those leather reproduction books with a fancy embossed cover, gilt lettering, and a ribbon bookmark stitched into the binding. She wasn't fooled. The book probably retailed for less than ten dollars.

She glanced up at Jeff. There was a gleam in his eye, and the corner of his mouth was curling just a tiny bit, as if he knew a secret he was bursting to tell. Did he think he'd found her a special first edition or something?

"Oh, this is nice," she said, trying to sound superenthusiastic, when she would much rather be hanging out on the beanbag chair drooling over Jessie Wilcox Smith's illustrations. Or, better yet, upstairs in bed drooling over Jeff.

"Open it," Jeff said, "to the marked page." Was there a tremor in his voice?

She opened the book to a three-paragraph story entitled "Brides on Trial." Right below the story's final paragraph, the book had been horribly defaced. Someone had cut a deep hole in the pages to create a secret hiding spot. And in the spot, with the ribbon bookmark threaded through it, was a sapphire and diamond ring.

Melissa's breath caught in her throat, and tears filled her eyes as she looked up at Jeff, the man who had become, in just a few short months, her best friend and the love of her life.

"Melissa," he said in his deep, quiet voice, "I walked into this enchanted place, and the minute I saw you, I knew I'd come home. I've patiently spent the last few months waiting for the right time to ask this question, and I don't want to wait anymore. I think I know enough about you to say that I never want to leave your side. You love Jessie Wilcox Smith, you know every story in *Grimm's Fairy Tales*, even the gruesome ones like the 'Heavenly Wedding.' You snore, you love margaritas, and you read romances when you think I'm not looking. Will you marry me?"

Like any fairy-tale prince, Jeff got down on his knee, took her hand, and kissed it.

"Oh my God, yes. Yes, yes." Melissa fell down onto her knees, too, and wrapped her arms around him. "I love you, Jefferson Talbert-Lyndon. And even though you are technically a member of the Lyndon family, I can't imagine spending my life with anyone else."

Jeff grabbed the *Grimm's Fairy Tales* off the counter

and sat on the bookstore's floor. "Sorry about defacing a book, but I figured it was for a good cause. And we'll be keeping this book forever."

He pulled the ribbon bookmark through the ring. "Do you like it?" he asked. "It's a family heirloom, but from the Talbert side of the family. It's my grandmother's ring."

"The cat-lady-on-the-Hudson grandmother?"

Jeff grinned. "The very one." He took her left hand and slipped the ring on her finger. It fit perfectly. "Grandmother would have loved you, Melissa."

And just then, Dickens and Hugo joined the group hug on the bookstore floor, one cat in each lap, proving—at least to Melissa's satisfaction—that Grammy would have loved Jeff too.

About the Author

Hope Ramsay was born in New York and grew up on the North Shore of Long Island. Hope earned a BA in political science from the University of Buffalo and has had various jobs working as a congressional aide, a lobbyist, a public relations consultant, and a meeting planner. She's a two-time finalist in the Golden Heart and is married to a good-ol' Georgia boy who resembles every single one of her heroes. She has two grown children and a couple of demanding lap cats. She lives in Fairfax, Virginia, where you can often find her on the back deck, picking on her thirty-five-year-old Martin guitar.

YOU CAN LEARN MORE AT:
HOPERAMSAY.COM
WWW.FACEBOOK.COM/HOPE.RAMSAY
TWITTER, @HOPERAMSAY

FALL IN LOVE WITH FOREVER ROMANCE

USA TODAY BESTSELLING AUTHOR

DEBBIE MASON

Driftwood Cove

"Heartfelt and delightful!" —RAEANNE THAYNE,
New York Times bestselling author

DRIFTWOOD COVE
By Debbie Mason

FBI agent Michael Gallagher never dreamed that his latest investigation would bring him back to his hometown of Harmony Harbor. Or that one of his best leads would be the woman he once loved. Shay Angel is tougher than anyone he knows, but she still needs his help. Even if it means facing the past they can't forgive...or a love they can't forget.

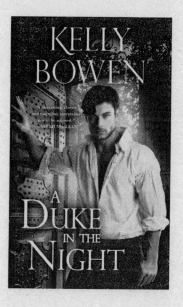

A DUKE IN THE NIGHT
By Kelly Bowen

Headmistress Clara Hayward is a master of deception. She's fooled the ton into thinking she's simply running a prestigious finishing school. In reality, she offers an education far superior to what society deems proper for young ladies. If only her skills could save her family's import business. She has a plan that might succeed, as long as a certain duke doesn't get in the way...

FALL IN LOVE WITH FOREVER ROMANCE

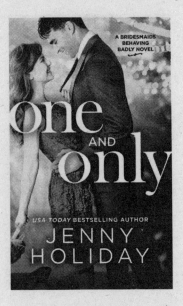

ONE AND ONLY
By Jenny Holiday

In this laugh-out-loud romantic comedy, *USA Today* bestselling author Jenny Holiday proves that when opposites attract, sparks fly. Bridesmaid Jane Denning will do anything to escape her bridezilla friend—even if it means babysitting the groom's troublemaker brother before the wedding. Cameron MacKinnon is ready to let loose, but first he'll have to sweet-talk responsible Jane into taking a walk on the wild side. Turns out, riling her up is the best time he's had in years. But will fun and games turn into something real?

FALL IN LOVE WITH FOREVER ROMANCE

SECOND CHANCE COWBOY
By A. J. Pine

Once a cowboy, always a cowboy in A.J. Pine's first Crossroads Ranch novel! After ten years away, Jack Everett is finally back home. The ranch he can handle—Jack might be a lawyer, but he still remembers how to work with his hands. But turning around the failing vineyard he's also inherited? That requires working with the one woman he never expected to see again.